THE GREAT CROSSING

L ong ago, before the gods walked among us, we were the No'Amatsi people. The people of shared love, of Thread-family. We lived in the northernmost stretches of the Fareastern continent until war chased us from our home.

We traveled west, following the Moon Mother, whose Threads were great ribbons of color across the sky. First she led us away from the war. Then she led us into the one place no humans dared to tread: the Sleeping Lands.

It is a vast expanse of snow where magic waits so thick in the air that those who go in, do not come out the same—assuming they come out at all. And although we, the No'Amatsis, did come out alive, we were markedly changed. The cold leeched all color from our faces; the magic turned our eyes golden and green.

When we finally left the Sleeping Lands and entered this new world, the people there did not welcome us. We had crossed the uncrossable. But much more alarming was the fact that we had magic.

In those days, only the gods had magic.

Those gods, however, did not fear us as their children did. Instead, they welcomed us. There was Owl, who watched over the creatures and plants of the Witchlands. Swallow, who controlled the seasons and the storms. Comet Bright, who gave us fire (but who sometimes lost their temper and spread it over the land). Old Uncle who protected the rivers and seas—if he could be bothered to wake up from his nap. Then Wicked Cousin, whose domain was the dead and the deadly.

And lastly of course, there was Trickster, who delighted in mischief and thrived off of chaos.

Soon enough, the No'Amatsis became the favorite of all the gods. They were fascinated by our Thread magic—so different from how magic worked in the Witchlands. But that favor only made the locals hate us more. They wanted to know why we, people from afar, were more favored than they? Why were we more beloved than they who had worked and toiled for an eternity to please their gods?

Then one day, the unthinkable happened: the gods turned on Moon Mother, led by the one who'd always claimed he loved her most.

Trickster.

After that, magic flowed through the earth into everyone. Each soul in the Witchlands received the power which previously had been only divine. Some received more than others; hierarchies formed; the powerful dominated those with less; and war spread across the Witchlands.

Worst of all, a shadowy sickness began to appear—oily and thick. Fast and violent. "Cleaving" it was called, for it seemed to sever a soul directly from its body, too fast for anyone to stop. And too fast for anyone to escape, for when one person cleaved, many more were likely to join them.

To no one's surprise, the No'Amatsis were the ones blamed for the transformation across the Witchlands. Before you came, the world was not like this! You are the reason we cleave and suffer and die! *And so our people withdrew from the world that had briefly been our own. Hunted again. Chased away by war. Except this time, we had no Moon Mother to guide us. No new continent toward which we could flee. So we hid ourselves in the forests and the mountains, behind morning glories and bear claws, and we waited for a time when the gods might one day walk among us again.*

And when our Blessed Moon Mother might return, her Threads blazing forgotten colors across the sky, beacons for her children to follow home.

WITCHLIGHT

For a recap of the Witchlands series,
head here:
SusanDennard.com/recap/

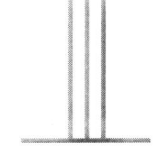

PART 1

Initiate

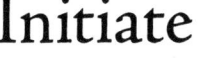

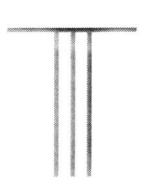

Kullen,

I hope the Goddess releases you from your sleep soon—and I hope there are enough pieces of you still inside to understand why this diary is lying on the ice before you.

Do you remember me? Do you remember everything we went through? How I found you in the mountain, no name, no memory? How I found you again in Nubrevna, and we lived for a time like nothing could hurt us . . .

But the inevitable caught up to us; your Paladin soul couldn't be ignored forever; and the Raider King forced you to his side. At least until Merik lured you into this sleeping ice, at the cost of himself in the ice beside you.

He has awoken again, though.

You have not.

Like before, I don't know what these pages will show you. I only know what I've written and what I hope the words reveal. Then you can make the right choice when the sleeping ice releases you.

I have gone deep into the Sightwitch Sister Convent—all the way into the lowest levels of the Crypts—searching for explanations of what has happened to you. Surely, in all of those thousands upon thousands of Memory Records, there is *someone* who has experienced what you're going through. Why has Bastien's soul taken over yours?

I don't think this is a possession, in which souls are bound to bodies not their own. Because you *are* Bastien—or rather, you carry the same reincarnated soul of the Air Paladin that Bastien did. This is what all Paladins experience: they reincarnate again and again, each new iteration able to remember the past lives that came before. When Paladins reach a certain age, something in their lives will "trigger" all the memories to awaken.

We went through your trigger together, do you remember? When we were trying to escape the mountain a year ago, and you discovered the blade and glass.

But remembering the past lives is not the same as *becoming* the past lives.

I will keep searching, Kullen, and I *will* find an answer.

Also, I must warn you: the blade and glass are no longer inside the mountain. Stacia Sotar and Admiral Kahina of the Red Sails have them in their possession. They are both Paladins, and they have both gone to the Raider King's banner.

I begged Stix not to. I begged her to see that the Raider King will destroy the Witchlands, but she disagreed. Something about him has convinced her he knows what is best for our future.

Who is right? Who is wrong? Who will bring terror to the Witchlands? Who will save us from it? I will keep searching for clues in the Sightwitch Crypts. I am the only Sightwitch Sister left, so if I can't crack this puzzle, then who will?

At least I'm no longer alone. The Rook found me today, swooping into the Convent as if he'd never left me a year ago. I cried at the sight of him. And I will cry even more at the sight of you, when you find me again.

If you do awaken and find this letter—if you are Kullen and not Bastien's eternal fury—then come to me in the Crypts. I have drawn you a map so you can find your way through the mountain. And I will have the Rook keep bringing these messages to your tomb.

I love you.

—Ryber

ONE

✳

Prince Merik Nihar could not get his footing on the ice inside this mountain. It reached for Merik with frozen claws, just as it reached for the storm hound pup at his side.

Merik dodged and dove. He'd come to this tomb to trick Kullen into the frozen, hungry ice. It had worked, and Kullen was still there.

Merik no longer was.

Nor was this storm hound—a blighted *storm hound*—whom he'd only just been told that he must raise. Told by two little girls who found him in the ice, no less, because somehow *that* made sense.

The hound yelped and galloped beside him. Aurora, he'd named her five minutes ago, because five minutes ago, a new dawn had seemed very symbolic. Poetic, even. Then the ice had decided to kill them both, and now here they were at the highest level of an enormous nautilus-shaped tomb of ice, both trying not to die.

"Watch out!" Merik shouted as ice launched down from the ceiling, but the puppy didn't understand. The ice pierced her left wing and pinned her to the cavern floor. Aurora screamed.

Merik blasted out his magic. His winds cracked against the ice, freeing her wing—but it was like throwing chum in the water, and now the sharks were coming. The ice sensed his power. It surged at him with double the force. It crunched over his feet like shackles.

Merik punched out more winds, shattering the ice. Then he swept air beneath him and grabbed hold of himself and Aurora. Awkward, frantic winds, but enough to launch them upward . . . before toppling them off the path and into the open core of this spiraling ice.

Merik fell, Aurora fell. And Merik felt as if he were trapped inside a frozen seashell as countless curving floors blurred past.

Aurora howled as blood striped upward from her wing. She couldn't seem to fly—or maybe she hadn't learned yet—and Merik could barely manage flight either. He grabbed and reached and strained for more winds. Just one burst, one burst before they crashed on that ice—

Air whooshed under them. *One burst.* Merik slowed their fall.

The storm hound hit first in a thunderous crack. Merik hit a split moment later, breath punching from his lungs and muscles ripping from impact. But the pain was so distant. He and Aurora weren't dead, they weren't shattered—so they must keep moving.

Merik hauled to his feet before dragging up the massive pup. Her wing gushed blood now. She whimpered and whined.

But she also resumed her clumsy gallop, trusting Merik to lead her to safety. He prayed to Noden that he would be worth that trust. He prayed to Noden that there was a way to survive this. Why else would he have woken up from the sleeping ice? Why else would those strange girls speaking riddles in their ancient tongue have given him a storm hound and told him to leave?

During his time with Esme the Puppeteer, Merik had learned of one line from "Eridysi's Lament": *Fissures in the ice always follow the grain. Unless something stops them, something blocks them, something forces them to change. Then the fissures in the ice will find new ways to travel.*

There are no coincidences. Except when there are.

He had followed fissures in the ice to get here, into the icy tomb that had swallowed him whole. He had lured his Threadbrother Kullen into that ice that had always been singing—that sang even now, begging Merik to return to its embrace. *Come, my son, and sleep. Come, come, the ice will hold you.*

Now he followed the fissures a second time, all these shadowy veins, like ore through a mountain. And ahead, the end of the tomb opened before them.

He and Aurora reached it, bursting into the enormous, eternal cavern Merik had come from before the ice had claimed him. He skidded to a stop, shoving in front of Aurora before she could topple off a ledge into a spinning galaxy of stars hundreds of feet below.

If the nautilus-shaped ice tomb was strange, this massive star-filled cavern was far stranger.

Behind them, ice crackled and reached. It left the tomb in a trail of chasing hoarfrost. Aurora whined and pressed against Merik, large as a draft horse. Blood stained her golden fur. She pushed her wet nose into his neck.

"I know," he murmured. "Let me think." The frost was coiling over her tail, over his feet, and although he kept shifting his weight, it kept simply skittering apart like ants disturbed in their mound. Then it would converge again to claim them.

Merik needed a way out of here. He needed one of the magic doorways that had first led him into the mountain. At this point, he didn't care where it led. But gone was the ice bridge he'd crossed when Kullen chased him; now the whole cavern was filled by filamentous ice.

Aurora keened louder and withdrew. *Now,* she seemed to say. *We need to move now.*

As if in answer to her, a sound filled the cavern. A strange sound that made no sense here. *Caw, caw.* The cry bounced and echoed. *Caw, caw.* A bird flapped by, wings black and glistening.

A crow or raven, Merik thought as he watched the distant bird wheel and dip around ice webs—moving in a path that, if he was fast enough, Merik could follow.

He sucked air to him. In through his nose. Out through his mouth. And on the exhale, wind lifted him and Aurora simultaneously. Hoarfrost crackled and released them.

Aurora yelped as they flew across the cavern, chasing after the black bird. They wheeled and dipped exactly as the bird had, until eventually Merik saw where the bird was aimed: a door with a thin stream of water pouring from it.

Merik knew that door. It was not the one he wanted—even if it was where the girls in the tomb had told him to go. He wanted to go through any door *but* that one.

But here he was: stopped, blocked, forced to change.

The bird swept through the door. Blue magicked light sprayed. And it was as if the sleeping ice suddenly seemed to realize it might lose Merik if it didn't act *now.* It lurched toward him in thick strands that wanted Merik and Aurora to sleep while the ice embraced them.

Aurora shrieked, her wings flapping ineffectively and spraying Merik in her blood. Merik slung out two winds at once. One wind he used to propel Aurora toward the door—hard and fast, and although she screamed, she also instinctively curled herself into a ball to avoid the pain of impact.

She hit the door's opening.

She disappeared just as the black bird had.

The second wind, Merik shot at the ice. An outward blast to keep it off him while he plummeted onto the tiny outcropping before the wet, glistening door.

Power roiled across him. This was *not* the door he wanted. This was *not* safety.

But Merik would follow the grain.

Panting, he threw one final look at the cavern where nothing made sense—where magic was both incalculably strong, yet also weak and starving. He could see now just how much ice was coming for him, lancing across the cavern like shots from a Firewitched pistol.

Merik dove for the door, curling as Aurora had. Then magic clamped over him. He left the mountain behind.

TWO

✴

There were few people the Bloodwitch Aeduan hated more than Purists.

Noblemen happened to be one of them.

Particularly noblemen who believed big swords made up for an absence of spines. "I have told you three times now," Aeduan said without inflection, "this is not a negotiation. Give up the castle and swear fealty to Her Imperial Majesty Safiya fon Cartorra."

"Demon," snarled one of the two men currently frozen in place before Aeduan.

"Monster," hissed the other.

Aeduan would have rolled his eyes if he were that sort of man. Around him, the ancient stones of the empty Hasstrel estate groaned. Wind shrieked through holes in the shutters; a rat scurried down a nearby hall, her blood singing of freedom and shadows. The two fon Grieg sons had been granted this estate when Eron fon Hasstrel had been arrested. Since the dom's release and his niece's ascendancy to the throne, fon Hasstrel had decided he wanted his castle back.

Which was why Aeduan was here, instead of a hundred miles east with a silver taler that smelled of his own blood.

Sweet wine and lathered horses. Cut emeralds and sharpened steel. Both fon Grieg men smelled of wealth. And both bore the lingering cold iron scent of the Hell-Bard Loom, for although they were no longer bound to it, it would forever taint their blood.

Aeduan let his Bloodwitchery swirl into his eyes. Let his lips lift to reveal his canines while a fresh gust of winter wind flipped into his new Carawen salamander cloak. He might not be a dramatic man, but he also wasn't above a bit of theater when the moment demanded. With his left arm outstretched, he furled in his fingers.

And watched as less and less blood reached the two men's brains. "I can kill you this way," he said. "I just keep tightening"—another inch with his fingers—"and tightening until there is nothing left to keep your brains functioning. Or I can set you free." He released, though only slightly.

Both men gasped. The right brother's eyes shuttered.

"Your choice."

"Our father," rasped the one on the right. Redrick or Redris or something comparably bland and Cartorran. "Was given this castle—"

Aeduan tightened on the man's blood again. Aeduan was tired, he was hungry, and he hated this part of his new job. "Your father," he countered, "has already offered his fealty to the new empress. As well as all of his soldiers . . . which, I believe, include the two of you."

The brother on the left—whose name might as well have been Shitpants fon Grieg for all Aeduan knew—let his eyes close again. Defeat practically sang off his blood. Redrick or Redris or whatever he was still would not relent, though. He pulled back his own lips, the snarl of an angry mongrel used to getting his way. *"Demon,"* he repeated with extra venom.

This time, Aeduan did let his eyes roll. "Understood. I will leave you as you are, and maybe your smarter brother here can talk some sense into you." He released Shitpants, letting the shapes of sweet wine and lathered horses fly free in the man's veins.

The man promptly collapsed to the stone floor. A second rat chittered from the rafters. Aeduan lowered his hand. *One, two, three . . .*

There it was: Shitpants grabbled to his feet and drew a sword. A fine blade with rubies of Hell-Bard red to adorn the hilt. He charged Aeduan while his brother watched on, unable to move.

Aeduan let the man come, waiting until Shitpants was so close he could spot a patch of hair the man had missed shaving. Aeduan spun sideways. His cloak snapped. In one movement, he unsheathed a blade of his own: small, sharp, always within reach at the top of his baldric.

He shoved the knife into Shitpants's hamstring. The man collapsed again, but now with blood spurting and a scream ripping from his lips. It was the sort of sound that would have given Aeduan no pause a year ago. Because that Aeduan had never met a Threadwitch named Iseult or a child named Owl (who was not a child at all).

But the Aeduan of today, the one who *had* met Iseult and *had* saved Owl and who *had* sworn his vows anew to the Carawen . . .

He did pause before this sort of thing.

Aeduan felt his molars grind. Felt his chest expand with cold breath. *One need not be evil to become it.* He'd thought that once about his father. Now he, Aeduan, was no better.

With a strangled growl, he swiped the stiletto on his sleeve and resheathed it. Then he grabbed once more on to Shitpants's blood. Here were the lathering horses, here was the sweet wine. He froze both, although only in the places nearest to the hamstring wound, where the tang of fresh blood wanted to burst forth and taste air.

Meanwhile, twenty paces behind Aeduan, the other brother he decided he would simply call Red was still frozen in place.

And the rat still chittered overhead. He was a hungry little beast.

Aeduan stepped in front of Shitpants. "You know you cannot win this."

"*You*"—Shitpants spat the word—"are a symptom of all that is wrong with the usurper. She took away our noose. She took away *our* castle, and now she threatens us with a monster?"

"Your noose." Aeduan glanced at Red. "Why would you want to keep that?"

Red didn't answer, and Shitpants was only just gathering steam. A pot boiling off rage that had simmered too long—certainly longer than this unfortunate moment inside a crumbling castle could have prompted. "It was an honor to serve Emperor Henrick. People feared us—and *you* would have feared us, for your foul, Void-tainted magic would not have touched us then. We would have skewered you."

Aeduan gave up. With a sigh, he clenched his fist. The man's blood froze, hamstring wound and all. His mouth ceased its spewing, his brain ceased its thinking, and he toppled over. Not dead, but deeply, stupidly unconscious.

Aeduan glanced again at Red. "Your turn. Make your choice."

"You," he croaked out, "are not a Bloodwitch."

Aeduan tensed. Not because he was bothered by Red's words, but because they were so unexpected, so illogical in this cold, stony hall with its whistling wind and scuttering rats.

Red continued: "Bloodwitches cannot do this. They cannot control people like this, freezing them. Killing them."

Aeduan walked now, his magic still clasping the man's blood as he advanced. "I assure you, I am a Bloodwitch. And I also assure you: I *can* kill you." He came to a halt before the man. Unlike Shitpants, Red had a beard. Neatly trimmed, clean like his velvet suit and fur cloak—and all of it so at odds with this barely upright ruin around him.

"No," the man insisted. "*I* am a Bloodwitch. Before the Loom, and after it. But my magic is bound to Water, and you—what *are* you?"

Now Aeduan frowned. The words remained unexpected, but now they were undeniably interesting. And undeniably unsettling, even if Aeduan thought he'd stopped caring about his witchery long ago. He'd never met another Bloodwitch. It was a rare enough magic that he'd never even heard of others like him existing outside of old tales.

Aeduan let his power rise, let his senses sharpen and prong deeper into the man's blood. And yes, there was a coppery tang that he recognized. Bright and fresh like his own.

"I do smell it on you," Aeduan admitted, his voice flat. "Which means you must smell it on me. But if you're trying to call my bluff, you need only look at your brother to know I *can* kill you—and I will."

Red swallowed. His eyes crawled with red, exactly as Aeduan knew his own did. "Oh, I know you'll kill me, *Monk*." His teeth bared just as his brother's had. "Not because you are a Bloodwitch, but because you are a demon. A monster. *I* can smell it on *you*: you're bound to the Void, a cursed beast with 'Matsi poison running in your veins. Tell me: was it your mother or your father who—"

Aeduan yanked upward with his magic. The muscles fired in his biceps and forearm. In his shoulder and chest. Then he snapped his wrist.

The second fon Grieg brother toppled down with a *thump!* Dust spiraled upward. Silence echoed. Even the wind seemed to hold its breath.

Then the man's feet twitched, since, like Shitpants, he was not dead.

Aeduan's nostrils flared. He inhaled all the way into his stomach, letting his witchery ease away like ripples on a pond. The blood off Shitpants's wound still keened in Aeduan's nose. The wind still tugged at his cloak. Nearby, the rats from the shadows and rafters were poking out curious noses. They were too hungry to be afraid, and there was a very real chance they would eat these brothers as soon as Aeduan got out of the way.

So Aeduan got out of the way.

THREE

✳

Vivia Nihar stared at the doorway before her, a sliver of blue light carved into limestone. Lush ferns hugged it close, brushing their fingers against the edges. A snag of grapevines too, with their leaves fluttering on a salted breeze. Cicadas clicked in the thick foliage. A gull cried overhead.

And magic rolled over Vivia, moving in time to waves off the nearby sea. Each caress made her hair stand more on end and her teeth grind inside her ears. She knew *of* these doorways, but seeing one was different from hearing about them. And having one simply appear overnight near Noden's Gift was downright alarming.

"See?" Cam said, motioning with his floppy limbs to the light. "That's it. That's a door that'll take you into the mountain. I don't know where it will take us, exactly, but I'm pretty sure once we're inside, I can find the under-city in Lovats."

"Pretty sure?" Vivia's eyebrows lifted.

"*Very* sure," Cam amended. The boy had come sprinting into the captain's cabin in Noden's Gift half an hour ago, hollering about *magic doors* and *secret tunnels* and *sneaking into Lovats, then Azmir with soldiers.* Then he'd half dragged Vivia and Vaness all the way to the seashore, just below the Origin Well perched atop its fox-shaped peak.

"It is . . . small." This came from the Empress of Marstok, who stood on Cam's other side. She had lately taken to wearing a Nubrevnan-style blouse tucked into sailor's breeches. It suited her. Softened her imperial lines—as did the sea and tides nearby, always tugging her hair from her braided bun. The only lingering reminder of her title and heritage were the iron bracelets she was never without.

Right now, they swiveled like snakes around her wrists. "I do not see how we can fit soldiers through there, much less the forces needed to claim back Lovats or Marstok."

"Right." Cam nodded as if he hadn't just proposed they do precisely that. "Well, we could go single file. Then . . . you know: hope the doors don't close up behind us."

"Right," Vaness said, mimicking him. "The doors closing up behind—a minor detail. Not worth fretting over." She fixed her gaze onto Vivia, eyes hooded. The heat of midday daubed color onto her cheeks. "As you know, I have traveled these doorways, Your Majesty. So while I certainly appreciate and understand their utility, I also understand their dangers. For one, if *we* can use them, then so can the enemy—which, you may recall, the Raider King *did* do when he tried to invade Lovats."

Of course Vivia recalled. And with stark clarity she'd prefer didn't haunt her sleep most nights. Ragnor's troops and his seafire had gotten much too close to destroying the entire capital. *Her* capital.

"For two," the Empress went on, "as Cam has already pointed out, these doors *do* have a tendency to open and shut without warning. You and I have walked by this spot every evening for a month, and only now is there a magic doorway appearing.

"And for three," Vaness finished, her voice regal and clear, "when I was in the mountain with Safiya fon Hasstrel and her Hell-Bards, the cavern was in a state of total collapse. Stones falling everywhere. Ice crawling and eating all in its path. It is not a space I would take anyone through, whom I wanted to keep safe. So not an army, and certainly not . . . you."

Vivia felt her face warm. Her chest too, and she had to force a breath through her nose. A big inhale that expanded her uniform and made old buttons wink in the sun. It was hot in this uniform at midday, but there were appearances to maintain. Vivia was queen, even if her father had fortified himself in Lovats and refused to give up the throne.

Vivia inched closer to the door. Magic scraped and tugged against her. With cautious fingers, she brushed aside a fern. Carvings appeared on the stone. Triangular shapes worn down by weather and time. Familiar, although Vivia had no idea why.

Think beyond, came a voice that sounded like her mother's.

"Are you listening?" Vaness demanded.

"Hye, hye," Vivia mumbled, although truth be told, while she'd certainly *heard* what Vaness had uttered, she'd also immediately discarded it.

Because this was the first change in fortune she'd had in a month. Serafin had lifted the siege chain, sealing off all of Lovats in a magical dome through which no enemy could pass, and for weeks, Vivia, Vaness, Cam, and Shanna, the lead captain from Vivia's Foxes, had tried to devise a way into the capital.

They could wage war directly at the Sentries of Noden, where the siege chain connected. Or they could send stealth units in through the Cisterns. Or they could turn their attention to Azmir and hope to reclaim Vaness's throne first.

But none of it had seemed viable, so instead, they'd done nothing. And the sitting still was proving a very, *very* quick path to madness.

Serafin was holed up in a city with only limited provisions and tens of thousands of refugees from across Nubrevna. The citizens would starve if Vivia didn't do something. Soon.

Wind snarled across her. Sand scraped her cheeks, and salt burned her nose. The ferns she held whipped and waved. "How do we know," she asked carefully, "that this goes where you think it goes, Cam? Maybe it doesn't lead inside your mountain at all."

He winced. "S'not *my* mountain, Majesty. It's the Sightwitches'. And . . . well . . ." He shrugged. "I don't know where it goes. But I could walk in right now. See what's on the other side, if you want."

"And what if you step into a trap?" Vaness snapped. "What if this was all designed by the Raider King? Or by the usurpers of Marstok and Nubrevna? What if you find yourself a prisoner—or worse, dead? *Then* what, First Mate?"

Cam gulped.

"Or," Vaness continued, the flush on her cheeks reaching her neck. Her ears. "What if this magic is simply fickle, as you yourself suggested, and the door seals up behind you? Then you will be stuck inside the mountain for all of time."

Cam blanched, setting off the pale spots on his face. He looked sick. He looked frightened. "You're . . . right. Of course you're right, Your Imperial Majesty. I'm sorry I even suggested such an idea. I wasn't thinking."

Vaness's iron faltered. "Well . . ." Her gaze flicked to Vivia's.

And Vivia pursed her lips in a way that said: *We discussed this, Vaness. You're supposed to be nicer to everyone.*

"You . . . should . . . not be sorry, Cam." Vaness tried to smile. It was terrifying. "It was a good idea. In theory. Just one that I fear is too risky. But, I *do* appreciate you thinking in new ways."

Think beyond, Vivia thought again, and she frowned once more at the door. At its bewitching glow. At the carvings she could almost—although only *almost*—swear she had seen somewhere before. *Probably in the undercity or the Cisterns.* Lovats had so many secret corners and ancient passages.

Including the underground lake surrounded by foxfire that only she knew about.

"We'll station guards here," Vivia said, finally withdrawing from the door. "I'll let Shanna choose who—unless you've an opinion on the matter, Your Imperial Majesty?"

Vaness rolled her eyes. "Of course not, Your *Royal* Majesty. I trust your Fox captain to choose wisely."

Vivia smiled and opted not to point out the thirty-seven times (and counting) that Vaness had very openly *not* trusted Shanna's wisdom. "Thank you, Cam," she told the boy as she released the ferns and backed away from the limestone. The magic's charge receded. "As our esteemed Marstoki Empress here just said—"

Vaness sniffed primly.

"—it's good for us to be thinking in new ways. So keep your ideas coming, please."

"Hye, Majesty." Cam saluted, fist over heart. "I'll try."

"I know, Cam. You always do."

It had become their nightly routine to sit beside the Origin Well and watch the sun set over the Jadansi. There were so many people who wanted a piece of Vivia's time. They demanded it even, these vizers and captains, sailors and soldiers and shop keeps. Then there were the supplicants too—and the sycophants, whose flattery was more dangerous than their desires ever were.

So Vivia's time beside the Well was sacred. *No one*, not even Cam, was allowed to interrupt it.

The Empress of Marstok always sat on a stool on the left; Vivia always sat on a stool on the right; and together, they watched the day end in the west and the night awaken in the east. The Water Well burbled behind them. The sea's breeze gusted ceaselessly, and the river that the Well fed into churned and chopped.

So much water. And all of it calling to Vivia. *Listen to us, Little Fox. Use us and control us.*

Vivia wished she could. Every hour, every second, the hunger ached inside her. A craving that could never be sated. A love that must remain unrequited. *Come, Little Fox. Be one with us, like you used to be.*

Vivia knew if she relented, it wouldn't be *she* who was in control. Because that had already happened against the Dalmotti navy. It had been too much. Vivia and Vaness had barely come back from that deluge of water and iron taking over their minds.

So, ever since, Vivia had avoided the salty, enticing currents in the Jadansi shouting her name. She'd avoided the river and the Well just behind. She could be *beside*, but she could never go in.

How Vaness kept iron always upon her body, Vivia could never comprehend. Then again, Vaness *was* the Destroyer of Kendura Pass. Her power had manifested young, and perhaps the thought of being without the iron frightened her more than the thought of iron claiming her soul.

It hadn't escaped Vivia's notice how often Vaness rubbed at her Witchmark. A square tattoo for Earth and a single vertical line for iron.

And whenever Vaness rubbed, Vivia automatically did the same. Like right now, her thumb massaged the upside-down triangle with a wave inside.

She dropped both hands to her sides. "I want to go through the door," she declared, lifting her voice over the breeze.

Vaness didn't look away from the flaming sky. Her hand didn't stop pressing at her Witchmark. "No."

"*Ahtset*," Vivia countered, angling toward the Empress. They spoke in Marstoki, as they always did on these nights. Silly as it might seem, Vivia felt she owed the Empress. In all ways, Vaness had made a true effort to adapt to Nubrevna: she wore the clothes, she braided her hair, and she spoke Nubrevnan all day long.

So a few words in Marstoki? It was the least Vivia could do. Besides, it was good practice for a queen.

"Don't dismiss the idea, Vaness, simply because you're worried it's a trap. What if it's *not* a trap? What if the door just opened up because the magic is fickle—and what if it *stays*? Then imagine the strategy we could have on our hands."

"I am imagining," Vaness said flatly, "and all I see is violent death." Her left bracelet slithered up her arm to form a band near her shoulder.

"Because you're assuming the mountain is the same as when you went through it. But what if it's like when Cam went through? What if it's not collapsing, and he *could* navigate us to Lovats? It's a brilliant idea—you have to admit that. Just as it was brilliant of the Raider King."

"I do not have to admit anything."

Vivia sighed at the Empress. With curt movements, she removed her coat, folded it—buttons gleaming—and set it carefully beside her stool. Then she unbuttoned the top of her uniform shirt.

The freedom and the breeze felt divine. She might not be able to touch the sea, but she could at least taste it.

"If I could sneak into Lovats," Vivia continued, "I could disable my father without any bloodshed. He would surrender the instant he saw me. It's why he lifted the siege chain: he is terrified to face me."

Vaness's right bracelet now slithered up like the first. Two armbands twining around her. But Vivia couldn't help but notice there was a stuttering rhythm—and she recognized that stutter because she felt it too, living inside the nearby tides.

Vaness stopped her iron. For several breaths, the wind batted loose tendrils across her face. Then she finally swiveled a cool expression Vivia's way. "Let us assume, for argument's sake, that your plan actually works. You face Serafin, you claim the crown. Then what? You cannot believe the navy and soil-bound will simply fall in line. The people of Lovats might have loved you once, but your father has painted you as a traitor."

This was unfortunately true. "All the more reason," Vivia countered, "to avoid bloodshed. I can remove my father from the throne, then confront the vizers. At least a few are loyal to me—especially now that three of their daughters have joined us in Noden's Gift. Then I will lower the siege chain and the magic barrier bound to it, so the Foxes and all our Dalmotti ships can finally sail in with food and goods and . . ." She shrugged.

And Vaness's face softened with something almost pitying.

Vivia hated it.

"Vivia." The Empress scooted her stool closer. She was always so careful to use Vivia's title when they were in Noden's Gift. But here, on their nightly talks beside the Well, she always used Vivia's name.

And Vivia always used hers. "Vaness," she replied.

"I think you overestimate how easily your father will back down."

"Maybe," Vivia admitted, although she didn't want to. It was bad enough having her own father turn against her. A man she'd loved. *Revered.* But he'd allied with the Dalmotti navy just to keep Vivia from claiming the throne that was her birthright.

And in all truth, if she'd actually believed Serafin was the better person to lead Nubrevna, she would have left him on that throne. But good leaders didn't cling to a crown. They didn't send an enemy navy simply to keep their own daughter out of a city. And they *didn't* lift a siege chain, effectively cutting off that city from food, medicine, fuel, or anything else they would need to survive.

Nubrevnans would die if Serafin didn't lift that siege chain. And Serafin didn't care at all.

The Empress leaned closer, reaching for Vivia's hands. Vivia let her take them. Let the Empress's warm fingers weave into her own. And she let Vaness dip all the way toward her until their foreheads touched.

"If we are going to do this," Vaness whispered, "then I think we should do so in secret. We can tell Captain Quintay what we intend, but we must leave her in Noden's Gift—and make it seem we are still there. The element of surprise against your father will not last long."

Vivia swallowed. Her grip tightened on the Empress.

"Cam will have to come, of course, as our guide. For although I was in the mountain, I was running for my life and remember almost nothing. But *no one* else can join us—and *no one* can know what we intend."

"But . . ." Vivia's voice broke slightly. "What if you're right? What if it *is* a trap?"

"Then we will use our magic." The two armbands coiled down. Down. Then slid across onto Vivia's wrists. For several long seconds, the two women were shackled together. "I know we both struggle to control and contain our magics lately, but we *are* still witches. And powerful ones."

"*Ahtset*," Vivia agreed, staring at the iron that bound them. A month ago, she would have been petrified by this nearness. Her heart would have lodged somewhere in her throat. Her mouth would have dried out, and her brain would have ceased all function.

But now she was . . . if not comfortable, at least accustomed. Something wound between her and Vaness. Vivia knew what she hoped it was, but it was not something she could act upon yet. Responsibility and crowns were a siege chain in their way.

Or at least, this was what Vivia told herself. That *this* was why she never leaned in a few more inches—and why the Empress never did either.

"Just promise me . . ." Vaness wet her lips. They were so red at this burning hour. "If we cannot get through the mountain—if it seems too dangerous for either of us or for Cam—then we will return. Immediately."

"I promise," Vivia agreed.

And the Empress of Marstok smiled. A sad, almost resigned thing. Her iron returned to her wrists. Her spine returned to steel. Together, both women angled their attention anew on the wildfire sky.

"Tonight?" Vivia asked after several minutes. There was so much she should wrap up before she left, but also so much that would fall into place if she could just get into Lovats again.

"*Ahtset*," the Empress agreed quietly. "Tonight."

FOUR

✳

Poznin had changed.

This was the first thing Merik thought when the magic of the mountain released him. Gone was the pond filled with dead bodies—although not the bodies. They were still here, but now frozen and slumped across the pond's empty basin.

It was winter now too, the world gray and white.

Aurora whimpered and Merik dragged himself toward her. Her golden fur was stained with red from where the ice had pierced her. Merik was bleeding too. A gash on his chest; a puncture on the back of his calf. They were lucky the ice had not killed them.

"Aurora," he murmured in a voice that felt too loud here, where cleaved bodies had frozen into bloated meat. "You're safe now." He laid a hand onto Aurora's back. Her spine protruded; her ribs too. "We're out of the ice now. You're safe."

Merik didn't actually know if this was true. So far, no Cleaved were approaching—and no Puppeteer laughed or cackled in his brain. She'd been mortally wounded when Merik had last seen her, but she might have survived. He had no way of knowing.

Carefully, he continued to stroke down the storm hound's back, feeling each knob in her spine, each ripple of young, malnourished muscle. Then Merik drew in cold air. It sparkled in his lungs, alive with his Windwitchery. *Maybe I can fly us out of here,* he thought. *Maybe I can summon enough winds to carry myself and Aurora far from here, across the Witchlands, all the way to Nubrevna, where I can . . .*

He didn't know. He'd spent so long trying to escape Esme, then trying to save Kullen . . . and then asleep in the ice. How long had he been frozen? How much had changed in the Witchlands since he'd left it behind?

Slowly, slowly, as Merik continued to stroke Aurora's back, she unfurled. Her body relaxed. Her whimpers ceased. She lifted her canine head and found Merik's eyes with her own of silvery blue. There was trust in those eyes, and strangely, inexplicably, Merik felt his heart break.

He'd only ever hurt those who'd trusted him. He'd only ever abandoned and betrayed them. His crew on the *Jana*. Kullen. Cam. Ryber. Safiya. And even Vivia. He'd tried to help, tried to *be* what he'd thought people needed from him . . . but he'd only ever been a disappointment. Just as his father had always said.

Aurora snuffed, her silver eyes blinking.

And Merik shook his head. "Dark thoughts," he told her, scrubbing a hand over her downy snout. "But as my father always used to say: *Sitting still is a quick path to madness.* Come on, little one. Let's move."

Aurora obeyed, stiffly rising. The wound on her wing was ugly, but it wasn't life-threatening. And Merik thought again of what the strange girls with their archaic speech had commanded. *There's one thing you have to do once you're free: you have to find our father. He calls himself the Raider King.*

That, Merik had already decided, was most certainly not what he was going to do. "This way," he said with more confidence than he felt. "I'll try to lead you around the bodies."

Aurora snuffed again. Her feet were clumsy like the puppies Master Huntsman Yoris used to raise in Nihar. But unlike those pups, Aurora had no interest in these corpses. There was no desire to nose around and root through the interesting smells. She seemed to recognize these bodies were not for her; that there was something inherently *wrong* with them.

Then they were out of the pond, out of the collapsed building, and emerging into the full cold of the day. Merik hadn't conceptualized how much the crumbling walls blocked out a winter wind. It crushed against him now, calling to his magic—and freezing him to his bones. Aurora seemed not to feel it. In fact, she visibly strengthened before Merik's eyes, and visibly brightened too. As if the power of the wind fed the Airwitched heart of her.

Merik knew so little about the magic creatures of the world. They were so rare, more often relegated to legend than ever seen. But he *did* know that creatures like storm hounds and sea foxes and shadow wyrms were creatures of pure elemental power.

Her snout wiggled in the air. The wind rippled and towed through her fur, turning the blood streaks into fluttering lines. Her wings stretched wide, and for several seconds, she looked like a cormorant drying in the sun. Then her injured wing began healing right before Merik's eyes—as if she was absorbing strength directly from the wind.

In a lurch of horror, Merik realized he should stop the storm hound. What if the Puppeteer sensed Aurora's magic? She might jump out and snap wooden collars around both their necks—

But then Aurora folded her wings back in. No longer injured. She blinked slowly at Merik as if to say, *We can go now.*

Merik swallowed. Food. Shelter. That was all he had to find—and without the Puppeteer sensing them. But which way should he lead Aurora? To the left, he could see the top of Esme's tower. He would *not* go that way.

The river? he wondered. *The forest to the east?*

East, he decided, would be safest, and he was surprised how easily he remembered Poznin and its streets. His imprisonment here had been so brief; his mind, his body, his magic so subjugated. Plus, winter had since sapped all color from the city, leaving snow to gather in steep banks along various corridors.

But Merik knew it, all the same.

Aurora kept her wings folded against her spine, lending her a hunch-backed look as she prowled forward. Her nose shoved into occasional snow-drifts. Twice, she pulled up a human body part: a finger. A foot. Like before, she didn't eat them. If anything, she seemed disappointed they weren't proper food.

When they reached a wider avenue through town, the Cleaved stood sentry. These were also as Merik remembered, untouched by time. People of all ages, all sizes, all genders and colors and castes. One tall man with a long, pointed beard reminded Merik of the Northman who'd stabbed Esme.

Merik hoped that man was safe. He hoped that man was headed toward his family now . . . or perhaps already there.

Merik was about to continue onward, when a sound hit his ears. A mere whisper beneath the wind's howl, and instinctively his gaze snapped to Aurora—as if she really were one of the hunting dogs he'd grown up with. Her ears swiveled forward; she heard the sound too.

Someone nearby was crying.

For several blinking heartbeats, Merik found himself not in Poznin but in a tiny room where he and Vivia used to play.

Merik is seven, Vivia is ten. He has just walked into Vivia's "fox's den," as she calls it—the secret room where they keep their toys. He likes to pretend Vivia's dolls are the Paladins from the old stories everyone says aren't true. But where Merik expects to find the den empty, he instead finds Vivia curled up beside the dollhouse.

She cries, with her hands over the top of her head and her face buried in her knees. The dollhouse is sodden, and a pitcher of water now stands empty on a table by the door.

"Vee?" Merik asks. He is afraid because Vivia never cries. And he is afraid because if she is crying, then he is not sure how he is ever supposed to keep himself from doing the same. Their father has already made it clear that Merik cries too much; he needs to be more like Vivia. "Vee?" Merik tries again, and he drops to the floor beside her.

She shrinks more tightly into a ball. Her tears fall harder. They are not the shattered sobs of a girl who has lost her mother, nor the carefully controlled tears she let fall while they threw autumn leaves off the water-bridges at Mother's funeral. They are a whimpering hiccup with an occasional sniff every few seconds.

Merik lays a hand on her arm. She stiffens. Then relaxes and raises her head slightly. Her dark eyes are almost swollen shut. She must have been crying for some time before Merik found her. "Don't tell Father." Her voice is hoarse and tired. "Don't tell him, Merry."

"Tell him what?" Merik asks, and it's an honest question. Is he supposed to keep it quiet that she is crying? Or that she has clearly, once again, lost control of her magic? Or is the secret that she was in here at all and playing with the dolls their father told her to leave behind a year ago?

"Don't tell him what you saw."

Merik recoils slightly, and a hot sensation wrings through him—a feeling he doesn't recognize and one he doesn't like. "What . . . did I see?"

She blinks at him. Then she swipes tears from her eyes. "Exactly." She pushes to her feet, nodding as if she is pleased by Merik's answer. Pleased by his understanding of something he most certainly doesn't understand at all.

But he likes it when she does what she does next: when she pats his head and even smiles a crooked smile that looks so much like Mother's. It's a smile that says, You're all right, Merry, and I'm glad you're here beside me. So Merik bites back his questions.

"I'm sorry about the dolls." She motions to the house, still dripping with water. *"It was an accident, and I'll go fetch a towel to wipe it up."*

"I'll come with you," Merik says, and to his deep delight, Vivia's smile widens and she offers him a hand. He takes it. Her palm is hot and clammy.

They leave their playroom like that. And Merik leaves his questions behind too, until the memory of that afternoon fades. Until he forgets he ever saw something he wasn't meant to see.

It was like a beam of sunshine punching through a storm. And as soon as the memory hit Merik, it was gone again—but the full weight and warmth of the moment remained. He remembered that day in Vivia's den. He did not remember what it was he'd supposedly seen and was meant to keep secret from his father.

It didn't matter now. What mattered was this sound of crying that was so like Vivia that it pulled at Merik's heart, as if a Thread already bound him to the unseen person.

Merik spun toward the whimpers. It was coming from within the rows of Cleaved—and by Noden, whoever they were, they must be terrified out of their skull. *Too fast, Prince*, he thought as he crept toward them, *and your prey will sense you long before you reach 'em.*

Hye, Master Yoris, you're right.

Merik slung his gaze left and right, searching for any movement in the Puppeteer's unmoving army. Dead grass and lifeless vines rattled and scraped beneath his bare soles. Aurora carefully kept pace beside him.

Until Merik spotted a noticeable gap in one of the rows—a hole where snow did not reach, as if someone had just left it there. As if one of the Cleaved had, as could happen, suddenly become fully human again.

The crying broke off, and Merik ground to a halt. "Hello?" He spoke Arithuanian. "Hello? I won't hurt you. I'm like you—I am a former Cleaved and lost."

Aurora stopped beside Merik, and it occurred to Merik that perhaps having a storm hound was not the best way to prove his trustworthiness.

"She won't hurt you. She's just a puppy who's lost too. Hello?"

He glanced around, searching shadows for where the child might be. But he couldn't see anything other than the usual bodies, the usual broken streets and drooping buildings of a city that used to be as prosperous and fine as the greatest capitals in the Witchlands.

Aurora snorted, sinking into a pointer pose, exactly like the hounds used to do with Master Yoris. Her whole body became a perfect line from snout to tail with a front paw crooked upward. Even her wings pressed back along her body to make her a white-furred arrow.

An arrow that pointed straight ahead toward a barren hedge tangling upward along a limestone building. Merik squinted toward it, and hye. There was a slightly darker shape tucked inside.

He lifted both hands toward it and started walking. "I won't hurt you," he tried in Cartorran this time. "I'm like you. I was a Cleaved. I promise I won't hurt you." When the hedge didn't move and the darkness tucked within didn't either, Merik continued his careful inching forward. And he kept on repeating the same phrases, over and over again, each time in a new language.

After Cartorran, he tried Dalmotti. Then Marstoki. Then broken Svodish and even more-broken Lusquan before he circled back to Arithuanian. When he was ten paces away, he could finally see the distinct shape of a child, dressed in velvet with gold rings upon his fingers. His brown skin blended more easily into the shadows, but the day's tepid sunlight occasionally winked on those rings.

The boy's knobby knees were pulled up just like Vivia's had been in her fox's den, and he must be about the same age she had been on that day Merik had almost forgotten.

With his hands still raised, Merik dropped slowly to one knee. His muscles shook; he lacked any of his former grace. "Can I sit?" he asked, shifting now to Marstoki. The boy's style of dress suggested he might be from the east. "I will tell you a story, if you like. It's about two fish who swam into Queen Crab's lair. Maybe you have a story like it wherever you're from."

Aurora, having eased out of her pointer pose, now circled twice. Then huffed down to the ground next to Merik—a welcome body heat. *Tell the story*, she seemed to say.

So Merik did, describing Fool Brother Filip and Blind Brother Daret. Then he told a story about a hungry Hagfish. And another that Evrane had once told him about a little monster who wanted to become a man. Cold burrowed into his bones. Hunger curled through his gullet. And the boy never unfolded. Only the wind broke the stillness as it kicked at the winter-stripped hedges and towed at the coattails and dress hems of an army that never moved.

After what must have been at least an hour of such stories, when Merik's throat was too dry to continue and his body too cold, he pushed to his feet. The world wavered. Blood boomed in his ears. Then he called out, "I am going to search for food and shelter. You can follow if you like. Your choice."

Merik turned away. Aurora went with him.

FIVE

*

They left when the full moon was at its peak. It was when the legends said Noden was at His strongest. Certainly Vivia's magic was. The Jadansi practically screamed at her as she, Vaness, and Cam carefully trekked to the magic door. *Little Fox, do not leave us! Use us! Take us! Carry us with you into the mountain!*

Vivia exhaled against it. *No*, she thought, while aloud she said: "Draw your weapons." The jungle around them thrummed with salted heat and cicadas. So loud, she didn't hear the sound of steel ringing when she unsheathed her cutlass.

She exhaled again, this time more forcefully as she shifted the weight of a pack on her shoulders. Food, healing supplies, water—three days' worth was within. Hopefully it would be enough for whatever waited ahead.

Because they were doing this. The water couldn't stop Vivia; nor could fear. Weeks of being trapped in Noden's Gift, and now she could *finally* move, flow into a new riverbank, return to the plateau she'd always called home.

The magic door shimmered before them. No guards because Shanna had summoned them away for a shift change. The new group of twelve would arrive soon.

The noises of animal life changed almost imperceptibly. The ferns thickened. The doorway glowed like the Jadansi under moonlight, silvery blue and wavering. "It's bigger," Cam said quietly.

"We can still turn back," was Vaness's reply, left hand kneading at the Witchmark on her right.

"No." Vivia's grip tightened on the cutlass, and with her free hand, she checked her collar. Her buttons. But all were in order. There was no reason to stand here simply staring. "I'm going in."

"No!" Cam barked at the same time Vaness hissed: "That is *not* what we agreed upon."

And it wasn't, but Vivia also had never *actually* planned to let Cam go through first. The boy had no magic and his comfort with a blade was nonexistent. So before he or the Empress could actually stop her, Vivia leaped through.

The magic took hold, sudden and staggering. Like diving into a frozen lake, all the breath punched from Vivia's lungs. All thoughts punched out of her mind. Even her soul seemed to depart momentarily as she was torn apart . . .

Then assembled again.

She almost toppled to her knees. She definitely dropped her cutlass. It clanged on stone as cold air wept against her, damp and ancient. She rubbed at her eyes, blinking.

It was a cavern—which she'd expected based on Cam's descriptions. But hearing versus seeing . . . Well, it had sounded like something out of a child's tale, and now that child's tale was real.

The cavern before her could have held the entirety of Queen's Hill inside it. Twice. And all of it was filled with fibrous strands of ice that looked like veins across a dying body. Some of the ice was a pure, almost glowing blue.

And some of it was black, as if cleaving.

Yet this was not the explosive cleaving Vivia knew, so much as the gradual, unabating kind that her spies said swept across the lands northwest of here.

Sheer dread rolled through Vivia. A feeling she recalled from the first time she'd seen the Sentries of Noden. *How can such things exist?* she'd asked her mother. *What magic can make something like this possible?*

Noden's magic, her mother had replied. *Anything is possible with a god on your side.*

At the time, Vivia had thought her mother meant that Nubrevna was divinely chosen. Now, though, she had seen too much of the world to believe such things. And she had met the enemy and befriended her.

It was hard to see Nubrevna as holy if that in turn made Vaness unholy.

You're thinking in circles, she thought. *Get up. Keep moving.*

A flash. A frizz. Cam stumbled through the doorway. "We"—*gasp*—"made it." He doubled over. His sword clattered to the granite next to Vivia's.

A heartbeat later, Vaness arrived too. Her flail swung. Her eyes bulged with incredulity, and like both Cam and Vivia, she gulped in air as if she were drowning. She, however, didn't lose her weapon.

Cam was the first to recover from the journey. He leaped up and whooped. A boyish bound, an effusive sound. One that the Empress immediately cut off. She lurched at Cam, grabbing his arm. *"Hush,"* she snarled. "This is a place of silence."

Vivia absolutely agreed. Cam's cry hadn't echoed, so much as pinged and plowed, skittering off their platform and vanishing into the abyss beyond—where she was almost certain the ice was now responding. It cracked. It groaned. It oozed frozen air this way with tendrils of white fog to drift toward them.

Vaness dipped closer to Vivia. "This is not how it looked when I was here," she whispered. "There was a storm raging—an actual storm, with lightning. And there were winds and rain. And rocks fell while the ground shook."

"It looks like I remember it," Cam inserted, his voice now a whisper too. "But the ice—that's new. It wasn't there before. Not like this, anyway. It was confined to the Sightwitches' tombs."

Cam had described those tombs. A place where Sightwitches went instead of death, so their goddess could take back the magic she needed.

Vivia retrieved her cutlass. She sheathed it, and noted that while Cam did the same, the Empress did not. Her flail remained a flail.

Vivia tiptoed to the edge of the platform surrounding their magic door. It was twenty paces long, and beyond was nothing. Only darkness and black-veined ice. "That's where the spirit swifts live," Cam whispered, joining her. "Or at least, where they used to be."

She nodded but didn't answer. Cold coiled off the strands of ice. Threatening. Hungry. Certainly no starry bird creatures flew there now. No magical beings made of pure Aether.

Vivia was almost glad not to see them. This place was already too disquieting and uncanny.

"Which way do we go?" She looked at Cam. Then motioned to the two paths that carved from their platform. One ascended sharply with rough-hewn stairs. The other hugged the cavern wall and remained blessedly flat.

"Give me a second, Majesty. It's . . . well, the cavern's the same but different." The boy started muttering to himself, striding toward the flat path. "Me and Ry came in over there . . . which means that's the way to the Convent. Then Ry took us . . ." He screwed his eyes shut.

And Vaness, who still stood beside the door where magic could radiate around her, frowned at Vivia. Her nostrils flared in a way that said: *Should we not have figured this out* before *we stepped inside?*

Vivia frowned right back. It wasn't Cam's fault the space had filled with ice since he'd come here two months ago.

"That way!" Cam flung up a hand, eyes springing wide. "The door to the Convent is that big shadow over there, and we went left outside of it. So the under-city must be between here and that shadow."

"Except there is nothing between here and that 'shadow,' Cam." Vaness sounded fully furious now.

"No, no. There is! I swear it, Imperial Majesty. It's just blocked by that column of ice."

"And how," Vivia inserted before Vaness could fume any more, "do we remove the ice, Cam?"

"I . . . don't know."

"Fine." Vivia kept her eyes on the Empress, warning. "We will determine that when we reach it. Let's move." She checked her pack. Checked her cutlass in its sheath. Then set off *without* checking if the others followed. Because of course they did, Cam with a noisy bounce in his stride and Vaness with lethal silence.

No one spoke as they moved onto the narrow path overlooking the abyss. The outcropping of granite was only as wide as Vivia's left arm was long, so she kept herself pressed as closely to the cavern wall as she could. She didn't look down; she looked only straight ahead. And Noden's breath, it was cold. Her fingers were soon numb from clutching at the wall.

For thirty paces she moved this way, until she reached a column of ice she would have sworn hadn't been there a few minutes before. She stared at the cold curling off it, at the fathomless blue of it striated with black. Vivia could fit around in theory, but it would be tight.

And it was a long way down.

Infinitely long, if Cam's stories were to be believed.

Vivia wished suddenly she'd thought to include a rope in her sack of supplies. Such an obvious thing to bring, yet she'd been so fixated on *after* the mountain—on Lovats and her father . . .

What a stupid, foolish oversight for a woman who wanted to be queen.

"Let me go first," Cam whispered, carving through her thoughts. Without waiting for approval, he wiggled past his queen and shot ahead. He reached the ice. He skirted easily around, graceful and lithe—if still too noisy. Then he reached the other side and offered a hand back. "I can help from the front, and maybe Her Imperial Majesty can help from behind."

Vivia swallowed. Shame spun through her. *Stupid, Little Fox.* She made herself nod. Made herself give Cam her right hand and offer Vaness her left.

Cam pulled. Vaness pushed. Vivia scraped ahead, and the ice blazed ineffably cold against her.

The abyss looked somehow too close and also too unreachably far. Maybe she did see stars down there. Maybe she did see spirit swifts.

She stepped again. Her foot planted on the granite just past the ice. One more step and she'd be on the other side.

The ice attacked. An explosion outward of tendrils and shards. It surged over Vivia's outstretched arms, over her legs and her face. *Come, come, the ice will hold you. Come, my daughter, and sleep.* It thrust into her ears, her mouth, her eyes.

Vivia screamed. Or maybe that was Cam, maybe it was Vaness. There was no telling what was what. The ice claimed everything. Cam tried to wrench Vivia to him, but she was frozen down. She was trapped.

"RUN!" she heard Vaness shriek, and abruptly, iron sheered upward. It cut the ice. It released Vivia's limbs and Vivia's brain. "RUN!" Vaness shrieked again, and now she was shoving at Vivia from behind.

They both toppled onto the other side of the column.

Already, the iron was buckling. Already the ice was clambering around its edges and reaching for Vivia and Vaness. It ignored Cam entirely. Not that Vivia noticed that in the moment. All she had mental space for as she staggered after her young first mate was the ice. The stone. The quaking that built beneath her feet. *Come, my daughter, come. Come, come, and find release.*

They reached a door. It was not a magic door, but rather an archway into darkness. *The big shadow,* she thought distantly as Cam towed her through, *that goes to the Convent.*

But Vivia didn't want to go to the Convent. She wanted the magic doorway to the under-city. She tried to swivel back. To see if the ice still hunted or if maybe she could carve a way through the ice and to the under-city door.

But she ran into Vaness, who gripped her tight and shoved her back into shadows. Ice lurched behind the Empress, a glowing blue tidal wave that sang of sleep and hunger. That filled the doorway Vivia had wanted to rush back through.

It crunched, it built, and finally it sealed them in completely.

"Your iron," Vivia gasped. "Can you use it?"

The Empress shook her head, lifting her wrists to reveal no iron shackles. No iron flail or shield. "Gone," she answered. "We are trapped here in this darkness."

SIX

※

The boy followed Merik, skittering and scurrying from shadow to shadow. Merik was careful to never move so fast the boy couldn't keep up. It was hard to stay slow, though. The wind had burrowed deep into his bones. Hunger was so pressing, he felt his stomach eating into his esophagus.

What Merik did not feel were signs of the Puppeteer. She was as inescapable as the tides. Her power seeped into every stone, every branch, every inch of plague-ridden soil. But there was nothing here now beyond wind and cold and these bodies that should be dead.

Bodies like his own. And like the boy still following him.

It was that thought more than any that propelled Merik onward until, at last, he and Aurora reached an intersection he knew too well. This was the way to the Puppeteer's tower, and if he lifted a numb hand to block the wind, he could see it right there: part crumbling relic, part testament to a history long forgotten.

Ancient things made new again. He'd thought that of the tower, where Esme had trapped him, tortured him, terrified him.

But she also had had a stove in there. Blankets too. And maybe, by some miracle, there would be food.

Years later, Merik would look back at this moment as one when the fissures in the ice had finally led him exactly where he needed to be— for there really were no coincidences. But in that moment, all he'd really known was that an unexpected peace settled over him. And it radiated stronger, stronger as he stumbled ever closer to the tower.

When he finally reached the gaping, open door, he paused long enough to look back. The boy was still there, although he'd stopped now. Which was fine; Merik knew eventually the boy would follow. Aurora certainly did, shoving past Merik to be the first into the tower.

She nosed at an old pile of kindling beside stone steps, startling several mice. She snapped them into her jaws; Merik winced at the sound. But then decided he'd rather she eat mice than people.

With a fresh surge of strength, Merik hurried upstairs to the top floor. *The* floor where Esme had made her home.

There was no one there now. There was only her desk, her books, her many slouching candles that hadn't seen flames since her passing. And of course, there was the corner where Merik had existed, bound by the Puppeteer's collar and her capricious, yet calculating whim.

The rags that had been his only warmth were still there. The collar that had blocked his magic was not. For several moments, a tightness gripped Merik's chest. As if his ribs had become a fist, as if they squeezed inward, trying to stop his lungs and heart from working.

Aurora whined. The moment passed. And Merik inhaled, laying a hand on the storm hound's warm head. "We should start a fire," he murmured, though he suspected she might understand his desires even without words. "And then we should look for food, and try to make a bed for that boy outside."

Aurora snuffed. Merik scratched. Ancient things made new again.

Hours later, Merik had found wood and coaxed a fire to life in the stove. He'd found salted meat that had frozen inside a barrel and a loaf of icy bread that the mice had never reached. So, after melting snow, he made a sad attempt at stew.

Then Merik hugged a rough blanket around his shoulders and with Aurora behind him, he climbed the final steps to the top of the tower. The boy had not yet braved the doorway, but he was still out there. Merik heard him shuffling every hour or so.

He would come eventually.

Or at least, Merik hoped he would. Night had fallen; the cold would soon be deadly.

The wind beat stronger atop the tower, and the winter sky was crystalline in a way it never looked on the Jadansi, as if the cold sharpened each star and darkened all the spaces between. There was a full moon tonight, which meant months might have passed since Merik had fled a dying Puppeteer and been swallowed by the ice . . . or it might have only been two weeks. Two weeks seemed unlikely though, given the dramatic change in temperature and snow.

And given the dramatic change in what waited beyond the walls of Poznin.

When Merik had been here as a prisoner, there'd been nothing to the east but swollen river and marshes for miles. Wet forests of beech trees, and plains rolling toward Cartorra. That was unchanged; the very earth there was still a sponge.

But the north and west held a landscape unlike anything he could have imagined. The plains that stretched endlessly to the north, all the way to the Sleeping Lands, were now a clotted patchwork of fires and tents and figures moving through the night. Black smoke drifted across the otherwise unmarred night sky. One plume in particular swept across the Sleeping Giant, diffusing its three bright stars into hazy smears of shadow-light.

Merik surveyed the various encampments. Although dark, the stars and the fires were bright enough—and near enough—to reveal red banners that marked Red Sail tents. Yellow banners that marked Baedyeds. And then loose, shapeless tents that seemed beholden to no one.

"Purists?" he wondered aloud. They had loved the southernmost stretches of Nihar, where poison and fire had drained the land of magic. And they had loved to tell Merik he was cursed for the magic he bore.

Merik strained to see some central spoke to the encampments. Some clear organization that would suggest where, in all those campfires and tents, he might find the Raider King—and this *must* be the forces of the Raider King. It was the only thing that made sense. But Merik could find no coherence, no structure.

The only consistent detail Merik did notice was that all the tents stopped at a very sharp, very specific distance from the northern wall of Poznin. It suggested the raiders and Purists were forbidden from setting camp any closer than that . . .

Or perhaps were too afraid to.

Aurora wagged her tail twice. A heavy thump on icy stones that prompted Merik to absently pat her head. He'd look more closely at this view tomorrow—see if this Raider King was out there . . . and then decide what his next moves should be. Perhaps he *should* do as the two girls had suggested and simply approach the man directly. *Why are these Cleaved still here? Can we do anything to help them?*

It was a foolish thought that disappeared almost as quickly as it formed. Of course Merik would not approach the Raider King. He had already come too close to death; he had no desire to tempt Noden's Hagfishes again.

Merik also would not stay in this place stricken by plague and shadows. These Cleaved weren't alive—there was nothing he could do for them. The boy, though, he could help. He would get the child out of here, and together, they would aim south. Because Nubrevna was home, and Nubrevna was where Merik needed to be.

SEVEN

✳

Heat roars. Wood cracks and embers fly.

"Run." Blood drips from his mother's mouth as she speaks.

It splatters his face.

With arms stained to red, she pushes herself up. She wants him to crawl out from beneath her. She wants him to escape. "Run, my child, run."

He does not run. He does not move. He waits, as he always does, for the flames to overtake him and the world to burn alive.

The wounds on his chest scream.

Aeduan thrashed awake. Thirty paces away, the Earth Well burbled, steam rising off its moving waters. Tendrils that lifted into the night, circling past beech trees with summer plumage despite the winter nearby. No snow touched here; grass grew; and the air was warmer than it had any right to be. Which had made it a logical place for camping.

Overhead, the bright column of stars that Cartorrans called the Sleeping Giant sparkled down, almost bright enough to outshine the moon. It felt bigger this high in the mountains, and there was a sharpness to it from the cold, as if the moon's yellow edges were chipped out of stone.

Aeduan's horse nickered. Then pawed at the first stones edging around the Well. Surefoot was a squat gray beast with a constellation of white spots across her rump and a comfort with mountains unmatched by any man.

Aeduan trusted her with his life. She'd carried him without wavering for almost a month now, one mission after another, always in the name of the Cahr Awen.

"I hear you, girl," he murmured as he hauled himself to his feet. "You're hungry again. You need to pace yourself, though. These fresh offerings from the Hasstrels won't last forever."

As despairing as the main estate had been, the stables had been clean, warm, and fully stocked. The fon Grieg brothers cared about their horses—a reminder that even the worst humans usually had a good side. (And the best humans almost always had a bad.)

After offering Surefoot fresh apples to go with the grass she'd already cleared, Aeduan turned his attention to the Well. He had never been here before, although he knew of it. Iseult had come here; she had healed these waters with Safiya; and what had once been dormant for centuries now thrived again—all because they really were the Cahr Awen.

Without thinking, Aeduan reached out with his Bloodwitchery. It was a habit. An instinct. A need. *Think of Iseult. Reach for the silver taler.* But she wasn't within the range of his magic, and Aeduan already knew that. She was a hundred leagues away, at a hunting lodge near the Solfatarra.

Aeduan ran his tongue over his teeth. One heartbeat passed. Two. Then he strode all the way to the Well's edge and stared into the waters. Despite never having been here, never having seen this Well or watched its waters roil, there was a familiarity that seeped through the night.

And the waters, he was quite certain, stared back at him. Because long ago these waters had been alive.

A thousand years ago, they had been Exalted Ones—not that Aeduan had known that when suddenly one of their souls had been shoved inside of him. All he'd known was that one moment, he was himself. The next, he was drowning and a Paladin named Nadje had controlled his body.

Once, as a young boy living near Saldonica, Aeduan had seen a bear forced to dance by a Herdwitch. All life had been sapped from the poor beast's eyes. There had been nothing left but broken resignation.

That was how Aeduan had felt when the Paladin had been trapped inside him. Nadje had been a Paladin of Aether before death had claimed him a thousand years ago. Now, fragments of Nadje still lingered inside Aeduan—not the man's consciousness so much as memories, hazy and illogical. Like a song from childhood in which the words are gone, but the tune still remains.

And that tune from Nadje had been one of pain. One of hatred and anger and, inexplicably, relief when the end had finally come for him. What end that was, though, Aeduan couldn't remember.

Nor did he want to remember. He wanted that cruel Paladin out of his mind, his bones, his blood. He wanted no memories or songs or fury to ever linger there. Iseult had told Aeduan that over time, these remnants of Nadje would likely fade. That these Threads, now unbound to him, would eventually drift away into the embrace of the Moon Mother.

But it hadn't happened yet, and it wasn't happening fast enough.

Aeduan sank to one knee at the Well's edge. Nearby, Surefoot stopped her chewing and snuffed. Aeduan ignored her, dipping his hand down. Gently, warily.

The water lapped on a sudden wave. It splashed against his fingertips, warm and welcoming. No sentience or hunger or hints of a soul from a thousand years ago.

Now Aeduan was the one to snuff, in a harsh, almost hateful laugh. Because he was being a coward. Of course this Well could not possess him. Assuming any ghost still endured as Nadje's had within the Aether Well, there was no Leopold the Fourth here to force such a being into Aeduan's body.

He is Trickster, Iseult had explained weeks ago, *from our legends. He can return souls to bodies just like the tale of the girl and her hedgehog.*

Aeduan had been too embarrassed to admit he scarcely remembered the Nomatsi gods, much less the fables and stories his father had once told him. The only one he recalled with any clarity was the monster and the honey—and he hated that story. *Collect the six pots of honey, little monster, and you can become a man.* In the end, the monster didn't become a man; because in the end, the Moon Mother broke her promise to him.

Aeduan swallowed. Wet his lips. Then, with an almost frantic speed, he stripped out of his clothes. Cloak, baldric, breeches, shirt, undergarments. Night air—winter laced with enticing heat—stroked his skin and raised chill bumps across him.

He dove into the Well. Water lashed into him, subsuming him with its wild churn. And with a sparkle that he had felt before, inside the Aether Well. One not of ghosts but of a healing embrace.

Within moments, Aeduan surfaced and let his legs float. He drifted on his back, the waters bubbling beneath him, sending him on a lazy course across the Well as he stared at the sky. At the Sleeping Giant, always pointed north.

A sky singing with snow, his magic murmured inside his chest. *Meadows drenched in moonlight. Sun and sand and auburn leaves falling.* It was not a scent Aeduan recognized, nor one he remembered ever having smelled before.

And it also was not a scent that was here. Instead, this was a memory plucked into being from the Old One, Nadje.

Inexplicably, the scent made Aeduan's chest hurt. His heart hollowed out in one sharp twist as if he'd lost a piece of himself—the *only* piece of himself that really mattered.

Monster. Demon. I can smell it on you: you're bound to the Void.
Run, my child, run.

Aeduan flipped onto his side. In four swift kicks, he reached the Well's lip. He pulled himself free, water sluicing off him. Then he sat on the stony edge, legs still in the water, and crooked over to study his chest.

The six old wounds had reopened. For years, they had bled and haunted. Then they had seemed to heal—or at least stop their recurrent bleeding after Iseult had saved Aeduan's life in the Aether Well.

But a week ago, the nightmares had returned and the wounds had begun their weeping again. They hurt too, as if the arrows from Aeduan's childhood once more flamed through his mother's body and into his own. He'd spent most of his life with that pain, just as he'd spent most of his nights with the nightmare of her corpse burning atop him.

Somehow, though, the intensity and cruelty of it all seemed far worse after two months of freedom.

Fresh waves lapped against Aeduan's calves, at odds with the cooling water that dripped over his chest and mixed with fresh blood. Dark rivulets gathered in the grooves of his abdomen and poured down onto his thighs. Onto the stones.

Aeduan waited. And he waited. The wounds did not close up, but the echoes of his mother's voice did fade, bit by bit. And the bleeding did slow. Then stanch entirely, while the pain eased into a softer heat.

Good. That was good.

After a quick scrub to clean away the blood, Aeduan stood. Winter air kissed and nipped against him as he strode to his discarded clothes. As he dressed, piece by piece, with Surefoot chewing audibly and watching him with drowsiness in her eyes.

"You can sleep, girl. I promise we're safe here, and we won't leave until first light—" Aeduan broke off. His bare toes had snagged on something unexpected. Something cold and slinking when there should be only stone.

A Hell-Bard's noose, he realized as he hastily scooped a golden chain off the ground—and not one noose, but two. Both were split apart, no longer necklaces but simply strands of gold to glint across his hands.

Aeduan frowned, lifting the nooses and expecting his witchery to latch on to the fon Grieg brothers' foul bloods. But no. These were different smells entirely, one of coastal storms and freshly turned soil. One of smokeless heat and a father weeping. Yet both scents also carried hints of the noose and cold iron.

Which matched the bloods of the two missing Hell-Bards: Zander and Lev.

For weeks, Safiya and Caden fitz Grieg—a bastard brother to Shitpants and Red—had been searching for these Hell-Bards. Aeduan himself had entered the Solfatarra three times to search for their bodies, since everyone had assumed they must be dead. They'd fallen from a flying machine; they could not have survived the acid lake waiting below.

But there had never been any corpses in the Solfatarra for Aeduan to find, and the mystery of Zander's and Lev's disappearance had stopped being his problem. He'd been sent away on errands. New coins, new causes, new Griegs with things the Empress needed.

Aeduan thrust both chains into a pocket on his breeches, and with hasty efficiency, he finished dressing. Already, his magic was peaking, searching, tracking. The Earth Well had left its mark inside his witchery; he would have no trouble tracing which way these bloods had gone.

After checking Surefoot possessed what she needed—a warm spot to sleep and a bucket of water—he gave her a scratch at the ears. Pressed his forehead to hers. "I'll be back soon," he promised. Then Aeduan set off, tracking the smells like the Bloodwitch he was, no matter what element he might be bound to.

EIGHT

✳

he only light in the mountain room came from the hungry ice. It glowed its vicious blue, radiating in threatening waves—but not entering the room where Vivia, Cam, and Vaness had fled.

How long this room ran, Vivia couldn't sense. Shadows laid claim so quickly beyond the door. She could see the room was tall, like the Battle Room in the Lovats palace . . . yet also oppressive. Claustrophobic. Closing in like a tomb.

She yanked her pack in front of her, and in seconds, she had their lone torch withdrawn. "Ignite," she whispered.

Flames whooshed before her. So bright, so warm. And so revealing. On her left was Vaness, austere and silent. She looked different without her shackles—not weak, but certainly exposed. As for Cam, he was spinning. Muttering. Stalking two steps forward, then three steps back.

"I'm sorry." He met Vivia's gaze through the flames. "I'm so sorry. Empress Vaness was right: we should've never come here, but I'll get us out. I promise."

Vivia lifted a trembling hand to silence him. Her lungs hurt. Her face too, where ice had clawed. "You were not the one who made the decision to come here, Cam. And there is no use in regrets. All we can do is keep moving."

"To where?" Vaness asked, her tone hissing and fanged. "I see no doors."

"No, there *is* one," Cam inserted quickly. "I remember this room— Ryber and I came right through it. It's called the Past, and there was a broken blade and a . . . a broken mirror on an altar." He pointed to the room's center.

Vivia and Vaness both squinted—but if there was an altar there, Vivia couldn't see it with only this one torch for light. By the Hagfishes, *why* did she bring only one torch? What other vital items did her foolish self leave behind?

She rubbed at her forehead. *Stop. Breathe.* Now was not the time for storm clouds to fill her chest.

"If we go past the altar . . ." Cam hurried forward three steps. "We'll reach a door into a long tunnel that'll eventually hit some stairs, and then . . . well, it's a long walk, but it does get to the Convent."

"And how," the Empress pushed, "does the Convent help us, Cam? It's in the middle of the Sirmayan Mountains, is it not?"

"Enough," Vivia bit out. Her voice was weaker than she wanted, because her lungs were weaker. This wasn't Cam's fault—none of this was Cam's fault and she would not let the Empress take such a tone with him. *She*, Vivia, had chosen to come here, so it was *she*, Vivia, who should be the target of Vaness's rage.

"No regrets," she repeated. "We keep moving. Lead the way, please, Cam." Vivia lifted one leg to shuffle onward.

Until Vaness lashed her words directly at Vivia: "I refuse to move."

"What?"

Vivia rounded the torch at her. Flames cast crude shapes on the Empress. On Cam. And on the walls, where carvings looked as if they scuttled and seethed.

"I refuse to move," Vaness repeated, "unless I know that forward is the safest way out of here."

"Well, we can't go backward." Vivia flung a hand at the ice. "It's sealed off and certainly *not* safe."

"We have supplies. We can wait for the ice to move again."

"Unless it never does. Then what? Do you expect us to wait here for the rest of time? Be reasonable, Empress."

"I *was* reasonable." Her nostrils flared. "And you did not listen. Now here we are, in a dark, cursed room in a dark, cursed mountain with only one path forward that will probably lead to more ice for all we know."

"Majesties," Cam mumbled. Neither woman heard him.

"Is this because you lost your iron?" Vivia demanded. "Is that why you're upset? Noden's breath, here. Take my cutlass." She unsheathed her blade.

"That is steel," Vaness clipped out. "Not iron. It takes time for me to separate the iron from the charcoal and manipulate what I need. You know that I only do that for the most important—"

"Majesties," Cam repeated.

"Take the cutlass anyway." Vivia shoved it toward Vaness. "Then at least you're armed. Or would you rather carry the torch? What would make you move from this room toward the other doorway—"

"Majesties!" Cam butted between them, his arms rising. Torchlight flashed on his dark eyes. "I forgot: the tunnel out of here has sleeping ice in it too. Although . . . maybe it's not the hungry kind? There are all these shapes inside—which Ryber told me are the Sightwitches. So maybe, since the ice has already . . . been fed . . ." He trailed off, grimacing as both rulers gaped at him.

And there was the panic again, a thunderstorm in each of Vivia's lungs. *Always so stupid. Why did you come here, Little Fox?* She wanted to scream at those words. Or maybe she wanted to hide. Vaness had warned her, but she hadn't listened.

"Perhaps," she squeezed out carefully, "the best course is to find out if this other ice is indeed hungry. Once we have an answer, we can make new plans."

"And if it *does* try to eat us?" Vaness asked.

Vivia didn't respond. Instead, she sheathed her sword—since Vaness wasn't taking it—and met Cam's wary gaze head on. "Lead the way, please, Cam."

He gulped. Glanced once at Vaness. Then nodded and obeyed his queen. "I'm sorry," he whispered as they strode side by side, leaving the Empress in blue-dappled shadows. "I'm so sorry, Majesty."

"Hush" was all Vivia replied. Now that her eyes had adjusted to the darkness, she could see the altar—although it was really nothing more than a simple table hewn from stone. Boring, empty, and with no sign that anything had ever been there.

"They're gone." Cam hurried toward it. "The blade and glass that used to be here—they're missing."

"Is that bad?"

"I don't know." He grimaced. "This is where we found Stix, though. She was staring at the blade like it was precious. Or more than that—like it was the answer to everything she'd ever needed. But Ryber told her not to touch it. That it would kill her in a way nothing else could. So Stix dropped it and we left."

Vivia had heard this story before—weeks ago, when Cam had first appeared in Pin's Keep babbling about raiders and Stix and danger in the under-city. But like everything Cam had shared, it had all been impossible to imagine. So much so that Vivia had even assumed most of it wasn't true. Not because Cam *wanted* to lie, but because memories often got distorted by pressure, by fear, by chaos.

Plus, Stix had never come back. Two months later, and Vivia still had no idea where her longest friend and closest companion had gone.

Vivia clenched her jaw. Adjusted her sleeves. Thinking of Stix was not what she needed right now. Much like with the waves always shouting at Vivia, the little fox couldn't go that way. The little fox had to resist if she didn't want to drown.

The room's end came into view, a black square in the center that must mark the door into the tunnel. But that was when a vibration ripped out. A rattle, a rumble, a surge side to side. Vivia fell; Cam too; and far behind them, Vaness screamed.

In seconds, Vivia was scrabbling around. Trying to reclaim her legs in a room that was now moving. *And not just the room.* The ice was moving too. A distant glowing shiver that oozed this way like blood from a scab.

Vaness ran. Her own stride was as wobbling and wild as Vivia's. They fell into each other beside the altar. The ground shuddered. The ice throbbed closer.

"It's moving." The Empress clung to Vivia for balance. "The ice is coming into the room."

"Not quickly," Vivia said—which was at least true, if little comfort. Assuming they couldn't leave through the ice tunnel, then they really were trapped here.

"Majesties!" Cam screeched. "Majesties, *look!* There's a hole in the wall! It just opened up in the quake—I'll go through! See where it takes us."

Oh no, Vivia thought. She met Vaness's eyes, huge and shining in the torchlight. Then as one, they leaped from the altar and chased after Cam's figure, already vanishing into a sharp slash newly hewn thirty paces away.

When they reached that hole, having shouted after Cam as they ran— having *bellowed* at him to come back—Vivia pushed Vaness into the new tunnel ahead of her. Cam wasn't answering them; they were going to have to trust that was a good thing.

For the ice was lumbering this way, and with it came sounds. Ones that sang directly into Vivia's brain, *Come, come, daughter, let me hold you.*

And there were other sounds too. Real ones that somehow felt more impossible than anything Vivia had encountered in this mountain so far: laughter. One voice, high-pitched like a child's, followed by a second that echoed in strange angles around the room. *There are no coincidences,* the voices trilled. *Except when there are.*

"Stop," Cam whispered. "I hear people." This was the first thing anyone had said in ten minutes. Maybe twenty. Or maybe an hour, for all Vivia could tell. The "path" Cam had found was more like a fissure in the stone, following the grain. It slanted, it dipped, it shrank and expanded in a way that might have made sense to the mountain, but held no guiding principle Vivia could follow.

At least there was no quaking now.

And no ice.

Vivia took up the rear, her torch wavering in angles that often left Cam blind and calling out, "Can you shine it this way?" But the last stretch had been smooth. Not a true tunnel, but at least a straight line with only the occasional upthrust of stone to get in the way.

Now here they were, a hole in the floor visible thirty feet ahead—and voices most definitely coming through along with more orange firelight. Not children's either, like Vivia had heard earlier, but adults'.

"They sound Cartorran," the Empress whispered, her head cocked and fingers scrubbing at her Witchmark.

Vivia agreed, but said nothing. Her pulse was gaining speed, a stochastic drumbeat fueled by excitement *and* fear. If there were people ahead, that might mean there was an exit from this mountain.

But of course, people also meant potential enemies. Potential danger.

"I'll move to the front," she inserted after several moments of careful listening. She snuffed out her torch. "You take up the rear, Cam, and have your blade ready."

"Hye, Majesty," Cam agreed, squeezing himself against the stone so Vivia could pass. Vaness did the same, her eyes holding Vivia's. She was cast almost fully in shadow. It softened her.

Vivia handed Vaness the unlit torch.

"Be careful," the Empress murmured, her fingers sliding around the grip.

"I always am," Vivia replied.

Which earned her a quiet scoff that was unexpectedly bright in all the darkness. It made Vivia think of all she and Vaness had faced and fought together. And it gave her heart iron when she needed it most.

Ahead, the hole in the floor was just as jagged as the "path" they'd taken through the mountain. It too must have opened in the quake. Vivia crept closer; the voices pitched louder. Two people. A man, a woman, and speaking with an urgency that suggested panic.

"No," the man said, his voice a warm, rounded thing. "I swear that's the way we came. It just looks different after the quake."

"Naw, naw," the woman replied, her voice harsher. Less polished. "You've gotten twisted around. That rock hit you hard—"

"Not *that* hard."

"—and if we head down the steps, we'll hit the big cavern again. See, look. There's a tunnel on this map."

A map. Vivia's excitement tripped higher. She hurried to the hole's lip, craning her neck—inch by careful inch—until she could see the edge of a boot. Then a black-clad leg. Then a sheathed weapon and buckler with a double-headed eagle stamped upon it. Which meant these were Cartorran soldiers.

She yanked out of sight. The Cartorrans were in the midst of upheaval. And while Vaness swore the new leader, Safiya fon Hasstrel, would help the Marstoki cause and Vivia's too, Vivia had yet to receive any actual confirmation of this.

"I wish the commander were here for this mission."

"He's a captain now, Lev, remember?"

"He'll always be a commander to me."

"Don't let him hear that." A snort. "And also don't be so hard on yourself. I think you're doing well for your first command."

"Yeah, yeah. The prince wouldn't have appointed me if he didn't think I could do it. You keep tellin' me that."

"Because you keep doubting it."

Noise rustled behind Vivia, the faintest shift of fabric and scrape of shoe. Then suddenly it was not Cam behind Vivia, but the Empress again. Her eyes were even bigger now. "I know those voices," she whispered. "They're Hell-Bards."

Vivia scrabbled farther from the hole. "And that's good because?" She was so quiet, she more mouthed these words than uttered them.

"Because these are the Hell-Bards who were with the Truthwitch when we were imprisoned in Saldonica. I could not have escaped without them— nor escaped Azmir during the coup, either."

"But why would they be here?" Cam now thrust in, his voice as hushed as Vivia's. "That seems like a real coincidence."

There are no coincidences, Vivia thought. *Except when there are.* She cleared her throat. The hairs on her neck pricked tall.

"I will go first," Vaness said.

"No, wait." Vivia grasped at her shoulder. "We should be cautious."

"Of course. But we also have no reason to hold back. Especially since"— here she smiled and her eyes turned murderous—"they have iron on their bucklers and armor. So if I do not like what they say, I need not listen."

She tugged free from Vivia, and with her usual grace, she dropped through the hole. Her feet landed a half heartbeat later. "Hello, Hell-Bards."

Vivia didn't hear what came next. She had reached the hole and was climbing through. Her pack scraped on stone. Her landing was decidedly ungraceful, and jolted through her ankles, her knees, all the way up to her teeth. By the time she'd wobbled to standing, Cam had plopped down beside her.

The Hell-Bards meanwhile ogled the new arrivals. The walls and ceiling were sharply square; the stairs worn but well carved. Firewitched lanterns guttered in sconces nearby, but twenty paces up and twenty paces down were shrouded in total darkness.

"Empress . . . Vaness?" the Hell-Bard woman asked, her green eyes so wide they pulled at scars fanning across her cheek to her ear. She was young with a heart-shaped, pale face. "Is this real? Is that *really* her, Zan, or am I seeing those nightmares the prince warned us about?"

"I . . . think it's her, Lev." The man's eyes scrunched. He was a giant, his neck so wide it gave him the illusion of having no neck at all. Meanwhile, his short hair was the same color as his browned skin, while a new beard sprouting across his face gleamed fiery red.

"It *is* me," the Empress said in Cartorran, lifting her hands appeasingly. "I am no nightmare. And these are two friends of mine. Cam." She waved to the boy. "And . . . Livia."

Well, Vivia supposed it *was* wisest to avoid revealing her true identity. However, as far as aliases went, *Livia* was blighted bad. And the woman Lev clearly agreed. Her eyebrows crooked high. "Livia, huh? And a Nubrevnan admiral too, who looks a lot like how the rightful queen is described."

Vivia sighed. She was glad to hear the word *rightful*—and frankly glad she wouldn't have to pretend to be someone she wasn't. Her brain couldn't handle any more tumult right now. "Yes, you're right: I am Vivia Nihar, rightful queen of Nubrevna. Cam here, though . . ." She laid a hand on the boy's shoulder. "He really is Cam, but he doesn't speak Cartorran, so if you might be so kind as to explain why you're *here* in the middle of this mountain, then I will translate the situation to him."

"It's simple," Lev answered, shrugging at Zander. "We were supposed to use the magic doorways in the mountain to travel, but. Well, the ruttin' mountain changed on us—twice. We've been wandering around ever since. It's almost . . . what, two days now? Kind of impossible to tell, honestly."

"Travel to where?" Vaness asked as Vivia translated softly. The boy, his mouth agape, just listened and wagged his head.

"Nubrevna, of course." Lev said this in a way that suggested both Vivia and Vaness should have known. "Because we have letters. For you." She looked at Vaness as she said this. Then twisted toward Vivia. "And for you."

Vivia stopped her translation. "A *letter*? From whom?"

It was Zander who replied, his voice somber and practiced: "From Her Imperial Majesty Safiya fon Cartorra. She requests your aid immediately in Poznin, and in return, she will give you all the soldiers you need to reclaim your rightful thrones."

NINE

✳

By the time Merik finished his pitiful but blessedly warm stew, he and Aurora had company.

The boy clung to the safety of the stairs, ready to bolt at the first sign of danger. But there was also an air of awe around him as he took in the sight of Aurora, tail wagging and drool hanging like ribbons from her mouth.

"She won't hurt you," Merik assured, still using Marstoki. "Her name is Aurora. It means *dawn*. What's your name?"

The boy didn't answer—nor did he flee. So Merik shifted back to his cycling of languages, just in case he had judged the boy's clothing wrong. Cartorran. Dalmotti. Arithuanian. Marstoki. It was in Merik's third attempt at Marstoki that the boy finally reacted.

"Revan," he said, his voice surprisingly strong. "My name is Revan. What . . . *is* she?"

"She's a storm hound. Just a puppy though. I found her much like I found you. She needed someone to feed and help her, so I did."

Aurora's tail wagged faster. The boy risked a smile, though it died almost as soon as it arrived when a shiver rattled through him. He was better dressed than Merik for these elements, but he was still just a child. "Where are we?"

Merik inhaled at that question. A drawn-out, audible breath to steel him against what he was about to say: "Poznin. It's very far from where I assume you must have come from. Which is where, exactly?"

"Tirla."

Very far indeed. And the boy must be son to one of the powerful merchant families there; it would explain the fine clothes and rings. "Do you remember anything?" Merik asked. Aurora meanwhile rolled onto her back.

It made the boy smile again. And in turn, Merik's own attempt at a smile widened. "Have you ever had a dog?"

Revan shook his head.

"Then come. I think she'd like her belly rubbed, but it'll take two sets of hands."

Revan didn't move. Merik's smile wanted to falter, but he kept it pasted on. "Like this." He demonstrated, and the scratching sound of his palms on Aurora's belly—as well as her contented grunts—filled the tower.

Revan still did not come in. "There used to be a lady here, didn't there?"

Merik nodded. *Scratch, scratch, scratch.*

"She was bad. She brought me here. And my mother too. But I don't see my mother out there. Just all those . . ." He hesitated. Then uttered a word Merik had never heard before: *Kyrestiri.*

"Kyrestiri?" Merik repeated, letting his ministrations to Aurora pause.

"*Ahtset,*" the boy replied, his eyes drifting to Merik for half a moment. Then to the open window behind him. "The Kyrestiri. The ones that the mountain spits out. It is what we call them in Tirla. Sometimes, the mountain shakes and people change. So is my mother like that? Is that what happened to me?"

Merik was careful to keep his brow smooth. He knew he was prone to frowning, to letting dark thoughts play across his face. "I don't know if your mother is Kyrestiri, Revan, but yes. You were. And I was too."

"And . . . Rora." Revan pointed at the storm hound, who had flopped back over to her side. She stretched one of her wings behind her and nudged it against Merik's knee. "Rora was Kyrestiri too?"

"Yes," Merik answered, even though this wasn't true. Aurora had never been cleaved . . . yet she *had* been spit out by the mountain, just as Merik had.

"Would you like to come closer? I have stew—albeit not a very good one. But it's warmer here by the stove, and then you can tell me everything you remember. Maybe we can find your mother."

Revan inhaled, a furrow sinking across his forehead. Then, with a nod more for himself than for Merik, he finally stepped into the tower. "You never did tell me your name. Sir." He added the title almost as a reflex.

Definitely the son of wealthy merchants. Tirla was certainly full of them. "Merik."

"Oh." The boy's eyebrows shot high. "Like the prince who died in Nubrevna?"

A soft laugh escaped Merik's throat. It was a bitter sound that made his chest ache more than it had any right to. "Yes, just like the prince who died in Nubrevna. Luckily for both of us, though, I'm still alive."

It was clear from Revan's wincing that despite the hunger that must cramp inside his gut, he was accustomed to better fare than salted meat boiled in water.

"I'm sorry." Merik offered a wince of his own as they sat before the hearth. He and Revan were alone now. Aurora had lumbered out of the tower once Merik had served the stew, and he'd felt her take flight in a combination of winds and wings.

He kept checking the window though. Looking for her in the gray skies. Would she be foolish enough to fly toward the raider encampments? Would she be foolish enough to go back toward the mountain and the hungry ice?

While Merik and Revan slurped the hot, salty water and gnawed at the slightly softened meats, Merik managed to pry more information from the boy. His family *were* wealthy merchants, and he actually spoke all of the languages Merik had tried on him.

"Why do you know so many?" the boy asked. He was pulling another face as he tipped back more "stew." Or maybe the face was a commentary on Merik's person, for the next thing he said was: "You don't *look* like you'd know so many."

Fair. Merik set down his empty bowl. "My clothes have seen better days. I was . . . what was the word? Kyrestiri? I was Kyrestiri for a very long time."

This made Revan's face fall. His shoulders slumped too, and he finished eating in silence. Merik left him that way while he moved around the tower and prepared sleeping mats for them both. He would need to get proper food—perhaps from the river to the east, where no raiders camped.

Or, he thought, as a memory struck, *at one of the Nomatsi shrines.* As soon as he thought the word *Nomatsi,* though, he could hear Esme snarling, *No'Amatsi.* Their shrines were all across the Windswept Plains, built for the ancient gods they still worshipped. And at two of those shrines, Merik had found food. It had been a different season then, the tail end of autumn, but maybe he could get lucky a third time.

He would go tomorrow night when he could fly without risk of being seen by the raiders. They must have lookouts; perhaps even this fire in the hearth was a risk . . .

A gunshot cracked through the city.

Merik lunged for the tower window to search outside. In the distance, a shadow trailed across the sky. It was Aurora, except her movements were ungainly.

"You have to help her," Revan cried, coming to the window next to Merik. "That's Rora!"

"Yes, but you—"

"I can hide if anyone comes, sir."

Merik swallowed. There was no denying the white-hot fury sparking inside him. It made his winds come easily; it made him feel righteous and strong. But he'd spent too many years letting that temper be his guide. He was not that man anymore.

A second gunshot pierced the night. The shadow that was Aurora lurched downward.

"I'll be back," Merik said, and just like that, the decision was made. He took flight from the window in an eruption of magic and winds.

Revan barked surprise, and Merik had half a moment for regret. He should have warned the child of his magic. Should have made a point to show him the faded Witchmark on his hand.

Too late now, though, and Merik's regret was quickly swamped by anger. His winds had always been fueled by that temper, and now was no exception. Someone wished to harm Aurora. It was Merik's job to stop them.

He flew higher and faster. A third gunshot ripped out. It missed Aurora, but only because Merik had already blasted her with his own winds, cocooning her as Kullen used to do with him. His magic mixed with hers. It was like a spark to gunpowder. A charge ignited; lightning crackled. She rocketed out of sight.

And now Merik was directly over the people who'd shot at her. Three dark shadows in the night-shrouded city. He dropped straight for them, his fury gathering more power for these raiders who would dare prey on a city filled with Cleaved innocents.

They spied Merik. The two with rifles tried to reload, but their weapons were not Firewitched. It was a slow process—and Merik's winds were so much faster. He swatted the weapons from their hands. He saw no reason to be cautious. No reason to quell his temper. There was nothing between him and the violence he wanted to unleash against these raiders.

But then three faces came into focus. Young faces almost as haggard and hollowed as the Cleaved—and not much older than Revan.

Noden curse me. Merik yanked in his winds. It was like wrenching the lead on a large dog, and it required sheer force and full-body power to pull, pull, *pull* these winds that wanted to attack.

The three people gaped at him in horror. Their rifles had flung too far to grab, and other than a small knife in the hand of a scrawny young woman, they had nothing else to fight with.

She was just a kid, and like the other two with her, she wore Purist gray. *They're not even raiders,* Merik realized, and the last of his winds deflated in an unquenched sigh that sent air roiling off his body.

Dead leaves rattled. Gray homespun flapped on the three teens' hungry frames.

"You need food," Merik said. He tried Cartorran, since most Purists seemed to be from that empire—and his guess was a good one.

"Witch," the boy spat while the girl with the knife simply squeezed her hilt tighter.

The third teen, meanwhile, eyed Merik with a thoughtful look that reminded him very much of the way Ryber would gaze out at the world. With a wisdom that came from having seen too much.

"You got food, then?" she asked, and at once, the other teens looked to her. A subtle movement that showed right away she was their leader.

"No," Merik admitted to her. "But I can get you some. You have to put down that knife first, though." He addressed this to the other girl. Then to the boy: "And no more shooting at my storm hound."

"*Your* storm hound?" the leader asked. She seemed impressed by this, instead of horrified, and it occurred to Merik that although she *dressed* like a Purist, she didn't seem to possess the prejudices of one.

"Well, Aurora is *my* storm hound in so much as any storm hound can belong to someone." He dipped his head toward the other girl. "Now about that knife . . ."

The leader nodded at her, and the girl finally lowered her blade.

"Sheathe it, please." Merik motioned to the leather case at her belt.

Her lips wrinkled back to reveal a chipped tooth. "No."

"You can't expect us to *totally* trust you," the leader said. She shrugged with her hands, a smooth movement from a girl who seemed used to getting her way. And in that moment, Merik felt the slightest tug inside his chest. A little nudge that said, *Oh, she's reasonable. Do as she says.*

Merik did not do as she said. Instead, he felt himself smile. She was a Wordwitch, and he'd wager she had no idea. Or maybe she *did* know and it was why she was not so viciously spiteful toward Merik as her companions were. After all, a Purist with a witchery was a Purist with a death wish.

"Knife gets sheathed," Merik countered, "or you don't come with me for food."

"Come on," the boy urged. "Just do it, Ulga." He was practically salivating.

"I don't listen to you, Birdy." Ulga glared. Then turned to the leader. "Sky? What do you think?"

The leader, Sky, laughed, and it was a surprisingly buoyant sound. One that said, *Ah, he won't fall for my tricks then, will he?* "It's fine," Sky declared. "Sheathe the knife, Ulga, and let's see where this fellow might lead."

TEN

✳

As Vivia read the letter from the Empress of Cartorra, she forgot entirely that she stood in a magically lit stairwell in the middle of a crumbling, ice-filled mountain.

> *For Queen Vivia Nihar: I write to you to offer my assistance in reclaiming your throne from your father.*
>
> *In return, I ask only that you send your current forces east to aid me. You will see a map below with the best route north via sea and river to Poznin, and your recently acquired Dalmotti cannons would be of great assistance against the Raider King.*

The rest of the letter was a detailed description of how the Cartorran Empress would use Vivia's Foxes in direct battle, followed by how Safiya would in turn help Vivia reclaim her throne.

It was absolutely mind-boggling, and it took all of Vivia's mental power to simply remain upright with the letter held toward the light. The Empress seemed to fare no better.

"By the waters of the Fire Well," Vaness swore several paces away. Then, with an almost breathy laugh, she told Vivia, "According to this letter, Safiya already has an agreement with General Fashayid to return my throne to me. No fighting or armies are necessary."

How? Vivia wanted to ask. *How is that even possible?*

And suddenly, it was all too much. Vivia was inside a *blighted mountain* having run into two lost Hell-Bards after sleeping ice nearly ate her and a quake opened up a *direct* path to them. And on top of that, these Hell-Bards had been actively seeking Vivia and Vaness.

There are no coincidences.

Except when there are.

It felt as if the stairs had flipped and the cavern was opening wide beneath her. Vivia dropped the letter and sank to her knees, trying to breathe. Now was not the time for an attack. Now was *not* the time to let the oppressive weight of an entire mountain haul her down. *Be a bear, Little Fox. Be a bear.*

"Majesty," Cam murmured, sitting beside her with worried speed. "Majesty, are you all right? Let me take the pack. I'll get you water. Food."

"I'm fine," she tried to say. "I just . . . need . . ." *To breathe.* Her chest felt like storm clouds. Her mind felt like hurricanes.

A second person sat on her other side. The Empress's scent of citrus and iron tickled against her. "Breathe," Vaness said in Marstoki. "Breathe, Vivia." Her fingers laced into Vivia's. She held fast.

And Vivia breathed. One, two, three. Then she pulled on her mask and became a bear. "You . . . have a map." She dragged herself to her feet. Her fingers were still woven into Vaness's, and the Empress rose with her. "Give it to us."

The woman, Lev, immediately obeyed, pulling a thick vellum scroll from a tube on her belt. But rather than accept it, Vivia glanced at Cam: "Take it. You know this mountain better than anyone else here. See if you can find a way out of this place."

"Hye, Majesty." A sharp salute. Then he snatched the map and scurried toward the nearest Firewitch sconce.

The Hell-Bard Lev's lips pursed, like she was biting back a laugh. And some of Vivia's mask became real; some of her protective bear instincts flared hotter. "The boy," she said in Cartorran, "might be young, but he is one of our best."

"Oh, I believe it," Lev replied. "Because he reminds me of this guy"— she cocked her head at Zander—"when he was first starting out."

The giant only smiled. Of everyone in the stairs, he seemed the most serene. The least worried or unsettled by the total darkness and endless stone surrounding them. Air spiraled down from the hole in the ceiling, exhaling frost every few minutes with a low, almost imperceptible sigh.

Vivia turned away from him and joined Cam beside the sconce. It was an ancient lamp, the glass warped and bubbled. The wick within requiring no fuel to feed it. And around the flames were more of those triangular shapes Vivia had first seen carved on the magic door into the mountain.

"Majesty," Cam whispered in Nubrevnan as she joined him. "I don't like this."

That makes at least two of us.

"It just feels too easy," he went on. "The hole opening up, us finding the Hell-Bards—and even this map." He tapped a part labeled the *Way Below.*

"This isn't what it looked like before, when I was here with Ryber. And not just because the mountain's changing right now—I mean, it's *all* different."

"How so?" Vivia frowned, first at the map. Then at Cam's puckered face.

"Look. See all these doors drawn here in Paladins' Hall? There are nine doors in that cavern. But these seven here—they're the magic portals that lead across the Witchlands. This one is the portal we took, and it even says *Nubrevna*." He tapped at one on the right edge of the map. "We were supposed to go through this one labeled *Lovats*, but we got sidetracked over here."

"Hye," Vivia said, eying the room labeled *The Past*. "And I assume this spot labeled *The Future* is the tunnel you spoke of? With the ice inside and frozen Sightwitches?"

"Exactly. And look, right here, in the middle of the Future." The urgency in his voice suggested Vivia was missing something obvious.

"It looks like more doorways."

"Hye, *magic* doorways. They're drawn the same way as the ones over here, and they're labeled too. This one says *Windswept Plains* and this one says *Contested Lands*."

"All right," Vivia answered slowly. "And those magic doorways are not supposed to be there?"

"No, they're not. I went in that tunnel with Ryber, remember? And there were no portal doors. Not to mention, I know where the original seven go. They've never led to the Plains or to the Contested Lands."

"I still don't understand, Cam." Vivia lifted a helpless shoulder. "What does it mean if there are two new doorways? You said yourself, the mountain is changing right now."

"Yeah, but not like *this*. The mountain can't just make new doors. The first portals were built a thousand years ago by *Paladins!*" His voice had risen. He hastily yanked it back down to a whisper. "That's what Ryber told me. She said only a powerful witch can do the necessary magic. It also requires big stones and Threads and . . . and complicated stuff."

"I see," Vivia said on a sigh—and she did. "You think someone is building new portals."

"Exactly, Majesty. And then they're putting those portals on a map."

"Could it be Ryber?"

"Maybe," Cam acknowledged, but the slant to his brow suggested otherwise. "But I just . . . I feel it in my gut that it ain't. I know I've led us wrong once today—"

"Please stop blaming yourself, Cam."

"—and I don't want to do that again. But really . . . I've got a bad feeling about this map. And"—he dropped his voice to a mere exhale—"I've got a bad feeling about those Hell-Bards."

Hye, Vivia agreed. *Me too.* Aloud she said, "Thank you, Cam. I appreciate your insights. Now if you could pick a direction to get us off these stairs, then we can get moving before all this standing still leads me to madness."

ELEVEN

✳

For several miles, through evergreens and snowdrifts, Aeduan let himself sink into the hunt. He was a collection of thoughts. Of actions. He was not his mind, he was not his body. He was nothing more than the coastal storm and weeping father of two blood scents he wanted to catch up to.

The course ran downhill. Then uphill. Then zagged around thickets and past holly bushes pocked with red. Always, it trended westward. Higher into the Ohrins, and always it followed the easiest course through forest and stone.

The scents grew faint though, weakening by the second.

Until they ran out entirely. Six miles, Aeduan calculated, and almost to the edge of the lands that belonged to Eron fon Hasstrel.

Aeduan sniffed. Flexed his fingers at his sides. If the trail ran cold here, then that meant this was the way the Hell-Bards had come *from*. Not gone *to*. It was useful information to have, which was why he'd followed it this far. But it was not his targets nor their end destination. So he spun on a heel, kicking up snow, and returned, faster now, to the Well. Surefoot's ears swiveled as he raced past. She opened groggy, long-lashed eyes. Recognized him. Snorted. And sank once more into slumber.

This time, the trail moved eastward, and the scents grew stronger with each claimed footstep. So strong, in fact, that Aeduan expected he might come across the Hell-Bards at any moment. If he was lucky, they too would have made camp for the night.

Aeduan was not lucky. Instead Lady Fate abandoned him a mere mile later, as sharply as if she had dropped the knife herself. All blood scents broke off and Aeduan found himself in a clearing filled with snow. At the heart was a granite slab several feet taller than Aeduan and three times as wide. Thick drifts hugged it; ice had gathered in its cracks, creating lines like the Cleaved.

Aeduan hurried behind the rock, hoping the blood scents would continue. But they didn't, and Aeduan could guess why.

This must be the secret doorway into the mountain. The doorway Iseult and Safi—and their Hell-Bard companions, including Zander and Lev— had used to reach Cartorra many weeks ago. There were several such doors scattered across the Witchlands, each portal leading into a mountain filled with stars.

When Iseult had described it to Aeduan, he had struggled to imagine it—until flickering memories from Nadje had surfaced to show him the scale. The spirit swifts flying inside a crevasse with no end. The glowing blue that marked the seven portals carved inside the mountain.

Now Aeduan was faced with such a doorway, except it was shut. There was no magic to radiate off the granite, no bright hole through which he might crawl. The Hell-Bards must have done so, but the door had somehow sealed up behind them.

Aeduan and his hunt were finished already.

He lifted his chin to study the stone from the bottoms of his eyes. His orders were to continue westward, for there were two more pesky doms resisting their new Empress's rule. But those orders had come from Eron fon Hasstrel and Monk Evrane. And although Safiya might have agreed that Aeduan's skills were useful for a task of the violently persuasive nature . . .

He was certain she would much rather know that her missing Hell-Bards had been here. Recently, too, and alive.

Iseult is also east, Aeduan thought, and once more, he cast out his Blood-witchery, reaching for a scent like fireflies stained on a silver taler. It wasn't there, no matter how much he might wish it to be.

Aeduan's nostrils flared. He tapped at the knives strung across his chest. He could easily use a Voicewitch to send this news of the Hell-Bards; as much as he might wish for it, there was no reason for him to return to the Solfatarra and deliver the information in person.

He lowered his chin, decision made—even if it was one he did not look forward to. However, as he twisted to return to the Well and to Surefoot, a third blood scent trickled into his nose. Skated across his magic. Likely it had always been there, but only by reaching for Iseult had Aeduan caught a whiff of it. *Clear lake waters and frozen winters.*

Leopold fon Cartorra. The Rook King. That Paladin of Aether who had cursed Aeduan with a soul not his own—*he* had also been here. Either just before the Hell-Bards, or more likely alongside them.

It was unsurprising, for if Aeduan were the broken bear from Saldonica, then Leopold was the cruel Herdwitch who always made him dance.

Because Leopold made everyone dance. It was his nature. It was the truth of his Trickster self.

Aeduan sniffed again, just to confirm there was no deeper scent here nor the possibility of tracing the former prince's path. But there was nothing, and already this one sliver of Leopold's blood was fading into the night.

Within seconds, Aeduan lost hold of it entirely. And within seconds, he was charging back toward the Well—now with a new urgency. A new excitement. For as furious as he was to discover Leopold lurking and scheming and forcing more bears to dance, this was not news that could be sent via Voicewitch. *This* was a message and a story Aeduan would have to deliver in person.

"Sorry, girl," he said once he reached Surefoot's side again. "I lied. We are traveling tonight. But at least, on the bright side, it will be almost entirely downhill."

TWELVE

✳

Cam chose *up* as their destination because *up* was away from the tunnel filled with ice—and the new doors—and *up* would eventually lead to the Sightwitch Sister Convent and freedom from this mountain.

Vivia insisted the Hell-Bards lead their ascent, and they were amenable. If they sensed Vivia or Cam didn't trust them, they gave no sign of it. And when Vivia probed them about who had made their map, they only ever had one answer: *It came with the letters.*

And who gave you the letters?

Safiya fon Cartorra, of course.

There was a missing piece there—Vivia felt it. As did Cam's gut, since the first time Zander answered this question, Cam hung back to whisper: "There's somethin' wrong about that reply."

"Any idea what?"

"No, Majesty." A grimace on his shadowed face. "But I'll let you know if I think of anything."

The boy thought of nothing before they left the stairs. Nor did Vivia. In fact, soon all her focus was on simply *not passing out.* The stairs weren't steep, but there were hundreds upon hundreds of them, always cast in sputtering firelight and darkness. Vivia's thighs shrieked at her. Her spine too, under the weight of her pack.

Eventually the stairs gave way to a snaking tunnel lit with foxfire. It was roughly hewn, almost a circle in the earth like a giant worm had once come this way.

After taking a brief pause to drink from Vivia's single canteen and the Hell-Bards' two water bags—almost empty now—Cam spotted Vivia frowning. "Don't worry," he told her. "There's water in the workshop. We can refill there."

This was a relief, and Vivia quickly translated Cam's words for the others. Which prompted Lev to moan her joy before draining off the rest of her water. Zander, however, only nodded soberly. And also only sipped once, before returning the bag to his hip.

He caught Vivia watching him as he did so, and she took the chance to say something she'd wanted to from the start: "You are Hell-Bards no longer. We heard the magic that bound you was destroyed. That you're all witches once more."

"Yes," he agreed with a bow of his head.

Vaness stiffened nearby. "You can control plants once more, Zander? And Lev, you can heal?"

"Sort of." Lev grimaced as she buckled her water bag to her hip. "It comes in spurts. We aren't comfortable with it yet, are we, Zan?" She glanced at her partner, and it hadn't escaped Vivia's notice that Lev was the chattier half of their pair—yet when Zander *did* speak, everyone homed in to listen.

Just as they did right now. Even Cam, who couldn't speak Cartorran, slanted toward the giant.

"I miss being outside," Zander said. The foxfire throbbed around him. "But being here, without grass and trees and leaves, is still so much better than it ever was without any magic at all."

Vivia's shoulders tensed toward her ears at those words. She'd spent weeks fighting the temptation of her tides. It had not been easy, and she'd wished so desperately that this deluge might cease so she once more could savor her tides and rivers and rains.

Even that, though—that pained resistance that *she* chose—was infinitely better than having no connection to her magic at all. Right now, she could feel the water in Zander's bag. Just a few mouthfuls that sang to her, as did the water in her own pack. But what would it feel like if those songs were gone?

Without her Tidewitchery, she was nothing. Not a little fox, and certainly not a bear.

She rubbed at her Witchmark—as did the Empress a few steps away—before murmuring that Zander and Lev could keep walking. Vivia wanted out of this mountain. No more breaks, if she could avoid it.

It was another half hour before they reached the room labeled *Workshop.* Cam's guidance had led them true. With multiple floors and stairwells, with shelves and tables and books in countless shapes and sizes, the space was everything Vivia could imagine might fill an experimental laboratory. Papers, glass bottles, metal contraptions. All of it perfectly immobile, perfectly untouched by time.

And all of it lit by foxfire. Hundreds of fungal fans climbed over the space, on the walls and ceilings and shelves. The glow was so bright, Vivia had to squint at first to even see as she stalked inside. Her hands came to her eyes.

A child giggled.

Vivia snapped her hands down. Her breaths turned scattershot as she glanced around, searching the shadows. But there was no one there. Only Cam and Vaness hurrying in behind her. Then the Hell-Bards too.

"Water!" Lev cried as she launched through the workshop to a series of pumps on the walls. "It looks just like the prince's lab, doesn't it, Zan? Maybe we can find a flying machine in here too. Although, I guess that wouldn't be too useful if we can't get out of the mountain."

Zander didn't respond, and rather than follow Lev to the pumps, he turned to stare at Vivia. His eyes, which had seemed auburn in the stairwell's firelight, now looked green. His beard too, and his faintly freckled skin.

She had the sudden suspicion he might have heard the child's laughter as she had.

"There's a spell on the room," Cam said in Nubrevnan, nudging in closer to Vivia. He hugged his arms over his chest. "A preservation spell. That's what Ryber told me, and it's why there's no dust, no spiders, no nothing. It's all exactly like Eridysi left it."

"Eridysi," Vaness repeated, and now she huddled to Vivia's other side. "How is that even possible? How is *any* of this possible?"

Vivia wondered the same, but where such questions struck awe in the Empress, Vivia felt only horror. Eridysi was a woman who'd written a sad song a thousand years ago; she was a Sightwitch no one really remembered; she was as relegated to legend as Lady Baile or the Fury.

Which meant she was not supposed to be *real*, and her Lament wasn't supposed to be real either.

Vivia shook herself. "I don't want to stay here. Let's keep moving."

"Hye," Cam agreed. "The door's straight ahead. Through that hallway across the room. I'll show you." He scampered ahead. Vivia trailed behind. Zander too.

The sheer size of him made Vivia want to cower—which wasn't his fault. And nothing about him cued aggression. Yet Vivia found her strides lengthening to get away from him. The foxfire fans wavered as she passed. The air seemed too thin.

She was ten steps into the hall when she heard a barking cry. *Cam,* she thought, and now she fully ran while Zander galloped behind. They rounded a curve. They saw the boy.

He was fine. Or at least, he wasn't suddenly dead or eaten by ice. Instead he leaned against a massive wooden door, his head hanging in his hands. "We can't get through," he mumbled as Vivia skidded to a stop beside him. The boy didn't look at her. "We can't get through, Majesty. This"—he punched a single fist against the planks—"needs a special key that only Sightwitches have. Unless we can find one of those keys in the workshop, we can't get through."

Vivia stared at the door, trying to process Cam's words. There was no knob to turn, and only a single hole where a key was clearly meant to slot.

"It doesn't open?" Zander asked, joining them. He spoke in his rounded Cartorran.

Vivia nodded. "Locked," she said numbly.

"May I . . . try something?" He gestured to a spot between Vivia and Cam.

And Vivia simply shrugged. "Sure." She gripped Cam by the sleeve and towed him out of the giant's way. But where she thought the Hell-Bard would fling his enormous body against the door, he instead placed both hands upon the wood. His fingers splayed. His eyes closed.

The foxfire brightened toward blinding. So much so that Cam recoiled and Vivia had to shade her eyes. Yet she heard . . . then *felt* as the wood responded to Zander's magic. She hadn't known such a thing was possible— any Plantwitches she'd ever met in Nubrevna had only ever worked with *living* plants. But long-dead wood? Long-*carved* and -*nailed* and -*hidden* wood inside an ancient mountain?

This Hell-Bard must have incredible power.

A groan filled the hall, like metal bending against stone. It was impossible to see in all the light, but Vivia thought the door might be opening. Splitting down the middle as wood fought against hinges.

Then it was done. The light receded, and now Zander was the one to groan. His knees gave out beneath him. Vivia and Cam darted forward, but he was so big. So limp. He crashed down, knocking wood and splinters on the way.

"Zan!" Lev shouted, trampling into the hall. "No, no, *no*, you stupid man!" She dropped to his side, and Vivia dropped with her. Together, they hauled Zander onto his back. He was bleeding from his nose. Gushing, actually.

"Vaness!" Vivia bellowed toward the workshop. "Get the healer kit from my pack! *Now!*" She knew what to do here. This was the same curse that struck the Empress if she used too much power. They had tools to help . . .

But the tools never reached Vivia or Zander or Lev. Instead, the ice did. Black-veined and hungry, it screeched in through the broken door at a speed no human could ever match. Vivia tried. Her arms shot high, her legs sprang her upright to flee. But such instincts were useless against an enemy that wasn't alive and never had been.

The ice covered Zander, entombing him in a single heartbeat.

Then it claimed Lev. And it claimed Vivia too, embracing her, caressing her like a mother coaxing her into sleep. *Come, come, the ice will hold you.*

The last thing Vivia sensed before she lost all sight and sound was the presence of two little girls. They giggled and clapped and watched as the ice did its work.

"The queen of hounds, the queen of hawks, and the king of bats," the taller one said in a language that was familiar enough to understand, but too foreign to identify. "That sounds like it should start a joke, doesn't it?"

"Not a very funny one," the smaller girl replied.

"It *will* be funny, though. Once all the six are together, everyone will have to laugh." As the last slivers of ice shrouded over Vivia's eyes, the taller girl smiled—at Cam, Vivia thought, although she couldn't turn to see. "Oh, hello," she said. "You must be the Nine of Hounds. Do not be frightened. Nine is sacred inside this mountain, for only with nine can one ever think beyond."

Kullen,

I have found some clues, but Goddess, it has taken me too long. On the thirty-first level of the Crypts, the ghosts found an old record from when the twelve Paladins still lived and were the only people with magic.

It was an old text about the differences between Void and Aether—and how the line distinguishing those two powers is thin. I've copied the words of the record on the next page, but suffice it to say that I have a theory: What if you are not possessed but merely a puppet?

You must remember when you began cleaving on the Nubrevnan shore a year ago. There was a vast, wicked storm. You cleaved, and I sang "Maidens North of Lovats" to bring you back to me. At the time, we both believed the cleaving was mere chance—the nature of magic and its growing instability.

Now I have no doubt it was done on purpose. The Puppeteer wanted to control you by binding you to her Loom, which in turn forced you to join the Raider King's forces. But you are no ordinary person with an ordinary soul. You are the Paladin of Air, filled with hundreds of lifetimes.

What if, by cleaving and binding you, one lifetime grew louder than all the others inside of you? The lifetime that belonged to Bastien. What if his strong emotions, his strong *fury* allowed him rise to the surface?

And what if I could instead awaken strong emotions from *you?* From my Captain, my Kullen Ikray?

I will keep searching. The ghosts of the Crypts are used to me by now, and they lead me to new records every day. And as for Skullface and the Death Maidens on the lowest levels, they seem almost glad for my company. They run to me whenever I arrive, and then they linger while I study and read.

I once wondered if they were ghosts or guardians created by Sirmaya Herself. Now I think it's the latter. Their . . . well, *clinginess*, for lack of a better word, makes me think they sense something in the mountain isn't right. And they want *me* to find the solution.

I will. Just as I will keep sending the Rook to your ice tomb.

I love you.

—Ryber

The Six Elements and the Magic Associated Therein

A TREATISE BY
SISTER KOMLA INHAR

It is a misconception to say that Aether Paladins possess power over mind and soul while Void Paladins possess power over flesh. In fact, both types of magic can manipulate Threads—but it is the end result that differs.

An Aether Paladin uses Threads to transfer a soul into a body other than its own. Typically, these souls belong to the dead, and typically, the Aether Paladin will restore those Threads to their original corpse, thereby bringing a person back to life. However, there are records in which Aether Paladins have attached the Threads of the dead into a new body— almost always without the consent of the host.

Control, meanwhile, is the domain of the Void Paladins. They can manipulate a person's mind by weaving a soul against its own desire. In turn, this causes the body to act in ways it otherwise would not.

To put it simply, a Void Paladin creates a puppet. An Aether Paladin creates a possession.

THIRTEEN

✳

Iseult det Midenzi knelt over the dying man. He had been fine two days
ago, his wife said, but now he had these shadowy lines across his body.
Please, are you the one who heals the Cleaved? Please, can you help him?

Iseult couldn't help him.

She had tried. Since dawn, when the woman had first found her at the
imperial hunting lodge, Iseult had tried to weave this man's Threads back
into life as she had done with the Hell-Bards a month ago. *Living, living,
breath and living. Threads that heal, Threads that thrive.* But it was early afternoon now, and still his Threads had not responded.

It made no sense. Iseult *should* be able to control these Threads. She
should be able to heal this slowly cleaving man. Yet it was as if, by destroying Corlant, the very nature of cleaving had changed. Gone was the quick,
vicious death that bubbled up from the core and burned a person from the
inside out, magic turned molten and cruel. Now it was this agonizing thing
that crept over a person for days, sucking the life from them.

It was horrible to witness, and Iseult hated that none of her tools as a
Weaverwitch could stop what Moon Mother had decided must be.

"Iseult," Safi whispered, kneeling beside her. "You're exhausted. You
need to stop."

"I c-can't." Iseult's hands trembled as she wove them through—again—
the man's Threads. Strands like burning silk. Here were the ones that bound
him to his wife and his three daughters. Here were the ones that bound him
to his work as a blacksmith. And here were the Severed Threads eating him
alive.

They seared against Iseult's palms, as Severed Threads always did, except now she couldn't control them. She was going to have to turn to this
man's wife and say, "I'm sorry. I'm so, so sorry."

It was the third person in as many days Iseult hadn't been able to heal—
and the fourth person in a week who'd had no magic but had begun cleaving all the same. *Why?*

"Come," Safi repeated, and this time, she gripped Iseult's elbow, gentle but unrelenting. Iseult didn't fight her Threadsister; there was no point, and Safi was right: she was exhausted.

"I will come back soon," Iseult told the wife, a lie on two fronts. First, because *soon* wouldn't save the man. Second, because Iseult was leaving *soon*. Tonight, in fact. She and Safi were leaving this eastern corner of Cartorra to brave the Windswept Plains.

Still, it gave the woman hope to offer promises. It made this woman feel like someone cared enough to do something—and Iseult *did* care. And she *was* going to do something. "Keep him warm and make him drink water."

"Thank you," the woman replied. The lines around her mouth and eyes were stark with exhaustion and fear. And with love too, for the Threads that bind etched deep marks upon the soul.

Yet as the woman offered Iseult jars of lanolin meant for oiling blades, as a thank-you, Iseult spotted faint shadows within the woman's weathered hands. They followed her veins, and were it not for Iseult's magic—her constant connection to Threads and the corruption that can work inside them—she would never have noticed. But she did notice, she did recognize, and her heart broke for the second time that day.

It was spreading. This slow, incurable cleaving was spreading.

"Th-thank you," Iseult murmured to the woman before her weak grasp on stasis could give her away. Then she hurried with Safi out of the woman's home.

They mounted their horses, a chestnut named Dandelion and a gray named Cloud, and set off into the afternoon. Half the morning had passed while Iseult bowed over that blacksmith. Wasted time with no one saved or healed.

Her throat ached. Her tongue felt sluggish behind her teeth.

"The w-wife is cleaving too," she said once they had left the small village behind. Snow dusted the road, hiding potholes along the edges. Knowing Safi, she would send Hell-Bards to fix those holes later today because, even if she kept saying she was not Empress—even if she and Iseult were *leaving* at midnight, Safi couldn't seem to let the responsibilities go.

It had been a month since Safi had taken full control as Empress of Cartorra. They were calling it a military coup in Praga, and already domnas and doms gathered to oppose Safi. Little good it would do them. Many of the Hell-Bard forces backed her, and although they were no longer bound to a Loom or impervious to magic, they were still the best soldiers in all the Witchlands.

Thousands of newcomers arrived each day to the lodge, Hell-Bards and soldiers summoned from the capital, servants and nobility Safi's magic told her could be trusted, and of course, the necessary craftsmen that followed large crowds and war.

Including that blacksmith and his wife.

"Evrane will go in your stead," Safi said over the whip of wind through barren trees. Over the *clop-clop* of Dandelion's uncrushed gait. "She will comfort the man more than you can. Her magic can at least soothe his pain."

Iseult leaned forward to pat Cloud's neck. The gray mare's breath fogged. Iseult's did too. "Maybe I can still find a solution. We haven't left yet."

"You said that yesterday." Safi's tone was sharp, her Threads fluttering with impatience. "And you said it the day before too, Iz. I don't see how twelve hours will change anything. Which is exactly *why* we're leaving: because you know what we have to do to help people."

Yes, Iseult did know. She and Safi must heal the final Well. They had to heal all magic in the Witchlands, and only then could this cleaving end.

And only then could she and Safi finally step away from the noise, the Threads, the expectations. They were both so tired all the time.

Safi was especially exhausted, what with the added pressure of running an empire—not to mention the Cahr Awen souls stuck inside her. They gave her headaches, bulging her Threads to clotted thickness. Safi never complained, nor even mentioned the pain. But Iseult could see it so vividly.

And Iseult knew there was only one cure for it.

Ahead, the road split: one way toward the imperial hunting lodge, the other south to circle around the Solfatarra. A wagon trundled toward them; a square of Hell-Bards trotted north toward the lodge.

The girls sank into their hoods, fur-lined and drab brown. *We are nothing more than standard travelers on the road. Look the other way, please.* Certainly, their cloaks were finely made, their boots a supple black, and their horses too well tended to be steeds for the road-weary. But as Mathew always taught: people saw what they wanted to see. As long as Iseult and Safi hunched with exhaustion, as long as they kept their horses moving at a shamble, they were invisible.

The wagon's driver nodded at them. The Hell-Bards never noticed they were there. And at the fork, they ambled Cloud and Dandelion south, away from the lodge and all its demands. At this distance, it was nothing more than a lump of white blending into the snow and sky.

A quarter mile down the new road, a trail veered into thickets and trees. Safi reined Dandelion that way; Iseult followed with Cloud. Few people traveled south, and fewer still aimed toward the Solfatarra. Within minutes, a new lump appeared—this one a daunting, shadowy place that both locals and newcomers avoided.

Cursed, they called it, and they weren't far wrong. This ancient, half-collapsed tower was where Iseult had broken her Threadstone and Safi's too. That act had freed all the souls and power that now thundered inside Safi's brain.

It was also where Corlant had died, at the altar in the center. His body was gone, his blood had long since soaked into the earth. There was nothing to show he had ever been here, had ever lived at all—nor anything to show how often Iseult and Safi had visited. For the snow always fell anew. It always erased their passage.

Iseult's cheeks were cold, her toes numb as she and Safi dismounted beside the tumbled stones at the tower's edge. Each girl removed sacks from her horse's saddle before striding into the tower. Past the altar they strode, and into a shadowy corner beside the curved remains of a staircase. Here, a massive mound of snow awaited. The girls each grabbed a corner of a waxed tarp.

Yank. Snap. Snow flew, spraying into Iseult's face. Flaying her cheeks like blades as she and Safi flung the tarp aside and revealed crates to the winter morning. Ten of them, each carefully organized.

"Don't you dare put that there," Iseult snapped as Safi moved toward a box on the left. "That's our camping supplies, and your pack is filled with food."

"Right, right." Safi scowled. Her Threads flashed with russet annoyance. "Food goes . . . here?" She kicked at a bottom box.

Iseult gave her a flat-eyed stare.

"Here?" Safi kicked at another.

More staring from Iseult.

"Here? *Here?*" She kept kicking, red suffusing across the entirety of her Threads with each failed kick. "What about here? Here?"

"Oh, don't kick that one, Safi! That's got firepots inside!"

Safi flinched back. But then promptly resumed her kicking, if more gingerly now. "Here? Here? Hell-pits, Iz, what about *here*?" She had reached the literal last crate.

"That," Iseult answered with a stately nod, "is the one for food. Well done, Safi. You clearly have a knack for this."

"Oh, shove it." Safi stomped to the box. "It's all going to get mixed up on pack horses anyway—"

"It absolutely will not."

"—so who cares where I put this dried meat and wheel of cheese? Maybe it'll taste better if it's with the firepots."

"We've come here at least eight times in the last week, Saf." Iseult shuffled to the first crate Safi had kicked. "How do you *still* not know where things go?"

"I'm a doer. Not a planner."

"Painfully accurate." Iseult wedged off the lid and dropped her own supplies inside: a Firewitched candle that could burn even in high winds, a blanket of salamander fibers, and finally, the newly acquired lanolin jars.

Once it was all inside, she returned the lid, then joined Safi several paces away. It was clear from the way Safi eyed the crates that she still didn't know what was inside them. "What else are we missing?"

"Not much," Iseult said. "Just the Aetherwitched troop map, which *you* need to get. And then a tent . . . wh-which *I'll* get tonight when I go to the tribe." She now leveled her whole attention onto Safi—who pointedly avoided that gaze. "In other words, Safi: you n-need to talk to Caden. Now."

A fresh flare of annoyance on Safi's Threads, but this time it was tinged with mustard shame and a rusted gray dread. Because Safi knew what she had to do, and understandably, she didn't want to do it.

Iseult could hardly blame her for that. If she had to do to Aeduan what Safi was about to do to Caden . . .

Well, there was a reason Iseult had timed their departure for when Aeduan was away.

Safi swiped a hand across her hair, brushing snowflakes off the row of short braids she'd made along the top. "Yeah, yeah. Talk to Caden. I'll do it, Iz."

"Now."

"Eventually."

"*Now.*"

"I'll start with the map first."

"Safi, if you k-keep putting this off—"

"Yeah, yeah, Iz. I *know.* But I promise I'll get it done before you go to the tribe tonight. Does that satisfy you?"

Iseult grunted. It didn't satisfy her at all, but she knew when she'd nagged enough.

Safi heaved a sigh. It was a sound so weary, it briefly veiled all her Threads in bruise-like despair. Her spine slumped. "Why does it have to be us, Iz?"

"What do you mean?" Iseult bounced on her feet; her toes were getting numb standing here.

"Why do *we* have to be the Cahr Awen? Isn't it bad enough that I've got to be an empress? Now I also have to heal a thrice-damned Well surrounded by raiders?" Safi opened her arms to the crates. "I mean, surely the goddess could have found better candidates than us."

Iseult snorted, but it was a humorless sound. She didn't like the worry twining through Safi's Threads—and she liked even less the way the Cahr Awen souls swelled those Threads to twice their usual size.

"If you're getting cold feet, Safi, it's kind of l-late for that."

"I don't have cold feet. Well, I do *literally*." Safi lifted a booted toe. "But not about our plans. We'll leave tonight. I promise. I'm merely wondering philosophically why it has to be us? You know, it's like asking why the sky is blue. I realize there are no easy answers."

"The sky is blue because sunlight gets scattered by things in the atmosphere. Goddess, Safi, didn't you listen to any of our lessons from Mathew?"

A pause. Then a huff. "Of *course* I listened. I meant blue as in *sad*. Why is the sky so sad?"

"Because you keep disappointing it w-with your lies."

Safi laughed, her Threads brightening with pink, warm in a way the tower around them never could be. "Gods below, Iseult det Midenzi, it'll be nice when it's just the two of us again."

"And by the Moon Mother, Safiya fon Hasstrel." Iseult smiled back. "I agree."

The girls and their horses retraced their route. Back to the main road, back to the fork, back toward the crowded lodge, where hundreds of Threads coalesced like a quilt upon the horizon.

When the bridge over the dark-watered moat to the lodge came into view, one set of crimson, furious Threads stood out: Caden fitz Grieg.

Ever since three searches of the Solfatarra had failed to turn up his Thread-family, Zander and Lev, the Hell-Bard had become a walking firepot. And he'd taken to expressing his frustration at anyone who so much as looked at him wrong . . . which was, more often than not, Safi.

It didn't help either that Caden's Firewitchery, which had been culled from him by the Hell-Bard Loom, was now returned. He and countless other Hell-Bards were suddenly brimming with powers they hadn't felt or used in years.

He spotted Safi across the drawbridge and kicked into a canter her way. His Threads pulsed like storm clouds. "How many times are you going to do this?" he demanded once she was in earshot. "I realize you've no concern for your life, *Your Imperial Majesty,* but have some concern for mine."

"I didn't ask to be an empress," Safi retorted.

"And I didn't ask to be your guard, but here we are."

And this, Iseult thought, *is why you should have spoken to Caden sooner.* She had heard this argument so many times in the past month, she could now recite it by heart. Next, Caden would say, *If you leave the lodge—*

"If you leave the lodge," Caden barked, twisting his horse into step beside Safi, "you need a square of Hell-Bards around you. That is the rule."

"And the rule is stupid. I can handle myself. Besides, I have Iseult with me." What Safi didn't add was what they all knew: *And she can easily kill almost anyone.*

"Ah yes," Caden said, taking on a calm, thoughtful tone. "The other half of the precious, irreplaceable Cahr Awen."

Iseult sighed. She had better things to do than waste her time and energy watching Safi and Caden rehash the same argument. Especially since Safi's own temper was fueled by grief. She knew what she had to do—and she absolutely didn't want to do it.

Iseult spurred Cloud into a canter. The horse's hooves clattered into a three-beat rhythm on the road, and neither Safi nor Caden noticed her departure. The Threads that bound them had turned fiery with mutual irritation, mutual unspoken pain. There was little space in their Threads for anything else.

Iseult did not look back.

FOURTEEN

✳

Safiya fon Hasstrel knew that her pacing bothered her uncle. But if she didn't pace, then all this energy wriggling in her body was going to come out through her fists. Back, forth, back, forth across the long room that had once held feasts and feasters, but now held all the missives, tomes, and ledgers necessary to run an empire. The dining table that stretched almost thirty paces was now invisible beneath maps of the empire—and, more importantly, maps of Poznin.

Those were the maps that interested her. Every day, more figurines were added to them, just as every day more were added to the area representing the Solfatarra. And wherever those figurines were placed, corresponding images would appear on smaller Aetherwitched maps that were given to the spies or soldiers who needed them.

Understandably, these maps were closely guarded, because they revealed not only Ragnor's troops but Eron's as well.

"Safi, are you listening to me?" Eron demanded when she reached the midpoint of her usual path alongside the windows overlooking a courtyard.

"No," she admitted, even as her magic whispered, *False*. She always listened—sometimes she even cared. But when she'd told her uncle she had no plans to be Empress, she had meant it. It was bad enough being the Cahr Awen; she couldn't do *both*.

She frowned up at a portrait above the central window. It showed Henrick's mother, a woman with a comparable underbite to her son's. "Do you think," she mused, "the artist *tried* to emphasize her jaw that way or was he just bad at shading?" She glanced at her uncle. "You knew the woman, yes?"

"Gods *dammit*, Safi." Eron hauled to his feet, and Safi felt a twinge of shame at the stiffness in his rise. At the grunt of exertion he tried to hide, but couldn't swallow back.

Turn around, she willed at him. *Turn around.*

He didn't turn around.

Scowling, Safi planted her hands on the table opposite him and forced herself to recite, word for word, everything he'd said: "The Carawen monks and their new Abbot Lizl will leave their Monastery in one week—although only if the snows continue to hold off. You would almost prefer the snows arrive, however, and slow them, because at this point, we do not have a reliable supply chain from Ontigua. Thus, when the monks do arrive, we will be forced to ration."

For several moments, the only sound was the crackle of the fire in the two hearths at either end of the room. Then Eron matched Safi's scowl—the same slouch to his brow, the same sideways curl of his lips, and the same thoughtful gleam in his Hasstrel blue eyes. Clearly she had learned this expression from *him*, and that only made her own scowl sink deeper.

"The problem with our Ontiguan supply chain is the Hell-Bards," Eron continued, pointing shakily toward the map next to the stack Safi needed to pull from. "With half of them leaving the service, our forces are—"

"Weakened to the point of useless. Yes, Uncle." Safi straightened. "I know that's why you sent the Bloodwitch on his special errand."

"And if Habim and Mathew do not succeed on their offensive here . . ." Eron stretched toward another map, using a quill to gesture at the Sirmayans. "Then we will be on tight rations the entire winter. Which is why you must return to Praga. You and Iseult, before the Carawens can reach us." Eron wiped at his brow. His skin was too pale. He needed to sit again, and his scowl was now shifting toward one of personal frustration. He was glad to be alive, but he was not yet accustomed to the body the acid-thick dungeon had left behind.

True.

Unfortunately, Safi couldn't let him sit again.

"The best way to recruit new soldiers is to show them for whom they fight."

"Yes, and for what they fight." Safi scrubbed a hand at her eyes as she walked the length of the table again, her tan breeches rubbing against the wood. The map of Marstok showed ample soldiers in Habim's forces, but all were blocked by mountains thick with blizzards. The one pass the Marstoks could cross was still held by the Raider King. His people would die. The Marstoks would die. Cartorrans would die, and even the Carawen monks. And for what?

War, war, war. All in the name of peace. All in the name of the Cahr Awen.

But then, that is why we're leaving.

"Your plan was such a foolish one," Safi said, her voice fuzzy as she tried to count just *how many* people would die—or how many she might be able to save. "So many years," she went on, "and so many people. How did Mathew describe it? *There are big wheels in motion. Wheels your uncle and many others have spent years rolling into position.*" She shook her head. "What a waste of your time and energy."

"Stopping a war is a waste?" Eron's voice wasn't, for once, angry. Nor even insulted. If anything, he sounded surprised—and mildly amused.

"The way you did it, yes." Safi turned to face him.

"Except that war in the Witchlands *has* ceased, hasn't it? Marstok no longer fights; Cartorra no longer fights; and Dalmotti has withdrawn after a rout at Nubrevna. So I should think my 'foolish plan' has actually succeeded."

"The Raider King still remains, though. Blood will be shed to stop him. A war's worth."

"Yes," Eron agreed. "But once he is gone—once you and your Threadsister have healed the final Well, peace will reign."

"And you think I am the naive one?"

There—that finally did it. Eron set his jaw and turned to face the window. He stared over the soldiers, over Hell-Bards, over the servants and tradesmen rallied to an imperial banner.

In seconds, Safi was back at the map of Poznin and Arithuania. Of *course* the stack she needed was stuck beneath the primary map littered with the Aetherwitched figurines. She gripped the edge, hoping to slide it sideways—

"There has been some good news from our spies in the north."

Safi snapped her gaze toward her uncle. He wasn't turning around—thank the Twelve. "Oh?" she half squeaked. "And what is that?"

"Baedyeds are leaving the Raider King's banner, now that Habim has agreed to their demands in Marstok."

"So they will get back their Sand Sea?" Safi tugged again at the map. Figurines wavered on the top, and she recalled a street performer she'd once seen. The woman had snapped a cloth off a table without disrupting a single dish or saucer.

Safi, meanwhile, was disrupting everything. Three of the Red Sails figurines fell. One of the Baedyeds too. "But what of the people who live in the Sand Sea now? What will happen to them? They will be displaced just as the Baedyeds were a century ago. Have Habim and Mathew made accommodations for them and their families?"

Eron shifted as if to turn.

And Safi gave up on stealth. She yanked like the street performer had, but without the grace. Six more figurines toppled. Then the map was in her grasp. She instantly dropped it to the floor.

"Crap!" she barked, right as Eron finished his aching turn. "I, uh . . . knocked over your toy soldiers." She pasted on a face of contrition.

Eron, meanwhile, didn't respond. He simply sighed, all antagonism sliding off his face. He was once more a tired man doing his best to run an empire. "Safi, please: Will you at least consider traveling to Praga? Discuss it with your Threadsister. I'm sure she understands how much it will help our cause."

Safi rubbed at her forehead. Now that she had what she'd come for, a headache was coming on. One of the monstrous ones that never let her sleep. "I promise to make a decision," she murmured. *Lie,* her magic frizzed. Because her decision had already been made.

"Thank you." Eron opened his hands. They trembled. "Your consideration is all I ask for."

Safi didn't respond. Instead, she dug her fingers into her temples. The pain was building fast behind her left eyeball. Soon it would leap across to the right. "I need to lie down, please."

A flash of understanding—possibly even sympathy—crossed her uncle's face. Though Safi had never directly told him of her headaches, they all must have noticed how often she vanished into her room. And the servants certainly saw the blindfold she'd fashioned out of velvet. It had become her nightly routine to tie it as tightly as she could around her head, until the pressure on the *outside* of her eyeballs felt as if it matched the pressure within.

"We'll continue this conversation tomorrow," Eron said. "Over breakfast."

"Yes," Safi agreed, even as her magic skittered and clawed: *There won't be a tomorrow! There won't be a breakfast!* She swooped down, and after sliding the map into a loose sleeve, she gathered up the fallen figurines. "Sorry," she said as she dropped them onto the map.

And once more, Eron sighed.

For a brief moment, as Safi departed and the door clicked shut behind her, she considered if perhaps she should offer her uncle a good-bye. A proper ending after so many years as antagonists. After all, this might be the last time she ever saw him again.

Love and dread, Safi thought. That was the fon Hasstrel motto, and never had it felt more perfect for this family that was not really a family at all. But Safi couldn't make her feet turn. She couldn't make her muscles swivel back. She simply walked away toward the main stairwell. And although her magic shrieked at her for all the lies she was telling herself—*I don't need Eron, I won't miss him*—she pretended not to notice. She pretended not to care.

On the floor above the dining room, elegant bedrooms overlooked the forest. One such room, small but finely appointed, had been repurposed to house Henrick fon Cartorra. Iron bars were now fastened over his windows; a bewitched lock had been bolted to his door, and four Hell-Bards stood watch at every hour of the day.

"I will not be long," Safi told them as they slid aside so she could reach the door. She and Eron were the only ones who knew the lock spell's rhythms and words. Six beats and five pauses, then the silently mouthed *Goat tits in a piss storm.*

Safi had chosen the password, of course, and she'd chosen it with relish knowing how much her uncle would hate it. Even now, a smile cut through the headache gripping her left eyeball.

The door's locks clicked apart. Safi pushed into the bedroom of evergreen upholstery and wood paneling. At a lone armchair beside a fireplace—one that Henrick had to tend himself—sat the former Emperor. He wore chains around his wrists and ankles, yet on his lap was an open book.

It was the one freedom Safi allowed him: he could choose books from the lodge's library to keep himself busy. Otherwise, he had to remain here for all the rest of his days. Or at least for all the days it took Safi to figure out what else to do with him.

Eron wanted his head on a pike. A logical desire, since Henrick had killed Eron's sister and brother-in-law—Safi's parents—and he had ruined Eron's life along with countless others while cruelly controlling the Hell-Bards.

Safi knew she was supposed to feel the same hatred, the same fury. And certainly her disgust for the man ran deep. Henrick fon Cartorra was the reason she was an orphan; he was the reason she'd been forced into the noose; he was the reason she had lived most of her life on the run as a Truthwitch.

Yet even the most hated men could offer use somewhere.

Iseult had been impressed when Safi had told her this; Safi had been, quite frankly, impressed with herself too.

It helps, she thought as she stared down at Henrick's face—at the cleverness he no longer veiled behind his dark eyes, *that we aren't married and he is powerless.* The man had settled into a complacency that bordered on obsequiousness—all of it genuine according to Safi's magic. This was a man who had accepted his fate and his lack of any future. His mistress and bastard children were taken care of, since Safi wasn't heartless, and so what was there for him to fight for?

"I have only one question for you tonight."

"Hmm?" Henrick grunted, and he shifted in his chair. The wood creaked; it did not sound comfortable.

"There is a negotiation we have with Lusque. They have the better end of the deal, and I want to know why you agreed to it."

"Ah." He nodded and closed the book upon his lap. The title read, *The Great Mystery of "Eridysi's Lament."* "You mean the grain agreement?"

"Yes. They get the grain at such a deep discount. Why would you approve that?" This was a genuine question on Safi's part. One that was not even the slightest bit pressing considering her plans for later tonight . . .

But a question that had gnawed at her for days—and would keep gnawing at her, even on the roads to the east of here. Because for all Henrick's attempts to trick the world, he was not *actually* a fool. And he did nothing without adequate reason.

A fact which was proven yet again when he answered: "There was another deal for shipbuilders. It was old—before I came to the throne, and before my mother too—but it hinged upon intimidation. *Build us these ships or we will invade* was essentially how it read. The grain agreement was my attempt to smooth the waters. Literally."

"Ah." For a brief second, the pain behind Safi's eyeball receded. There was not only logic in this contract, but diplomacy. "And where is the shipbuilding treaty? I haven't seen it."

Henrick lifted his hands. "That, Your Imperial Majesty, could be anywhere. There are so many places I kept such things."

Safi sighed, and just like that, the headache punched back in. "Could you be a little bit more specific?"

Another shrug, this time with a wince that was neither *genuine* in its apology nor totally false.

And Safi heard her teeth grinding, a scritching sound to fill her skull. It was moments like these when Henrick revealed a bit of his old ways, although she didn't think he was intentionally difficult. It was more like the pain in Safi's foot that never quite went away after Empress Vaness had smashed all the bones with iron. Mostly the injury was healed, mostly Safi had adapted to a slight change in her gait to avoid irritating the old pains . . .

But sometimes she forgot. Sometimes she landed badly or twisted too fast because the muscles still remembered how they used to be.

That was how Henrick felt: he had been emperor so long, he could not fall into total complacency overnight, even if he wanted to.

Head on a pike! Eron would have barked were he sitting here. Safi only dropped her hand and said: "I'm leaving tonight, Henrick. In secret."

He bowed his head, as if this were only to be expected. "You go to the Well?"

"Yes." How strange that she could be honest with this man, but no one else in the lodge or her empire. "I'll leave orders that you should remain as you are, but . . . well, accidents happen."

"Accidents happen," he acknowledged. "Thank you for the warning." He bowed his head, a truthful gesture. "And I wish you luck on your journey. May I offer a word of advice?"

Safi twirled a hand. "Clearly you're itching to do so."

"Do not underestimate the Raider King. He amassed incredible power in a short amount of time because I let my attention get distracted."

"You mean *I* distracted you." Safi lifted an eyebrow.

"Yes." A bounce of Henrick's shoulder. "Whoever leaked the secret of your Truthwitchery so that it would reach my ear . . ." He opened his hands. "It helped the Raider King these past months."

Indeed. Safi's nostrils flared. She was certain the leaker had been Leopold. Why he'd done such a thing, however—that question still plagued her. Polly had worn the face of a friend for over a decade, carefully dancing around her magic . . .

Then he'd let his masks fall and his treachery land.

Just thinking of him made Safi's head hurt twice as much as before. She cracked her neck. Worked her jaw. Then said with an air of nonchalance that wasn't at all true: "Good-bye, Henrick. Do try to remember where that shipbuilding agreement is."

"May I have another book?" he asked hastily, as if this was the greatest potential tragedy in his near future. "I will likely finish this latest stack tomorrow—"

"Don't push your luck." Safi glared. "And if you really need something to do, then try considering all the lives you've ruined. Then ponder how very lucky you are to have survived this long when almost every person in this lodge wants to remove your head from its shoulders."

"Ah," he replied.

"Ah," she agreed, and now, pleased she'd said enough, Safi walked away. The locks magically bolted shut behind her. The Hell-Bards resumed their perfect square around the door.

FIFTEEN

✳

Caden was not at his post outside Safi's bedroom.

On the one hand, Safi was glad for this—it would actually be easier to confront him outside the lodge. On the other hand, she was furious. Truly, *furious*. He dared to boss her about, but then he was the one sneaking out as soon as he had the chance?

She knew exactly where he was.

Through the veil of a snow-dusted evening, she could just make him out, riding at a brisk canter ahead. *Ah, the hypocrisy,* Safi thought as she nudged Dandelion faster—although never fast enough to catch up.

They were two miles west of the lodge when Caden finally left the road, as Safi knew he would. Cold bit her face, while snow gathered on her lashes. Her fingers and toes ached with numbness. But she did not slow, because Caden did not slow.

Another quarter of an hour passed before the first snarls of the Solfatarra reached Safi's nose, strong in stench and barbed with acid. Another five minutes, and the acid was thick enough to choke. Her eyes watered. The Solfatarra's sulfuric edge must be near . . .

Yes, there it was. If she squinted, she could just see a pallid fog erasing the forest and killing all it touched. And there was Caden too, no longer mounted but instead striding on foot toward it.

In seconds, the fog swallowed him.

Safi hopped off Dandelion in a wide clearing where gray sky frowned. Nearby lay Leopold's ruined flying machine in splintered pieces. Snow covered what little had not been scavenged for wood and sailcloth. Soon enough, snow and the need for kindling would decompose it entirely.

Safi had come here since the crash, of course. The Bloodwitch had too, searching for two Hell-Bard scents he'd never found. So why Caden thought he might have better luck, why he kept insisting on walking into that acid fog . . .

Safi didn't understand.

Liar, her magic frizzed. *You would do the same for Iseult. You would do the same for Caden.*

After roping Dandelion beside Caden's horse—in the shelter of a towering pine—she marched to the flying machine's corpse. It was on that Windwitched invention that Safi had realized Leopold couldn't be trusted. She'd had inklings before, of course, but it was only upon the *Eridysi* that she'd realized just how much he was not on her side.

Her fingers fisted. How clever Leopold must have thought himself, bringing Safi and the Hell-Bards to his workshop. Showing them an invention the *real* Eridysi must have helped him design a thousand years ago, when he'd been the Rook King.

She hated him. Gods below, she *hated* him.

Footsteps stomped at the edge of her hearing. She whirled about right as Caden coalesced from the fog. He aimed for the pine tree with the horses. Then paused when he spotted Dandelion. Moments later, his gaze found Safi.

They stared at each other. He was covered head to toe in scarves that now bore holes, and a pair of lenses protected his eyes. She was covered simply in snow.

"Well?" she called.

"Well," he replied. His head began shaking as he strode toward her. By the time he reached her and the crashed *Eridysi,* he'd removed his lenses and scarves. Acid had gotten him in multiple places, despite his defenses. There was a line of blisters around each eye, and along the bridge of his nose.

"Well," Safi repeated. "What do you have to say for yourself, Hell-Bard?"

"Nothing, Heretic." He shook his head again. "Only that you shouldn't have left the lodge without a square of Hell-Bards to protect you."

Safi snorted. "Let's dispense with the horseshit, please. Why are you here? *Again?* As your empress, I forbade you from entering the Solfatarra. You do remember that, don't you?"

"And as your Hell-Bard captain," he countered, "I forbade *you* from leaving the palace without protection—"

"Don't." Safi stamped a foot. Snow kicked up around her. "Caden, we have to talk about this. Although, could we perhaps do so while returning to the lodge? I'm freezing."

Caden winced. First at Safi's request, then as snowflakes landed on fresh blisters. "You forget," he offered eventually, "that I am a Firewitch now . . . or rather, *again.* I can get us warm and we can talk here."

There was so much contained in that one sentence: the fact that Caden's magic had returned, the fact that he still wasn't accustomed to it . . . And the fact that he was subtly refusing to obey her because he wanted to remain beside this graveyard.

"Fine," Safi said eventually. "Let us burn what remains of the *Eridysi.*" *And let me finally have this conversation I've been avoiding.*

It took Caden three times to get his magic to spark—and that was only after he and Safi had cleared away as much of the snow as they could. Then it took another three times before the *Eridysi's* wood, damp and cold, would listen to his witchery and feed his magicked flames.

Now the wood burned like a funeral pyre, and Safi had to admit there was something healing about the flames. It must have cut Leopold deep to see his precious creation crash. She hoped this blaze could be another twist of the knife. A sprinkling of salt on a thousand-year-old wound.

Neither Safi nor Caden sat, but instead stood near the fire and let the smokeless heat roar against them. It added color to Caden's haggard cheeks. It made his new blisters gleam orange.

Far, far in the distance, chimes clanged out the eighteenth hour. "I think you should leave," Safi said. *False,* scratched her magic. "I think your time with me is done."

He stared into the flames, silent.

"You want to search for Zander and Lev, don't you? Beyond the Solfatarra? Because you must know they're not here."

Caden shifted his weight, and for the first time since being cornered, his posture relaxed. "I *don't* know they're not here or I wouldn't keep searching. But yes, I would . . . like to look farther abroad."

True.

"Why haven't you asked for permission to do so?"

"Because." Caden glowered at the pyre, his thumb tapping against his collarbone—where a golden noose used to hang. "I'm still a Hell-Bard captain. My duty is to protect you, and I take that seriously."

False, Safi's magic warned at the same moment it murmured, *True.* She moved toward him, and with gentle care, she pulled his hand from his neck. He didn't resist, and so they stood there, hand in hand. "But that isn't the only reason you've stayed, is it?"

For her, this was a conversation between friends, yet she knew that for him—no matter how close they might be, no matter how much hellfire they might have fought through . . . For him, it would always be a conversation between a captain and his empress. She might be his Thread-family, but he could not shed duty. He could not shed his vows.

Sometimes, she wondered what Caden had been like before his father had sent him to Hell-Bard Keep. She saw glimpses of that boy from time to time. Certainly the Chiseled Cheater who had first swindled her out of coins was part of that old persona—the same charming, almost mocking man who could navigate a fraught card game with an admiral in the Red Sails. Who could say *Good enough* even as the world literally burned around him.

It was a personality like her own. Someone who laughed easily and enjoyed a good drink; who reveled in mischief and teasing, yet would never intentionally harm.

But that person was not who Caden was any longer. The Hell-Bard Loom scraped people of their essence, stealing their color and their life. Safi had only been bound for weeks, yet she was forever changed by that Void magic. Small divots had been left upon her soul; they would heal and they would scab, but the scars would never go away.

Caden had lived as a Hell-Bard for so much longer. He'd been consigned to the Loom so much *younger*. And no matter how often he might say that phrase—*Good enough*—Safi didn't think it was true anymore.

"I've crafted a mission," she said, "which will allow you to search for Lev and Zander." *True,* her magic whispered at the same moment that it whispered, *False.* Because she *had* made a mission—but it was not merely so Caden could search. It was mostly so he wouldn't be in the way.

"No." Caden reared away from her. "You can't give me special treatment, Safi. People disappear all the time, and we don't go looking—"

"Of course we do." Heat from the pyre licked against Safi's side.

"Well, I won't do it. I won't accept the mission."

"Even if I command you to?"

Caden set his jaw. The scar on his chin shone, a white line from some blade that didn't quite hit. "You will have to discharge me, Safi. I will not obey."

"And if I do discharge you? Then what? Will *that* make you search for them?"

His forehead cinched down.

"They are your Thread-family, Caden, and until you find them—or at least learn what happened to them—you'll never be whole."

His forehead sank lower. "You think me *unwhole*?"

"Yes." She tugged him closer; he did not resist. Snow tumbled between them. "You're gruff and withdrawn. You don't sleep. You don't enjoy the revelries like the other Hell-Bards, and when I offered everyone a chance to exit the service, you were the first to bark, *No*."

"Because I want to protect you."

"Lie," Safi spat, planting her free hand over her heart. "I can feel it right here"—her fingers curled into a fist—"that this is a lie, Caden. One you don't even believe. You stay here because you have no one else to care for and nowhere else to go."

His eyes flashed with a spark she hadn't seen in a long time. It wasn't anger so much as insult. She had hurt him.

And that, in turn, hurt her. She needed him to leave—she *wanted* him to leave. And as much as Lev and Zander were deeply important to her, they were only a secondary motivation. A distracting left hand while her right hand cut the purse.

Caden tugged free from her grasp to stalk four paces away. "*Most* Hell-Bards have no one to care for and nowhere else to go."

"And you are not most Hell-Bards." She chased after him, matching his drawn shoulders and set jaw. "If I have to discharge you to make you search for your family, then that's what I'll do. But *please* don't make me do that, Caden. You've done nothing dishonorable, so I'll have to tell a terrible lie, and we all know how much I hate lying."

This startled a laugh from him. His brown eyes softened. "Tell me: Does your magic catch *you* when you lie?"

Safi grinned—even if inwardly she grimaced. "I don't want you to go." *True.* "You must know that, Caden." *True.* "But I think you have to." She reached up and cupped his face.

He sighed and settled into her hand. Once, Caden had been her enemy. Now he was her Thread-family. Safi didn't *want* to send him away. She didn't *want* to be away from him. But Lev and Zander did need finding.

And where she was going, Caden couldn't follow.

"If you won't do this for yourself, Caden, then at least do it for me. Lev and Zander are out there, somewhere, and you need to find them."

Another sigh. His eyes closed, and he leaned his forehead against Safi's. She smelled the day on him: steel and snow, Solfatarra and horse. Above all, though, Safi felt the truth of him: strong, reliable, real. "Where do I even start, Safi?" Caden's voice was gruff, and the crackling of the fire almost stole his words. "I have no leads."

"No," she agreed. "But Iseult has an idea—a good one that I can't believe we didn't think of sooner: Threadstones."

Caden's cheeks twitched. "You mean the things Nomatsis make?"

"Yes. Iseult's mother and her apprentice Alma are both Threadwitches, and they've agreed to bind your Threads to stones. It will let you find your Thread-family."

Caden's breath caught. "And . . ." He wet his lips, his head still pressed to Safi's. "Why would they do that for me? What must I do in return?"

"Travel east with them. To Saldonica. They could use a trained soldier at their side."

"So you've already set this up, I suppose." An observation, not a question.

"Yes, I have." *A whole week ago, in fact.*

Caden didn't answer, and for several dragging moments, Safi could see him mentally mapping out what all of this might mean. Traveling with Nomatsis; guarding them while they built him a Threadstone; using that stone to find Lev and Zander . . .

"So this is my mission? And I have to comply?"

"No, of course you don't have to comply." Safi cupped his face again. "But Caden, I want you to. I *want* you to find peace, and I don't see any other way to give it to you." Her eyes burned with tears as she said this, and her magic sang with truth. "I will miss you, Hell-Bard. You know that, right?"

Caden sighed and leaned once more into her touch. "And I will miss you, Heretic."

"Does that mean you will accept the mission?"

He nodded against her.

"Good." Relief poured through Safi now, mixing with her magic—and prickling more tears into her eyes. "Just promise that after you find Lev and Zander, you'll come marching right back to me. After all, who else is going to nag me when I don't have a proper escort?"

Caden didn't laugh, nor even smile. Instead he laid his hands over Safi's. "I will, my Empress."

"Toward death with wide eyes," Safi murmured as she pressed her lips to his forehead.

"All clear," he answered softly. "All clear."

SIXTEEN

✳

Snow fell, thick and white. Iseult's boots left tracks as she trudged through the forest toward the Nomatsi encampment a mile away. Caden's too, five paces behind her. His Threads were alight with nerves, and she could hardly blame the man. Navigating a deadly trail toward a tribe of people who might decide to kill him instead of letting him join?

Oh, yes. She'd be nervous too.

Actually, Iseult *was* nervous. She had only visited the tribe three times in the last four weeks. Not merely because the Solfatarra breathed poison nearby and she had to follow this Nomatsi trail through it—a trail that was constantly changing—but because for all her newfound understanding of her mother, things were not suddenly easy.

Plus, there was Alma, and what was Iseult supposed to say to a girl who'd died by her hand and then come back to life by her hand too?

"Shit," Caden yelped behind her. "Is that a *bear* trap?"

"It is." Iseult wanted to laugh. Instead, she kept her face flat. "And there are more lurking in the shadows. Stay close, Hell-Bard."

"Right." He tugged his wool cloak to him. Then shifted so his heavy pack rested differently. Then seemed to realize Iseult was already striding onward without him, so he scooted after, plowing up fresh snow.

The encampment was quiet by the time they reached it. The sun was setting; most of the Nomatsis were in their tents, preparing end-day meals. Smoke coiled toward a snow-clouded sky. Horses snuffed and pawed, layered beneath blankets. Goats bleated.

Iseult had timed this arrival well. It had been challenging enough to convince Alma and Gretchya to accept Caden as a guard; she was absolutely not up to the task of convincing the entire tribe.

She found Gretchya's tent, the largest at the center of the encampment. A fresh pot of borgsha simmered, oozing out spicy, fatty scents that slithered over Iseult as she shoved inside. Lanterns flickered near Gretchya at the clay pot of stew; Alma worked at a traveling desk covered in gemstones.

Both women looked up at Iseult's arrival. Then their attentions quickly latched on to the man following just behind.

Caden looked absurd inside the tent. He was a tall man by Cartorran standards, and even more so by Nomatsi standards. His Threads, though, were what really shrank the tent down three sizes. The erratic newness of his magic, fiery and fierce. The sputtering pale discomfort of being in a place he'd never expected to be. The green determination encasing all the other shades because although he hadn't expected to be here, he would make the most of it.

There were also bolts of white fear. A sign he knew perfectly well that his emotions were visible to these women. A sign he wished it were not so. He might be used to Iseult, but strangers reading his mind too?

Iseult couldn't blame Caden for such feelings; it was how *most* people felt when meeting a Threadwitch and one of myriad reasons Nomatsis were so hated across the Witchlands.

"Welcome." This was Alma, rising from the desk, because she was ever the diplomat—and also, the more adept at fashioning her Threadwitch face into the expected emotions. Were they her real feelings? Iseult still didn't know. But at least now, Iseult no longer let her confusion bother her.

Alma swept toward Caden, her Threadwitch black gown twirling and sucking up all light. He had paused at the ring of stools that always fill a Threadwitch's home. "I am called Alma," she said in Dalmotti. "And this is Gretchya. Your bag—I can take it."

Caden bobbed his head, the discomfort quavering toward a teal certainty in his Threads. "Caden fitz Grieg. And I can handle the bag. It's heavy." He did let it slide to his feet. Then squared his body toward Gretchya and did exactly as Iseult had taught him: with his hands at his sides, he bowed and said in smooth, lilting Nomatsi, "Thank you for welcoming me to your tribe."

The reaction was instant. Alma smiled—a real one, Iseult suspected— and Gretchya's posture at the pot relaxed. She had not wanted an outsider to join them. But the truth was Gretchya *couldn't* say no. Caden's presence here was a favor to Her Imperial Majesty of Cartorra, and that Imperial Majesty of Cartorra had thrust so much coin, food, weapons, and horses onto this makeshift tribe that Gretchya felt indebted to her very Threadwitch core.

Gretchya dropped her stirring spoon and wiped her hands on her gown. Then she approached Caden in the same way Alma had.

"Welcome." This was in Dalmotti. "Sit, and we will feed you, Caden."

She glanced now at Iseult, her face carved into its usual Threadwitch implacability. "You too, Iseult. We have much to discuss with this visitor, and the night could run long."

The conversation that followed went better in many ways than Iseult had prepared for. Caden's Threads settled into a calmness that spoke well of his adaptability. She'd known the man had been sent on countless missions across the Witchlands, to strange situations ranging from conning a Truthwitch out of coins in Dalmotti to capturing that same Truthwitch in the Pirate Republic of Saldonica. But he'd been so consumed by grief these last weeks—and his new, unsteady magic—that Iseult had forgotten this other side of him.

The Chiseled Cheater, Iseult kept thinking as she watched him turn on the charm in much the way Safi or Mathew would. He had a mission again; it would hopefully bring him to his friends.

Gretchya and Alma could interpret Caden's Threads too, and although they themselves might not wear any Threads Iseult could see, she knew her mother well enough to sense Gretchya was warming to Caden as they sat on their stools and pored over a map of the Witchlands.

"The River Tine will get you south," Caden murmured in Dalmotti, "but it is usually iced over here, where blizzards funnel out from the Windswept Plains—although you should have almost a full month before that happens. Winter comes more slowly in the south."

"We will have to leave the Tine before that, I believe." Gretchya tapped several spots near the map's center. "These cities here are well known for hostility against Nomatsis."

"Right." Caden's Threads moldered with both shame and frustration. He swiped a hand through his chestnut hair. "In that case, we can disembark here."

We, Iseult noted. *Not you.* A quick transition—and she suspected Gretchya and Alma heard it too. She sipped at her borgsha. Then frowned at the half-eaten stew. The horse meat, taken when the beasts died at the Moon Mother's will, was overcooked and greasy. She'd never enjoyed it.

"Not to your liking?" Alma asked. She sat two stools away, her face cast in firelight. Gone was the golden green of her eyes; now, they were pure silver. As pale as the icicles gathering on the trees outside.

"I have gotten spoiled off food fit for an empress." Iseult flushed.

"As have we. Safiya has given us so much. But . . ." Alma slid over to the stool beside Iseult. This near, her eyes practically glowed. "You will have to adjust your tastes once you are on the road."

Iseult tensed.

"When do you leave?" Alma asked.

Iseult's tongue fattened in her mouth. "W-when Dom fon Eron d-decides our armies are large enough."

Alma's eyebrows arced. She didn't believe Iseult at all, but she also didn't contradict her.

So Iseult gave up. "How did you know?"

Alma dipped closer. "Because Rikra, who is selling you a tent, ratted you out. Although, to be fair, she only said something because I cornered her and asked."

Iseult sighed. "I see."

"This is not a bad thing," Alma insisted. "She was going to sell you a broken tent for too much coin, and I will give you a good one for free. *And.*" She leaned closer. Then she half whispered: "I have assembled more things that might be useful. We Nomatsis travel so much, you know. We have useful tools that weigh less and pack smaller. It's all in a bag behind the tent. I've covered it with pine branches."

Iseult didn't know how to respond to this. It felt so much like a moment a month ago when Alma had followed her through the forest east of here and given her a satchel of supplies. Iseult had asked why Alma had helped then, and Alma had answered: *Because Moon Mother always protects her own.*

Iseult didn't ask Alma why she helped this time. She knew the answer would be the same—but now they both would remember the time Iseult hadn't helped Alma at all.

"Does m-my mother know?"

"I have not discussed it with Gretchya, but I would think she can guess what you intend. After all, there is no other path before you."

No, Iseult thought. *There isn't.* She and Safi might not have known it, but they'd been locked into the future from the day they were born.

"I saw her, you know," Alma continued, still so near. Still so quiet. "She was surrounded by stars and shadow. And I felt whole. I felt unafraid and loved to the core of my Threads." Alma's glowing eyes held steady on Iseult's face. "But she is dying, and I fear these new Threads, this new slow cleaving—it is her attempt to take back what little power she can."

"Yes," Iseult agreed on an exhale.

"Until you heal the final Well, none of us are safe. Any of us might be the next target Moon Mother takes from."

Iseult nodded.

"So it is good that you go now to heal the Well. And if there is anything more I can do to help you along your way, then you need only ask."

"Ah." Iseult sighed again, a sad, heavy sound that sank into the earth. There was *so much* building inside her. More than her lungs could contain. More than her heart or chest could hold.

She forced her throat to swallow. Then she clasped Alma's bicep. "Y-y-you . . ." She paused. Tried again: "*You* have already done too much, Alma. I will ask for no more."

"It is not for you that I make this offer, though." Alma's lips twitched in a way that might be a smile, or might simply be annoyance. "It is for Moon Mother, because if you do not heal the Well, we all will suffer."

Iseult let her hand slide off Alma. "In that case, all I ask is that you keep my mother safe. And . . . well, Caden, too."

"I will watch over them both, Iseult. With every tool and weapon I have."

There was the swelling again, but now it pushed against Iseult's skull. She wiggled her nose—once, twice—before standing. It stretched a distance between her and the girl who could have been her sister if only Iseult had let her in.

Caden did not look up. His Threads were fully concentrated on the map. Gretchya, however, did. She blinked at her daughter, her eyes nearly orange in the firelight. And she nodded once, knowing. Or perhaps there was something else, something almost sad, almost frightened.

But something that her Threadwitch training still couldn't let free.

Iseult twisted away. "I w-will find you and my mother again in Saldonica," she promised Alma. A simple good-bye before she left the tent. Left the tribe.

The night and its moon whispered a Nomatsi good-bye as Iseult found the pack Alma had left beneath furry branches. It was a proper Nomatsi pack, with structural rods meant to be hefted onto the back or alternatively reshaped across a horse.

Alma had added a Nomatsi shield too, a wooden square meant to protect one's body when on the run.

Iseult's lungs compressed, pushing air from her chest as she hefted the pack onto her shoulders. Snowflakes fell anew, tender things. Hesitant even, as if they weren't sure the world was ready for them.

Iseult wasn't sure either, but she set off into the night anyway. Cold embraced her. Snow swallowed her footsteps.

SEVENTEEN

✳

Safi knew she needed to finish packing. She'd gotten the map; she'd han-dled her Hell-Bard captain; all that was left was to gather her travel clothes for the night's departure. And eat—she should probably eat.

However, all Safi was *actually* able to do was to stagger through the lodge toward her bedroom. Tears over Caden had accumulated in her skull. And worse, always worse, the Cahr Awen were being noisy.

Relentlessly noisy, but in an incoherent way that resulted from a hun-dred souls mashing together with no single language and no real grasp on reality. It was like having a beehive for a skull. They buzzed, they droned, they never wanted to sleep.

Tonight, they were especially rattled. *Do something* seemed to be their message—but that was as much clarity as Safi could glean from them.

And gods below, her head hurt. All she wanted to do was curl onto her bed with her velvet band across her eyes. Surely the souls would quiet eventually, and maybe, if she was lucky, she could get a few hours of sleep after that.

Unfortunately, Safi didn't reach her door before Monk Evrane cornered her. *So close,* Safi thought, gazing at her nearby square of Hell-Bards.

"Excuse me," Evrane said, holding a satchel the size of two fists. "I have a healer's kit here that Iseult requested. But she is not in her quarters. Per-haps I can give it to you?"

"Of course," Safi forced out. *Be polite. Don't cringe.* "That's very helpful of you, Monk Evrane. Thank you." She tried to move past.

But the monk cut into her path. "I thought perhaps Iseult was injured, but now I suspect *you* are the one who is actually hurting." Then she quickly added, "Your Imperial Majesty."

Evrane was a woman accustomed to titles and royalty, and as such, she hadn't once tried to cross the barriers of Safi's crown since joining them. A wall had come up around Safi that only Uncle Eron and Caden seemed comfortable enough to cross. And Iseult, of course.

Although, to be fair, Safi *did* avoid Evrane as often as she could, giving the woman no opportunities to even pass within her imperial cage. Safi's brain hurt all the time. She didn't want Evrane nagging her precisely as she was doing now.

Liar, her magic nudged. *You know that is not why you avoid her.*

"No pain," Safi lied, "I am fine." Her voice didn't sound convincing—and Evrane clearly didn't believe her, because for once, the monk pushed against Safi's cage.

"Are you injured?"

"No, I'm fine." Her magic scratched at her spine. *Lie, lie, lie.*

And Monk Evrane nudged once more: "I can ease pain, you know. Or craft you Painstones that will help whatever it is that ails you."

Painstones. Safi had tried one of those a week ago. It hadn't helped at all.

"Or," Evrane continued, advancing a single step closer and dropping her voice, "I can help you fall asleep."

Ah. Now they had gotten to the crux of the matter. "It's the Cahr Awen souls, Monk Evrane. All the souls that are trapped inside me from the broken Threadstones. They . . . push." Safi dug her fingers into the left side of her forehead, as if this motion might somehow explain how it felt. "It hurts and makes sleep difficult."

"Hmm," Evrane agreed, as if all of this made sense to her. "I cannot relieve your burden, Your Imperial Majesty, but I can attempt to dull the pain—and I can certainly give you enough relief for sleep. That is . . . if you will allow me into your quarters?"

Safi swallowed. She didn't want Evrane in her quarters. She didn't want Evrane talking to her in this voice accented by Nubrevnan. Most of all, she didn't want to open her eyes and meet the dark Nihar irises she knew were standing *right there.* Inescapable.

Safi swallowed a second time. Then, after several seconds of only taut silence to fill the hall, she twisted away from Evrane. "All right," she said, finally letting her eyes open. "You may come inside."

Safi didn't bother to remove her day's clothes, filthy though her shirt was and even filthier the gray breeches. Even her boots she kept on. The flames in her hearth rolled heat through the room and flickered orange light over a tall, many-paned window with a desk beneath it and a wide canopied bed several paces away—a bed onto which Safi now flung herself.

"Do what you will," she said with a flip of her hand toward the monk who'd followed her. Then Safi closed her eyes and waited. She couldn't look at Evrane closely. She *couldn't*.

Evrane didn't move for several seconds, and Safi could easily imagine the indecision the monk must feel. She adhered so strongly to formality. To ritual and station, to bows and titles and of course, the holy adulation she afforded both Safi and Iseult. All her life Evrane had dreamed of finding and supporting the Cahr Awen, now here was the chosen pair. Now, here were all the Wells being healed one by one.

But in the end, Safi was still just a girl with a headache who hadn't slept in so very, very long. And in the end, Evrane was a healer witch.

Safi heard when Evrane moved: a slight clinking of belt buckles and blades, a soft swish of her white Carawen cloak as if she pulled it back from her shoulders. Safi felt the weight of the monk easing onto the mattress beside her.

"It is your head that hurts? Anywhere else?"

"No. Just the head. And . . . well, the neck in turn." Safi was careful to keep her eyes clenched shut. Evrane was very near. Nearer than she had been in the hall. Nearer than she had been since returning to Safi's company a month ago.

Almost as near as her nephew had been during their brief encounter inside a mountain.

"I cannot draw out the souls that cause the pressure," Evrane explained, lowering her voice to a gentle intimacy. "I will do what I can to dampen the pain by reducing the swelling in your brain—only by a small amount, of course. But it should help relieve the pressure. And then I will send a sleeping wave through your body. Will that be all right, Your Imperial Majesty?"

Again, Safi nodded. It was all she wanted; it would make her days so much more bearable. It would make the pain and the pressure more bearable too, since they were not a burden that *anything* could relieve other than healing the final Well.

Which I am about to do, she reminded herself—and reminded the souls in turn. *In a few hours, I am going to do what you want.*

But that didn't appease them. It never appeased them. They were bees trapped in a barrel, and now they simply buzzed worse than before.

"I will touch your head," Evrane said. "But my hands are cold. I am sorry."

"Cold is good," Safi murmured, and it was true. Sometimes, when the weight of her blindfold wasn't enough, she would tuck cold stones beneath her velvet wrap so they pressed against her eyes.

Evrane's hands laid upon her, and *ah*. There was the wave, like a sweet tide on the Jadansi. For several minutes, as pain dripped and dropped out of her skull, Safi felt as if she were back in Veñaza City. Back beside the sea forever lapping against the wharf where Mathew's coffee shop lived.

It made her throat choke up. Made her entire rib cage ache. How long had she and Iseult been gone? Could she even measure how much their lives had changed? They would never get a place of their own now. They would never get to *escape* and simply *be*.

Despite Safi's best efforts, she was less free now than she'd ever been. She had a crown upon her head—and it weighed almost as heavy as these souls trapped inside her. Meanwhile Iseult had a power so vast, she was stuck forever on a knife's edge, afraid that if she moved, the knife would cut and kill all she loved.

At some point, Safi wasn't sure when, tears started to slide down her cheeks. And although she knew where the tears would lead her . . . although she *knew* she would have to wipe her cheeks eventually . . .

Safi opened her eyes and looked at Evrane. The monk's hands were on Safi's brow—no longer cold—and the fire behind the monk lit her hair into a silvery halo.

"He's not dead," Safi said in Nubrevnan, and there it was. The words Safi was afraid to say. "He's not dead, and I saw him."

For several seconds, Evrane did not move. Her gaze was fastened on Safi, her pupils large and unfocused while her magic still floated through Safi. Then Evrane's eyelids shuttered halfway. She breathed, "Oh."

Her hands withdrew. The caress of her magic did not. "How do you know?"

"I saw him inside a mountain," Safi said simply. "It was filled with ice and winds and shadow, and although he was scarred and . . . and . . ." She motioned to the right side of her face, to where burns had changed the prince into someone almost unrecognizable. "I knew him in an instant." *I knew his eyes, so very much like yours.*

"He isn't dead," Safi repeated, more forcefully this time. "Merik still lives." She pushed upright, a wobbly movement that sent Evrane grabbing for her and shoving pillows behind her back. But Safi didn't need pillows. She felt better than she'd felt in days. *Perhaps,* she thought vaguely, *because this was a pressure that needed releasing too.*

"I don't know where he is now, and I'm sorry I didn't tell you sooner. I don't really understand what I saw or how Merik came to be there. For a time, I thought maybe I'd dreamed the entire thing. Except, I know . . ." She pressed at her stomach. Then her chest. "I just *know* in the very core of my magic that it wasn't a dream. Merik's alive, somehow, and he's out there." She waved ineffectually toward the window, as if Merik were merely on the ramparts. As if he might turn up at any moment, scarred but still himself.

Evrane nodded slowly, a thoughtful triangle forming between her brows. It was clear she didn't understand what Safi was saying—and how could she when Safi didn't understand it herself? But it was also clear she was overjoyed to learn her nephew lived. Safi didn't need to be a Thread-witch to spot this.

"Thank you for telling me, Your Imperial Majesty." A pause. A swallow. "I will . . . will send word to all my contacts so they may search for him."

Safi exhaled a soft *Hye.* Then she added: "And I have already asked all the spies in Henrick's . . . or rather, in *my* vast network to search for him too. Hopefully we can find him. Hopefully you can see him again."

Evrane didn't answer. Her thoughts currently lived in another place, her fingers splayed across her lap like sea stars in a tidal pool. She looked older than she was. And tired. Neither monk nor healer witch, but simply a woman who'd lost too much.

Then, as if watching the tide rise up—as if watching the sea stars climb back into the waters they knew best—Evrane's demeanor changed. "Sometimes I marvel at how selfish grief can be. Are we sad for those we lost? Or are we sad for what we did not remember to do?" She fastened her dark Nihar eyes onto Safi, and with the same gentleness from before, she eased Safi onto the pillows.

Then she laid her hands on Safi's forehead, and the soothing, salty tides swept into Safi anew.

"I know you hate your uncle, Safiya, and I suspect that in many ways, Merik feels the same way toward me—and likely Aeduan feels it too, for I raised him with as much harsh care as I gave Merik. But in the end, nothing can change that we do the best we can with the tools we have. Sometimes we use our tools wisely. Sometimes . . ." Evrane shook her head. "Sometimes our best is not enough."

The tides swept in more strongly, but they were not drowning waters. Nor rough and stormy. They were gentle currents meant to carry Safi's floating body out to sea, where healing and sleep awaited.

"I hope that I see Merik again one day, if only so I may tell him that he has turned out far wiser and far fiercer than I could have ever dreamed he would be. Now sleep, Safiya, and dream of peace in your mind, peace in your body."

Safi sighed. Her muscles softened. And there it was: the true sleep that had eluded her for days.

The last thing Safi heard before she sank under was: "Thank you, Light-Bringer, for this gift you have given me tonight. It was the reminder I needed that the path I am on is true."

EIGHTEEN

✳

The moon was fully risen by the time Iseult navigated the Nomatsi trail again. She did not return to the hunting lodge, but instead made her way to the ancient tower with its altar inside. The pack weighed heavy on her back, but it was steady. Comfortable, even.

She scanned the tower, full of shadows. A world of black and white. Snow still skated languidly down, and a barely perceptible wind whispered every few seconds. But something was wrong. Something had changed since Iseult had come here with Safi that morning.

There were the supplies, tucked into the darkest corner with the blanket above. Snow had once more banked around the crates.

There was the altar, only ten feet away. Still, silent, timeless.

There were the crumbling walls and broken staircase and winter trees beyond.

Iseult shifted her weight, splaying her toes in her boots, trying to find warmth. The pack shifted with her. She should add its supplies to the organized crates in the corner. Open up the leather and catalog exactly what Alma had given her.

But Iseult didn't move. Instead, she eased the pack off her back, letting it land directly behind her. A bulwark against cold—and against the strangeness still huddling around her.

There were no Threads here, so she did not fear humans. And she didn't fear animals, since they, like men, avoided this place. Of course, there were ways to hide Threads. Ways to travel that even a Threadwitch could not see . . .

Wind pulled at her hair as she withdrew Eridysi's diary from a leather pouch at her belt. She always kept it with her, for its words were too precious, too dangerous to ever leave untended.

Iseult lowered to the snow-covered earth, folding her legs beneath her before laying the diary on her lap. She closed her eyes. She slipped into the Dreaming.

It was so easy here, in this old tower where the walls between this world and the Old Ones' were thinner. She only had to imagine the Dreaming, and suddenly she was there. The night hazed around her. The edges of her vision blurred into gray nothing.

"Leopold," she called. "I know you're here. Show yourself."

She sensed his emergence before she saw him. A heaviness where her periphery smeared—a slowing of time that made the snow drift differently, as if gravity no longer operated by the same rules.

She turned toward him and found he was not Leopold at all, but the purest distillation of his Paladin form. He stood at the tower's entrance, a ghostly figure. Almost insubstantial, yet also many people at once, many genders and many races before all the incarnations of his Paladin soul finally settled into the version Iseult knew best: Leopold fon Cartorra.

Except now he wore the Rook King's silver crown, and his cloak was black and bulky, adding breadth to what she knew were lean shoulders.

"This is a welcome surprise." His voice and Threads indicated it wasn't welcome at all. "I did not think I would see you again, Dark-Giver."

"Don't c-call me that." It was Iseult's title as the Cahr Awen, but Leopold always made it sound insulting. She rose to her dream feet while her physical body remained behind. "Where are you? I know you must be near." The last time she had seen Leopold in person had been here, after he'd stabbed Corlant in the back.

Leopold paused at that altar now, inspecting the precise spot where his blade had cut through Corlant's spine, as if he were an artist looking upon his work. "Is it so strange to want to see how the Cahr Awen fares?"

"Yes."

"I have spent a thousand years trying to heal the Wells. Give an old soul this . . . *pleasure.*"

"Except you were the one who betrayed the Six. Oh yes, I've read the diary in full now, Leopold. Eridysi writes that you betrayed the Six so that the Exalted Ones knew of your plans. The Six were going to kill the Exalted Ones, but you warned them. And so the Six failed."

"And Eridysi was wrong. I was not the betrayer, Iseult." A pause. A contemplative twirl of Leopold's Threads as he motioned toward the altar. "I was, in fact, the one who *ensured* the Exalted Ones were slain."

"Portia was not slain."

"Was not, but now is." He smiled, and although he didn't add it, Iseult could practically hear him saying: *Because I slayed her. She was in Corlant's body, and I killed Corlant so you would not have to.*

"Why are you here, Leopold?" Iseult spoke more forcefully now. "Why are you in this tower, lurking so I'll find you? I w-want an honest answer. None of your charm or lies."

"Ah, but charm is a prince's only weapon, remember?"

"And you are not a prince anymore."

He laughed. A twinkling sound that clashed with the brutal frustration in his Threads. "I am here because it would seem that you and Safiya are leaving. Abandoning all the forces Dom fon Hasstrel and Monk Evrane have assembled for you."

Iseult wanted to recoil. Wanted to gasp. *How does he know? Who has he told?* But she clung to her Threadwitch training. She was stasis through and through.

"It will be a march to your death," Leopold continued. "If you travel east, just the two of you, you will not survive long enough to heal the Well. You will not even reach Poznin, for that matter. The Raider King is not a man to be trifled with. He is the greatest strategic mind of the last millennia."

Iseult presented a thoughtful silence. One breath. Two. Then she said coolly: "I'm surprised you would say that about someone who isn't you."

A snort and a flash of Threads that, for once, actually matched the amusement on his face. "Why do you think I made him my general? I know what my strengths are, and they are not battlefield tactics. Meanwhile, Ragnor has both knowledge and experience that span generations."

"So why not kill him?" Iseult flipped a dismissive hand. "Why not use a-all your sneaking and shadowy tricks to eliminate him, Leopold?"

Another snorting laugh, this time with Threads of violet disappointment. As if Iseult was a particularly slow pupil. Against her will, heat burned in her chest.

"Trust me, Dark-Giver: I have tried to kill him, but he has accounted for every strategic possibility—including assassination. So only brute force will get you through his armies."

"Brute force," Iseult repeated. "Meaning people will die. Countless people—on his side and ours. Don't you care about that at all?"

"Not particularly." Leopold opened his arms. The black of his clothes smeared like wings. "Either we lose thousands of lives now or we lose the entirety of the Witchlands when Sirmaya dies. Tell me which sounds preferable to you."

"Funny how you never put *your* life at risk, though."

A sneer carved down Leopold's handsome face. His Threads, however, remained placid and unperturbed. "You have no idea what risks I've taken. I have done *nothing* but help you and Safiya. Please recall who found you in Tirla, all alone. Who reunited you with your Threadsister in Cartorra. Who *gave* you an army, that you foolishly set free—"

"Because Hell-Bards are people, not tools."

"—and who killed your father so that you would not have to." Leopold strode toward Iseult, closing the distance between them until all she could see was his face. All she could feel was the icy core of his Threads, crackling with static and cold. He had a Paladin's Threads. Overwhelming in power and violent in their intensity.

"Everything that has gotten you and Safiya this far—it has been *my* doing."

"No." Iseult cocked up her chin. "It has been your manipulation. Because you work forever behind the scenes, never willing to take direct action. Why is that, I wonder?" She canted toward him. Closer, closer, until only inches separated them in this cold, hazy place of nothing. "I think you avoid direct action, Leopold, b-because then, if you fail, you can absolve yourself of any blame."

The silvery core of his Threads dilated. The sneer carved deeper. But Iseult wasn't finished yet.

"Tell me, Leopold, how many Cahr Awens have you nudged along and given armies to over the last thousand years? How many of them failed and died because you refused to ever work with them directly?"

"I will not let you and Safiya go alone to Poznin. I will not let you leave this lodge without an army."

"And what will you do to stop us?" Iseult motioned to her body, still seated in the real world with the diary upon her lap. "Stopping us would require you to act, and I don't think you're capable of it."

"Do not underestimate me, Dark-Giver."

"Do not underestimate *me*, Trickster."

The sneer fell away. In its place, a smile spread over Leopold's lips, like an asp coiling to strike. His Threads folded outward in a meteor shower. "Trickster," he purred. "Yes, that is what you so love to call me. But what is it the Nomatsis say? *May the Moon Mother light your path, and may Trickster never find you.*

"Well, I have found you. And I have acted in a manner that is quite direct and not at all conducted behind the scenes." Now Leopold was the one to motion, although not toward Iseult but rather to the dark corner where her supplies awaited.

They were not so dark now.

"Enjoy the flames, Iseult. They burn so brightly in this ancient place of memories." Leopold backed away. The charge of him receded, his body fading like smoke into the sky.

Iseult lurched out of the Dreaming, her body crudely trying to remember how muscles connected to ligaments connected to bones. Heat billowed, orange and blue, fed by the fuel of Iseult's and Safi's supplies.

They were all on fire.

Somehow, while Iseult was distracted in the Dreaming, Leopold had ignited the crates, and now they all burned.

Iseult half crawled toward those flames, toward the smoke and heat billowing above it all. She didn't think to cover her mouth or face, nor did she think to protect herself in any way. Not until she made it five steps over and suddenly remembered what was *inside* the crates.

Firepots.

Iseult flung herself around. She crossed five steps in only two bounding leaps. Then she jumped, headfirst behind the altar.

The first firepot exploded. A mere stutter, a mere *crack!* before the rest of the cataclysm joined in.

Fire, heat, noise, and stone. It convulsed over Iseult, rippling with power and rage. She was midair, reaching for the snowy banks behind the altar—when the force of the explosion slammed her down. Right into snow and stone. She lost all hearing; she lost all sight; she lost all sensation in her limbs, her lips, her skin. She could do nothing but lie there, facedown and limp, while heat and shockwaves boiled across her.

She thought of how Safi had described being trapped beneath a flame hawk. She thought of earthquakes and Sirmaya and all the power of a Firewitch contained inside a single clay pot. Inside fifty clay pots.

The tower burned.

Iseult burned with it.

Until suddenly she was being moved. Someone was rolling her over. Then tugging her to him. There was so much smoke, her eyes streamed. She coughed and gasped. She couldn't see her savior, but she knew who he was anyway.

He had no Threads.

"I'm here," he told her—or at least, she thought he told her that. Everything was echoey and vague. Fire and smoke swirled like Threads. Her body hurt where Aeduan held her. As he carried her step by steady step out of the tower.

Then it was not fire, but snow.

It was not smoke, but starlight.

Cold air beat across her. Aeduan solidified into sharp specificity: fire-flap across his face, eyes glittering like bloodied ice. He walked and walked until the tower became nothing more than a distant torchlight. Until they were beside a stream, frozen save for one patch where ice had not laid claim. There was no light to create reflections upon the black, burbling surface.

Here, Aeduan eased Iseult down. She had, by now, reclaimed her senses. Reclaimed her mind too, and a thousand questions crowded in: *Why is Aeduan here? He should not be home yet. What will this do to our plans? What can we do if we have no supplies?*

But there was only one question that really mattered in this immediate moment. She coughed and scrubbed ash from her eyes. "Where is he? Where is Leopold? F-find him, Aeduan, before he can get away."

NINETEEN

※

Aeduan didn't need to be told twice. He had smelled the prince near—both of the man's blood scents—and if Leopold was the one who had set off the explosion . . .

Then Aeduan would destroy him.

With nothing more than a nod of obedience for Iseult, Aeduan abandoned the stream. His muscles flamed with strength, pumped there by his magic. Faster, faster through the trees. He sprinted and veered. Any direction his witchery sensed the prince, Aeduan followed. Two bloods to track.

Leopold fon Cartorra: *New leather and smoky hearths.*

And the Rook King's: *Clear lake water and frozen winters.*

There it was, the Paladin scent. Paces away, but to the left. Aeduan halted so hard, his cloak cracked like a whip. Then he turned and followed Leopold anew.

He knew that he was once more that broken bear from Saldonica, and Leopold was forcing him to stomp and spin wherever he desired. Yet what else could Aeduan do? He couldn't rest if the prince was here. He couldn't rest when he knew Leopold might try to hurt Iseult again.

Wind slammed against Aeduan, dismantling snow drifts. Singeing his eyes. He almost missed when the forest changed. The trees went from spaced and natural to a tunnel of nearly locked branches. Footsteps tracked inside.

Aeduan swerved after them.

Faster, harder. Not his mind. Not his body. A collection of seamlessly interacting parts—although . . . He was also inexplicably flagging too. Worse, his old wounds were pricking awake.

But the prince was so close. Aeduan could feel the imminence of capture. The lure of prey that could not get away. Any rising pain was a mere distraction. *Not his mind, not his body.*

Except halfway into this uncanny tunnel—with the clear lake waters and frozen winters *right there*—the highest two wounds on Aeduan's chest erupted with such fire, he gasped. He stumbled.

Run, my child, run, came his dead mother's voice.

Aeduan's vision wavered. His rib cage felt as if it were collapsing, and he could do nothing but gulp for air while Leopold's scent sidled away. Aeduan had had these wounds since childhood, yet never had they tortured him with such brutality. It was as if his dead mother had fallen atop him all over again. As if the six arrows that had punctured her were now puncturing into him again too.

Run, my child, run.

The pain eased. Reluctant, sluggish. Then urgent and freeing. Aeduan regained his footing. Resumed his forward hunt.

Not that it mattered; his prey had flown, and soon the stink of the Solfatarra snaked into Aeduan's nose. Flickers of rotten eggs and acid before the fog, thick and deadly, rolled into the branch-woven tunnel.

Leopold's boot prints strode right into the fog.

So Aeduan strode in after him. His chest wounds still ached, but with a throb he could once again ignore. Especially since the acid mist that trawled over him ate at his face wherever his fire-flap didn't cover. It ate his hands too, and any other part of him not protected by salamander fibers—although even the cloak couldn't resist this acid forever. And as fast as Aeduan's magic healed the blistering parts of him, it would never be fast enough to outrun the Solfatarra forever.

Water splashed beneath Aeduan's boots, a sign he'd reached the poison lake at the heart of the mist. He had no choice now but to stop and abandon his pursuit.

Yet again, the prince had won.

Yet again, the Rook King would fly free.

Run, my child, run.

For several seconds, Aeduan stood there, listening to the silence of the Solfatarra. Feeling the acid burn, scrape, carve into his lungs . . . Then it came: a laugh. Soft, ghostly, unreachable. A mocking sound from a Paladin who lived for mischief and games.

Aeduan's fingers moved to the sword at his hip. *Come,* he dared the prince. *Come so I may end you.* His lips ached where a hole was forming in the flap. His eyeballs were on fire.

But the prince never came, because in the end, he was a coward. Forever working from the shadows. Never stepping into the light. He might make the bear dance, but he would never dare face it head-on.

No man could avoid Lady Fate's knife forever, though. It would come for Leopold eventually. It would exact all payments owed.

And Aeduan only hoped it would be his hand holding the knife when the prince finally paid up.

None of the supplies survived the blast. All of the carefully accumulated food, kindling, blankets, weapons—all of Iseult's and Safi's things, right down to the crates, had been destroyed. Only embers and splinters remained, and scraps from a salamander blanket that would not burn.

Somehow, Iseult preserved her calm as she limped through the tower, searching for anything that might be salvaged. In the end, only the Nomatsi pack from Alma was still intact, thanks to the Nomatsi shield attached to it. But even that was now pocked with holes along the top, where the shield had not protected it.

Perhaps the worst blow of all, though, was Eridysi's diary. It was gone. Not because the flames had claimed it, but because Leopold had. And in its place was a new book, hidden by rubble. A History of Arithuania's Rise, Iseult read as she wiped off melted snow and ash. It was an old book, written from before the plague had wiped out the entire Republic—and now it was filled with handwritten notes and drawings.

Leopold clearly wanted Iseult to have this. And given how he'd left it where it could have been easily destroyed, he also clearly hadn't expected to almost kill Iseult in the blast. He might have known about her and Safi's supplies, but he hadn't known about the firepots.

Grim as it was, Iseult was almost satisfied by his miscalculation. What would he have done if he *had* killed her? How would he have proceeded then? And how much more would he have hated himself for such a vast mistake?

Iseult held the new book toward what few flames still burned. She'd seen Leopold's neat scrawl before, and now it was crammed so small she had to squint to read it.

One page in particular was thick with annotations: a fold-out map of Poznin, except it was the city as it used to be fifty years ago, before the roads and buildings had been flooded, then eaten away by despair. Leopold had marked all the locations that the Raider King might utilize in his favor. Streets where Ragnor would *probably* move troops, where he would *probably* reinforce walls, where he would *probably* guard most heavily against an attack.

And it was clear the Raider King could defend Poznin and the Air Well for weeks, if not months. The only thing that could possibly defeat such strength and such magic (for Ragnor had many, many witches at his disposal) were numbers. Exactly as Leopold had told Iseult in the Dreaming.

And Leopold had also laid out exactly where to direct such numbers. While the bulk of the Cartorran and Carawen monk forces could attack head-on in a dizzying, aggressive onslaught of bodies against a siege, in the hidden background, the Cahr Awen could infiltrate the city using ancient tunnels that the Raider King had not yet discovered.

In other words: with one hand the armies would distract while the other hand cut the purse.

It was a good plan; Iseult couldn't deny that. From the arrangement of Cartorran forces upon the field to the use of long-forgotten passages beneath Poznin. But as Iseult had told Leopold less than an hour ago: the cost was too high. She couldn't do it. She *wouldn't* do it. And destroying all of her and Safi's supplies was not going to force the Cahr Awen to change course.

Iseult clenched her eyes shut. Her fingers moved to a Threadstone that was no longer there, and for half a moment—on a pause between smoky breaths—she felt the Threads that bind. She *felt* Safi miles away inside the hunting lodge.

Or at least, that's what Iseult imagined she was feeling.

And she imagined too that she wasn't here. That instead, the heat sweeping against her was from sunbaked cobblestones in Veñaza City. That it was just her and Safi, two Threadsisters facing off against the world. The only thing they'd wanted in those days was to get enough money to forge out on their own. For years, they'd had adventures and made mischief and cared for nothing but what the next day might bring.

Now here they were, hundreds of leagues and countless lifetimes away. So much had changed in the last few months. *And yet nothing has changed at all.*

At that thought, a plan assembled in Iseult's mind, slicing through her brain as clearly as Leopold's drawings upon the page—except these were *her* thoughts and *her* visions of a terrain that waited ahead. Planning had always been her greatest strength. Logic, organization, careful strategy. These were the skills she used to complete all the wild, impulsive schemes that Safi initiated them into.

And while Safi might not have started this particular scheme, that didn't mean Iseult couldn't find a way to finish it.

Her hand fell from her collarbone. She closed the book on Poznin history. It was thinner than Eridysi's diary, but only by half an inch. Otherwise, its dimensions were nearly the same—meaning it slipped easily into the case at Iseult's hip. She fastened the buckle with a click, then crouched over to grab the now-pocked Nomatsi pack. The weight settled across her shoulders with creaking ease. The shield, however, was no use anymore, so she left it behind. One more artifact for this tower to claim.

Threads raveled at the corners of Iseult's magic. Hell-Bards and soldiers, she assumed, wondering why an inferno had erupted into the night. She didn't want to explain, and she certainly didn't want to be caught with this pack upon her shoulders or crates of supplies aflame.

So she left behind the tower where she had almost died—more than once now—and she felt no regrets over the wreckage. Instead, she felt only cold fury and hard, indomitable determination.

Safi awoke thinking that war had come. *Cannons,* she thought. *I hear cannons.*

But there was no follow-up boom, and she was not on a battlefield or trapped on a warship. She was simply in her room, the shadows complete because someone had banked her fire and blown out her lamps.

She felt drunk as she tried to rise. *Why did I hear cannons?* The bed spun. She was still dressed.

A knock at her door. "Come," she growled, her throat fighting her as much as her mind and body did.

A Hell-Bard shoved in. "There's been an explosion in the forest, Your Imperial Majesty. About half a mile from here. We don't know if it's an attack or something else."

Something else? Safi wanted to demand. *What the tits else causes an explosion?* But she only waved at the man and barked, "Update me as soon as you know."

He bowed. He turned to leave.

"Wait. What is the hour?"

"The twenty-third chimes just sounded."

So late? Safi waved at him again. The word, *Dismissed,* was beyond her current capacity—and he seemed to understand, for he said, "Should I send for Monk Evrane?"

She shook her head. Then regretted that movement. Then waved even more emphatically for the Hell-Bard to go. This time he obeyed.

Once her door clicked shut, Safi gulped in air and probed at her head with her fingers. The Cahr Awen were still in there, but so was Evrane's magic. It wanted to suck her back into sleep. It wanted to roll her out to sea on the tide.

But if it was almost midnight, then it was almost time for Safi and Iseult to leave. So Safi dragged herself from her bed. Surely whatever had just happened in the forest would not affect Iseult. Surely at any moment her Threadsister would shove in wondering why Safi wasn't ready for the road.

Except . . . *Cannons. War. Explosion in the forest.* Safi's stomach plummeted. Her breath punched from her lungs. Suddenly she knew exactly what could set the night on fire.

As did the Cahr Awen souls. Already, she could feel them reawakening. The barrel of bees stirring, wanting to sting and buzz and shove back into the cracks of her brain. *You must leave. Do not let this stop you! Do not stay here!*

"Yes," she snarled, staggering toward her closet—and toward the clothes she had already chosen to keep her warm on the road.

Her fingers moved for her Threadstone. But it wasn't there, because it hadn't been for weeks. Safi still felt incomplete without it.

Gods below, she hoped Iseult was all right. And gods below, she wasn't about to wait here to find out. She let her hand fall. She had a secret way out of the castle—one she and Iseult had used whenever they needed to evade Caden and his Hell-Bards.

Thinking of Caden made Safi's ribs hurt.

Thinking of Iseult made them hurt far more. But the girls *did* have a backup plan in case the worst happened. A spot to meet, where they could regroup, recalibrate, and reevaluate without the controlling eyes of Eron or Evrane.

In minutes, Safi was dressed. All beige, all wool or fur or leather meant to withstand the Windswept Plains and their ire. A scarf cloaked her face, gloves warmed her hands. She was boiling in her bedroom, but she'd be glad for the extra heat as soon as she slid through the hidden doorway tucked in the closet's back corner. It was a spot Henrick had told her about because why not? It was no use to him anymore.

Once she'd strapped a sword and a parrying knife at her hip, Safi tugged the final piece of preparation she needed for the night. It was not intended for the road; it was nothing more than a letter folded over and sealed with Hasstrel blue wax—and the Hasstrel mountain bat stamp. *Love and dread,* she thought for the second time that day as she placed the letter on her desk.

Cold air coiled off her window. Snow billowed and spun outside. And in the hall, a three-beat rhythm that heralded Uncle Eron and his cane stomped out. "Let me in to see Her Majesty."

Sorry, Safi thought. *You're just a few seconds too late.* She spun from her desk, reaching her closet just in time to hear the *bang-bang-bang* of a furious fist against the door. She slunk into her closet, wedged behind a shelf, and found the hidden bump that marked a hole in the stones.

Knock, knock, she thought as she tapped out the secret rhythm. The stones vanished. Frost billowed against her. Her bedroom door cracked open and Eron called her name, an edge to his voice that meant he suspected what she was up to.

But he was too late to stop her. His empress had escaped. The night and freedom had claimed her.

TWENTY

⁂

Iseult went to a new spot in the forest. It was beside the same stream where Aeduan had left her, but a different clearing. A mere patch of shore where trees hadn't grown. This was the secret backup spot to meet Safi, in case things went wrong.

And things had gone very wrong.

Here, there was no hole in the ice to reveal dark waters. Here, the snows had not banked quite so high.

Iseult dropped the Nomatsi pack, reaching for the taler at her neck. This was her chance to slip away. She should have removed it at the tower . . . but she hadn't. She should have removed it at the tribe, but she hadn't. She should have removed it at *any* time in the past week, but she hadn't.

For all that she had criticized Safi, Iseult was absolutely no better. And even now, she didn't remove the taler.

The night was too quiet around her. Too real after the sensory overwhelm at the tower. Iseult's senses were so keyed up, she felt raw. Overly receptive to the wind's bite, the stream's burble, the snow's talons. She heard Aeduan long before she saw him. And she felt how incensed he was, as if Threads really did weave above him, revealing all he felt while he stalked from the trees.

She just hoped it was not with her that he was incensed. He would have every right to be.

"I lost Leopold," he told her once he was near enough to be heard. "I am sorry." He came to a stop beside Iseult on the shore, his cloak swishing around him. His cheeks were red with exertion, his eyes red with magic. "Are you hurt?"

"No."

His gaze flicked to the pack. Held there for three breaths. Then flicked to Iseult's face again. "Why did Leopold try to kill you?"

"I don't think he meant to. He was . . ." Iseult wet her lips.

"Trying to keep you here."

"Yes."

"You were going to leave for Poznin."

"Yes."

An expansion of time. A stilling of Aeduan's chest as he studied Iseult. His witchery drained from his irises; the usual pale blue returned. "And now? Will you still go?"

"Yes."

His nostrils flared, but he said nothing more. He didn't ask if he could come, he didn't insist that Iseult should stay. In the distance, a crow cawed into the night. Ice popped and groaned on the stream, while the overwhelm of Iseult's senses ratcheted up another notch.

The snowflakes were too cold on her cheeks. Her breath was too big in her lungs. Her clothes were too constrictive across her body.

And Aeduan . . .

Aeduan felt too dangerous. There would be no escaping him now, and she couldn't believe she'd ever wanted to. That she had ever convinced herself that *leaving* him would be the right course. *There is no we, there is no us.* He had said that to her in Tirla, and it had broken her heart.

Now she had planned to do the same—and standing here, facing him in a clearing made of winter, she couldn't pretend she hadn't known it would cut him. That even though his face wore no expression, inwardly, he was bleeding.

"I . . . did not want . . ." Iseult bit out each word. Carefully. *Clearly,* so there could be no confusion. "To leave you. But . . . I saw no o-other way."

Aeduan didn't reply. The exerted flush from his cheeks was fading, blending the pallor of his skin into the pallor of his eyes into the whiteness of his cloak—and into the snow tangling around them.

"You should not have to face your father," Iseult continued. "I d-don't want you to have to choose."

"I have already chosen."

"Yes, but . . ." Iseult gritted her molars. "No one should have to kill their parent. And wh-*what* if it comes to that in Poznin?"

Aeduan's jaw clenched. His eyes glinted red. "Then I will choose exactly what I chose before."

Yes, and that is the problem. For Iseult could not deny one powerful thing: she was glad she had not killed Corlant. She was *glad* Leopold had shoved that blade through her father's spine so that she wouldn't have to. Wretched as it was, it had been a gift.

And Iseult wanted to give the same to Aeduan.

"I will stay here," he said flatly, "if that is what you want from me."

Iseult's eyes screwed shut. She could feel Aeduan retreating into himself. Closing off emotion as adeptly as a Threadwitch. She understood that instinct because it was a match for her own: reject that which might reject you, for it hurt less if you were the one to act.

You can lie to yourself, she'd told him in Tirla. *But you cannot lie to me.*

She opened her eyes. "I don't w-*want* this. Of course I don't want this, Aeduan."

A pause. A gnarl of fogged breath. Then: "So do not do it." Fabric rustled, snow crunched, and in a sweep of speed, Aeduan closed the space between them. He knelt before her on the snow. "Please, Dark-Giver. Please . . . Iseult. My blood I offer freely."

Iseult reached for his face.

"My Threads I offer wholly."

Yes, she wanted to say.

"Claim my Aether."

Yes. She ran a knuckle down his jaw.

"Guide my blade."

Yes. She gripped Aeduan's chin and forced his head to rise. Forced his icy gaze to meet hers as he uttered the final words: "From now until the end."

Yes. Iseult sighed. *Blood. Witch. Blood. Witch.* The words pulsed through her in time to her heart. In time to her blood. How had she ever thought she could leave him behind?

"Come with me," she finally offered in Nomatsi. Quiet as the fireflies that had once floated with them beside a different stream in a different forest far away. "Come with me, Monk Aeduan, to Poznin."

Now his eyes were the ones to shutter, and he was the one to sigh. He sank into her hand. "Yes. I will come." He slid his fingers around Iseult's wrist, and pressed his thumb into the place where her pulse did not flutter so much as boom. *Blood. Witch. Blood. Witch.*

She softened her grip on his chin. His breath was warm against her fingertips, so at odds with the winter night around them. Iseult's muscles moved without conscious thought. Her thumb stretched long. She touched Aeduan's bottom lip. Stroked down.

His eyes snapped wide. His breathing ceased, as did hers.

Then he tugged at her wrist. More request than command, but it made Iseult's legs collapse all the same.

Her knees hit the snow. Her eyes came almost level to his, and there was a look on his face she'd never seen before. As if he were afraid to hurt her. As if he feared he might break her if he made any further move.

But didn't he know Iseult better than that? Didn't he *know* she had gone through seafire to save him and broken a Well to heal him? This frozen moment could do her no harm.

Then it struck her: Aeduan didn't fear *she* would break at his touch. He feared that he would. So she leaned in. An inch. Then two. Closer, closer, slow enough that he could pull away if he wanted to, needed to.

He didn't pull away. Their lips grazed. Their breaths mingled. And at last, the Threads of the moment gave way. The red strands that bound them snapped taut.

At the touch of Iseult's lips, Aeduan broke in two. A stiletto in his heart. A breaking of his spine beside a lighthouse. He felt his magic surge. Inexplicably, because he'd never been able to sense Iseult. Never felt his witchery respond to her nearness. Yet it swelled and burned all the same. No pain in his old wounds, nor even an awareness of the wounds in the first place.

There was only Iseult, pulsing and here.

A moan unraveled from her. The vibration of it curled into Aeduan's mouth, into his chest. His fingers dug into her wrist; her fingers turned to claws against his chin.

She swiveled her hand in Aeduan's grasp—a move he had taught her months ago, in one of their many sparring sessions across the Sirmayans. It broke his grip and forced his entire arm to follow wherever she led it.

Which was above him. Then behind him, so that he abruptly toppled backward onto the snow. Iseult toppled with him, bracing her legs on either side of his body with such ease Aeduan would have been vexed by her win—if he weren't so transfixed by her above him. Had she always looked so powerful? Had she always felt so strong, with her face of shadows and moonlight? Her lips shuddered with each breath. Her hair flew on the breeze, and her thighs trembled against his waist.

"I will stop," she murmured, "if you want me to."

"*Te varuje*," he replied.

And there was that smile of hers. Subtle and disarming. It sent a thrill into Aeduan's gut. Made his witchery and his desire respond in turn. He flipped her.

She saw it coming, of course, but he was much too fast for her to stop. His hips bucked; his right leg swung out; she fell. Yet before her back could hit the snow, Aeduan caught her and eased her down. She grabbed his baldric in two white-knuckled fists. Then he settled her onto the cleared patch of snow his body had left behind.

"You shouldn't waste energy," she told him, "on showing off."

"And you should not challenge someone more skilled than you."

"Then teach me," she replied, and she yanked Aeduan to her. Their lips touched a second time. Their teeth and tongues too, while Aeduan's mind, Aeduan's body, and Aeduan's magic shattered all over again.

TWENTY-ONE

※

Caden fitz Grieg knew his own weaknesses. Intimately. And one in particular had always bothered him: he was not well educated. Wasn't it bad enough to be a nobleman's bastard? Why did he have to be an ignorant one too? He'd found ways to compensate, of course. He couldn't recite every emperor that had come before Henrick III or what the architectural style around the palace courtyard was (he thought those curvy things might be called buttresses?), but he could read people. He knew what their emotions were as plainly as if they'd been written on their faces.

He'd asked Iseult det Midenzi—half in jest, half in seriousness—if this was what Thread magic was like. She'd said no, but then, in that thoughtful way of hers, she'd added: *Though I suppose that makes you even more dangerous than we are.* He hadn't been sure what she meant by this, and now weeks later, he still didn't know.

What he *did* know was that the Nomatsis didn't like having him in their tribe.

And honestly, he couldn't blame them.

Caden stood in the empty clearing where the tribe had disassembled their camp. Tents had been folded down to their component parts, then rolled tightly into packs for all the mules and horses. The cooking fires were long gone, no smoke to linger in the frostbitten air, and if the Nomatsis bustling about felt any disdain for the brown-haired, freckled Cartorran in their midst, they weren't showing it. At least not in obvious ways.

Caden felt their secret glares. He *felt* their nervous confusion, and although he'd tried to ease it with a few smiles, he only ever got hostile stares in return.

Thank the hell-gates I'm not traveling with them anymore.

He'd been grateful for the idea, and he *would* have followed through. But then the Bloodwitch had shown up at midnight with Lev's and Zander's nooses. Monk Aeduan had found them right beside the Earth Well, so that was where Caden now planned to travel. And honestly, Iseult's mother had seemed as relieved as Caden that he wouldn't be staying with the tribe.

Gretchya had, however, insisted she at least give him the promised Threadstones before he go.

So here he stood, awkward, stiff, and cold while he waited for the apprentice to walk his way. She was beautiful. Unnaturally so. Like a sculpture carved from ice: he could look and appreciate the attention to detail, but ice didn't make good company. "Come," she said in accented Dalmotti. "We are ready."

Caden nodded, and feeling the stares of literally *everyone* in the tribe on his back, he traced after Alma through the camp's remains to the only two things still intact in these old ruins: a Threadwitching desk and low stool. Light and color flashed from tens of gemstones that lay before Iseult's mother. She sat with her eyes closed until Caden was near. Then her hazel eyes snapped wide and fixed onto the space above his head.

One breath. Two. Her gaze lowered to meet his.

And Caden forced himself to stare. *I know you see what I'm feeling, but I'm not afraid of you.*

"We see what you feel," Gretchya said as he came to a stop at the table, "but we do not see what you are thinking. Your mind, Hell-Bard, remains your own."

These words didn't comfort Caden much, but rather than say, *I'd prefer if my feelings were my own too,* he simply bowed his head. "Tell me what I must do."

It was Alma, again, who spoke: "In order to find your Thread-family, we will need to craft three Threadstones. One will be for you, then two will be for your friends."

"Choose," Gretchya commanded, "three stones. Let your hands guide your arm."

Don't hands always guide arms? Caden frowned at the jewels. The attention of the tribe watching him was like a frozen wind he couldn't wriggle out of. If he thought he'd felt tall and discordant in the middle of the camp, now he felt like the gap in a coat of armor.

He knew of Threadstones, of course. His fellow soldiers had loved to acquire them—sneakily, since Nomatsis weren't welcome in Cartorra. For safety, for love, for beauty. But Caden had never had one for himself. And he'd never wanted one.

"May I touch the stones?"

"Yes," Gretchya answered. "In fact, it is better if you do."

Nodding, Caden reached out with both hands. At first, he felt nothing beyond general foolishness. He was waving his hands over a bunch of precious stones in an absolutely freezing forest while people gawped at him and pretended they didn't. To make it that much stranger, he would have gladly stolen every one of these jewels as a child. Even today, so many years later, there was a part of him that itched to take things that weren't his—fine things that would buy his mother food and firewood . . . and buy himself a warm meal or twenty.

As Caden thought about that childhood—about how he'd actually met Zander on the same streets, well before either of them had been pressed into the Hell-Bards—Caden felt a stirring at his fingertips. It was a subtle warmth in all this cold, and it made him think of sunshine and green things. His left hand moved down, down, seemingly all on its own, before plucking up an emerald.

Meanwhile Caden's other hand felt tingly. Scratchy. Like the fuzzing of wool before an electric *crack!* is set free. Then the spark came, and it was above an opal.

Both stones were rough, uncut, muted in color and wild in shape. And both felt instantly *right* as soon as he grasped them. *Ah,* his heart seemed to say. *Here is your Thread-family.*

"Well done," Alma murmured, and for the first time since meeting her, Caden sensed a slight waver of emotion. She was excited he'd found the stones. She liked this part of her job.

"One for you still," Gretchya reminded. No feelings roiled off of her, no indication of how she'd known *these* stones belonged to Caden's friends and not to him.

Caden drew in a long breath. "Good enough," he replied. More to himself than to them. It was what his mother had always said: *Good enough, Cay. Good enough.* And he'd liked the solid, reliable way she'd said it. As if, although life might not be perfect, perfect was never what she'd wanted anyway.

His hands paused over a red rock that might have been a ruby.

He swallowed.

Clearly these gems—or perhaps these witches—were like fishing lines. They reeled memories to the surface. His past, his person, his promises, and he'd be lying if he said this process didn't frighten him. It sounded so very much like being bound to the Loom. Woven into something completely outside himself.

Except it all happened so quietly, so seamlessly. While Gretchya grabbed the opal and the emerald, Alma retrieved the ruby. Then they both withdrew spools of colored thread from large pockets in their coats and with fingers that were deft despite the cold, they wove and they wound. They whispered and they worked.

Bind and bend, build and blossom, family fills the heart.

They spoke in Nomatsi, of course, but Caden wasn't entirely new to that language. Owl had spoken so much of it to Zander in Praga, and that giant man with his kind heart forever projecting outward had spent hours practicing it whenever he could.

Alma finished her stone first, since she only made one Threadstone. The Threadstone that was meant to be Caden's. With small, focused movements, she tied off a braid of dark and light green threads, attached them to a leather thong, and handed it to him.

Now all of the tribe was openly watching, and many people had clustered in like an audience. Caden couldn't decide if it was better than the sneaky scrutiny or not.

Alma rolled onto her toes so she could drape the threaded necklace around Caden's neck. He had to bend deeply so she could reach him. Her breath ruffled his hair. She smelled like campfire and laurel. Then the leather was around his neck. . . .

And he felt exactly the same as he had a few seconds before. If some great magic had just happened, he wasn't sensing it.

"Rubies," Alma explained, "stand for honor and love, which you must have in abundance. And Threads in these shades represent focus and determination—which you will need to find your family."

Caden swallowed. "And . . . the emerald?" he asked. "The opal?" Gretchya had just finished tying pink threads around the stones, and now she handed them to Alma.

"Emeralds stand for certainty," Alma explained. "The man this stone represents is like an anchor in a storm. Opals, meanwhile, are for loyalty, and the woman this connects to would die for those she loves. The threads around both stones are the shade of deep, unbreakable family."

Alma moved in once more, and Caden leaned down again to meet her. "I don't feel any different," he told her quietly. "Should the stones do something?"

"They are." Alma made a slight, *barely* there smile. So tiny, Caden was certain only he spied it before it smoothed away. "The stones are now bound to your Thread-family. That means you can find them."

"Right." Caden wasn't entirely sure what else to say. If he felt nothing while he wore these, then that wasn't going to do much for him as he trekked west into the Ohrins. If anything, three gems of such size were going to make him a prime target for the criminals he'd once aspired to be.

"Well, uh, thank you," he started. "I appreciate the stones, and—" He shut up. The stones were suddenly winking in the morning light. At first he thought it was sunlight playing over them, reflecting color into his eyes. But there was no sunlight today; the clouds let none through.

And now Alma was pushing in close again.

"They're in trouble," he rasped, as she grabbed all three in a fist. "That's what that means, isn't it?" Caden remembered how Safi's Threadstone had warned her whenever Iseult's life was at risk. "What do I do?"

"We follow," Alma answered, eyes still shut and her face taut with concentration. "And quickly, for we do not know how much time we have."

"We?" Caden asked. But the question was lost in the sudden clatter at the desk as Gretchya shot to her feet.

"But what of Saldonica?" she demanded. "The tribe cannot wait for you, Alma." Gretchya spoke Nomatsi, but there were enough words there for Caden to understand.

Just as he understood what Alma replied: "I know." Her eyes opened, but rather than look at her tribe's leader, she gazed only at Caden with eyes of pure silver and ice. "I do not expect you to wait for me, Gretchya, but I also cannot let this Hell-Bard go alone. I will take him where these Threadstones lead."

Ah. It wasn't at all what Caden had wanted, and yet it was also deeply and desperately what he needed. "I will make sure she gets to Saldonica," he told Gretchya in Dalmotti. "Whatever it takes, I will get her there."

Gretchya didn't respond. Nor did the rest of the tribe. If Caden had been able to see Threads, he imagined they would all be stretched like bowstrings about to snap. Until Alma, again, offered him a secret, almost-nothing smile.

"Tell me what to do," he said to her. The stones were still blinking, beams of color to flash through gaps in her fist. "I don't want to waste a single moment."

"Nor do I." Alma turned from him to bow, hands at her sides, at Gretchya. "I will see you again soon. May Moon Mother light your path."

"And may Trickster never find you," Gretchya replied.

It was all they exchanged before Alma laid her cold hands on Caden's wrist. "Hurry, Hell-Bard. There is no time to waste." She pulled, Caden moved, and the sun rose, unseen, behind thick clouds above them.

Dear Uncle,

Iseult and I are leaving to heal the Well. I know you'll send troops after us, but please don't. You won't catch us—not before we reach Poznin, anyway. And the movement of your troops will only alert the Raider King that something comes his way.

You trained me for this moment. You, Mathew, and Habim. And you trained Iseult too, claiming it was because no one else could protect me like my Thread-family . . . But that wasn't the whole story, was it? I see that now. My magic sees that now.

You knew all along what we were and what we were meant to do.

So please let us do it. Let us heal the final Well on our terms as the Cahr Awen. And if I don't make it back, I hereby decree that you are my heir. A bit unorthodox, I know, but you're the only family I have, and you're a much better leader than I ever could be.

Just don't screw it up.

—Safi

P.S. The crown is in my closet at the bottom of the trunk filled with those hideous gowns you insisted an empress needed.

P.P.S. Don't kill Henrick. He's actually pretty useful, if you give him enough books to read.

Kullen,

There are two new doorways in the mountain. The portal kind like Eridysi made a thousand years ago. On top of that, the *old* doorways have reopened again—the ones I destroyed two months ago.

It shouldn't be possible. I broke the Standing Stones in the meadow beside the Sightwitch Sister Convent. I severed the Threads that bound Sirmaya's magic to those megaliths. That power was gone. The doorways were shut. So who could have opened them again? And who could have built new ones, too?

Part of me wants to leave the mountain right now and check the Standing Stones. See if I can find a clue. To build a magic doorway, you need a stone from the destination—a *big* stone. And then you need to anchor Sirmaya's Threads to that stone. Eridysi figured out how to do it a thousand years ago, and it's not easy magic. In fact, no one but a Sightwitch should be able to do it, and since *I* am the last Sightwitch Sister . . .

I cannot leave my work in the Crypts to go searching for answers. Things are so unstable in the mountain. Quakes rattle through every few hours, and the sleeping ice covers everything. Any magic it can find, it tries to claim.

I only know of the new doors because the Rook has brought me a map—*the* map I drew for you. But someone has added these doorways. I sent the Rook to check, and he tells me in his bird way that they are real.

Goddess, I wish you'd wake up. I wish Sirmaya would release you. But now I'm really starting to fear that will never happen. Not while she needs every scrap of power she can claim. Otherwise, all the Witchlands will die. All the Witchlands will cleave.

But *you* are my focus. The taro cards tell me so, every day. *Lady*

Fate, the Cleaved Man, and *the Paladin of Hounds.* That is all they will ever show me when I draw from the deck. So I will stay focused on you.

You're important. I always knew that, and I only grow more certain of it each day.

I love you.

—Ryber

TWENTY-TWO

✳

For three days, Iseult pushed everyone as hard as their horses would allow. After all, Eron must have sent people after them; they needed to be so far ahead, his riders could never catch up.

In some ways, it was good they had nothing more than three Nomatsi packs to sustain them. They were lighter, faster. And in some ways, it was *very* good they had Aeduan. Without their food supplies, now burned to ash, his magic let them find rabbits and fowl that would otherwise stay hidden in the snow.

Occasionally, the trio passed camps at the roadside. Sometimes, they spotted smoke on the horizon. Twice, they found traveling caravans of traders. Yet no one ever bothered them; no one ever asked, *Why are you traveling east into war?*

On the fourth day, the gusts that had howled off the Windswept Plains softened, and for the first time since leaving the imperial lodge, they let their horses slow to a walking pace. But clouds hung like frowns on the horizon, and it felt to Iseult like the brewing storm waited for a moment when she might look the other way. Then it would strike with all its might.

It reminded Iseult of the storm Corlant had conjured, when he had cleaved the very sky to chase her.

On the fifth day, they rode hard again. Poznin was close now, three days at most if this blizzard would hold. The lands rolled with uneven, unpredictable hills, as if some god had left their shallow footprints across the plains. It made seeing ahead difficult.

As did the grass that hugged the highway, high as their horses' chests and spanning as far as their eyes could see.

Halfway through the fifth day, they spotted smoke. Black coils had blended into the storm clouds. Aeduan drew up his mount, letting Iseult and Safi trot to a stop beside him. Then they all waited, their horses' breaths pluming into the cold as their masters gazed ahead and wind beat against them.

That same wind scattered the smoke, taking thick, black clots and shredding it to papery tendrils.

"That's more than just a campfire," Safi said. Her Threads were a muddied mixture of suspicion and worry.

"And the highway goes right through it." Aeduan, whose face was hidden within his Carawen hood, pointed to the road's dip and rise. It would indeed take them directly into the smoke and fires. "We will have to circle around."

Neither Iseult nor Safi responded to this. Instead they met each other's eyes. "Someone might be hurt," Iseult said. Cold stung her cheeks and nose.

Safi lowered the scarf across her face. Her freckled cheeks shone red. "We can't risk finding that out, Iz."

Iseult's nose twitched. She knew Safi was right, but that didn't make it better. *Either we lose thousands of lives now,* Leopold had said in the Dreaming, *or we lose the entirety of the Witchlands when Sirmaya dies. Tell me which sounds preferable to you.*

"All right." Iseult nodded to Aeduan. "Lead us off the road."

He bobbed his head, eyes flaring red within the shadows of his hood. Then he steered Surefoot into the tall grass. Safi followed atop Dandelion, while Iseult took up the tail with Cloud. This was their usual arrangement, for Aeduan could reach ahead for blood scents while Iseult could reach behind for Threads. The grass was a new challenge, though, slowing them severely.

Which turned out to be the point.

Threads suddenly wavered at the edge of Iseult's magic, closing in fast. "*Raiders!*" she shouted at the same moment Aeduan roared, "Attack!"

Then the raiders were there. Tens of Threads zooming in from all sides in an ambush that couldn't be escaped. Some Threads bore magics. Some only a thrill of cruelty. Yet all wore a shade like violent iron, and there was no stopping the response of Iseult's magic in kind. The bad side of it that liked to sing, *Sever, sever, twist and sever.*

She squashed it down. Hard. That magic was only for final measures. Only in situations of last resort. Iseult had blades; she would use them.

Aeduan was already off his mount. Safi too, their blades unsheathing as figures manifested in the grass, hulking shapes lit by brutality.

Threads that break, Threads that die.

"Aeduan!" Iseult shouted. "Can you freeze them before they arrive?"

Aeduan glanced back. His hood had fallen, his eyes glowed red. "Some, but not all."

"Then do it," Safi barked, her Threads blazing with imperial expectation.

"Yes." Aeduan stretched out his arms. His eyes flamed so red it sent lines across his face. And Iseult watched as the nine nearest raiders became statues within the golden grass. Their Threads burst with panic and surprise.

But they didn't pass out. Instead of Aeduan's usual magic to dominate them, his hands began to quaver—and already, there were more raiders crashing this way.

Iseult rounded toward Cloud. The horse sensed the tide of violence barreling toward her, but she was trained for war. She made no movement as Iseult freed her weapons from the saddle. First a moon scythe of sharpened steel. Then a second scythe from a mountain bat's claw. It was the only remnant of Owl that Iseult had, and every time she held the hilt—every time she felt the claw radiate with ancient Threads of earth and stone—she thought of the little girl who wasn't a little girl at all.

Long ago, when the gods walked among us.

Iseult turned to Safi, and without another word, the Threadsisters launched themselves at the first raiders finally toppling through the frozen grass.

All Safi saw were Red Sails. Because of course it was Red Sails. When the slaughter was at its ugliest, they were always near.

And this slaughter was ugly. Eight raiders stormed from the grass toward Safi and Iseult, and there was no missing the blood and soot across their vicious faces. Whatever that smoke was from, people had died there—and here were their murderers.

Two men at the front split apart to try to flank Safi and Iseult. Fools. She and Iseult had been trained for this. The reactions lived inside them, written onto their bones by a Firewitch general who accepted no failure. It was a dance, a rhythm, a gliding arrangement of steps that required two partners. And although it might have been months since Safi had fought with Iseult, they were still Threadsisters. Still sun and moon, light and shadow, two halves forever orbiting each other.

The raiders reached the girls.

Initiate. Safi ducked for one man's knees with her shoulder. He went down while her blade went up. *Complete.* Iseult bounded over Safi, both moon scythes extended toward the second raider.

Neither man had time to react before steel sliced through and blood sprayed. Hot blood that seemed to sizzle the instant it was exposed to air—as did the organs oozing out with it.

Their bodies hit the snow, but two more raiders were already leaping up from the grass. Safi and Iseult twirled toward each other. Iseult swiped with her mountain bat claw at the first. Safi attacked with steel at the second.

And somehow, as the incoming raider growled at Safi with savagery, as his blood-smeared cutlass swung at Safi's head, she felt her own sword become the truest steel that had ever sung. It was as if her magic responded in that moment, reaching down her arm, her fingers, sliding into the hilt and blade.

She'd bound her witchery before. First, when she'd made the Truthlens in Marstok. It had required careful study, using the book *Understanding Threads* to make the correct knots and braids, loops and weavings.

Second, when she'd turned the lens into a necklace. She'd only had intuition and memory then. It had been slow work, but satisfying.

And now, here she was a third time, and it required almost no effort at all. Here were the Threads of her power; here was the Arlenni Loop, exactly as she'd once seen it on the page. Then the Vergedi knot—harder to make, but stronger in the end.

All of this happened in the space between seconds. The stutter between heartbeats. Then leather and fur split apart, followed by muscle and bone. With a single, frictionless movement, Safi carved off the man's head.

He went down, his head following a split second later—and with the same expression of shock scored onto it that Safi must be wearing as well. How had she done that? And without any thought at all, only instinct?

No time to wonder or contemplate. Another raider struck, lashing out with a long, pointed blade. But when his steel connected with Safi's parry, the blade snapped in two.

This was as unexpected as the decapitation—although it shouldn't have been. She'd imprinted her magic onto the steel. Now it was a blade so true, nothing could stand in its way.

Safi kicked the man in the groin. Flung a flat fist to his chin. Then she levered her leg behind his, and a heartbeat later, the man hit the ground beside his fellows.

The snow in the clearing had turned red. "Incoming," Iseult yelled, darting away from their miniature battlefield as another clump of raiders tumbled from the grass.

Three froze mid-stride, then collapsed. Safi didn't need to look back to know Aeduan had joined them. His magic, strangely weak before, seemed to have returned in full force. Which was why, rather than careen directly for the remaining five raiders as Iseult was doing, Safi cut left toward an exposed flank where raiders coalesced in the grass.

Two toppled toward her. They were easily dispatched with her sword that could apparently slice through spine and steel now. *True, true, true.*

But that was when a third raider whom Safi hadn't noticed—a man who must have come at her from behind—sprang. The force of his tackle crumpled them both to the earth. Knocked her sword from her grasp. She rolled and wiggled, but her winter furs slowed her.

The man's face was the only part of him Safi could see. It was thick with stubble. His breath—hot, foul—panted over her. He was trying to pin her to the ground, both his hands pushing her arms into cold tundra.

So Safi let him. For one breath, she relaxed fully and let him get into the position he *thought* would give him power. *False,* her magic seemed to laugh. *False, false, lies.* Then the breath had ended and the man was leering down. Spit fell from his lips. He wasn't much older than she.

Safi grinned at him before bracing her feet against the man's, then hefting up her hips and flipping him sideways. He fell, and Safi used the moment to roll the other way. He grabbed for her legs. His fingers clamped onto her calf, and he tried to drag her back. But she had her sword now.

Pivot. Swing. It cut through the arm that held her. At the elbow, clean as a butcher's knife through fresh meat.

He screamed. His blood sprayed.

And it was then, in the frantic moments while Safi scrabbled to her feet and another raider sprinted toward her, that she saw something she hadn't noticed on the other raiders: this man's blood wasn't truly red. It was too dark. It should have been scarlet upon the snow, but instead it was almost black.

He was cleaving.

No time to assess what that might mean for this fight. The next raiders had arrived, and Iseult was facing a woman who was just as nimble and fast as she was. Worse, she was drawing a Firewitched pistol from her belt. She aimed. Safi dove. The single shot cracked out.

Pain lanced across Safi's left shoulder. Down to her fingers, up into her skull. Had she been holding her sword in this hand, she would have dropped it. As it was, though, nothing vital was damaged—so despite pain bright and burning, the fight still pumped through her like a sunrise.

Safi ran for the woman with the pistol as the woman tried to reload.

The cold made her slow. Or maybe the intensity of it all made Safi fast. Either way, she reached the woman before the pistol winched high again.

"Big mistake," Safi snarled, and in two arcs of her blade, she carved the pistol from the raider's grasp—and carved away half her hand too. Then she aimed the sword at the woman's neck.

Iseult, her cheeks flushed and blood-splattered, now staggered to Safi's side. "Get on the ground," she ordered the raider. "Now. Or we will put you there."

TWENTY-THREE

✳

Their blood was the wrong color.

Iseult had noticed it as soon as she'd cut into the first raider with her moon scythes. But it wasn't until now, with the battle won and twenty-seven raiders scattered across the snow, that she could finally see it was not merely blood that was corrupted. Their Threads were the wrong color too.

All of them were cleaving. Just like the blacksmith and his wife and all the countless others she hadn't been able to save. Every one of these Red Sails possessed faint Severed Threads at the heart of their beings.

"Why have y-you attacked us?" Iseult asked the woman with the pistol. She was the only raider still conscious.

"Because you were in our way." The woman smiled, revealing teeth coated in blood. Her Threads hummed with a disturbing satisfaction.

"And is that smoke in the distance from you?" Safi clutched her right arm to her side, the pale furs marred with her blood. Red, all of it red, and from a wound that would need tending. "Over there—did you attack others?"

"They had the plague," the raider answered, as if this explained anything. "So we had to."

Iseult frowned at the black smoke choking the sky. Then she frowned at Aeduan, who crouched over two raiders. One by one, he was freezing the blood in their veins. Any who were still conscious, he pushed into sleep.

He was tired though. Iseult could see that even from here.

"She's telling the truth, Iz." Safi bent closer to Iseult. "Or at least she thinks she is. She really believes whomever they just killed had the plague."

Iseult's frown whittled deeper. She supposed it made a tortured sort of sense: the plague had marked the end of the Republic of Arithuania, and burning bodies *had* stopped its spread. But the dark blood of these raiders, the Severed Threads mingling across this clearing . . .

"Why do you think it's the plague?" Iseult asked.

"Because they have the same pustules. The Raider King told us what to look for, so we do."

Safi's expression—and her Threads—turned grim. Cleaving, of course, made pustules. "So the Raider King has sent you to kill anyone with the plague?"

The woman spat shadowed blood onto the snow. Her Threads settled into a stubborn forest green. There was a hesitancy to them, though. A fear, even, that made Iseult think perhaps Ragnor did *not* know how many they were slaughtering to eradicate this so-called plague.

Safi sighed. "You have two choices here. Either you can cooperate with us, and we'll leave you and these other survivors with healing supplies." She turned a meaningful glare at the nearly thirty bodies scattered about. "Or you can choose *not* to cooperate, and we'll leave you here with nothing."

The woman sneered.

"Storm's coming." Iseult pointed to the sky. "I d-don't think you want to be stuck here."

The woman looked neither worried nor impressed, so Safi gave a lopsided shrug. "Good enough. The gods can't say we didn't try." She turned away, flickers of pain wincing in her Threads. "Come on, Knifey," she hollered at Aeduan. "We're leaving these bastards behind."

Aeduan straightened. His eyes pierced Iseult's. One heartbeat. Two. *Blood. Witch. Blood. Witch.* Then his attention skated to the sneering raider.

Her Threads flashed with blue comprehension. "Hells, you're him, aren't you? The Raider King's son. Which makes you two . . . Oh, this is rich. He's going to be so happy. He told us to be on the lookout, now here you are."

Two things happened in that moment. First, Iseult saw the woman's Threads blare with a new shade, one that spoke of Aether magic and connections spanning miles.

Second: the woman's whole body locked up. So fast it made her muscles crunch inward like a dead spider. Then she *did* die. Iseult saw her Threads snuff out moments before she went limp against the black-striped snow. Iseult spun toward Aeduan. His arm was raised, his fingers flexed as his eyes—now pure red—once more pierced hers from across the bloodied grass and snow.

"What the rut, Knifey!" Safi exclaimed. "We needed her!"

"No," Iseult said. "He did the right thing, Safi. Look." She knelt beside the fallen woman and tore the glove from her right hand.

A Witchmark winked into the gray light. A hollow circle with a scripted letter inside. "Voicewitch," Iseult said.

"Well, shit." Safi wiped her bloodied blade on the snow. "Shit in a gutter, shit on my ancestors. Was she able to send a message before you stopped her?"

"We have to assume so." Aeduan's voice was inflectionless. He was the least exerted of their ranks, and also the most detached. But just as Iseult did not need to see a wound to know it was infected, she didn't need to see Aeduan's Threads to know he was agitated. Not from the fight, although that certainly contributed . . .

But by what the Voicewitch had said. The orders she'd described from the Raider King to kill anyone who might be sick. That was his father, after all. A man he'd once followed and trusted.

"We'll have to stay off the road," Safi said.

"Yes." Aeduan blinked slowly. "The horses ran off, but I will find them and bring them back."

"No." Iseult reached for him before he could stride away. She didn't touch him, though. "We should stay t-together, Aeduan." *Do not lock up your feelings and walk away.*

His lips parted. One heartbeat stuttered past. Two. Then his spine slackened ever so slightly. "As you wish. We will stay together."

The last thing Iseult saw before she followed Aeduan and Safi into the grass was a bloodied head fallen atop the snow. Empty eyes stared into frozen nothing. *Sever, sever, twist and sever.* For all that she had avoided using her magic and avoided taking control . . .

People had still died here. The wickedness had come anyway.

It slowed them considerably to be off the road. Snow fell. Small, hard flakes that found their way into gaps in Iseult's clothing. The high grass whipped against the horses. Night was fast approaching. It also slowed them that Safi was hurt. It wasn't a life-threatening wound, but it was bad enough that it would need tending—and bad enough that nothing but curses had left Safi's lips for almost an hour.

Until she abruptly groaned out: "What's that?" Safi pointed with her left hand; Iseult squinted into the darkening sky. Something thrust up from the grass, almost like a tree except it was only the trunk.

Aeduan was the one to answer: "A shrine." He had once more tucked himself inside his hood. His voice was muffled by snowfall and salamander fibers. "There are many of them across the Plains."

Iseult nodded; she knew of these shrines, for Nomatsis often stopped at them to pay their respects to Middle Sister Swallow. "Is it safe to make camp there?" she asked him. "Or will N-Nomatsis stop there too?"

What she didn't add was that most Nomatsis had taken up the cause of the Raider King, so she couldn't even trust her own people.

"I think we can stop for the night." Aeduan's hood swiveled, as if he sniffed with his Bloodwitchery. But there was no one for his magic to find, just as there were no Threads to brush against Iseult's magic. And this time, Iseult *really* reached—even as it drained her. Even as she felt her other senses get muddy and numbed.

She couldn't let them be ambushed again. She didn't think they could survive another fight like that.

Soon, they were near enough to the shrine that grass and snow could no longer hide it: a stone pillar poking from the soil, twice Iseult's height. Winds had kicked all the snow to one side of the clearing, carrying with it offerings: food, trinkets, coins, and the uncut stones of a Threadwitch. The Nomatsis feared Swallow's fickle temper on the Plains; these gifts were meant to appease her.

Safi was the first to dismount—stiffly and with no attempts to hide her pain. Not that her Threads could hide it anyway. "Sit," Iseult ordered, pointing to a smooth, smaller stone rising up from the snow. "Aeduan and I will make camp."

Safi scoffed. A sound that was loud enough to reach across the winds. "You've got tits for brains if you think I'll let you do this alone. I'm injured, not useless."

Two seconds later, a snowball hit Safi's head—and Safi's laugh split the falling night.

In the end, Safi did help Iseult and Aeduan by using her heels to drive Nomatsi tent stakes into the earth. Then they guided the horses into the tent, arranging them at the back and using the remaining space to lay out a single pallet for Safi. This would not be the first night they'd shared their tent with the horses, but it would be the first night someone was injured.

Safi was worse off than she claimed—a fact which became obvious as soon as she tried to remove her cloak and her arm wouldn't lift higher than a few inches. It made her face and Threads crumple with pain. So Iseult helped her peel off layers, each one more soaked with blood than the last. It filled the tent with a coppery scent that overwhelmed even the smell of the horses.

"Well, that doesn't look great." Safi grimaced at her arm in the light of a Firewitched lantern. They hadn't made a proper fire; the smoke would be too dangerous. For now, the warmth of so many bodies would have to be enough. "It didn't hurt that much when it happened."

"Could you not sense how bad this was getting?" Iseult aimed her question at Aeduan, her voice sharp. "Why didn't your magic alert you?"

He didn't answer right away. He was rubbing down the horses, and his ministrations to Cloud continued uninterrupted. Gentle, steady. Until at last he paused near Cloud's hindquarters and said, "Yes, I sensed the blood, but it was not a life-threatening wound."

"And it still isn't," Safi insisted. "I've had worse." She grunted and shifted her weight. The lantern wobbled.

"Sit st-*still*, Safi." Iseult studied the gash. It was an ugly shredding of skin and muscle that hadn't sliced cleanly through. Bits of cloth and fur were stuck in the open flesh, and although Iseult had brought Evrane's healing kit . . .

Well, maybe they should have simply brought Evrane.

"We've switched places." Safi's voice was light, joking—but her Threads gave her away. "Only a few months ago, you were the one with an injury, and I was the one taking care of you."

Iseult was willing to play along. "You mean *Evrane* took care of me."

"I helped her."

"Sure. By pissing off a prince, attracting sea foxes, kidnapping a Firewitch healer—"

"Yes, yes, I did all of that too." Safi laughed, but it rang false. And no matter how many times Iseult murmured *Relax*, Safi couldn't seem to soften her muscles or deepen her breaths.

After tending the horses, Aeduan brought a second lantern to Iseult's side. All of their camping gear was now from Alma, which meant all was easily stowed and carried.

At Aeduan's whispered *Ignite*, flames flared, while outside, the winds briefly flared too. The tent wavered and flapped. Drafts of frosty air swirled through the gaps.

Iseult smeared a Waterwitch salve on Safi's arm, meant to keep the blood in her wound pure. Then a Firewitch salve to heal Safi's muscles, and finally an Earthwitch salve for the skin. Scents of lavender and calendula soon replaced the smell of blood. And soon, Safi *did* relax, just like the winds outside.

"Thank you," she mumbled once Iseult had wrapped the wound. "I owe you one."

"You owe me hundreds." Iseult tried for a smile. "But I stopped counting years ago."

Safi matched her smile.

"Do you want a Painstone?"

"No." Safi bit her lip. "Let's save those, in case I need them to, ah, you know . . ."

Iseult nodded. *In case you need them to get through a fight. In case you need them at the Well.*

They were so close to Poznin now.

After unrolling two sleeping pads, Iseult helped Safi lie down. Then they shared the cold remains of a rabbit caught the day before. Once Iseult was satisfied Safi had eaten enough, she layered a blanket over her. "Sleep." She tried again for a smile.

This time, Safi didn't match it. She simply closed her eyes, and in seconds, her Threads hazed into sleep.

TWENTY-FOUR

✳

Aeduan was furious with himself. Beyond furious. Irate. Seething. He had not sensed the raiders until too late. The Cahr Awen had nearly died. How could he forgive himself for that?

Worse than his rage, though, was his fear. It was not an emotion Aeduan felt often. After all, as he'd once told Lizl: *I do not know what fear is, so I can never be brave.*

Right now, he knew fear. For if his father had been warned the Cahr Awen were coming, then it was only a matter of time until Ragnor caught them. He had witches; he had weapons; and he had numbers. The only advantage Iseult and Safiya had possessed was the element of surprise, and now they'd lost that.

Because of Aeduan.

Because the old wounds were getting worse. Crueler. And he'd been trapped in a rout of scalding pain when the raiders had arrived.

At least once a day now, the six holes in his chest would detonate. Like firepots loosing. Like pistols shot at close range. Sometimes he could barely move from the intensity of it. When Aeduan was atop Surefoot, he could hide the onslaught. Mask the sudden collapse of his spine with a pat for Surefoot's head or a casual checking of his saddle.

But if he was trying to sense ambushing raiders . . . Or if he was in the middle of a battle against such enemies . . .

He'd almost killed the Cahr Awen with his lapse.

And now he was so angry. So afraid.

It was too cold, here on the Windswept Plains, to peel off his clothes and examine the wounds. He knew what he'd find anyway: blackened scabs that hadn't been there before—that he *knew* had healed in the Well, but now were opening up again.

Aeduan had thought perhaps he was cleaving. After all, so many now suffered from that slow spread of oily black lines. It could strike anyone; it could strike him. But he had no lines; he had no shadows or pustules burbling beneath his skin; and the stench he'd smelled on those raiders had been death come early, a song cut short. Aeduan's blood had none of that.

It was just the old wounds, returned after a brief respite. A cruel pause he'd thought would last forever.

The world was quiet around Aeduan as he stalked in concentric circles around the camp. Around the shrine. The night sky hung low, a ceiling of gray. No stars, no Sleeping Giant. With the lanterns snuffed out in the tent, there was only the snow to brighten the world. Everything became black and white. Everything became a threat.

Aeduan would not lapse again. He would *not* let this awful, inexplicable pain consume him.

He scanned the tall, endless grass around them. This shrine was too vulnerable to raiders. *And to Itosha too.*

That name—*Itosha*—was not one Aeduan knew. It had clawed up from the depths of his memory, where the marks of Nadje would never be scrubbed free. And while Aeduan could conjure no face, he could hear a cackling, hateful laugh.

Itosha. The Exalted One.

Nadje had feared her, and illogical as it was, Aeduan now felt that ancient fear too.

He spurred his magic wider. Harder. And for hours, he only ever sensed Safiya and the horses. And of course, the silver taler Iseult always wore around her neck.

Which eventually stirred within the tent, and moments later, Iseult revealed herself. Her eyes were thick with sleep, her face creased from a bedroll. "The first watch ended an hour ago," she scolded. For once, the winds had softened on the plains—as if perhaps one of the many offerings here had finally appeased Middle Sister Swallow. "You should have woken me."

"You need the sleep, Dark-Giver."

"As do you, Bloodwitch." She stepped toward him, picking her way through cleared snow. "Let me take over."

"No."

"Please. Aeduan." She'd rarely said his name since leaving the hunting lodge. They had both been careful to adhere to their roles. He was a Bloodwitch monk; she was the Cahr Awen he served. *Or failed to serve.* Formality was safest when so much was at stake.

And yet . . .

"Forgive me." Aeduan felt his face crease inward while his feelings reached outward in a way he didn't want to place upon Iseult. "For earlier. I failed you and the Empress."

"How?"

"I should have sensed the raiders coming. But I did not, and I failed you."

"You failed no more than I did. I d-didn't sense them either."

"Yes, but *you* have not sworn vows to protect me. This is my one duty. The reason I'm here."

Iseult's golden-green eyes thinned. For several seconds, she simply stared at Aeduan. Then she murmured: "Maybe I should, though."

"Should what?"

She didn't answer, but instead claimed another step toward him. "Have you ever *not* had a master?"

"I . . . don't understand." It was true: he didn't understand. He also didn't like how instantly his abdomen tightened.

"You became a monk so young. Have you *ever* existed w-without some outside force telling you what to do? First it was the Monastery." Iseult waved vaguely east. "Missions that sent you out for coin. Then it was Guildmaster Yotiluzzi. Then it was your f-father. Then . . . the Old One." She shivered here. "And finally . . . me."

Aeduan's abdomen knotted tighter. "You forget the times I disobeyed." Now he was the one to approach. To claim a single step. "I broke orders to help you find Safiya. To search for Owl and her tribe. To get you from the Aether Well to safety. And now . . ."

"And now," Iseult replied. Her face pinched up. An inward frown that sent her gaze to the snow. Made her head wag with a self-loathing he recognized. "I don't like it. I know I accepted your vow at the lodge, and I know I a-agreed to bring you—"

"Do not make me go back."

"No." Her gaze shot to him again. "But I want to know: if you could do anything, Aeduan, what would it be? If there was no Cahr Awen, no Well, no Raider King or slow cleaving or war across the Witchlands. W-what would you do?"

He sucked in sharply. Frozen air sliced his throat, his lungs. He felt the six old wounds throb as if they too awaited his answer. *Run, my child, run.*

"I do not know," he said eventually. It was an honest answer, if a bleak one. "I . . . do not know."

Iseult sighed. It was a sound of sadness, of grief, of pain. "Then I will make a vow to you." She closed the space between them. Her fingers came to touch his jaw; they were cold, but then so was he.

Her eyes bored into his, a shade like the sun through forest leaves. "When this is done, you'll serve no one but yourself, and we'll find what you want. Together . . . i-if you will have me."

Aeduan's heart skittered. More frozen air cut deep. Then he scoffed and shook his head. "Stupid."

Iseult blinked. "My vow is stupid?"

"No. Wondering if I will have you is stupid. Have I not made it clear?"

Her lips twitched with a nearly imperceptible smile. "Made . . . w-what clear?"

"In Lejna, when I told you to trust me as if my soul were yours—I had never said that before. Yet I was compelled to do so. I still am."

The smile widened. "Then you accept my vow?"

"Stupid," he replied before kissing her. Deep, full, with all the fury and the fear that still pulsed inside him. He had failed her hours ago by the road, but he would not fail her again.

He pulled away within moments. It was his only choice; otherwise, he *would* get distracted. He would lose sight of the plains and the bloods and the cold, gray night. "Go back to sleep," he told her.

Her lips were parted. Her eyes wide. "No."

"I will keep watch."

"No."

Now she was the one to kiss him. A brittle, urgent thing. Before she too pulled away. Then pointed at the tent. Her hand, Aeduan couldn't help but notice, trembled slightly. "I *will* take second watch, Bloodwitch. I command you to sleep now, and please remember: I am your master, so you must obey."

He sniffed. He could argue if he wanted, but truth be told, he was exhausted. Now that his wrath had quieted, there was only gaping fatigue left behind. And the wounds, of course. Always those six old wounds.

So Aeduan bowed his head, "As you wish, Dark-Giver." Then he kissed her on the forehead and returned, pace agitated, to the tent.

TWENTY-FIVE

※

Now bad is it?" The Truthwitch's voice rasped through the tent, and when Aeduan turned from where he checked Surefoot, he found her gazing up at him. Her face, much too pale, glistened with sweat. Her freckles stood out like constellations.

Aeduan didn't try to help her as she sat up.

"Earlier," Safi continued with a grunt, "you said you sensed my injury wasn't life-threatening, and that was a lie."

Yes, it had been a lie.

"So how bad is it?"

"Better now."

Safi rolled her eyes, a move that was barely visible in the shadows. She finished sitting up, her hurt arm hugged tightly to her chest. "You know you can't lie to me, Knifey. So I'll ask again: How bad is it?"

Surefoot snuffed. Dandelion stamped. But there were no sounds to suggest Iseult was near enough outside to overhear them.

"It's more than a surface wound," Aeduan said honestly. "And you should be resting." He tried to turn away, to resume his careful checking of the horses. But Safi leaped to her feet, surprisingly agile for someone with an injury as bad as hers—and it *was* bad. She had lost enough blood that the mountain ranges and cliffsides were nearly swallowed up by the meadows filled with dandelions and the truth hidden beneath snow.

That didn't mean her magic had suddenly become stronger, but rather that all those Cahr Awen souls inside her were crushing down on the pieces that made Safi who she was.

Her arm muscle was also ripped apart. Aeduan was no healer, but he would wager there was bone damage—and also that she had the start of a fever. It did not radiate off her yet, but there was a certain shallowness that hit blood when infection took hold.

Safi's was beginning to throb that way.

"You can't help me." The way she said this was more statement than question. "You, who controls people's bloods . . . you can't do anything to help me."

"No."

She staggered toward him. Aeduan tried to withdraw, but there was nowhere to go. And in the shadows of the tent, her blue eyes had become storm gray.

"Because you will not or *cannot?*" She crooked toward him, her voice lowering until it was almost lost to the winds outside, until not even the horses could hear her. "Make me a promise: if I cannot walk to the Well, then you will walk me there. You will take control of my blood and move me like a puppet every step of the way."

Bloodwitches cannot do this. They cannot control people like this.

Aeduan swallowed. "We have Painstones."

"Not many." Safi's right hand whipped out and yanked him close. The feverish gleam in her veins was unmistakable. "Not enough to last us two days and carry us through armies. Which means, Knifey, that when the time comes, you *will* take control of my blood. Whatever consequences might come from that magic, we'll reckon with them after the Well is healed."

Aeduan did not answer. He took in the sweat on Safi's forehead, the faint scar above her brow. He took in the intensity of her eyes and the strength of her grip upon his cloak.

He didn't like this Truthwitch. Perhaps he never would. She was rash and loud, spoiled and obscene. But there was a steel in her he recognized, a determination to do what had to be done no matter the cost to herself.

And, at the end of the day—at the end of everything that was careening nearer and nearer—Aeduan had sworn his vow to the dark-giver *and* the light-bringer. "Yes," he said at last. "I will take control if I have to."

Demon. Monster.

Safi nodded. Her shoulders relaxed and her grip on him too. As she drew away, her muscles shook. But Aeduan didn't let her get far before asking: "What did you mean by consequences?" It was a flat question, almost bored.

"Since we left the lodge, there is something off inside you." She wiped sticky hair off her brow. "My magic senses it."

"Like . . . cleaving?"

"No." Her breaths sawed in. Out. "Something different. Something else . . . wrong."

I can smell it on you: you're bound to the Void, a cursed beast with 'Matsi poison running in your veins.

"Clearly you don't want Iseult to know about it. And I don't want her to know about me. So." She gestured at her hurt arm. It made her whole body sway. "You will tell her I am healing quickly. Do you understand?"

It was a threat, and against his will, Aeduan found his estimation of the Truthwitch rising. Iseult was their Sleeping Giant, forever pointing north, and if they lost her, then both Aeduan and Safi would have nothing left to follow. No reason to keep traveling to Poznin. When Iseult had called herself a "master," she hadn't been far wrong. But it wasn't because she *forced* people to follow. It was because everyone who met her felt compelled to.

So Iseult had to keep going because it was the only way Aeduan and Safi could keep going too. Yet Iseult would stop immediately if she thought either Aeduan or Safi were hurting.

Aeduan bowed his head at the Truthwitch. It was the closest to an agreement he would offer Safi, and she seemed to realize this, since she finally released him. But rather than hobble back to her bedroll, she reached to her neck and withdrew a length of silver chain from beneath her many layers. Bits of quartz and brass dangled off it.

Aeduan's fingers flexed. "The Truth-lens."

"Yes, Knifey. Good job at stating the obvious. I . . . want you to take it. The person I made it for is in Nubrevna, according to Uncle's spies, and in case I don't survive this . . . Well, it's your job to deliver it to her."

When Aeduan didn't claim it from her, Safi sighed. Impatience set her muscles into motion. She shoved it against the skin of his neck and wrapped it around like a scarf. Against his will, he staggered back. "That is . . . overwhelming."

True, sang the crystals and glass. *True, so very true.* It was a heady feeling that buzzed like a hundred Painstones in Aeduan's skull. He ripped the necklace back off again and thrust it at Safi.

But she flipped out a weak hand of refusal. "You don't have to wear it, Knifey. You just . . ." Pant, pant. "Have to deliver it if I can't. I'd give it to Iseult, but then she'd know what's wrong with me. So just . . . shove it in your pocket and deliver it to Vaness if I don't make it out of the Well."

"You will make it out of the Well. I already said I would control your blood."

"To get me *to* the Well, yes." Her eyes scrunched. She wiped clumsily at her brow. "But neither of us knows what will come after that."

There is something off inside you.

Demon. Monster.

The necklace glinted and swung in Aeduan's grasp. The wounds on his chest throbbed. He didn't nod or agree, but he did slide the lens into his pocket where it couldn't affect him.

"Good," Safi said, though nothing in her voice sounded triumphant. "Now, I can sleep." She slogged back to her bedroll—and snorted loudly when she got there. "I agree," she declared as she folded herself back into the covers. "This tent is way too small for this many bodies. But I promise it's not me that's stinking up the place."

Aeduan had nightmares after speaking to Safi. He saw the Cahr Awen ghosts inside her skull, pushing at her like too many crabs inside a basket. He saw Iseult with her abdomen carved out and Threads crawling from it like worms. He saw the Truth-lens, but on each bit of quartz or glass was a shadowy face he couldn't recognize.

He saw a mountain filled with stars where shadowy ice clawed for anything it could grab on to—except for him. It never dug into him.

He saw four Exalted Ones in quick succession. Ferisien on a mountainside. Itosha on the plains. Rakel beside the sea. And, most violent of them all, Lovats spreading flames. That Exalted One was the one they'd all feared, even Portia with her power over Void. And certainly Nadje, who had never quite known which side he ought to choose.

Then Aeduan smelled it, poignant and inexorable: *A sky singing with snow. Meadows drenched in moonlight. Sun and sand and auburn leaves falling.*

"Run, my child, run," said the voice like his mother's while heat roared, wood cracked, and embers flew. Blood dripped from her mouth. "Run."

Aeduan did not run. He did not move. He waited, exactly as he had as a child, for the flames to overtake him and the world to burn alive.

TWENTY-SIX

※

The next day, Safi wasn't doing well.

On the bright side, she hadn't suffered a single headache since leaving the hunting lodge. Her brain felt keen, her body a thousand pounds lighter. And only in the absence of that pressure and that pain could she fully grasp how much agony she'd been living under.

On the shitty, not-so-bright side, Safi's arm felt like a volcano bleeding lava, and it was basically the only thing she could think about. The sharpest heat radiated from the hole in her arm, where the iron shot had pierced skin. But the pain wasn't contained there; she hurt all the way from her left ear down to her left fingernails. And while she was pretty sure she'd stopped bleeding now, she was also *pretty sure* she might die.

Because what she hadn't told Iseult—or Aeduan either—was that it wasn't a normal iron shot that had pierced her. It had been a Firewitched pistol, and the shot itself had been Firewitched too. As in, bewitched with a magic that would create flames inside her body, slowly burning her from the inside out.

She'd learned of such weapons as a child. Habim, after all, was a Firewitch and such weapons were a favored tool of the Marstoki Empire. Safi had also seen plenty of these Firewitched weapons up close during her time in the Marstoki Empire as Empress Vaness's personal Truthwitch.

In other words: she knew when she was screwed.

Each jolt of Dandelion on uneven terrain made Safi's brain melt. Each gust of wind across the plains made her skin burn. She was boiling inside her furs, but she knew the fever was a lie. If she took off her clothes to relieve the heat, she would freeze . . . and she wouldn't even feel it happening.

She did lower her scarf out of desperation, savoring each icy gust of Arithuanian winds. Pretending that those winds were cooling her, healing her, helping her.

At lunch, she was half tempted to take the Painstone Iseult offered again . . . but if things were this bad now, then she had to assume they were only going to get worse. So Safi gritted her teeth, forced out a smile—*false, false, false*—and refused the magical relief that was offered to her.

By midafternoon, she was starting to worry that losing consciousness might actually be the greater risk. In fact, she was quite certain the only reason she hadn't yet collapsed was because the Cahr Awen souls inside her wouldn't allow it. They were so close to the Air Well; they would not let her turn back. It literally felt like they solidified her muscles, her spine and limbs. *You will stay upright and you will keep riding. That pain is unimportant. All that matters is the Well.*

Yes, Safi agreed—although only because she *had* to agree with them. And to keep herself distracted and awake, she made herself turn all of her attention onto Aeduan. The monk rode diagonally behind her, his posture unrelenting on Surefoot's back. His white cloak a billowing, intimidating thing around him and his face hidden inside his hood.

Really, Safi had no idea what Iseult saw in him. He was bad at cards, worse at smiling, and worst of all at conversation. Admittedly, he'd stayed true to his word last night and said not a thrice-damned thing about Safi's fever or her weakness or all the agony he must be smelling on her blood. But still, he was so *boring.* The only way to get any glimmer of character out of him was to pester him until he cracked.

"You tried to kill us," Safi said, nudging Dandelion up to Surefoot's side. "Several times, in fact." Each word that came out was stronger than the last. "I think you owe us an apology. Me and Iseult, I mean. I'm sure the horses are fine."

"No." This was all Aeduan said.

"Come on now, Knifey—"

"Don't call me that."

"—it isn't hard to admit wrongdoing. They even say it's good for you. Healing for the soul, apparently." Safi pressed her uninjured hand to her chest. Her clothes were slick with sweat, but at least she was having fun. "I don't know how true that is since I myself have never done anything wrong, but I do trust advice shared by the general *they.*"

"No." This time, Aeduan rolled his wrists—and Safi couldn't help but smile.

"You tried to kill us."

"I tried to capture you."

"Which almost resulted in our deaths, making it the same in the end."

Aeduan's fingers tightened on Surefoot's reins. "It is not my fault you were inept."

"Inept?" Safi gasped. "You do recall that Iseult and I are the Cahr Awen, so by default, we are the opposite of inept. We are . . . ept."

"I don't include Iseult in my assessment."

Safi scoffed. It came out weaker than she wanted, and her vision smeared with the effort. *Not good.* "If you won't apologize," she made herself continue, "then how about a thank-you? I am, after all, the one who introduced you to Iseult, and you two seem to like each other very much."

Now Aeduan's eyes flashed red. An excellent development. "No."

"Knifey, you have to work with me on this. We're going to be together a long time, I think. Assuming you and Iseult really are—"

"Leave him alone," Iseult barked from Cloud's back. She yanked her scarf down to give Safi the full severity of her death glare.

And Safi hoisted her eyebrows innocently. "Well, why don't *you* thank me then, Iz? Someone here owes me some gratitude. At the very least, these are all *my* horses from *my* imperial stables."

"I take it you're feeling better?"

"Much." *Lie,* Safi's magic scraped—and as if in agreement, the flames in her arm fanned hotter. She had to fight to keep her face from changing. She prayed her Threads wouldn't give her away.

A frown tightened on Iseult's forehead.

"I *am* ravenous, though," Safi continued. *Lie, lie, lie.* "When do you think we'll stop to make camp?" She batted her lashes. Innocent. Pure. She was not dying by degrees, but rather a hungry Truthwitch who liked the beating wind against her face.

Iseult glanced at Aeduan, and he—to his credit—stared straight back with all the enthusiasm of a dead fish slowly rotting on the Veñaza City harbor. *Well done, Knifey,* Safi thought at him. Iseult might not trust Safi's reactions, but she definitely trusted Aeduan's.

And while part of Safi felt dishonest, manipulative, and generally terrible for lying to her Threadsister, most of her was simply glad that Aeduan was willing to ally with her in this. They *had* to reach the Well.

"We should travel as far as we can before nightfall," Iseult answered eventually, gesturing to the horizon. "That storm is getting closer, and I'd like to reach the forests east of Poznin before it breaks. Can you ride any faster, Safi? The hills ahead are less overgrown. We could pick up the pace."

No! Safi wanted to scream. *My gods, no!* But she couldn't scream that, couldn't scream anything at all. They had to keep moving forward; she couldn't—*wouldn't*—be the reason they slowed enough for more raiders to ambush them.

"Yes," she gritted out. "Let's ride." She waited until Iseult had turned her attention to Cloud before looking again at Aeduan. He drew back his hood, just enough that Safi could more easily see his face in the grayness of the day.

"Well?" she said with more edge than he deserved. "Are you going to help?"

He blinked—a movement Safi was starting to recognize as an acknowledgment. But rather than do as Safi expected, with his eyes glowing and his magic taking hold of her, he simply leaned toward her, hand extended.

A small chunk of rose quartz glittered on his palm. A Painstone. He must have snuck it from the healer kit when Iseult wasn't looking. "Use it," he commanded softly. "And I will save the other measures for later."

Safi swallowed. Somehow Aeduan's arm was completely still beside her, even though Surefoot ambled beneath him.

The Painstone flashed and shone.

Safi yanked it to her and shoved it down the front of her shirt. The quartz touched her damp skin. Relief soared through her. Up her chest, into her shoulder, and then down, down into the flames. The magic wouldn't heal the injury, but it would deplete the fires of air so they couldn't blaze quite so brightly.

"Go," Aeduan now ordered. "Before Iseult notices us."

Safi nodded. She didn't say thank you, she didn't say anything. Her voice was caught somewhere in her abdomen, the relief from pain so great she thought she might start crying. She dug her heels into Dandelion and let her gelding shoot her forward. *Jolt, jolt, jolt.*

Behind her, the Bloodwitch followed, Iseult trailing last.

Iseult knew Safi was lying. She wasn't a fool; she could see Safi's Threads, for one, and for two, she knew Safi's false bravado as intimately as she knew her own. Where Iseult would become more stoic, more centered to push through pain . . .

Safi just got louder.

Iseult had seen Aeduan give Safi the Painstone, just as she'd seen when he took it from the healer kit. Why Safi would accept it from him and not Iseult, Iseult decided not to ask. For now, she was simply grateful that Aeduan apparently had greater powers of persuasion than she, since there were two potential paths Iseult saw before them: they could continue going slower, stopping often to accommodate Safi's pain. Then the storm would almost certainly crack down right overtop their heads. Or else the raiders that must be hunting would catch up.

Or their trio could push through Safi's pain and try to reach the safety of a distant forest before the storm unloaded and raiders arrived.

Option two was clearly better, and now that Safi's Threads had changed—gone were the skittering, frantic lightning bolts of pain, replaced by something muted and calm—Iseult felt as if they could finally push hard.

So she rode them all as fast as the terrain would allow. Each league their horses carried them, the closer they got to the storm clouds. The winds bared their fangs. The temperature plummeted. When Iseult finally spotted a darkening line on the horizon—a shadow to disrupt the endless grass and snow—she cried out with a sound of uncharacteristic exuberance. Because there. *There.* They would make it, and they could finally pause their relentless, ruthless ride. Safi could rest properly. The terrain would protect them from storm and raiders alike.

Cloud's hooves churned over the grassy earth. A thunderous beat. Faster, faster. The horse saw what was ahead; she understood that in the forest she too would find relief and rest and safety.

But the wind fought against Iseult and Cloud. It brought tears to Iseult's eyes. It threatened to rip her scarf from her face. She glanced back to check that Aeduan and Safi were coming. That they too rejoiced in the forest ahead—

A funnel of wind tackled her, so hard it almost knocked her from Cloud's back. The horse veered like a drunkard.

And that was when Iseult finally sensed it: Threads hurtling toward her, not from the Windswept Plains, but from the sky. She looked up, time sagging. Her vision smearing. *Again?* They would be ambushed again?

"Windwitches!" Aeduan roared, and yes. He was right. Two shadows streaked this way.

Iseult had been so focused on avoiding raiders in the grass like yesterday, she had failed to keep vigil on the sky.

For half a moment, Iseult gazed at the forest—so near, yet still impossibly far. If she pushed their horses to the brink, could they reach those trees ahead?

Logic quickly thrust in: *You cannot outrun a Windwitch.*

"Control their bloods if you can," she commanded Aeduan, yanking Cloud to an unkind stop. Then Iseult was on the ground, frozen grass snapping beneath her.

Aeduan dismounted too. Safi did not. Her Threads were past suffusion by pain and verged on unconsciousness. It was a wonder she was still on Dandelion's back.

Iseult reached with her magic, latching her focus on to the Windwitches. Four sets of Threads, each vibrantly yellow from their magic. She spread her fingers, teeth grinding against the heat she knew would come when she grabbed their lives, their emotions, their powers . . .

It had been a month since she'd last done this; she had sworn never to do it again. But sometimes Threads made decisions the mind could not. *Sever, sever.*

Her fingers twined into Threads. One Windwitch, two. Both were fully visible now, and their arms high. Their Threads bright with an imminent attack.

Iseult hauled the Threads to her mouth and chomped down.

There was the heat. There was the skittering from the wild electricity of their power. And oh Moon Mother, *there* were the Severed Threads of the slow cleaving. These people too were dying. Fire cut into Iseult's teeth, into her gums. Through her eyeballs and down to her toes. These Windwitches were so close to cleaving on their own, she barely had to bite to finish the job.

Except now, as Iseult tried to hold on to them—as she tried to *claim* some of their witcheries as her own so she could fight any other forces that might be coming this way—she found she couldn't. The Threads wouldn't obey her. They wouldn't stay woven around her fingers. Instead they were shriveling, burning like fuses downward.

And these two fully cleaving Windwitches were about to crash into Iseult, Aeduan, and Safi. "*RIDE!*" Iseult roared at Safi as she slapped Dandelion's hindquarters.

The horse bolted—and Cloud too, just behind. Only Surefoot stayed back, seemingly unafraid of the hot, unnatural winds tornadoing this way.

Aeduan stood beside Iseult, his eyes aflame as if he searched for their blood scents. The winds had ripped back his hood, and now shadows slid across his face from the snow and debris carried on unnatural winds.

But he had no more success than Iseult did. The Windwitches arrived: two women dressed in furs not so different from Iseult's own.

Nomatsis, she realized as she watched them crash to the earth . . . then writhe back to their feet. Somehow, this was the worst thing to have happened so far. To be faced with two women of *her* heritage. Two women who prayed to the same Moon Mother.

Iseult couldn't look at them. She lowered her head, pressed herself into their winds, and unsheathed her mismatched moon scythes. She charged the two Cleaved as they rushed her. Pustules erupted on their faces, spewing tar into their winds. Their lips curled back like they were feral animals, desperate to feed. And that was what they were, weren't they? They were *hungry* for pure magic, good magic.

Just as their goddess was.

Iseult reached the taller of the two Nomatsis and swung at the woman's throat. The furs split apart, then the throat split apart too. But Iseult didn't get all the way through to the spine before the second Windwitch was upon her.

Iseult toppled to the earth. So fast, she didn't have time to withdraw her claw scythe from the first Windwitch's neck. Snarls filled Iseult's ears. Oil and heat razed her skin. She grappled and fought, both with her body and with her magic. Maybe she could control the Threads. Maybe she could still run.

The woman went completely stiff atop Iseult. It took her several booming heartbeats to notice—to *see* that the woman was choking and her eyes were losing clarity.

The Windwitch died like that, on top of Iseult. Her winds sliced off, and for half a lung-crushed breath, there was no sound but the wavering grass to fill Iseult's ears.

Then Aeduan was there and dragging away the woman his magic had ended. "We can't stay," he said. His eyes blazed red as a funeral pyre. "More witches are coming. Raiders too."

Iseult flung out her magic, grasping across the earth and hills and sky. He was right: at least a hundred people marched this way, clearing paths through the grass and snow.

Panic clogged her throat. She felt as she had when the Marstoks had taken Safi away in Lejna. When Emperor Henrick had carved away Safi's magic to make her a Hell-Bard. When Corlant had looked at Iseult beside the Solfatarra and crooned *My daughter*.

She was helpless. Completely helpless, no matter how wicked she let herself be. The Threads would not be twisted. She could cleave, but she could not control. She could kill, but she could not dominate.

"I c-cannot control them," she said as Aeduan helped her stand.

"Then let's ride." He tried to pull Iseult toward Surefoot, but she resisted.

"Safi," she told him. "Go after Safi and keep her safe. I will buy us time."

His head reared back, eyes widening. The blood within them draining in a single heartbeat. "No." He reached for Iseult with more urgency. "There is no reason for that. Come, and we can both get away."

"No, listen to me." She clutched his bicep and pressed her face close to his. His eyes were such pure, icy blue, she'd once thought them the color of Threads of understanding.

She *needed* him to be understanding right now.

"I can't c-control their Threads, Aeduan. I can't force them to fight for us. All I can do is cleave as many as possible, then h-*hope* they attack each other."

"No." He fumbled for her face. His fingers were so cold. "I won't leave you, Iseult."

"And I won't give you a choice." Winds thrashed harder; Iseult felt the charge of untamed magic on the way. She touched her forehead to his. "Go, Monk Aeduan. I command you: find the light-bringer and keep her safe until I can come after you."

Aeduan didn't move. The war brewing inside him was visible in the quaver of his pupils. In the hardening of his touch against her cheeks. He wanted to disobey Iseult. He wanted to fight with all he had inside him to keep her safe.

But in the end, he had taken his vow. He had named the dark-giver his master. He *knew* he had to let Iseult claim his Aether and guide his blade.

She laid her hands over his, feeling the frozen skin. The muscles below. His hands had held her in so many ways. As enemies, as allies, as friends.

"I love you," she said. "*Te varuje.*" She kissed him. He stiffened for half a moment against her . . . then he leaned into her lips. One hand clutched the back of her head, fingers curling in her scarf. He held her tighter, tighter against him. A panicked kiss with clashing teeth and no time—*no time.*

Iseult broke away first. "I love you," she told him again.

"I will find you" was all he replied.

TWENTY-SEVEN

✳

When Safi had been young, she'd gone swimming in a lake near the Hasstrel estate. The night had been hot, and there'd been guests at the estate she hadn't wanted to deal with. So after sneaking out of the family castle, she'd hurried through the nearby evergreens and embraced the shadows.

Once at the lake, its surface a perfect mimicry of the starry sky, she'd stripped off her clothes and dived in. Down she'd swum. Down, down, savoring the silence. Relishing the cool. The pressure increased against her skull. Her eyeballs were compressing and her lungs felt like bursting.

It was a good feeling. A *living* feeling after too much time indoors hiding her magic.

Until something brushed against Safi's leg and terror lashed through her. Then she writhed and kicked. She'd still been young enough to believe in the tales of mountain bats, and everyone knew they sometimes liked to swim when there were children nearby.

But Safi was too deep for the stars' light to reach her. She saw nothing.

So she tried to surface, tried to swing her arms and haul herself upward . . . but she only made it a few strokes before she realized she had no idea which way was up. She'd swum so deep and lost so much air from her lungs, she wasn't floating. For all she knew, she might be swimming toward the night or she might be swimming deeper.

Panic really set in then. It was as if the Void itself had swallowed her, and now she was going to die. Who would find her body? Would it be eaten to bits by a mountain bat? Would anyone even *notice* she was gone?

Her toes hit something hard. She stretched longer, and yes. That was substrate. Rocky, glorious substrate.

Without another thought—there was no time—Safi kicked hard at the lakebed and swam. No mountain bats ate her, and soon, the shadows shifted as bright mountain stars cut through the water.

When she surfaced, her lungs were a conflagration. She gulped. Her vision spun. There was a very real danger she might pass out, so she made herself flip upward and lie on her back. *Breathe. Breathe. Float. Float.*

Eventually, Safi made it back to shore. Eventually, shivering and broken, she hauled herself onto the rocky edge and lay there until the stars stopped shaking and her lungs stopped aching. She hadn't needed Habim or Uncle to inform her how stupid she'd just been. For some reason, Lady Fate had opted to spare her that night, and Safi never—not ever—swam alone or swam that deep again.

Yet now, here she was, trapped in the same shadowy unknown, and with no substrate to guide. *True, true, true.* She was in a forest with soft earth and barren winter beech trees. There was almost no snow here and even less undergrowth, and Dandelion listed and zagged so much in his panic, Safi had no idea which way would get them out of here.

Worse, her arm was on fire again. The Painstone's numbing powers were finished, and the blaze was so much hotter than before—no longer confined to just her left side but sparking into her skull, into her chest and abdomen.

Safi squinted upward, trying to ignore how it made bile rise in her esophagus, but there was too much winter gray for the sun to pierce through. She couldn't gauge which way was north. There could be no desperate final kicks to guide her home.

You can't pass out, the Cahr Awen clamored. *You're so close to the Well. Just a little bit farther.* But even those souls were not as powerful as the Firewitchery that had claimed Safi.

With a groan, she hauled herself off the saddle. Her left arm jostled. Pain stabbed, dazzling and fresh. She had to screw her eyes shut and wait for the wave to pass.

When she lifted her lids again, Dandelion was staring at her expectantly. His breaths whitened the air; he looked as lost as Safi felt. And Cloud—she was no better. She had moved closer to Dandelion, her ears swiveled forward as if she awaited her next command.

No, Safi thought as Dandelion's ears also swiveled. *They hear something.* Iseult and Aeduan—it had to be Iseult and Aeduan. They had followed her tracks and were here to rescue her.

Except when no sounds actually reached Safi's ears, she realized that whomever approached was moving with such quiet care, they could not possibly be an ally.

Cloud whinnied, and Dandelion's tail flipped in a way that said, *I don't feel safe here.*

"Me neither," Safi croaked, and for several moments, she felt stronger. Clearer. She unsheathed her blade. It sang with such truth that for several seconds, it was the only sound she heard. An empowering echo that shivered inside her ear canals.

Another whinny, this time from Dandelion, and when Safi spun toward him, she spotted four figures rushing her way. They were dressed in gray, faces hidden behind scarves like her own, and they moved with the concerted strength of trained military. Gone was any attempt at quiet. Now they were coming for her.

Shit. She could not fight four soldiers. Even on a good day, those would not be odds for a betting woman like herself. And on a bad day? Hilarious to contemplate.

Safi dropped her blade and lifted her good hand. "I surrender!" she shouted. "I surrender. Take me to the Raider King."

Aeduan's worst fears had come to pass. He'd failed again, and now the consequences were so much worse.

He should have sensed the witches approaching. He should have killed that Windwitch before it could attack Iseult. He should have moved faster, thought faster, reacted better. And he should not have been born the son of the Raider King. It was that, above all else, that haunted him. Where had his father gone so wrong? Why had he, Aeduan, served his father for as long as he had without seeing it?

One need not be evil to become it.

Aeduan thrust all his power into Surefoot, pushing the mountain horse to speeds she could never sustain without his help. It was not a magic he used often, if he could help it. For one, animals' blood was a challenge to control. The freedom in their bloods ran wild; it took twice the effort to manipulate an animal as a human.

For two . . .

Well, that same freedom sparkling and alive only ever served to remind Aeduan that what he did was wrong. *Demon. Monster.*

He thought of Boots.

He thought of crocodiles.

Then he squeezed the reins more tightly on Surefoot's blood and told her where to go. She trusted Aeduan; she didn't resist his magic and she didn't resist the speed he pulsed into her muscles.

In some ways, it was good that he was on her back. It meant he had to focus so completely on propelling Surefoot faster that he couldn't look back or second-guess Iseult's command.

No one followed him toward the forest.

He hadn't thought they would. After all, Aeduan's father wanted the Cahr Awen. His son was merely a disappointment who now stood in the way.

There was a part of him that wondered if he should try to return to his father again, claim he had been serving the cause this entire time. Then he could do the one thing Iseult so badly wanted to protect him from: he could kill his father.

Except going to Ragnor was not the command Iseult had given Aeduan, and Safi would die from her wound if Aeduan didn't find her. His jaw ached. His knuckles too. He gripped Surefoot's reins as if they were driftwood in a storm. *Go after the light-bringer and keep her safe.* That was all he had to do. He did not have to plan ahead. He didn't have to debate whether he should be here or he should have followed Iseult instead.

I love you. Te varuje.

Why hadn't he said the words in return? Why was he obeying her instead of chasing after? *Coin and the cause, coin and the cause.* She'd been right: he had no idea how to live without someone else to command him.

The forest ahead was a black haze across pale grass. Never had he seen trees look less welcoming. The storm that hung above siphoned all light. All life.

Distantly, he wondered *why* this storm never broke.

At last, he and Surefoot reached the trees. The ground softened and flattened into a forested floodplain. The winds stopped their constant howl, and Aeduan was able to ease his control over Surefoot's blood.

She slowed. Then stopped entirely.

Aeduan slung off her back, worried she might collapse. That he'd pushed her too hard, and it would be one more creature he had failed to save. But when he studied Surefoot's face, he found her unharmed. Her breaths were overloud in the sudden silence of this forest, her eyes were wide and terrified . . . but she was all right.

She was all right.

Aeduan lifted his nose, forcing his magic to rise again. He wanted to reach for Iseult's silver taler first—then he would reach for Safi's blood. But that was when the six old wounds decided to awaken. Spasms of torture across his chest. He cried out. He slumped over, eyesight crossing and ears ringing. And the fire—the *flames*. They started in the wounds but didn't stay there. They lanced outward like wildfires spread by wind.

He imagined he saw arrows with fletching poking from his ribs. He tried to grab one. To yank it out. But of course, there was nothing there.

Surefoot's face butted into Aeduan's. She snuffed; her hot breaths steamed. Slowly, the ringing receded. The pain and cold too.

He rasped in air. Again, again, feeling how his heartbeat shuddered through him. Into his lungs pierced by arrows, down toward his abdomen. What was this weakness? This curse? Safi had said it wasn't cleaving, but it *was* wrong. Was it some lingering effect from the Old One, Nadje? Or some new ailment he would never escape?

You're bound to the Void, a cursed beast with 'Matsi poison running in your veins.

Aeduan grappled once more for his magic.

This time it obeyed. Weakly, sullenly, but there for the commanding— and Aeduan's command was to search for the silver taler. He reached until he felt the faintest stirrings of his own blood smeared on silver.

Iseult had moved. In fact, she was aimed for a different part of the forest at this precise moment. That was all Aeduan could sense—not if Iseult was alive, safe, running, or fighting. But it gave him energy and hope. She was near; he would find her after he found the Truthwitch. Then they would all leave this awful forest together.

For Aeduan understood now why this place might have been left un-guarded by his father. There was something else at work here. A different danger. An uncanny force he didn't want to reckon with.

Surefoot whinnied quietly, as if to say *Hello? Human? What are you doing?* He stroked her neck. Then forced himself to straighten and turn away from the silver taler, away from the dark-giver . . . and toward the light-bringer.

The Truthwitch could not have ridden far in her current state. She had a vibrant blood, made all the more unmissable by her wound and bloom-ing fever. Yet when Aeduan sent his magic stretching out again, he sensed nothing. Yes, Safi had left traces of her blood. Remnants floating like moths. But the physicality of her was nowhere nearby.

Aeduan swallowed and let his hand fall from Surefoot's warmth. He let his magic fall too. It shrank inward, tail between its legs. *I am too tired for this. Give me rest and peace!*

He couldn't do that. He had sensed Safi's scent to the east, so east he aimed, guiding Surefoot with him. Once at the spot where he'd sensed Safi's blood, he hauled out his magic anew. *Reach, stretch, find. There.* He let his magic hide again; he resumed his tired trek with Surefoot.

Twice he wondered if it would help him to dig out the Truth-lens. Maybe it would sense its creator; maybe its magic was still somehow threaded to Safi.

But Aeduan resisted. He didn't like the way that witchery felt. He didn't want to have to stare directly in the face of truth.

So on and on he and Surefoot traveled, and bit by bit, they made progress. The undergrowth vanished in some places to reveal hoofprints that must have come from Dandelion or Cloud. Or he would snag a taste of the Truthwitch's blood scent and know she'd gone this way.

He lost sense of daylight. The forest and its ever-present storm felt beyond the passage of time. Here, it was gray whether night had fallen or not. Here, the wind did not reach and the world did not change. Only the river, expanding and growing and sinking into the porous, hungry earth, had any power.

It made Aeduan think of his time trapped and drowning inside his own body. When Nadje had ruled him and he'd felt no hope. Could that Exalted One be the source of this bloodied weeping from his chest?

A sound reached his ears: horses huffing, stamping. A clink like tack. Then a soft whinny to curve and slide around beech and pine trunks.

The Truthwitch.

Aeduan shoved ahead, leaving Surefoot behind as he kicked into a run. He grabbed hold of his magic, yanking it out with almost painful cruelty. *There are the mountain ranges and cliffsides, there are the meadows filled with dandelions and the truth hidden beneath snow.* The blood scent was weak, but then Aeduan was weak too.

He spotted shapes in the forest ahead. Two horses. One a splash of brown, the other a smear of gray. They both nickered, and one reared slightly as Aeduan stomped through the undergrowth toward them. He was close enough now to see their eyes widening and ears perking. He was close enough to know they were afraid of his rapid, wild approach . . .

And then he was close enough to see the clearing held only Cloud and Dandelion. There were markings and boot prints in the snow, but no Safiya.

Aeduan cast his magic wider. He grasped and felt . . . but Safi was gone.

The gelding reared as Aeduan came to halt before him. His eyes rolled, and Aeduan lifted his hands. "Whoa, Dandelion. Whoa." His voice was much too loud. The horses were much too loud. This was not a place for hope or life. Here, everything drowned.

Surefoot trudged into the clearing. She needed rest. So did Cloud and

Dandelion. Aeduan would have to continue alone. His worst fears might have come to pass—and Lady Fate's knife might have turned against him—but he couldn't abandon the cause yet. The light-bringer needed him. The dark-giver needed him.

Hope dies last, he thought, knowing instantly that it was not his own thought, but a ghostly memory from Nadje. *Hope dies last.*

Aeduan set off again.

TWENTY-EIGHT

✳

After binding Safi's hands, Safi's captors hauled her onto a horse—one of their own, since they left Dandelion and Cloud behind.

For some reason, this made Safi want to weep. She'd thought she could feel nothing but magma right now, yet an oceanic hole split her chest. She had to fight the tears, had to pump false authority into her voice: "How far are we traveling?" She spoke in Marstoki, of course, for these raiders spoke Marstoki—and she had to assume that meant they were Baedyeds.

The woman riding with Safi blatantly ignored the question.

"I only ask," Safi continued, "because I'm in a lot of pain. I got shot in the arm—by a Marstoki one-shot pistol, actually. And you know how much damage those can do. This one was even Firewitched, so not only have I lost a lot of blood, I seem to be cursed as well." She paused here, having to suck in a breath. "It's quite unpleasant."

False, her magic laughed. *It is so much more than unpleasant.*

"There should be a healing kit in my gelding's saddlebag," Safi added. "As well as some Painstones. If we could just go back to get him—"

"Shut up," barked the Baedyed riding at the fore. He glared, his eyes dark holes surrounded by pale scarves. First he looked at Safi. Then at the woman riding with her. "If she speaks again, gag her."

Safi grimaced. A gag would *not* do right now. She was already on the verge of vomiting; a gag would make that worse. So she bit her tongue and tried very hard to focus on what little horizon she could see through the forest. The trees were beeches, the underbrush mostly moss over peat. But the ground, she couldn't help but notice, was softening, eating up each hoof fall.

They must be moving west toward the river, toward Poznin.

And therefore toward the Raider King.

Gods below, everything had gone to goat tits, hadn't it? Clearly the intel on the Raider King's forces had been wrong. *Or else*, her brain prodded with surprising clarity, *the Raider King was simply being smart.*

An old lesson from Habim percolated to Safi's mental surface: *If the enemy is too small to target, then restrict their range of movement. Make them come to you.* This was a battlefield tactic for dealing with stealth units that larger battalions struggled to fight—and it would seem it was precisely what Ragnor the Raider King had done to Safi, Iseult, and Aeduan. He had attacked them from one direction, which had sent them running into a trap.

Safi frowned, her gaze fastening on the Baedyed riding ahead. Then on the raider walking across the earth in front of him.

When Habim had taught her and Iseult about battlefield tactics, he'd used real-world examples from the battles *he* had led. Against Baedyed raiders in the Sand Sea. These raiders right here.

She compressed her lips. It was one thing to learn lessons about faceless, distant enemies. It was quite another to ride with those enemies and realize that not only did they, in fact, have faces . . . but the reason those faces were here, in Arithuania, was because of the strategies General Habim Fashayid had used against them.

Do not vomit. Do not vomit. She fell forward. Her arm burned, her stomach revolted.

"She is fading," her companion barked. Then arms slid around Safi to hold her upright.

The man walking at the front called back, "Ride on. We will catch up to you."

The horse beneath her kicked into a fluid gallop, and the entire forest bled into a hazy, dreamlike blur. The pain was so intense in Safi's arm that it felt as if her consciousness had simply given up and said, *Nope, this is too much for me.* But rather than drag her into darkness, it clambered outside her body and watched the scene unfold from a distance.

Tree trunks muddled past, the barks shifting from shapeless beeches to shapeless alders. The ground sucked up all sound. The canopy overhead thickened, not with leaves but with branches that wove and braided until they were almost a ceiling.

And onward the horse galloped. Steady, true. A three-beat rhythm that rocked through Safi in a disconnected unreality. Even the flames in her arm seemed to fade, until she found herself cold. So, so cold.

This is what we call death, she thought, but she lacked the strength to escape its widening arms—even as the Cahr Awen souls were waking up again, were shouting and jostling and clamoring: *NO. YOU NEED TO STAY ALIVE AND REACH THE WELL.*

It was only when the Baedyed reined their horse to a stop that Safi realized she was no longer in a forest. That snow no longer covered the ground, but only mossy peat and mud. And that the shapes and shadows surrounding her were not trees but instead makeshift tents and hovels.

And people. So many people. They were dressed in all manner—some in Purist gray, some in Nomatsi-style furs, and others with no discernible faction to mark them. They watched Safi pass, aggression on a few faces, but most only wearing fear.

The Baedyed woman dismounted, and a different woman, her blond hair in thick braids, strode up. She hauled Safi down, not roughly but not gently either. Safi's vision crossed. She doubled over as soon as her feet sank into the earth. She was so cold. She was going to collapse onto the welcoming moss of this strange settlement and then she would never wake up again.

NO. YOU NEED TO STAY ALIVE AND REACH THE WELL.

Safi's left arm was limp and agonizing. She wished the *thrice-damned* Cahr Awen souls would shut up and let her sleep. She wished she could vomit or pass out. Anything to end this pain.

Then, as if the souls were actually listening for once, they did quiet. Abruptly. They scattered from her skull like flies from a corpse, and Safi felt their fight drain from her body. The world around her silenced. She swung her gaze upward, stars flashing, to find a path had cleared through the people so a single man could pass. He was cast in shadow, but Safi didn't need to see his face to know who he was.

The Raider King, she thought. *Finally we come face-to-face.*

He was not a towering man—the Lusquan woman stood taller—and he was thin. Rangy, even. He wore no crown, no adornments to glitter in the dim light. He was just a man, and distantly Safi appreciated that.

Her eyes sank shut. She let her head loll down, let the mossy earth take her. She wanted to fight, but there was nothing left in her to fight with. The Raider King had won, and this was how her story would end.

She didn't even have the energy to feel grief or regret anymore.

The Raider King's boots reached her. Worn brown leather that blended into the dark peat. A chime like buckles clinking. A huff like someone who was tired and . . . of all things, *amused.*

Then the man crouched before Safi and warm skin brushed her chin. "Domna," he said softly. "Stay awake. A healer is on the way."

For several moments, Safi didn't understand what she was hearing. *Domna? The Raider King must have heard I am no longer a domna.* She dragged her eyes open. Forced her pupils to find the king's face. It was veiled by such deep shadows that it had become half shadow itself. His hair was dark and cropped close, his eyes . . .

Ah, his eyes.

"Prince," she rasped, her voice a tragic, dying thing. "Is it really you?"

"Hye," he murmured as her magic suddenly woke inside her and sang with a warm, blissful truth. "It's me, Safi."

That was the last thing she heard before Merik's arms scooped beneath her and blessed unconsciousness swept in.

TWENTY-NINE

※

As Aeduan prowled and searched the unnatural forest, he had the gradual sense he was not alone. He smelled horse; he smelled dirt; he smelled old river and sulfur . . . But never did he smell humans.

Animals, he decided. *Wolves, maybe.* He scanned the trees with his sight. But he found nothing. Only snow falling in a slow, half-hearted twirl, as if the storm clouds overhead had given a tired sigh and expelled whatever they couldn't still hold on to.

Aeduan reached carefully, silently for the knives across his chest, for the largest blade that hung at one end. All of his muscles were poised, his heart pumping with a steady, reliable strength. No agony from his old wounds; just the dull ache that had followed him an entire lifetime.

A branch snapped behind Aeduan. He wheeled around, slinging his knife upward and thrusting his magic outward like a net. But still, he smelled no one.

The hair on his neck stood up. He'd learned as a boy about storm hounds on the Arithuanian plains. And he'd seen as a man what their cousin, the mountain bat, could do. He could not fight against such creatures, even at the height of his powers.

Aeduan crept around the trees, sniffing and squinting. Something was near. Something that could keep itself hidden.

Ghost, he thought, and his mind shot to other stories—ones his mother had shared of Threads that became detached from dead bodies; snippets of memory and Aether that lived on long after a person decayed. *The Sightwitch Sisters,* she'd told him, *have Crypts filled with written memories taken from the dead. Those memories sometimes break free, and they're drawn to the souls of the living. Not hungry in a violent way, but hungry in a lonely way.*

As a boy, he'd imagined a dark place filled with pale wisps of spirit. He'd imagined books that crawled off shelves as if they were spiders in search of a new web. He'd known now that his mother had meant to instill him with awe, but at the time, it had only frightened him. Given him such bad nightmares that twice he'd woken up screaming.

Suddenly he felt like that little boy all over again, for there was a pale spot forming in the forest now. Exactly as he'd imagined a ghost in the Crypts might appear. It scuttled away from him.

Run, my child, run.

Aeduan did not run. Instead, he drew in a long breath, feeling the air rise into his nasal cavity. Then slide down his throat and against his vocal cords. He was not his mind, nor his body, nor was he his fears.

And that was not a ghost.

His grip tightened on his knife, and with his left hand, he reached for his sword. But he never got a chance to unsheathe it before a scent abruptly clattered against him: his own.

Iseult, his brain fired out. *The silver taler.* It was here, and it was moving into the trees—while mingling with it was a second scent, of mountain ranges and cliffs. Of meadows laced with dandelions.

Both Iseult and the Truthwitch were nearby.

Wait! Aeduan wanted to shout, but no voice left his throat. Instead, his feet propelled him forward like shot from a cannon. He ran, horses forgotten. Ghosts forgotten too.

The forest folded him in, and the night stretched on.

Perhaps if Aeduan had not been so focused, so fully detached from his mind and body as he always became on the hunt, he would have paused long enough to consider how the forest changed around him. How illogical it was for Iseult and Safi to have traveled this way. Or perhaps he would have pulled out the Truth-lens and used it to assess the truth of what he followed.

But Aeduan was fueled by his own failure. And so he could not relent.

Aeduan really should have paid attention, though. He *should* have pulled out the Truth-lens, and he *should* have noticed how the trees were gradually replaced by stones. An illogical feature in a land made of damp earth—one made all the stranger when soon there were no trees at all but only boulders rising up in a way that reminded him of the Contested Lands.

The snow here looked almost like the asphodels that grew on that cursed peninsula. Small evergreens replaced the ferns. The gravel crunching underfoot could be the helms and blades from battles centuries ago.

The Contested Lands were cursed.

This place was cursed too. But the silver taler was so near—and the truth beneath snow as well. Iseult and Safi had come this way. Somehow, they were together and Aeduan just had to find them.

He didn't, though. Not before he came to a hole that finally *did* make all his senses clamor with alarm. It was a perfect circle carved into the earth, with a wide ramp descending on one side like the ramp within a fortress, meant for horses and men side by side. At the bottom of the stairs, a faint glow throbbed, blue and frizzing in a way that Aeduan had never seen . . . but that Nadje had.

This, the ghostly memories whispered, *is another doorway into the mountain.*

Aeduan stood still as the towering stones around him. He stared at that doorway twenty feet below. Something about this spiral was familiar. It made the six old wounds pulse and bleed—he could *feel* the blood trickling out once more. Sliding down onto his abdomen, where the wool of his garments rejected it.

Snow coasted languidly by, in no rush to meet the ground. Untouched by wind. Where it landed on the ramp, it disappeared. Not melting, not freezing, simply vanishing.

Aeduan let his magic unfurl cautiously toward the spiral. Then toward the blue door. *Bright and fresh and laced with fireflies.* The taler and its bloodstain had come this way—and mixed with it were the dandelions and the meadows.

So Aeduan must go that way too.

He jumped. A single coil and spring of his muscles that took him through the soft snow. Then down, past spiraling granite where all light and moisture disappeared. The light of the doorway shivered across him. His feet hit hard rock. He transferred the power into a roll.

And the magic of the portal reached him. It stretched him, ripped him, compressed him into a fraction of his being. Blood, muscles, ice. *Run, my child, run,* the voice said.

Then Aeduan was through. He was inside the mountain made of starlight that the Paladin Nadje had once known.

THIRTY

✳

seult had lied to Aeduan when she'd told him she would cleave the raiders. She had lied when she'd said she would follow him and Safi into the forest. She had lied as soon as she'd realized she couldn't control the Windwitches. She hadn't wanted to lie—she hadn't *known* she was lying, in fact. But it was as if the back of her brain had assembled a plan while the front of her brain simply fought to stay alive.

Then, once Aeduan had disappeared from sight, Safi already gone by then, the back of Iseult's brain finally decided to provide her with its new decision. A single bolt of logic that sizzled through her like Severed Threads.

Leopold couldn't kill the Raider King because he could not get close to him.

I can get close to him now that Aeduan and Safi are safe.

I can kill the Raider King.

Those were the key points of the plan—the primary thoughts that formed across her consciousness like music notes. And only now, as she was being escorted toward Poznin, did all the connections surface. The dots and lines that transform individual parts into a melody.

If the enemy is too small to target, then restrict their range of movement. It was a lesson Habim had once taught Iseult and Safi years ago—and it was what both raider ambushes had successfully done. But Habim had also taught the counterstrategy: *Make multiple, smaller targets.* If a group was already too weak to stand against massive numbers, then there was no reason not to separate. Break the hornet's nest into individual hornets, then the enemy couldn't contain *everyone*.

But Iseult wasn't merely trying to shrink their unit—she didn't *merely* want Safi and Aeduan to get away. She also knew that she had a unique opportunity to get close to the man leading everything. The heart, the brain, the strategic mastermind.

And if I do this, Aeduan will no longer have to face the possibility.

Iseult was careful to show no hostility as the raiders—of which there were at least a hundred—escorted her to Poznin. There was a threat that hung in their Threads. The raiders watched Iseult closely, and at any sign of violence, weapons would be drawn, witcheries aimed, and chains locked around her limbs. For now, she walked unimpeded—but that was only because they'd locked her into a heretic's collar.

The wood was smooth with age, the iron bolts cold on her skin. And although it was true: she couldn't use her cleaving magic, she *could* still see Threads. As if the collar, rather than eliminate her magic, had simply punted her from the Void and into the Aether. *Now you are a mere Thread-witch again.*

Which was good. Excellent even, for now all these raiders thought they were safe against her. They all believed her fangs were muzzled, forgetting she still had claws.

It took the rest of the day to reach the first outskirts of the Raider King's encampments. Iseult had of course *seen* all these troops and factions and small settlements on the maps Eron fon Hasstrel kept constantly updated. But dots and figurines upon a flattened surface could never capture the sheer scale of what actually surrounded the former capital of the Republic of Arithuania.

She felt it before she ever saw it. A change in her center of gravity, as if she were a rock rolling downhill. As if the weight of all these people and horses and tents and weapons and magics had sunk into the landscape and there could only be one path forward.

It was breathtaking and horrifying just how many troops the Raider King had beneath his banner—and there *was* a banner now: a simple black flag with a red crescent moon at the heart. It was a combination of the Red Sails and the Baedyeds—but it was more than that, too. The black felt like the black Threadwitches wore, and the red shade of the moon . . .

It felt gruesome. Like the Moon Mother reduced to arterial blood.

Leopold had been right: there was no way Iseult, Safi, and Aeduan could have gotten into this city without an army at their side.

Which made Iseult's new plan that much more urgent.

As she was led over a newly built bridge across the wide river that slid past Poznin and had overflowed its banks decades ago, Iseult reached for her Threadstone. It of course wasn't there. *And neither is the taler.*

Her hand stilled, stuck at the base of the heretic's collar. Then, for the first time since she'd been captured, terror sluiced through her body. She patted and scraped and searched under the collar for the coin, but it wasn't there. She'd lost it. Somehow, somewhere—it was gone.

This is good, she tried to tell herself. *You didn't want him to follow you anyway, and you were going to leave him at the lodge. This is good. A completion of what you'd tried to initiate with your first plan.*

But it didn't feel good. Iseult felt alone. And she felt small. Very, very small.

"Stasis," she mouthed to herself. "Stasis in your fingers and in your toes." She was a Threadwitch by training, and for once, a Threadwitch in magic too, since she could no longer weave. And as a Threadwitch, Iseult had no need for feelings or for fear. Logic had gotten her here. Stasis would keep her going.

When the bridge ended, soggy floodplain dusted in fresh snow squelched beneath her feet. High stone walls climbed from the earth ahead, stretching shadows across her. Until she was within the walls and the wind from the plains fell silent.

It was strange to feel stillness again. To hear only the sounds she was meant to hear, untempered by Middle Sister Swallow's howling. She examined the city around her; it was different than what she'd seen in the Dreaming, through Esme's eyes. More raiders, more tents, more Threads crammed into a city that had died fifty years ago from a plague that might still lurk in the soil and stone and waters trudging by.

Certainly there were Severed Threads here, thick as cobwebs. Everywhere Iseult's gaze landed, she could detect them, coiling and wriggling. *Threads that break, Threads that die.*

This close to the final Well, all magic had become poison.

As for Esme's actual army of Cleaved, Iseult spied none of them. Eron's intelligence reports had said they still stood here, yet on this particular wide avenue that led uphill with buildings like skeletons left upon a battlefield, there were no signs of her forgotten army.

"This way," one of the raiders said, veering Iseult toward a copse of trees grasping at the winter sky. A path with occasional flagstones cut through the forest and snow, until a small clearing appeared. Here stood a single domed Nomatsi tent.

Inside, Threads burned with such teal certainty, it was almost hard to look upon them. They were like Evrane's Threads, bordering on fanaticism. But they were also like Eron fon Hasstrel's: unrelenting and self-assured.

And swirling at the core was a knotted cluster of grieving Threads. Of pure cobalt and stark navy that were a perfect match for the Threads of a different man from a thousand years ago.

An undercurrent of darkness stirred inside Iseult. She was so close, it would be so easy. So quick. One death to prevent many. *I will not falter.*

"Stop," said the raider woman leading Iseult, and she dismounted with the expectation that Iseult should do the same. Moments later, a raider opened the tent flap for Iseult. Heat and orange light poured over her.

Once inside, flaps swimming shut behind her, it took several moments for Iseult's eyes to adjust. All she saw were the Threads. *Forest green determination. Cerulean preparedness. Rose calm.*

Blue, blue, devastatingly blue grief.

Until at last, Iseult also saw Ragnor Amalej.

And her resolve didn't merely falter, it shattered into a thousand pieces. For here stood a replica of Aeduan, except Aeduan of the future. Aeduan with Threads and silver-streaked hair, with hazel eyes and thick lashes. Ragnor was slender like his son, but dressed neatly in a black gambeson and breeches. Lines fanned out from his mouth, as if he'd smiled often long ago.

The undercurrent inside Iseult became a tidal wave, and suddenly her logic was drowned just as most of Poznin was.

Ragnor stood, his stool sliding over a rug, and with a deliberate, thoughtful frown, he said, "So the dark-giver has finally come to me. Welcome. I do not wish to kill you, but I will if I must." Then, to Iseult's shock and discomfort, the Raider King pressed his hands flat to his sides, hinged his torso at the hips, and bowed. It was a bow like Nomatsis gave to a Threadwitch, meant to show that Iseult had earned the respect of the tribe—and it was the same bow she had taught Caden only days ago.

She swallowed. Then swallowed again, harder, her throat clogging up. No one had ever bowed like this to her, and she had to brace herself against the floods. *Stasis! Stasis!*

When the Raider King rose again, his gaze leveled past Iseult toward the door. "Admiral," he called to someone outside, "bring in the food. Our esteemed guest has traveled such a long way, and we must show her proper hospitality."

THIRTY-ONE

✳

afi awoke sweating. *Thrice-damned city,* she thought blearily. *Why is it always so hot in Veñaza City?* She opened her eyes, expecting to see the top of her four-poster bed, to find she'd forgotten to open her bedroom window the night before . . .

But it was not a white ceiling above her, nor the wooden beams of an attic where heat could gather from Mathew's kitchen. Instead, Safi stared at densely woven branches lit by a hanging lantern. There was a scent in the air—a cold, wintery scent laced with peat and cedar. Outside, sounds of people clattered and clanked and hummed.

Her left arm pulsed, but with a distant throb like music that plays from several streets over.

Iseult. This was Safi's first thought once clarity wedged in. She'd lost Iseult. Where was Iseult? She tried to rise, but the movement defeated her. Pain speared through her. Then gentle hands pressed against her chest. A voice she didn't recognize murmured in Marstoki, "You are safe. You are protected."

The voice was attached to a brown face blessed with age. She smiled. "You are safe," she repeated. "You are protected. I am Riness, a healer."

Safi's magic hummed with the truth of this, even as the Cahr Awen souls argued, *But we need the dark-giver! We are so close to the Well!*

"I . . . don't care about me," Safi said. "Where is Iseult? And Knifey? I mean . . . the . . ." She had to pause. To gasp in air as her gaze fastened on her caretaker. "The Bloodwitch. He's a Carawen monk. I was with them."

"And my people will search for them," came a different voice. One Safi knew. One that made no sense yet comforted her all the same. "I promise we will find them," Merik said.

True, true, true.

It was exactly what Safi needed to hear. It didn't quell the Cahr Awen souls, but it did at least quell her own. Merik was here, Merik was true. He knew how to find Iseult and Aeduan, and Safi could have faith that he would. It was safe for her to sink back into sleep now and let the waves of Veñaza City heal her.

She closed her eyes. The woven ceiling vanished. The hands pressing on her chest withdrew.

Merik had spent most of his life trying to control the world around him. He could look back and see how this behavior had arisen in him. When your mother takes her own life, your sister blames you for it, then your father sends you away because your magic isn't strong enough . . .

Yes, it was easy to look back and say, *Ah, no wonder I grabbed on to anything that would obey me. And no wonder I was so angry when the world refused to listen.*

Safiya fon Hasstrel had been one of the first people who'd refused to listen. She had not, however, been the last. Nothing and no one Merik had met after Safi had followed his plans. And rather than accept this fact, he'd spent all that time seeing only what he'd wanted to see and never accepting what truly lay before him.

He didn't like thinking back to that version of himself. He didn't like realizing . . . and then *counting* how many people he'd harmed by being inflexible or letting his temper win. His greatest regret of all, though, was how he'd treated the boy Cam, who'd been nothing but loyal and true. Merik, in his stupid, almost *hateful* certainty, had refused to see what was actually right in front of him. With Cam, with Vivia, with his own awful hunger for revenge fastened onto the wrong enemy.

Now here Merik was, once more forced to accept that he had no control—that as much as he'd *wanted* to see only clear skies, Noden had actually prepared many waves and storms to fling his way. If he didn't bend like the palm trees of the Nihar lands, then Merik was going to break.

An empress. Here, in the middle of his secret camp—and claiming she was also half of the Cahr Awen. *Surely* Noden was laughing at him.

"The raiders ran off," Birdy said, leaning against Merik's desk in that slouchy way only a young man could. All sharp angles and lines. "Soon as Rora came down out of the sky, her storms goin', they ran."

"Retreated," Ulga inserted, an edge to her voice. "They *retreated.*" She tried so very hard to be a proper lieutenant to Merik and his makeshift forces. It annoyed her to no end that Birdy didn't care. "We watched until they were gone, sir, and then we watched a bit longer. We returned here once we were sure they weren't doubling back."

"And Aurora?" Merik asked. "Where is she now?"

"Gettin' fed." Birdy grinned. He found it hilarious to watch Aurora eat since the entire affair involved a lot of mess, a lot of slobbering, and a lot of whining afterward for cuddles.

"Good." Merik nodded at Birdy. Then at Ulga too. "Thank you both." Despite their age, they had become two of his closest advisors—if *advisors* was the right term for the ragged crew who helped him. For weeks, the Raider King had not noticed Merik in Poznin . . . until one day, all the forces had moved in. From outside of the city, they'd shoved in like ants discovering a forgotten carcass. Merik had barely gotten his new people out before the whole of the crumbling capital had been overrun.

Yet rather than flee, they had dug into the wet forests east of the river. Revan had found a tunnel near the Puppeteer's tower. Following it had led them into this forest, into a strange place where the trees had been woven into structures and no one who might fly overhead would spy them.

It seemed too perfect to be real. As if Noden had created these buildings *just* for Merik to find. Some of the trees even looked recently woven, their branches green and pliant.

So Merik and his people had stayed.

After all, so many of Merik's new people had families trapped in the Puppeteer's cruel stasis or still loyal to the Raider King. They wouldn't leave, and he wouldn't leave without them. So he had named this place *Last Holdout*, and everyone had thanked their assorted gods for the safety of these strange trees.

Merik's base of operations—his captain's cabin—was like all the other buildings here: a crude assemblage of woven branches, roots, and vines. He had layered it with canvas and furs and whatever else he could find to keep out winter and wetland. Then he'd done the same to all the buildings, packing soil and dirt into walls and layering dried rushes across the earth.

Merik had rushes on his floor now too, and a brazier burned in the corner beside a mound of furs that made the space moderately comfortable. His greatest luxury, however, was a large desk salvaged from the city, upon which he'd laid out maps. Each day, he updated the maps as new people arrived at Last Holdout.

He also updated them as his nightly forays into the city afforded new intelligence on the Raider King's forces.

"Where's Sky?" Birdy asked. "And Loulou?"

"*They*," came a new voice, sanguine and cocksure, "are already back." Sky shoved into the tent, dressed in a wintery thick camouflage like the

Baedyeds. Loulou—one of those Baedyeds, whose real name was Loued—shoved in behind Sky. He was a short man, stocky and square jawed. His thick fringe of black eyelashes and glossy black curls softened him toward a beauty that Merik suspected Sky was slightly in love with.

And that Loulou was completely oblivious to, given he was ten years her senior.

With their powers, they were easily Merik's most important advisors. "We saw where the horses went," Loulou said in Marstoki, flipping his right hand toward Merik—and as such, flashing his Witchmark to the room: a square for Earth with an ox horn for Herdwitchery.

"In the . . . *other* part," Sky added. She spoke a rougher Marstoki, recently learned because her Wordwitchery sponged up new languages as easily as the earth around them sponged up water. "We walked in a few hundred paces too, just to be sure, but there were no hoofprints. No horses, and definitely no people."

Loulou nodded. "I could find only the usual wild animals willing to exist in that . . . place."

Merik felt his breath expel at those words. *That place. The other part.* If Last Holdout and its unnatural buildings were strange, the *other part* of the forest was far stranger. It was an area in the east where the air felt wrong and night's shadows lurked long after the sun had risen each day. Merik had been there once, just to see why his people were so afraid—why *those* trees frightened them when Last Holdout did not . . . And he had promptly rushed back out again.

So if Iseult and the Bloodwitch were in there, then it would not be easy to find them. He twisted his attention back to Ulga and Birdy. "And you saw no signs of a monk or Nomatsi woman with the retreating raiders?"

"No, sir." Ulga shook her head emphatically while Birdy's face scrunched up momentarily. Then he too wagged his head. "Naw, no one that looked like prisoners with 'em."

Sighing, Merik massaged his temples. Dramatic flourishes marked the corners of his map, while the city itself had been drawn with unnecessary detail. But who was he to tell Revan to keep it simpler? Who was he to deny distraction to a boy who just wanted to find his mother somewhere inside all those remaining Cleaved? Plus, the boy made good maps, so long as Merik had the patience to wait for them.

He reached down and removed an acorn from the fringe of forest where the raiders had just attacked—and then retreated. All the forces on the map were denoted by acorns or walnuts. "I want a patrol sent out," Merik said, directing this at Loulou. "Tell them to comb the other part of the forest for the Threadwitch and the monk with her. I know not everyone is willing to go in there, but—"

"I'll do it." Ulga blurted this with far too much eagerness.

Merik studied her. Then Birdy, who less enthusiastically muttered, "Yeah, me too."

They were neither of them great fighters or trackers, but they'd proven themselves loyal as any sailor, soldier, or guard that Merik had ever commanded. And loyalty was something he'd learned by now never to waste. "Hye," he said slowly. "I will let you go, but not alone. Bring anyone willing to search with you. If you find them, bring them here. If you don't find them, search for signs of why."

"And me?" Sky asked, glancing sideways at Loulou—who seemed to have forgotten (again) that she existed.

"Rest up, Sky," Merik answered. "You're coming with me into the city."

THIRTY-TWO

※

It was a Firewitch who came into Ragnor's tent, and her Threads were like Owl's, like Leopold's, like the ancient creatures of the Witchlands who did not simply *possess* elemental powers but were created from them.

A *Paladin*, Iseult recognized, and this one held a quiet, imposing power with her dark skin and gray hair pulled into a loose bun. With her salt-roughened red coat that somehow made her look more commanding because of its worn edges and occasional rips.

She gave Iseult a smile that wasn't unkind so much as amused, her Threads shivering with subtle laughter. Like this whole thing was a joke, and she couldn't wait for the punchline. She also carried a bowl of steaming stew, and if she minded the drudgery of the task, she showed no sign. She simply set the bowl on a lone desk beside a lone cot, then left again with a sailor's rolling stride.

It was only as the Paladin slipped through the tent flap and torches outside flickered light across her hands, that Iseult noticed something on her thumb: a jade ring.

Suddenly, Iseult knew exactly who this woman was. *Admiral Kahina, leader of the Red Sails.* She had controlled the fates of Safi and many Hell-Bards in Saldonica, and she only let them safely escape the Pirate Republic once Safi had agreed to a deal.

Anything I want, I will one day collect from you.

Safi had a scar around her thumb to mark that bargain.

How such a woman had come to have a ring or lead the Red Sails, Iseult couldn't possibly guess. But she also knew better than to underestimate anyone with a witchery as powerful as a Paladin's.

"You may have my tent for a time," Ragnor said once Iseult returned her attention to him. "I have work in the city that will take many hours. You should rest, if you can. The linens"—he waved to his cot—"are fresh, if you wish to sleep." He moved to pass Iseult, his Threads alighting with new focus for whatever task lay ahead.

And in the brief span of two seconds, Iseult had enough time, enough nearness, to kill him. She could reach for the sword at his hip and stab him.

Instead, she faltered. Instead, she failed and only said: "W-wait."

Ragnor paused, ten paces away. Iseult could still make a move, if she was quick. If she was quiet.

Still, she did not. "It isn't plague," she told him.

The Raider King frowned.

"You've sent raiders out to kill people with black lines on their body—but it's n-not plague. They're cleaving."

The Raider King blinked a slow acknowledgment, a gesture Iseult had seen Aeduan make countless times. "Yes," Ragnor replied, the word carefully uttered in Nomatsi. Then: "That is what the plague always was, Iseult det Midenzi. This city has been poisoned for as long as the Well has been dead."

Iseult's posture wavered. "But then, if the plague is caused by dead Wells—why do you want to *cleave* all the Wells? That will only spread the poison farther."

"Will it, though?" Ragnor's question was not harsh, so much as impatient. "There is much for us to discuss and share, but I cannot do so now. I promise, however, that all your questions will be answered—and I think you will then see that we are not enemies in this fight. We are simply tools who refuse to be discarded." With those words, he finished his march from the tent.

The flap swung shut, sealing out winter and Threads and the noises of life beyond. Iseult's body felt separated from her mind. Her Threads, if she could have seen them, felt as if they were somewhere three feet to the right. She had already faltered; she had already lost. *Why didn't you kill him? Aeduan will die. Safi will die.*

"S-stasis," she gnashed out, prying so tightly at the heretic's collar her nails dug into wood. Cold, smooth, imprisoning. "You know why you are here. You know what you must do." The Raider King and his Firewitch Paladin were moving beyond her magical range, but four people stood guard outside the tent. Another fifteen people patrolled just beyond, each with the disciplined, united Threads of soldiers bound in duty.

Why didn't you kill him? Why did you falter?

She forced her hands to release the collar and her arms to return to her sides. Then with feet she barely felt on the amber rug, she made herself spin and examine the tent.

The cot had linens and a wool blanket fine enough to have come from the imperial hunting lodge. A brazier coughed meager smoke toward a gap in the tent's ceiling. No wind stole the smoke, only the natural force of warm air grasping for cool.

On the Raider King's desk, her stew waited beside letters and maps and drawings and ledgers. A compact version of Eron fon Hasstrel's table in the dining room—and all of it just sitting there. Right where Iseult could read anything, could *destroy* anything if she wanted to.

The Raider King is not a man to be trifled with. He is the greatest strategic mind of the last millennium.

Yes. Iseult believed that now, having seen the numbers that had swelled this city into a bloated corpse. And also having seen how easily Ragnor deflected her attempts to speak. Surely he knew why she had surrendered. Surely he *sensed* she had come here to kill him. Yet he had "opened" his house to her, then walked away.

She looked down. The collar blocked her view of her feet, but she didn't need to see her toes to know she'd found stasis. In four long steps, she carried herself to Ragnor's desk. Here was a map of all his forces, laid out exactly as she'd found them on her ride into the city. But now she could count exact numbers, study exact placements.

Either Ragnor had left all of this out for her because he wanted her to trust him . . . or this was a trap Iseult couldn't yet see. It didn't matter which. If he wanted her to study it, then study it she would. *Evaluate your opponent, analyze your terrain.*

She sat on the Raider King's stool, a humble throne of creaking pine. Then she withdrew the book still inside her satchel—the one Leopold had left for her, filled with what he'd *thought* would be the Raider King's strategies and plans.

"Let's see how accurate you were, Leopold."

Iseult got to work.

Safi had no idea how much time had passed when she awoke again. All she knew was that the room felt smaller, darker. There was only the one lantern, still burning, which cast an orange glow over the odd wooden room.

"You're awake."

Safi twisted, swallowing at a mouth that was too dry. And there he was: Merik Nihar, hunched on a stool and staring at her as if *she* were the ghost instead of he.

"Am . . . I dreaming?" she rasped.

"Not a very good one, if you are." He smiled, but it was a pained thing that pulled at the burn scars all along the side of his face. "We haven't found your Threadsister or the Carawen monk. But my people are still searching."

"Your people," she tried to say, but all that came out was coughing. Vicious rattles that sounded as bad as they felt, churning up from her abdomen.

Merik moved close, slipping a hand behind her. He helped her sit with a familiar strength. A water bag reached her lips several moments later, and she gulped it back greedily.

Never had water tasted so good.

"Not too much," Merik murmured, stealing the water away. "I'm under orders to hydrate you slowly." He set the bag on a second stool beside her bed—although *bed* was an exaggeration. It was more like a stack of thick furs and rugs.

There was a child's tale Mathew had once told Safi, about a mouse living at the base of a tree. That was what she felt now—like that mouse. Because everything in this room was mystical and storylike, from the rushes on the floor to the crude chest beside the door hung with furs . . . And most of all, to the scarred prince seated on a stool beside her.

Here he was ruling over a settlement that had clearly not been assembled by hands, but rather by magic, while people of mismatched backgrounds obeyed him as if they'd known him forever and would follow him through hell-fires.

She leveled a gaze onto his face. He was so much thinner now. Gaunt, even. Yet strangely, illogically, it suited him. Now he looked less like a boy and more like a man wizened by a world that had fallen apart around him. His eyes had always held a weight in them—the weight of a crown, the weight of people depending on him—but now they held wisdom too.

"I thought you were dead," she said.

"And I thought you were dead."

"I'm close enough to it." She tried for a smile, but she felt it failing her. Frizzing with falseness across her face.

"As am I," he answered. *True, true, true.* "But you will survive your wound, Safiya fon Hasstrel, thanks to our Baedyed healer. She was able to repair the muscles in your arm. However . . ." A pause. A swallow. "There will be scars on the skin."

Safi lifted a single eyebrow. "Scars do not bother me, Prince."

"I see."

It was like watching a storm clear at sea. For the first time since she'd awoken, Merik seemed to settle beside her. The waves that tormented him softened toward calm.

"How are you here?" The question emerged from Safi's throat like a breeze.

"It's a long tale, Domna."

"And I have time for listening."

Merik hesitated, and for half a moment, Safi thought she saw a bit of the boy he'd once been. An uncertain boy, afraid to make the wrong move with so many people watching.

"Please," Safi pressed. "The last time I saw you, we were both inside a mountain. I need to understand where I am. How you're here. Who these people are that are out there searching for Iseult."

"Still as impatient as ever," Merik murmured, and a real smile towed at his lips.

"And you're still as stubborn."

His smile turned sad. "I hope not." He shook his head, wiped a hand across his face, and finally straightened upon his stool. "It started when assassins came in the night to the *Jana*. I thought my sister had sent them, and so I traveled to Lovats to confront her . . ."

THIRTY-THREE

✳

As soon as Aeduan came out of his roll inside the mountain, he caught flickers of a blood that his witchery instantly snarled at: *Clear lake waters. Frozen winters.* But he was too late to turn around—to leap out of this bear trap before iron fangs closed.

He dove for the magicked door, but already the light was shrinking, fading, vanishing. His hands hit stone, and although static charged through him, he did not topple back out the other side.

He was stuck here.

"No," he growled at the granite, pounding it. Then louder, "*No.*" He grabbed at triangular carvings around the door. He pressed them, he scratched them, he shouldered into them until it left bruises that his magic had to tend to. But nothing happened; the stone remained stone. Aeduan could not get back through.

If Aeduan had been angry with himself on the plains and irate with himself in the forest, it was nothing compared to what plunged through him now. He had danced like the broken bear; he had fallen, yet again, for Leopold's games.

Aeduan spun away from the door. His Bloodwitchery surged, bolstered by fury, and he flung it outward in a wide, vicious net. Leopold was here, and Aeduan would find him. *Ahead*, his magic told him, so ahead Aeduan went. He wasn't surprised to find no floating remnants of the silver taler now. No mountain ranges or dandelions, either.

Iseult wasn't here. Safi wasn't here. They never had been.

And now Aeduan finally did what he should have done earlier: he pulled the Truth-lens from his pocket and slung it over his neck.

Like the first time Safi had placed it upon him, power roiled through him. It plucked down his vertebrae, it swelled inside his lungs. *This is truth, this is rightness, this is all that is pure and good.*

Then the intensity of it shrank, like a settling tide after an unexpected wave. And for several dragging minutes, Aeduan waited—and took full note of his surroundings. It was indeed the mountain where, supposedly, the sleeping goddess Sirmaya made Her home. *True, true, true.* Yet it looked nothing like Iseult had described to Aeduan. She'd spoken of storm and stone, lightning and earthquakes. Of a cataclysm filling a colossal cavern that wanted to kill all in its path.

Nadje's memories, meanwhile, suggested silence and stillness and peace. When that Aether Paladin had gone into the mountain a thousand years ago, the mountain had welcomed her children home. War had raged, yes, but it had not been the mountain's doing.

What Aeduan found before him was neither peaceful nor apocalyptic, nor even a cavern. He was in a tunnel made from the same uncanny granite as the spiraling ramp in the woods. Lanterns flickered, not with flame, but with foxfire casting the stone in green.

But that was all Aeduan saw—and all Aeduan felt. A single confirmation from the lens that yes, this was the goddess's mountain . . .

And now silence. Now nothing. Every few seconds, the tunnel shivered around him. A vibration that rattled through his feet and up into his eyes. Not a quake so much as a distant heartbeat. This too elicited no response from the lens.

"Useless," he said to no one as he tore it off again to return it to his pocket. Then he started, walking, aiming steadily through the tunnel while time bleared past. His Bloodwitchery latched on to Leopold.

Dance, little Bloodwitch, dance.

Slowly, the tunnel did change. Its corridors widened, the ceiling lifted, and the throbbing beat in the stone fell away. Gradually, a new light claimed the foxfire shadows: a bluish glow that leaked out of veins in the stone.

Aeduan's fingers flexed at the sight of it. At the cold, and his heart pumped out a melody he didn't recognize. Part lingering bewilderment from the weight and strangeness of the mountain. Part booming hunger because Leopold was here and pulling strings . . .

But most of all, Aeduan's heart beat with an atavistic terror that said: *You should not be here.* The veins that thrummed in the stone were ice, and inexplicably, his old wounds were responding to them. As if they'd heard their master calling and they'd waited so long for this moment to come. *Finally, you understand what we have wanted from you.*

Aeduan didn't understand at all.

The ice in the rock crackled and groaned, sounding almost like speech as Aeduan walked by. And with each forward step, the more thickly ice coated at walls. Climbed the ceiling. Frayed onto the floor.

Not your mind. Not your body.

Aeduan focused on his breaths, even as pain sharpened in his chest. Even as the six wounds began their oozing again, soaking him in blood. Aeduan breathed in through his nose. Out through his mouth. He could not let the wounds or the ice distract him.

Except there was one small problem: the farther he strode, the more blood scents began to waver against him. Five. Ten. Hundreds. Then *thousands*, as if somehow there were people all around him. Living and waiting in the stone.

He stumbled forward. The pain was stealing his grace, the cold was numbing his extremities. If Leopold had hoped to lose him with more trickery, then he would be disappointed. Aeduan could discard all scents he did not need. *Lilacs and apple trees.* No. *Rainstorms and salted fish.* No. *Gnawing hunger and empty eyes.* No, no, no. *New leather and smoky hearths.*

Yes.

Aeduan locked on to Leopold's blood and moved faster. His wounds barked; warmth streamed down the front of his body. But he wouldn't let Leopold distract or evade him. He was tired of this game. He wanted to stop dancing and to simply face the prince once and for all.

But soon, the entirety of the tunnel became ice, and soon, human-sized shadows appeared within the bright blue glow. Each possessed a blood scent. Each was a person that was still alive.

That was when the pain hit its peak. A brutal ambush from all six wounds at once. It stole all breath from Aeduan's lungs and replaced it with fire. Literally. He felt the flames overtake his lungs. He felt magma carve out from his chest.

His footing failed him. He slid on a patch of unseen ice and pitched toward the nearest wall, the nearest person, the nearest *tomb*. His hands lifted on instinct, but where he should have hit tunnel wall, he didn't. He kept falling. Mere fractions of a heartbeat that felt endless.

Then his fingers made contact. He finally collided with something. It wasn't ice, though. It was warm, pliable, *alive*. And it was speaking. Shouting: *"Blood on the snow! Blood on the snow!"*

As quickly as he'd lost it, Aeduan's footing returned. And the pain—it snapped off like a spigot had been turned. Suddenly he could feel himself fully, feel his magic too, and *see* what was right before him: a woman's robed body was exposed. Her face, wrinkled and brown, had wide, panicked eyes of burnished silver. She shouted again at Aeduan: *"Blood on the snow! Blood on the snow!"*

He retreated, clawing away from her. Except the ice gave him no purchase. Each time he tried to grab hold and pull, tried to dig in heels and flee, it sprinted from him like metal shavings from a magnet.

More bodies erupted from the ice. Limbs. Feet. Faces. Mouths all screaming at him with different decrees.

"That which is closest!"

"Winds of flame!"

"Knife with two sides!"

"Blood on the snow! Blood on the snow!"

Aeduan finally found a stride. He ran down the tunnel. Desperate, ungainly, with the unthinking terror of an animal facing its death. His muscles were not his own. His magic was silent. He was simply a child trapped in a nightmare that he couldn't escape. There were hands climbing out of the ice. That snatched at him. Ripped at his cloak and clawed at his skin.

"Fissures in the ice!"

"New ways to travel!"

"Knife with two sides!"

"No coincidences except when there are!"

Aeduan couldn't get out. The tunnel had no end. The ice kept thawing wherever he turned. The bodies kept tumbling out—always women. Always old. And always with eyes of moonlight that saw too much.

Run, my child, run.

He wanted to. Desperately, Aeduan wanted to wake up and find this was all a dream. Boots would be beside him, and his mother too. She would stroke his hair while his father crooned a lullaby or told him the story of the monster and the honey again. But it wasn't a dream, and Aeduan didn't wake up. Instead, when the tunnel finally ended, he found himself in an even worse place than before.

He was finally inside the mountain's cavern. Finally inside the storm and stone, the lightning and earthquakes. Worse though, was the ice. It zigged, it zagged, shrinking away as Aeduan ran toward it. Which was why he didn't realize until too late that he'd raced onto a stretch of ice no longer reinforced by stone.

He stepped off a cliff's edge.
He fell.

Heat roars. Wood cracks and embers fly.

"Run." Blood drips from his mother's mouth as she speaks.

It splatters his face.

With arms stained to red, she pushes herself up. She wants him to crawl out from beneath her. She wants him to escape. "Run, my child, run."

He does not run. He does not move. He waits, as he always does, for the flames to overtake him and the world to burn alive.

The six wounds on his chest scream.

THIRTY-FOUR

✳

Vivia awoke to screaming. An entire chorus of voices in a clamor of languages she couldn't split apart, much less comprehend. She couldn't see, and she was cold—so blighted cold.

"Move. Please, *move*." One voice severed through all the others, in words Vivia could understand. "You've got to get out of this ice—Zan, *help*."

Vivia felt her arms rip upward. Her muscles resisted. Her mind too, although it was starting to reclaim awareness in spurts. *You are in the mountain. That awful ice consumed you.*

She opened her eyes. It hurt—not merely from all the light, radiating off of ice and foxfire—but from frost crystallized across her eyelids. It had glued her lashes shut. Her vision was blurred and bulbous. As if the shadowy ice had pushed so hard against her eyeballs, it had changed their shape. *How long was I frozen? Why are we waking up now?*

"Zan," the woman named Lev cried again. "Help!"

The giant smeared into focus before Vivia. He dug his hands into her armpits, and he tugged, tugged, wrenched at her. Because ice had glued more than just her lashes in place.

Vivia kicked, she pulled, she fought against any ice pinning her down. Voices still screamed. She couldn't see where they came from; she couldn't get her mind to understand them. And the light—why was the ice so bright, even with filaments of darkness to slide through?

The last shards cracked away. Vivia fell into Zander's arms. "Cam?" she shouted. "Vaness?"

"We have the Empress. But not the boy."

Vivia spun. The door out of the workshop was still split apart, but now ice filled every space between the wooden panels. She found the Empress, limp on the ground with blood across her face—and with Lev stamping and tromping at ice trying to crack in and claim her.

But no Cam. *No Cam.*

And the ice wouldn't sit still. It wouldn't stop groping for new bodies. It had lost its quarry once; it wouldn't lose them a second time.

"Grab the Empress!" Vivia barked at Zander. The Hell-Bard obeyed, hopping over ice claws and swooping up Vaness. The movement looked harder than it should have been. The giant was tired and weak. They all were.

Nonetheless, Vivia and the Hell-Bards ran. Vivia hit the workshop first, Lev only steps behind. There was no ice here, thank the Hagfishes. But the ice *would* be here soon. It was following.

Vivia sprinted through the timeless space built for a Sightwitch she'd never believed was real. Whatever spell had kept it safe for so many centuries, it was failing now. The room shook. Dust fell from the ceiling. Entire fans of foxfire broke loose and toppled down.

And the Waterwitched pumps groaned.

Which gave Vivia an idea.

YES, her magic squealed. *Use us and attack. Join us and attack.*

I will, Vivia agreed, and the dam broke inside her. It was like an addict seeing Painstones after too long without. Vivia dove right in and lost herself to the power. No control, only channeling. Water exploded from the pumps in the wall. It slashed outward, forming sharp lines to snake and fly through the workshop. Waters couldn't stop the ice. After all, water had no shape. It only engulfed, eroded, flooded, or drowned.

But there were shelves here. There were ladders and tables and stone, and they could not resist so much power, so much strength.

The tides—tens of tentacles, each as strong as a bull shark—slammed into any surface they could find. Two tables flung up and launched at the archway through which ice clambered. A shelf fell. Hundreds of books and beakers toppled down. And wherever there was nothing solid, the tides settled in.

It was enough. The ice, for now, could not get through.

But Vivia found she couldn't stop the waters. She was so deeply bound to the magic spewing out of the wall, her mind was dissolving into it. After all, the waters never asked her to simply *use* them; they also asked her to *join* them. And like a sandcastle collapsing beneath a wave, Vivia lost control of everything.

"Take her," the woman Lev shouted from a hundred miles away. "I can manage the Empress. You take the queen."

Once more, Zander's arms came around Vivia. He was solid, he was safe.

No! the waters shouted. *He is confining. He is controlling. Do not let him stop us.* Against Vivia's will, the tides took aim. Whips and waves that flung full power at a Hell-Bard whose only crime was trying to carry Vivia to safety.

Before the tentacles could slice him, drown him, slay him, all the foxfire in the workshop moved. Fans that flew off the walls, off the shelves, up from the waves. They launched upward in an onslaught of glowing green that encased both Zander and Vivia together.

The tides smashed against the fungus. It shredded, it collapsed. Zander, however, did not, and in that moment while green smeared through her, Vivia was finally able to reclaim control.

"I'm sorry," she gasped out, clinging tightly to his neck. He was wet, bleeding. "I'm so sorry."

He didn't answer. He simply chased after Lev. Two Hell-Bards Vivia hadn't trusted who now were the only things keeping her and Empress Vaness alive.

They left the workshop. The waters, the foxfire. The sleeping ice too, and the screaming voices. Lev and Zander retraced their steps, through the winding tunnel where new foxfire flared at their approach, then faded at their departure.

Vivia wanted to carry herself. She wanted to help carry Vaness or do *anything* that wasn't simply clutching at Zander like a child. But the little fox couldn't find the mask labeled *bear*. The tides still cried out for her.

Down, down. The Way Below was endless and unchanging. Dust kept falling. The ground kept quaking. Vivia didn't notice when they passed the hole in the ceiling. She wanted to sleep. She wanted to fall back into the tide's embrace and never find herself again. To be neither little fox or queenly bear, but rather water, ever changing and free.

"Look," she heard Lev say. "The ice is gone in the tunnel. We can get through."

"How?" Vivia tried to ask, but the word was lost to a rising cacophony. Familiar now, in all its many layers. Many languages. This time, though, Vivia could understand bits—and this time, she saw faces attached as Zander stormed by her.

"Knife with two sides!"

"No coincidences!"

"Think beyond!"

"One by one, into the ice!"

They were old faces in every shade of skin imaginable, with hair of silver or white or no hair at all. Vivia heard languages she'd been taught growing up and others that were fully unknown. She heard clear crystalline tones; she heard voices murky and slurred. But the one thing every woman had as she fell or climbed or reached out of the ice was silver in their eyes.

"A door!" Lev roared. "That's a door!"

Vivia forced her head to turn and forced her sight to lock on to a glowing, frizzing archway hammered into a patch of wall not coated in sleeping ice. She recalled the doorways from the map. She recalled what Cam had warned about them. They shouldn't exist; they would lead her far, *far* from home.

"No," she tried to tell Zander, "let's keep going. All the way to the big cavern." But Zander didn't hear her. Or perhaps didn't understand, because he nodded as if he agreed and hollered, "Go!"

Lev, with the Empress of Marstok in her hands, leaped through. She vanished in a burst of crackling energy. Three staggering heartbeats later, Zander also reached the door. He charged forward.

The magic laid claim. Quivering, ecstatic, violent as it sliced Vivia apart like a chicken on the butcher's slab—her soul, her body, her thoughts, her Threads—and then sewed her back together again. She landed on a red stretch of dirt, where heat sweated in and white asphodels grew. At first, Vivia thought they were back in Nubrevna. That she was home, maybe even at Noden's Gift beside the Origin Well . . .

But then, as she coughed and gasped, the differences battered against her. Oaks instead of palms or cypress. Reddish-yellow soil instead of white. And just visible through the trees, a languid, murky river that did not move like any waters Vivia had ever met before.

Not that this stopped them from calling out to her like an old friend desperate to make contact.

They were in the Contested Lands. That name had been on the map, and this looked like every description Vivia had ever read.

She swallowed against the magic rising inside her. Zander was at her elbow; he helped her stand. Blood poured down his nose, and he was pale—too pale in this night surrounded by jungle.

"The Empress," she choked out. "Where is she?" Vivia spun, searching until she spotted Lev through the shadows. The Hell-Bard had carried Vaness into the trees, and Vivia instantly stamped after. Yet before she could reach them, her foot caught on something. She tripped. She fell. Small stones cut into her palms.

Then Zander was at her side again. He lifted what Vivia had tripped over and held it toward the Sleeping Giant sparkling across the sky: a rusted helm. "The Contested Lands," he murmured, voice gravelly. He wiped his bloodied nose on his shoulder. "I don't know how it's possible . . . but we're in the Contested Lands."

"Hye," Vivia confirmed, her voice broken and defeated. "These are the Contested Lands, and now we're hundreds of miles from where we need to be."

Kullen,

I have been missing something hugely important. All this time, I've forgotten one piece of the puzzle that is critical: Merik.

I'm ashamed to admit the idea didn't come to me on my own. Instead, it was the cards. They say what they've always said: *Lady Fate, the Cleaved Man, the Paladin of Hounds.* But there was a new card that kept itching its way in.

I don't know how else to describe it. It is a *fourth* card that's begging to be drawn, even though I've only ever used three cards to guide me.

The King of Hounds. Merik.

He is bound to you, as your Threadbrother. But also as your *king.* That bond matters, I think. You've always known, in your Paladin heart, that Merik would one day lead—even before you knew you were a Paladin. So what if that connection between Paladin and ruler is important here? Merik didn't die when he should have. His connection to *you* kept him alive. Why? *How?*

The ghosts have ideas, of course. They take me to a new corner of the Crypts, where there are Memory Records on the Hell-Bard Loom. And that makes sense to me: the Hell-Bards are people whose magic has been cleaved from them. But rather than die as unexpected cleaving causes . . .

They exist, trapped. Neither dead, nor alive. Neither magicked, nor magic-free.

I think that's what has happened to you and Merik. It makes *so* much sense, and I can't believe I needed the cards to help me see it.

The Hell-Bards have been freed, Kullen. That must mean I can free you too. So now my focus becomes how do I *unbind* you from the Puppeteer's Loom? Is that even possible now that she is dead?

And what will it do to Merik if I succeed?

I love you.

—Ryber

THIRTY-FIVE

✳

Years ago, when Iseult and Safi had first begun training with Mathew and Habim in Veñaza City, it had become quickly clear that the girls' methods for absorbing information were different. *You're two ends of a scale,* Mathew would always say. Safi needed to listen while doing; she couldn't sit still, but as long as she had something to keep her hands busy—like blades to oil or dishes to scrub—she could absorb most information given to her.

Iseult, meanwhile, had to write everything Mathew and Habim ever said. *Everything.* She would scribble and scratch so fast, she'd break nib after nib. Her handwriting would be illegible to anyone but herself, and she would miss entire phrases in her attempts to scrawl down what she thought, in the moment, seemed like the most important part of a sentence. Then later, she would read over everything she'd written . . . and she would write it all down again.

Safi always thought this was a colossal waste of time, and Mathew always insisted Iseult should *simply listen and write later.* Only Habim had had sympathy for Iseult, and he would often repeat phrases two or three times until he could see she'd written down the necessary words.

Iseult had always wondered why she needed the extra steps and extra agony. Was it because lectures were always delivered to her surrounded by Threads? So, although she could hear the lessons and information launched at her, she couldn't absorb them when emotions were battering her too? Or was Iseult's brain simply built differently than Safi's, so Threads or not, she would always need more time?

Either way, the Raider King could not have given Iseult more perfect circumstances for learning: she had access to information, she had an inkwell and a quill, she had a place to write down everything she discovered . . .

And she had time. Hours in which to let her logic rise to the surface and stasis claim her body completely. The world outside was quiet; what few Threads were nearby drifted harmlessly like kelp in the tide. What

Iseult discovered was this: Leopold's notes and ideas were accurate. Not perfect, but near enough, and certainly more accurate than any of the intelligence on Eron's table.

But the sheer scale of the operation—Leopold had failed to capture that. The Raider King's operation had roots dug in across the entire continent, so the numbers clustered around Poznin were nothing compared to what *could* come and what *would* come if the Raider King called.

He had Red Sails and Baedyeds, he had Purists and Nomatsis, he had smaller raider factions and criminal organizations tucked in shadows. Anyone who'd ever made themselves a target of the empires, he had recruited.

Yes, there were clear areas of setback in Ragnor's sweeping plan: in the Sirmayans, where the monks had ultimately won against his raiders. In Nubrevna, where he'd never gained a foothold. And Cartorra, where Hell-Bards had stood strong against his attempts for advancement . . .

But the other two empires were not so resistant. Marstok, destabilized by Habim and Mathew's coup, was ripe with anti-imperial minds. And the Doge of the Dalmotti Empire had written to Ragnor himself—assuming the wax seal on the letter Iseult found was authentic—to *open communications regarding continental dominance in the Witchlands.*

It was breathtaking just how many people the Raider King had found either sympathetic to his cause or hungry to stamp out Cartorra and Marstok. It made Eron's twenty-year plan seem childish in comparison.

He is the greatest strategic mind of the last millennia.

Ragnor Amalej. Aeduan's father. A Nomatsi widower who could have killed Iseult when his raiders caught her . . . yet had not.

More food was delivered to the tent. Iseult sensed the approaching Threads, so she had ample time to hurry to the cot and curl as if asleep. She waited for the person to place the tray on the floor beside her. She let them stare at her for several moments, feeling as their Threads burned first with an almost hateful curiosity . . . then melted into confusion.

Yes, I am the dark-giver, and no, I'm not very much to look upon.

They left. Iseult wolfed down the food—more hot, meatless stew, this time with hard bread for soaking. Then she returned to Ragnor's desk and resumed her work. There was so much to study; this wasn't merely a welcome into his home, so much as everything handed on a porcelain platter and wrapped in a pretty bow.

The man was creating an empire all his own.

And although Iseult didn't understand how, he clearly had a plan for cleaving all the Wells newly healed by her and Safi. The Earth Well first. Then the Water Well. Then Aether, then Fire, and lastly Void—which his notes indicated he knew the location of . . . but did not have access to. Yet.

"How?" Iseult kept murmuring as she read over his sketches of Noden's Gift on the southern coast of Nubrevna. Arrows pointed to an approach point, and circles showing where he had people to aid him. "*How* will you cleave all the Wells?"

Nowhere, in all these notes and drawings, could she find her answer.

And somehow, this open question was more chilling than any revelation that had come thus far. Ragnor could not be deterred. He was a spider that kept going even as its legs were snapped off. He had lost three Wells, yet he hadn't abandoned his cause. He had lost his *son* to the enemy, yet still he fought on.

Why did you falter? Why did you fail?

Iseult knew the answer was because she wasn't like Safi. Because she couldn't let only instinct guide her. But now, in this long, long pause, Iseult had learned her opponent, had learned her terrain. So now she could choose her perfect battlefield, target the heart, the brain, the king at the center of it all.

Yes, it might be a trap, but if Ragnor could keep going with his legs cut off, then so could Iseult. For Safi, for Aeduan, for all of the Witchlands and the Moon Mother sleeping below.

THIRTY-SIX

※

Merik called them *Wakers*, the Cleaved who'd returned to life. He found only a few each night, but *a few* had quickly added up to nearly a hundred. Sometimes the Wakers returned to life during the day, and those people often wound up in the clutches of the Raider King.

But any Cleaved who awoke at night—they were for Merik to find. For Merik to protect. Thus far, the Raider King hadn't learned Merik was slipping in, hiding himself in shadow and snow and city ruins. And Merik planned to keep it that way.

If Ragnor knew the Cleaved were being stolen away, he might make it so none of the Cleaved could ever leave again.

Tonight, Merik took the tunnel into the city. Occasionally, he would fly—but only if a storm churned to mask his approach. Usually, there was too much risk. Too much visibility in the sky.

As always, Merik would look for Wakers tonight. But first, he needed to fulfill his promise to the domna. *No, to the Empress.* That new title was going to take some getting used to.

"I hate these tunnels," Sky groused behind him. "Everything is so cursin' wet."

Merik didn't respond. Sky loved to hear her own voice, and she loved even more to complain. Plus, in the end, she wasn't wrong: everything *was* so cursin' wet inside these tunnels. She and Merik splashed through water that reached almost to their calves. So cold, it made Merik's bones ache inside his boots. Like Sky, he wore nondescript Baedyed gear—borrowed from Loulou and Riness—and the sand-scarves they'd wrap over their faces now clung like wet seaweed to their necks.

For the water not only burbled at them from below, but also dripped constantly from a collapsing ceiling. The python weight of the river pressed down, squeezing water into any cracks it could find. One day, this whole thing would fall.

But not yet.

Foxfire glimmered around them, casting the water—*drip, drip, splash, splash*—with a green glow. It made Merik think of Vivia. It made him think of a home that had never felt like home.

"Ugh," Sky groaned now. "I think that was an eel that just scraped me. I *hate* eels, Merik. Slimy little things that look too much like snakes—"

"All right," Merik cut in, trying not to laugh. Sky's complaining had a way of lightening the mood, and whether that was a function of her magic or just her own general good nature, he hadn't yet sorted out. "We're almost to the tower now, Sky. Time to wrap up and get quiet."

"Hye." She used the Nubrevnan word for *yes.* That was another language she'd been toying with recently. "I'll wrap this sodden scarf around me—which has basically become an eel itself—and then enjoy the way it freezes against my face as we sneak into the night. I can't wait."

Again, Merik found himself laughing. And his own scarf *was* ice against his skin, as he wrapped it in the style Baedyeds used to ward off their Sand Sea.

They traveled the remaining two hundred paces to the tunnel's end. Here, the river relented her hold on the land, and the water stopped falling. The puddles shifted into ice that crunched under their heels. As the tunnel's elevation rose, the floor turned to steps. The foxfire dimmed to darkness, and the final fifty paces were thick with shadows.

It reminded Merik of the Cisterns back in Lovats. Which in turn, always made him think of Cam. He wished the boy were with him now instead of Sky. Which wasn't fair to Sky, of course—she was loyal and useful. But she wasn't *home*, and home was all Merik dreamed of most days.

He shook his head, clearing the thoughts as if he were Aurora shaking off the snow. Then he rubbed once at his chest, a motion that was almost a Nubrevnan salute.

A king does not rule, his mother had once told him, *but serves.*

The steps stopped, and Merik stopped with them. Sky grunted, part acknowledgment that she was ready to move on when he was. Part annoyance because the ice on these ancient stones had almost tripped her.

She had quite expressive grunts.

The door before them was one that Merik had installed before they'd fled the city—and *door* was a generous term for it. It was more like an octopus's hoard: shells and rocks and strands of seaweed meant to hide it from sharks and men. Instead of shells, Merik had found ancient planks; instead of rocks, he'd gathered bricks; and instead of seaweed, he'd moved dead, dried vines together like nets.

The vines rattled as Merik pushed out of the tunnel, his eyes squinting to see beyond. They were in a building beside Esme's tower—a space Revan had found while poking around for useful supplies. It must have been a shop once upon a time. Perhaps even an illegal one, for why else would they need such easy, secret access across the river?

Either way, the shelves that had once clung half-heartedly to the walls were now what made Merik's door.

"No one's here," he whispered, before twisting sideways to squeeze through his arrangement of bricks. Wind plied him. His face, already half numb, turned to ice. In seconds, Sky was beside him and scooting toward the exit while Merik rearranged the planks and vines. When he glanced at her, she was waving an all-clear sign.

So far, so good. Now came the hard part—the part where Sky would take the lead. Normally, they would travel east from Esme's tower, aiming for the Well, where most of the Cleaved clustered, and therefore where most of the Wakers formed. But not tonight.

Merik strained onto his toes and peeked out the window. Then gave Sky the all-clear sign.

"Don't speak," she told him, moving to his side. "Leave it all to me." She spoke in Marstoki now.

And Merik glared at her—his eyes being the only thing she could see through his frozen sand-scarf. "I know," he grumbled, even though he hated saying it. Hated giving up control to her. "Just please don't get us killed, hye?"

Sky gave another expressive grunt; this one said, *Obviously.* She tugged at her scarf, checking it was in place, and without another sound or even a backward glance, she set off into the city.

Merik hurried behind.

Back when Merik had still been a prince of Nubrevna, back when he'd still had access to spies and intelligence, the origins of the Raider King had remained an empty space. A mystery no one had been able to answer, and even now—as close as he lived day in and day out to the man—Merik still had few answers.

For one, he had never seen Ragnor. Neither up close, nor from afar. For two, he didn't understand Ragnor's strategy. The Raider King had gone fast and hard against all the empires, yet now he was content to simply wait.

Waiting was never good for morale. It was why Sky, Ulga, and Birdy had been poking through Poznin that day Merik had found them: they were bored and too young to stay loyal without clear cause.

Merik hurried out of cover, Sky stepping lightly ahead. A large pool had hardened to ice on their left. Marsh reeds poked up, rattling quietly against the night's winds—and against Merik's winds too. Just the occasional gust to mask their footsteps. To kick up old snow. To draw ears toward other sounds instead of toward him and Sky hurrying past.

Not that his Windwitchery was reliable. It always stuttered and coughed when he came into the city and got too near to the Air Well.

But that is why Safi is here, Merik thought for the hundredth time. *Because the Cahr Awen is real. Because Aunt Evrane was right. Because somehow Safi and her Threadsister are going to heal the Well and save all the Witchlands.*

It was a thought that kept repeating in his brain without ever settling in. An assemblage of words that didn't make sense. He hadn't even fully accepted that Safiya fon Hasstrel was currently in Last Holdout, so how was he supposed to also accept she could heal all magic in the Witchlands?

Merik and Sky reached the first building where guards usually patrolled. They weren't there tonight. Clouds drifted overhead, tatters from the storm above the forest. They looked like fish escaping their school.

"I'm going to have to find better ground," Merik whispered to Sky, who crouched beside him. "I can't see ahead clearly."

"S'a bad idea." Sky's magic latticed around the words. Not on purpose, but because she felt her point so deeply, she wanted to convince Merik too. "We shouldn't split up."

"I'll make the signal when we can keep moving." Merik drew in his winds and vaulted to the building's crooked rooftop. He folded onto his hands as soon as his feet touched icy shingles. He could spy many rooftops now, most half-tumbled or entirely broken . . .

And all of them empty as far as Merik could see. He withdrew a spyglass from a slot on his belt. The rooftops sharpened through the lens. The snow and shadows lurched closer. But all was still empty, still silent.

Merik gave the signal. A whistle so soft, it could only be heard when he coaxed his winds to carry it down, directly into Sky's ears. Her figure was soon a vague shadow across the snowy ruins.

Merik floated to the next rooftop, repeated his scan through the spyglass, repeated the signal to Sky. Again, again, as the horizon remained clear. Soon, however, they were too near the Well—so Merik's winds began resisting his command. It forced him to choose a path with narrower gaps between rooftops.

He and Sky went half a mile this way before Merik finally found any life—but it was not the usual arrangement of raiders he'd seen in the past. These were not rows of protective sentries meant to keep out intruders, but rather camps of soldiers with only a few tired guards huddled around burning fires.

Orange flames beckoned with warm fingers. Merik shivered. There were entire streets left empty; it would be so easy to navigate between encampments. And that felt wrong. Why would Ragnor drop his guard *now*?

Merik didn't whistle to Sky this time as he took flight. Instead, he skipped to a rooftop next door where the shingles were black and devoid of snow.

He should have noticed that—the lack of snow. He should have sensed how warm they felt through his wet boots. But he was more worried over the absence of soldiers, more worried he and Sky were blundering into a trap.

A plank shifted beneath Merik's foot. A shingle scraped on wood, and the sound split the night like a pistol shot. Then came a groan, loud as Aurora baying, and suddenly the roof beneath Merik collapsed. It happened so fast—one moment, he was upright; the next, he was being eaten alive by splinters and slate and heat. He hit a floor he couldn't see and grappled for his winds. But of course they chose to fall silent. To slam their hands over their ears and ignore his desperate calls.

The heat of a stove clogged his lungs. There was pain too, in Merik's ribs, in his neck, and above all, in his leg. A splinter had gotten him. He was bleeding.

He grappled for purchase and tried to rise. He was in someone's bedroom. A crude space repurposed into something almost cozy.

He was also not alone.

A woman gaped at him. The gap between her front teeth was familiar, as was her pale hair pulled back like a Nubrevnan sailor's and the sharp, pointed tip of her chin.

"Stix?" Merik tried to choke out. "Stix, it's me." The words never left his throat. Not before ice rose over him, hungry as the ice from the mountain— but without the soothing song to accompany it. This was Stix's magic, as wildly powerful as Kullen's had been but with control over a different element.

The ice claimed Merik's chin. His forehead. *No, no, no.* He drew in a final breath before it claimed his mouth. *Please, winds, come to me. Please, break me free.*

They did not come. They did not help him.

THIRTY-SEVEN

✳

afi was under strict orders to remain in her bed, which meant that she absolutely did not. After confirming with a few steps back and forth across her hut that she was able to walk again, she hefted up a blanket and finagled it around her shoulders. Then, because she'd been caught too often unawares, she found her sword and fastened it—belt, hilt, and Truthsinging steel—to her hips.

Warmer and armed, she now stomped into Last Holdout.

It was her first time really seeing the settlement. The tree-branch canopy that seemed to block out the sky, the forest hugging them close like walls.

Safi's right hand flexed at her side. It was a movement she saw the Bloodwitch make often, and she had a sudden, visceral understanding of *why* he was always doing it: because if he didn't, his fists would form and someone might get hurt.

There was no one outside at this hour for Safi to hurt, and she couldn't decide if she was happy about this fact . . . or angry. With the pain in her arm reduced to annoyance—and the muscles themselves almost completely healed—she had nothing to distract her from everything else that had gone wrong.

The Cahr Awen souls knew the Well was near. They were awakening again, resuming their eyeball-squeezing song. *Why are you not moving? Why are you once more standing still?*

"Because," she hissed at them, "the other half of the Cahr Awen isn't with me, and what good am I for the Well if *she* isn't there to heal it too?"

The souls didn't answer, because they never answered. Iseult had told her they were just leftover Threads, floating around, no longer bound to the outer package that had been their bodies. They were just the forgotten edges of desire, of need, of hunger—hundreds of each emotion crammed inside Safi's entirely too-human brain.

She spun around, searching the empty passages between huts for signs of life. But there was no one awake, no one out, no one to ask, *Excuse me, where can I find your leader?*

She picked a direction and started walking. There was a vaguely central point where the woven canopy seemed highest—and where a shadowy column awaited. A tree trunk, she thought at first, until she was close enough to see it was made from the same stone as the shrine they'd camped beside last night.

Then Safi was close enough to see a carving on the stone. A huff of understanding escaped her nose. In four more steps, her blanket loosening on her shoulders, she reached the column and placed her hand on the familiar marking. It was an owl, Safi knew, just as there had been an owl under the imperial palace in Praga.

So many secret places across the Witchlands, and somehow she and Iseult kept finding them. Or perhaps it wasn't *somehow* so much as Lady Fate guiding them. Perhaps all these places had been built long ago for the day when a dark-giver and a light-bringer might need them.

A voice sheared through the night, bouncing against wooden boughs and sliding into Safi's ears. A boy's voice poised on the cusp of manhood. "He isn't back yet." He spoke elegant Cartorran.

"Obviously." This was another boy's voice, and there was a decidedly sulky layer to it. "We all got eyes, Revan."

What followed was a rapid-fire stream of Marstoki between the young boy and a grown man, but it was quiet—too quiet for Safi to easily hear beyond the words *tunnel* and *forest*.

Safi tipped her body around the column. Her blanket slid down her left shoulder; cold kissed her skin. Standing before one of the smallest huts (of *course* Merik would have chosen the smallest; she should have guessed that) were four figures. Three were hooded, and the fourth wore a fine, if enormous black robe.

And beside them was a horse, gray as a stormy sky with breaths to puff against the cold. "Cloud!" Safi scrabbled out from the column, half tripping on her blanket as she ran. "Where is the rider?" She flung this question out in Marstoki. "Where is the rider?"

"There was none." This came from one of the hooded figures, who drew back his hood to reveal a handsome face with thick, dark lashes. "We found this horse not far from Last Holdout—alone." He flipped his hand toward Safi to reveal a Herdwitch's mark.

But Safi wasn't impressed by his power or his words. "Great. Your magic found a single horse. Now I need you to find two more, as well as the people who were on them."

"They are gone. The two horses you seek have disappeared into the other part of the forest."

"The *other part?*" Safi sputtered. Then she tossed up her hands. "You know what? I don't care. Just show me." She reached for Cloud's reins. Her blanket slipped farther down her shoulder.

And the smallest person, the one they'd called Revan, hurried in. "No, no, Lady! You are not supposed to leave. Merik said you must rest and heal."

"Do I look like I need rest?" Safi snatched Cloud's reins. The horse snuffed; her ears swiveled back.

But the Marstoki man holding the reins only gripped tighter. "We will await Merik's return. I can describe what we found if that might help."

No, Safi was about to snarl. *It won't help.* This was Iseult's horse, which meant Iseult had to be nearby. Any other possibility . . .

Safi couldn't think of it. She wouldn't.

But right as she centered her strength to kick onto Cloud's saddle and spur straight out of this uncanny place, a dog's whine pierced the night. Loud, sharp, and with percussive, booming thuds to rumble beneath it.

Then everything happened at once. A creature rounded a nearby building, enormous and gleaming with wings that smacked branches and feet that churned up soft earth. Cloud reared, stealing her reins from both Safi and the Herdwitch.

And one of the other hooded figures shouted, "Aurora, no!" at the same moment the last hooded figure shouted, "Merik must be in trouble!"

Those words jolted through Safi, almost as intensely as Cloud's hooves did, now tumbling toward her face. Safi jolted sideways. The blanket fell. Cloud trampled onto it, while the Herdwitch started shouting, "Ho, calm! Ho, calm!" His commands thrummed with truth and power.

The two hooded figures, meanwhile, were already running—one with a rifle clutched tight and the other with his hood falling back to reveal a mop of brown hair. They chased after the storm hound thundering out of Last Holdout.

Safi launched after them.

Stacia Sotar had been here before. Not *here* in this physical space, but *here* in this scenario. Except the first time it had happened—the first time she'd come face-to-face with the Fury—the heat of late Nubrevnan summer had warmed her skin.

There hadn't been a fallen roof, nor shouts of alarm from raiders outside, nor a knowledge poking at the back of Stix's brain that said, *This isn't the Fury. You knew the real Fury as a Paladin, and he has been gone for centuries.*

Still, Stix had seen this man before. She *knew* him. Even without her glasses, she could recognize the scars on his face.

More than that, she recognized his magic. The winds that poured into the attic (which had been her bedroom until five seconds ago) carried with them snow and power. There was a charge to them, an electricity that she had felt before. Not quite human, not quite . . . *alive.*

The ice encasing the man shattered outward.

And on the floor below, voices boomed into the building. Vague words of alarm and calls for violence. The specifics didn't matter. People were coming, and Stix thought people ought to be good. She might not like the raiders who worked for Ragnor, but at least they were on the same side. This man frozen before her—who wasn't the Fury, yet *was* . . .

He was the enemy. He had to be stopped just as Stix had stopped him before. And Stix would use exactly the same techniques she had used at Pin's Keep when she'd first faced this specter. She stomped once, her boot thundering through the floor. All the ice she'd created turned instantly to burning fog.

"Stix," the man croaked, vanishing inside the world of white. "Stix, it's me."

Winds blasted her face. She rocked back. The man was trying to summon more power. He was going to escape.

Vibrations in the floorboards signaled raiders on the stairs, but they were slow. Stix had chosen this building because she liked its rickety passages and tiny rooms. It reminded her of her apartment in Lovats. It reminded her of her quarters tucked belowdecks on Vivia's old ship.

"Stix," the man repeated, hopping upward like a baby bird learning to fly. He would escape through the hole he'd made. She needed to stop him before he could do that.

Distantly, it occurred to her that this Fury-man knew her name. And distantly she wondered how the man who had stalked the streets of Lovats might be here, hundreds of leagues from where she'd first met him.

But these were thoughts that happened so deep inside her skull, they couldn't push to the forefront.

Stix flung out two water whips, using the fog to form them. They surrounded the man, freezing and banding his arms to his sides. Yet again, *somehow*, he was stronger than she. His winds blasted outward, shattering her ice. Then lightning cracked, so brightly it stole all her sight. Forced her to close her eyes and duck low to the floor.

And so loud, it was like a firepot had detonated inside the room. Stix felt unmoored. She felt sick. She felt as if her body had melted away and all that was left were her thoughts. Useless thoughts, too, about a Heart-Thread named Bastien and a prince who had died . . . And loudest of all, the words of the Fury carved into shrines across Nubrevna:

Why do you hold a razor in one hand?
So men remember that I am sharp as any edge.
And why do you hold broken glass in the other?
So men remember that I am always watching.

Stix had possessed that glass, hadn't she? And she had possessed that razor after claiming it from inside the sleeping mountain. Everything from the past was rooted in the present. Just as Ragnor had told her.

She herself was nothing more than legend. Lady Baile with her three rules and the cats that never left her. *The cats*, she thought, and that thought prompted her to move. To try opening her spectacled eyes and survey the world around her.

Were her cats all right?

She squinted. Something huge and golden flapped above the broken roof. It looked like the statues on the bridge into Poznin—except very alive and very *here*.

He really is the Fury, an old voice whispered in Stix's brain. *Bastien always could talk to storm hounds.*

But it isn't him, Stix countered. *You know it isn't really him.* She loosed herself, muscles pushing her to standing. Her ears still heard nothing, but her blurred sight was returning. *That isn't the Fury. Not the Fury I knew. That is the man I met in Lovats. And somehow, he is leaving this place with a storm hound.*

The door into Stix's room burst wide. Raiders poured into the room. "I need Windwitches!" Stix shouted, pointing at the hole in her ceiling. "I need Windwitches, and tell the Baedyeds to get their pistols ready. We have a storm hound in the city."

The closest raider, a Red Sail with her hair in two long braids behind her head, gave Stix such a crisp Nubrevnan salute, Stix wondered if the woman hadn't once served in the Royal Navy. The other raiders, less disciplined, just stood there gaping at the damage around the room.

Something nudged Stix's calf. She flinched, half expecting to find a storm hound's mouth chomping down . . . but it was only her calico, purring against her as if none of the chaos had just happened. As if he had come for his usual evening cuddles, and goodness, could someone please do something about that draft?

Stix smiled as she crouched down to pet him. *And always, always stay the night*, she thought. *For Baile's slaughtering.* One stroke across the cat's head. One scratch behind the ears. Then Stix left the cat and the damage.

Come, she told her magic as she strode for the stairs. *We are hunting.*

THIRTY-EIGHT

✳

Iseult stood outside the tent and watched the eastern sky. An alarm was sounding, and if she frowned hard enough that way, she could see flashes like heat lightning.

She could see Threads too. Wild, silvery Threads somehow visible, although they must be miles beyond her range. She thought of mountain bats and sea foxes, of shadow wyrms and the statues she'd seen on the bridge into the city. *Long ago, when the gods walked among us, Middle Sister Swallow found a dog and gave him wings.*

"Get inside," a voice called. It was the Admiral. "Get inside and stay there, Dark-Giver. There are dangers in the city tonight."

Aren't there always dangers in the city? Iseult thought back to Esme's Cleaved—which she still could see no sign of, sense no Threads from. "Where is the Raider King?" she asked instead. "When will he return?"

"Why?" Kahina's silvery eyebrows lifted. "Have you decided to accept his offer?"

"Offer?" Now Iseult was the one to lift her eyebrows—and the reaction was instant: Kahina's Threads caught fire with surprise. Then anger. She'd said something she shouldn't have.

"Inside," Kahina repeated, and now her anger overtook her magic, sending sparks puffing from her mouth.

Iseult bowed her head, biting off a smile. Ragnor had a proposal for her; the encampments were riled up; despite her incredible power as a Paladin, Kahina still obeyed the Raider King. This was all useful information, and when Iseult ducked back into the tent, she examined the space with fresh eyes. Whatever offer was coming her way, the information on that desk was meant to coax her into an agreement.

She was halfway back to the desk when Threads surged into her awareness. Frightened slate, focused green, and unexpectedly triumphant pink. The flap barely moved as a small Baedyed raider slithered in.

"Are you the Threadwitch?" they asked in shockingly good Nomatsi.

"You must be. You've got the scar and the Witchmark." They yanked down their mask, revealing a young, pale face and large teeth. "I'm Sky. Merik sent me."

Despite the near-perfect Nomatsi, the words were absolutely indecipherable to Iseult. She blinked. "Merik? The . . . prince of N-Nubrevna?"

"Yeah. Scarred fellow. Missing some hair. He's got a hideout on the other side of the river. For Wakers and anyone else who's left the Raider King's banner."

None of this was any more comprehensible.

"So is he . . . here?" Iseult sent her magic reaching outward.

The girl shook her head. "Naw, he just got himself caught. But don't worry. I think he'll get away. Probably. Maybe. And now we can get away too."

Iseult's nose wiggled. "We?"

"Yeah, you. Me. I'm Sky, remember? I just told you. Your friend—some nobility or something from Cartorra—sent us to find you. Since it looks like you're a prisoner, then I'm here to free you. Although . . ." The girl waved at Iseult's collar. "I can't help with that."

These words finally connected in Iseult's brain. "Safi," she said on a sigh. Her spine sagged. "She's all right? She's safe?"

"Mostly." Sky shrugged. "We have a good healer."

"And Aeduan? Um, a . . . a monk. A C-Carawen—is he all right?"

"We haven't found him yet."

"Ah." Iseult's backbone reversed itself, locking upward again.

"We got people searching, though." The girl glanced around, eyes big as a rabbit's. Iseult would bet she could be as fast as one too. "Look, can we get going? I've sent everyone away. Told 'em they were summoned to help with the alarm. But it won't last. They'll realize I was lying soon—maybe even realize I'm not Marstoki."

"I can't leave."

Sky's big eyes got bigger. Confusion swelled in her Threads. "You *are* the one we're looking for, right?"

"Yes, but you have to tell Safi I can't go yet. Tell her I have a way to end all of this cleanly and quickly—but when it's done, she'll need to be ready to get to the Well. I'll, uh . . ." Iseult hesitated here. All those hours of planning and study, and now here she was thrown on the spot again.

But the book isn't. The book has everything Safi needs to know.

In less than a second, Iseult had snatched it off the desk. Two seconds after that, she had the book's pouch unbuckled from her belt and the book slid safely inside. "Here, take this. Give it to Safi. Tell her to follow all the markings I've made on the map in the middle. It'll take her right to the Well and should keep her out of sight of any raiders."

"Yeah, but the raiders are on the move now." Sky's Threads were a rusted wariness. "They're all over the city."

"I know, but trust me: there are paths to get past the troops. And I'll meet Safi a-at the Air Well."

"When?" Sky fastened the book to her own belt. "It'll take me time to reach her, and then more time for her to get there."

"I know." Iseult's hand moved to her neck, to the Threadstone that wasn't there anymore, and where instead she found only heavy wood and iron. "But I'll be there," she said eventually. "If all goes according to plan, then I'll be there waiting for her when she arrives."

"I don't like this. But . . . if you say so."

"I do say so. Now quickly. People are c-coming, and I need one more thing from you. Tell me: Do you have any weapons with you?"

Sky's Threads blinked with surprise. "Just this." She slipped a small folding knife from her sleeve.

"Can I have it?"

"Won't do much."

"No," Iseult agreed. But it *would* fit in her boot, and that was all she needed. "Thank you," she murmured as she took it. Then seconds later, the girl was gone. Iseult was alone.

Outside, chaos gathered and brewed.

Aeduan was being moved. Dragged, actually, across a rough surface that indicated in cruel relief where each of his bones had been broken. Where each of his organs had been perforated and each of his vertebrae knocked into a place it shouldn't be.

"You," said a voice Aeduan hated, "are heavier than you look, Monk. Which is forcing me to reevaluate my own fitness—something I do not enjoy doing."

Aeduan tried to respond, but all that came out was a groan. And try as he might, he could only get a single eye open. Which revealed, as he'd expected, Leopold fon Cartorra.

Aeduan couldn't smell the man; his magic was too focused on healing a hundred injuries from which most people would never recover. But he knew that sharp jaw and mocking smile.

"Ah, you are awake." Leopold's smile turned harder. "Good. I did so want to apologize for how much damage I caused you inside the mountain. You were meant to simply follow me. Not wake up all the Sightwitches. Fortunately for us both, however, you are a man for whom such wounds will not kill, but merely slow."

Aeduan managed to haul open his other eye.

Leopold sharpened into something more human, with flushed cheeks and curls flying on a cold wind—a wind Aeduan recognized. There was a smell here he would never quite scrape off his bones.

In much the same way he would never quite remove the memories of the Exalted One who'd possessed him.

"No," he tried to say. *Do not bind Nadje inside me again.* But of course, such words would not come. Aeduan's left lung was flattened and his jaw was broken.

"Do not worry, Monk. I have no plans to bind an Old One to your body. It was a useful experiment, but it would not be useful a second time. That said," Leopold continued, still holding Aeduan's arms—the only part of Aeduan that felt intact, "you *are* correct that I have brought you to the Aether Well."

Leopold let go. Aeduan's arms flopped down. Pain crunched through him, and the six old wounds boomed like tectonic plates in an earthquake.

Overhead, the impenetrable gray of winter in the Sirmayans loomed, no sky to break through. Leopold dropped to a crouch beside Aeduan's head and blocked out even the clouds. He reached for Aeduan's face—and Aeduan was pleased when he could snap his head sideways. Press it into the snow that surrounded him.

But it wasn't Aeduan's face that Leopold wanted. It was his earlobe and the opal pierced within. "Clever me," Leopold murmured, sliding his thumb across it, "making these little stones all those centuries ago." He pinched the opal. His lips torqued sideways.

And Aeduan felt as the summoning magic in the stone sparked through him. A jagged sensation like a tapestry being separated into individual strands. The magic jetted outward, to every Carawen monk nearby. They would realize he was hurt. They would come running to his aid.

Since the Monastery was nearby, that would mean *many* monks would soon converge here.

Leopold released the opal. His frown turned stern and, inexplicably, sad too. As if he regretted all that had happened—not just between him and Aeduan, but for all of the world. "One last thing before I go, Monk:

whatever you might think of me, I am not your enemy. I swear it. Just like you, I have only ever served the Cahr Awen, and right now is no different.

"The dark-giver and the light-bringer are about to fail. They will not reach the final Well to heal it—not without help. A great *deal* of help, in fact. Which is why I . . . well, I suppose you could say I *nudged* you here in the first place. I need your fellow monks, and I need them quickly.

"So, once you are healed, you must take the new abbot and all her forces through the mountain." Here Leopold paused long enough to withdraw a scrap of cloth from his cloak. It was blood-soaked and sang of truth hidden beneath snow.

He dropped it, letting it flutter down to Aeduan's chest. Next, he tugged out a leather thong, which he dangled over Aeduan's eyes. Light glinted on silver. A scent like fireflies tickled Aeduan's magic.

"How funny that this was once my coin, yet now it is a little trinket between lovers." The way Leopold said this did not make it sound funny at all. "Since you cannot use it to follow your lover now, then I will tell you exactly where she is and how to find her. Though do not seek her out until all the Carawens have joined you. Otherwise, your life and hers will be lost."

Leopold dipped close now, angling his face so his mouth was near Aeduan's ear. His voice dropped to a whisper not even the Well could hear. "The dark-giver is with your father in the heart of Poznin. She thinks she is helping you by trying to kill the Raider King, but we both know your father is more likely to kill her first. So hurry, Bloodwitch, and finish healing. Then go to the dark-giver before it is too late."

THIRTY-NINE

✳

ky was in a bad way. She'd gotten out of the Raider King's tent, but her attempts to reach the old tower and its nearby tunnel were proving futile. She couldn't even reach the original part of the city, enclosed in its crumbling wall. Thanks to Merik and his misplaced feet on a rooftop, every street was crawling with raiders.

She blended in well enough with them. Her Baedyed clothes never earned a second glance, not even with a book now bouncing at her hip.

But blending in was little comfort, because the more byways and side streets she veered down, the more raiders she encountered. They moved with surprising order and frightening focus. Never had she seen anything like it. Baedyeds buried firepots, Purists laid hunting traps, Red Sails wedged spikes into the ground, and the Nomatsis . . . Sky didn't actually know what they were doing, but they wore masks over their mouths, and a thick fog rose up in the places where they focused their work.

What worried her most, though, were the carts. Tens of them being hauled uphill by mules and horses over the rough remnants of city roads. Barrels sloshed, a smell like tar burned into Sky's nose.

It had to be seafire. Unquenchable, undousable, unstoppable. Seafire burned as soon as air kissed it, and the Raider King's people were transporting *hundreds* of barrels into the old part of the city.

Sky watched a procession amble past. All the other worker wasps were laying their traps with a precise, if chaotic speed—like this had always been the plan, but now the timeline had gotten bumped forward. But the people working the carts and the barrels . . . They never sped. Chaos never touched them.

Sky untucked from a shadow, letting her shoulders rise and chest balloon. Her stride sharpened. Words assembled while heat gathered around her diaphragm—a sensation she'd always thought was just guilt because she wasn't blessed and she wasn't pure. *Now* she knew it was a witchery. *Her* witchery, bound directly to the Aether.

Merik might not have been the first person to ever see through her manipulations and tricks, but Merik *was* the first person to say, *Ah, now that's a useful skill, Sky. Why don't we use it for good things?*

Turned out, Sky liked doing good things.

And she *really* liked the idea of returning to Last Holdout tonight—if not for her own safety, then to relay the words the Threadwitch had passed on. So she marched right up to the nearest cart with six barrels in the back and twelve Baedyeds surrounding it. Most had their scarves down. Their breaths plumed like chimneys. Ahead, at a gap in the wall, the Red Sails were stamping spears into the ground. They had left just enough space for the cart—and the three other carts behind this one to finagle through.

So much seafire.

Poznin was going to burn.

But Sky couldn't think about that. She just had to get into the old city. She just had to reach the tunnel.

Although her stomach was twisting, Sky kept her chin high and her stride long. The Baedyeds in Last Holdout, she'd noticed, had a way of walking. *Rolling*, really, as if they were on the decks of a ship or crossing their Sand Sea. Loulou was especially fluid. Sky liked watching him walk. She liked following him around too, trying to imitate him even if he mostly ignored her.

All her practice had paid off. Only one Baedyed glanced her way, dark eyes lingering on her as she eased into careful step beside them. Then it came: "Why are you here?"

"To help." Sky pumped her magic up from that warm spot in her diaphragm. Across her vocal cords and over her tongue. *I am just like you. I belong here.* "I was ordered to be here in case you need more hands for the . . ." *Oh shit.* Sky trailed off as the word for seafire didn't appear in her brain. She'd never heard it used before; her magic—she was discovering—could only replicate that which she had *heard.*

The man's eyebrows lifted. "*Inhelysha?*"

"*Ahtset. Ahtset.*" Yes, yes. "*Se-inhelysha.*" Sweat gathered under Sky's scarf. She was glad he couldn't see her face. *Trust me, trust me. I'm just like you.*

He nodded. "As long as you are trained?"

Sky gulped. Then nodded. "Of course I am trained." She smiled under her scarf, hoping the crinkle that reached her eyes would convince him. It did. He grunted.

"Then follow behind. Everything must be ready before the Cartorran stone-shitters get here. We'll have a good surprise for them, eh?" He smiled now too, but his was genuine and revealed sharp, shining teeth.

He turned away. Sky's breath punched out. She knew the words *stone* and *shitter* separately, but she'd never heard them bolted together like that. And she didn't like the implication of his words. If this seafire was meant for stone-shitters, then that meant Cartorrans were either already here or else would be here shortly.

Oh Cursed Wells, Sky needed to get back to Last Holdout.

As she hurried behind the Baedyeds and their seafire, Red Sails and No-matsis, Purists and other Baedyeds all bowed aside like grass on the Wind-swept Plains, giving the carts at least a twenty-pace berth. Sky tried to count them, to gauge how many traps were being buried and stakes dug in. But of course, she could see only this one avenue. The rest of the city was a mystery.

Once through the old ramparts, the quiet ruins of the inner city stretched before her. The wind whipped louder, picking up old snowfall and mixing it with thick, wet flakes just toppling down. Here the Cleaved stood in long, unmoving rows.

In Cartorra, on the Purist compound where Sky hailed from, they'd had apple orchards. Every autumn she'd had to help with the harvest. And every winter, the stubby trees endured winter and snow and winds and misery. That was what the Cleaved had always looked like to Sky when she'd seen them: the apple orchards when all life had been sapped from them. The trees when they were simply dormant skeletons.

While Sky had appreciated Merik's commitment to rescuing Wakers, she'd always thought it was a lost cause. Now, she *knew* it was, for there were barrels of seafire planted every thirty or forty steps. Against the buildings, against *people* who'd once laughed and lived. If the barrels were ignited, every one of these people would burn. There'd be no waking after that. No chance at a spring rebirth.

Sky found she was panting inside her scarf. Hard exhales that sawed against cloth. The traps were bad enough, the idea of rutting *seafire* was bad enough, but this? It was sheer murder.

And to think, you once supported the Raider King. Except Sky hadn't. Not by choice, anyway. When the Cartorran emperor had taken her compound's orchards for his own, off they'd all gone to join Corlant and his mass of displaced and hungry.

Corlant in turn had taken them here, and Sky had just pretended these not-dead, not-living people hadn't bothered her. They were just apple trees, after all.

The carts in the procession peeled away at new streets. Her cart however cranked forward; the barrels kept sloshing and groaning. Then there it was: the tower of the Puppeteer coalesced in the snowy shadows. A horrible place that Sky had hated even when Merik had been its master. Filled with shackles and collars, with spiders and mouse droppings.

What she wouldn't give for spiders and mouse droppings right now.

The cart trundled to a stop, right beside the crooked alley where the tunnels wormed underground. "Here," a Baedyed called, their voice high and trilling. "Cover this street in barrels. Go into the tower too. And you." Their eyes, vivid green even in the predawn, latched on to Sky. "You will help me set the triggers."

Triggers? Sky thought, her lungs now gasping so hard, she actually feared others would hear. *Don't pass out, don't pass out. Trust me. I'm just like you.* When Sky reached the Baedyed's side—they too were fully scarfed like Sky was—she forced her throat and mouth to work in concert, her warm, magicked diaphragm to push air at a reasonable pace: "Why do we need triggers?"

The Baedyed hefted a spool of rough string from the cart's front, and Sky thought he was ignoring her. Until eventually an answer came, flat and efficient: "The Raider King says there is a subterranean shaft near here. If the Cartorran armies try to use it, well." They shrugged. "Then they will feel the fangs of the Sand Sea right before they die."

FORTY

✳

It was not the Raider King who came to retrieve Iseult. Instead, it was Admiral Kahina. "Follow me," she said, her Threads exhausted. Something had unsettled her in the last hour.

"Follow you where?"

Kahina only glared and strode back out of the tent.

Iseult followed. Her hips felt so light without the book or any blades. Meanwhile the knife in her boot was stiff against her ankle; enough so, she had to adjust her gait. But Kahina was sunk too deeply in her own thoughts to notice Iseult's stride. She had a pipe in her mouth; it glowed and puffed smoke.

Although clouds still hugged the sky—erasing the setting stars and moon—there was a sharpness to the world. A hardening of edges that hinted at sunrise. The city had changed since Iseult had been marched in—or rather, Ragnor's raiders had. Everywhere Iseult glanced, she found worried, focused Threads. War was coming.

No, war was already here.

At an intersection two blocks from the tent, Kahina crossed onto a wide avenue. Iseult glimpsed a placard on a crumbling building that read *City Hall*. This was a road on Leopold's maps and on Ragnor's. It would lead eventually to the heart of the city and to the Air Well.

Inexplicably, there were no raiders or Threads here. There was only snow that had turned to ice on ancient cobbles. Mist trailed off Kahina as they traversed the ancient city, as if the heat of her Paladin soul melted all it touched. Her Threads pulsed with weariness . . . and something else—something pinkish and warm.

It was *almost* the color of friendship, *almost* the color of family. Except frightened, as if someone she loved was in danger.

Kahina shivered. Her pipe flared. Then once more, mist formed around her head.

"You're the Paladin of Fire," Iseult said. She hadn't meant to speak, but it was much like being next to Leopold. Here stood history. Here stood *answers.*

The woman's silvery eyebrows rose. Her posture was stiff and military. "I'm Admiral of the Red Sails," she countered. "But yes, I also happen to be a Paladin of Fire." A wider swath of snow and ice melted around her. Then turned to fog.

"You were one of the Six," Iseult continued. "You knew the Sightwitch Eridysi. And Ragnor, b-before he was the Raider King. You were there when . . . when the world became chaos."

Now Kahina's jaw clenched until her pipestem creaked. "And the world has been chaos ever since. Which is why we're here. Why *you're* here, Dark-Giver. Now, enough talking."

Ahead, ramparts rose, marking where the oldest parts of the city still clung to a waterlogged earth. Beyond that, Iseult knew the road would curve and eventually take her to the tower were Esme had once dwelled—or, if she went the other way, to the Origin Well.

"Why?" Iseult pressed. The snow still melted and fogged wherever Kahina stepped; it felt like running through sea spray. "What went wr-wrong a thousand years ago? I've only ever read part of Eridysi's diary, so I only know what happened with the Void Paladin Portia. She and the other Exalted Ones used their power to enslave the land and rule. But *then* what?"

Kahina didn't answer. She walked faster instead, her legs longer than Iseult's and her body weighed down by fewer layers. A Firewitch, it would seem, didn't need furs against this cold.

Kahina reached the time-worn ramparts; a gate cut through; she vanished into the shadows, only her hair still visible like a guiding star across the night. Then they were through the gate and the ancient part of Poznin rose before Iseult. She had seen this on the maps as well, but the two dimensions of a drawing were nothing compared to the heft and texture of the real thing.

These walls have stood against winds and waters for a thousand years—and so has the woman beside you.

Soon, Iseult could see Esme's tower, a bent-backed haze in the gradually fading night. She also saw a second person waiting ahead: Ragnor the Raider King. He wore a uniform now, giving him the look of the general he'd been a thousand years ago. Of the tactical genius that Leopold spoke of.

He no longer felt small.

On Ragnor's uniform was the red moon on the black field. And just as he felt bigger, stronger, the sigil no longer looked gruesome. Instead, it looked like a moon wrapped in Heart-Threads. *I am bound to Moon Mother,* it seemed to say, *and she is bound to me.*

"Why have you brought me here?" Iseult asked.

"Why do you think?" His voice was soft. "I want you to see the Origin Well."

"You could have shown that to me hours ago."

A smile slid over Ragnor's lips, though it never reached his eyes. "But then you would not have had time to read what was on my desk."

Ah. Iseult let a smile of her own come, but it was one of stasis. One of cold detachment that would have made Gretchya proud. Especially because inside her brain, everything she'd thought she understood was once more reassembling. For there was something so chilling in the way Ragnor had said, *But then you would not have had time to read what was on my desk.*

Of course she'd assumed he *wanted* her to explore all his maps and missives, but she had also assumed it was to instill her with a false sense of safety. Like someone who coaxes out a cat by holding very still.

Now that Iseult faced Ragnor again, however, she saw he possessed such clarity in his Threads—such certainty of his own correctness and truth— that it made Monk Evrane's clarity seem fanatically unhinged and Eron fon Hasstrel's certainty seem naive.

For half a breath, Iseult felt as she did when she sparred with Habim, like she faced a master who was already three moves ahead of her. Like no amount of strategy or wiles could let her win here. *And that,* she realized with a sickening kink of her intestines, *is* actually *what he wanted me to see.*

"Walk with me," Ragnor commanded.

"Yes," Iseult agreed.

FORTY-ONE

✳

Safi reached the edge of Last Holdout, emerging from the bowed branches and protective trees to find chaos on the river beyond. The two people she'd followed stood on a soggy shoreline. Natural and magicked winds beat against them.

But it was what swept high above that held everyone's attention: a limp figure plummeting from a fall too high to survive—while the storm hound swirled and flipped around him. Lightning flared off Aurora's body before she wrestled hold of the figure.

Of Merik.

Then came a sound like gunshots to fill the night. Safi's attention snapped to the river—but it wasn't rifles or pistols she found. It was ice, crackling across the river like a ship cutting through waves. And at its helm was a figure with her arms opened wide.

Air kicked against Safi's bare face. Sleet too, needles to stab at her palms, her cheeks, her brows. But she didn't retreat from the river.

"Rifle!" Safi barked. "Shoot that witch on the ice!" She knew the winds would blow any shot wild, but surely an attack was better than watching idly as Merik and the storm hound fell.

The person with the rifle seemed to agree. They crouched. They aimed into the chaos. Yet before they could pull the trigger, something happened that, even years later, Safi would have trouble describing.

The forest came alive.

Tree branches stretched out like sluggish whips, the wood groaning so loud, it rattled into Safi's chest and overwhelmed the winds. Stones seethed outward too—even though Safi had never seen such stones here before. This whole place was made of soft earth, yet from somewhere, boulders, rocks, and pebbles launched across the river.

The unknown Waterwitch barely had time to raise a shield of ice. It stopped the stones.

It did not stop the branches.

The wood curled around the shield and onto the Waterwitch, who writhed and resisted. Until the branches had closed away all shape of humanity. Then those branches tugged, creaked, moaned backward into the trees that had birthed them.

The forest swallowed the Waterwitch whole.

Seconds after that, the full power of the storm hound's winds hit Safi, forcing her and her companions back into the trees. Lightning charged and sparked, and for what felt like an eternity, Safi huddled. She waited.

Until at last, at *last*, the clamoring storm settled into silence. But when Safi raced to the shoreline expecting to find a collapsed man waiting there with his storm hound coiled around him, she found only the hound—and only ice, quickly melting as the river surged by.

Aurora sank back on her haunches and howled into the dawn.

The branches were eating Stix alive.

The trees east of Poznin had always teemed with menace. The shadows didn't move when the sun did, and a storm hung forever overhead. Now Stix was in those trees, and it was worse than any child's tale she could have conjured.

White, papery bark scraped against her skin. Jagged branches poked into her mouth, her ears, her eyes. Leaves rustled and rubbed. While underneath it all was the bass grumble of rock grating on rock.

Stix had the sense that she was being moved.

She grappled for water, of course. Weren't plants mostly water? Was her magic not *the* most powerful water magic in all the Witchlands? But although the water answered her with tendrils from the river that chased along like snakes, with ice crackling then steaming then crackling anew, it was never enough to stop the wood or rock that carried her.

Until at last, as fast and as feral as she had been plucked from the river, she was dropped again. The trees released her. The stone melted away. And Stix found herself staring at the gray, baleful sky. Her chest shook. Her skin felt as if the trees still writhed against her. She wanted to weep, but she was too numb to feel anything beyond relief.

Or maybe she did weep. All that moisture against her face couldn't merely be from magic.

"I am sorry to be so rough," came a small voice. Incomprehensibly small against a forest so vast. Then a smell wafted over Stix, like fresh-churned soil and cold caves. It reminded her of a time a thousand years ago when she'd known what she was and the world had made sense to her.

Not to me, she thought. *It made sense to the Paladin soul inside me.*

"Yes," the small voice said. "I feel it too. Anytime we are together again." She slid her little body into Stix's view: a Nomatsi child, but with hair whitening at the roots. It was the same thing that had happened to Stix when she was a child.

How strange, her father had said. *Your hair is changing like mine.* Her mother had brought home a dye for her to try, if she'd wanted. But Stix *hadn't* wanted because she'd recently met Vivia, and the first thing Vivia had said to her was *You look like the moon at sea.* Then Vivia had flushed, embarrassed by her honesty, and Stix had known right away that Vivia was special. That she wasn't just a princess hungry for a crown like people believed her to be.

Now this girl hovering over Stix had the same thing happening to her hair. It was not as silvery as Stix's—there was more warmth to it. An *earthiness*, like the soil left behind when a field had burned to ash.

"You're Saria." Stix's voice was a cough, and she was surprised when the language that came out wasn't her own. *It is yours, though, because you are Baile and she is you.* And Baile, Stix was quickly realizing, didn't trust Saria. Stix couldn't recall a reason, but there was a rift there. Some betrayal tucked in Stix's Paladin past.

"I'm Dirdra," the child corrected. "Although I like to be called Owl. But yes, a thousand years ago, the soul inside me was named Saria. And you were Baile." She tipped backward, forcing Stix to crane her neck—and to finally see where the forest had taken her: a wide clearing, with jagged rocks punching up from the ground. Except one of the rocks, Stix realized as she squinted with her unreliable eyes, was moving. There was a claw. There was a tail. And there was a head, swiveling sideways.

"His name is Blueberry," the girl explained. "I almost sent him after you, but you had the river on your side. I didn't think he could match both of you, so I had to send the forest instead. Which was violent, I know. The trees are . . . bored. The rocks too. They have waited such a long time for me to return to them."

"Why did you attack me at all?" Stix shoved herself into a seated position. The movement revealed cuts in her uniform and across her skin. She glared at them. Then glared at the girl, who stood as still as the giant rocks nearby. She wore a simple black coat lined with fur.

"I couldn't let you kill the man you chased. For one, he isn't a threat to you. For two, he's important. One of the ones we're supposed to protect, not to harm."

"We?" Stix drew in her legs. A giant hole now slashed across her pants; the skin beneath was already bruising. "So you are on the Rook King's side?"

The girl didn't answer. The mountain bat—Blueberry—snuffed. It was a sound like laughter.

"I do not *oppose* you," the girl said carefully, "if that is what you are asking." She watched Stix with large hazel eyes. Her face held the wisdom of countless Earth Paladins; her skeleton carried more years than it was ever meant to sustain. She had come into her knowledge young, and Stix pitied her that.

"I didn't ask if you oppose me." Stix stood. The clearing and its rocks swam unfocused around her. "I asked if you are on *his* side. The Rook King's. He killed us, remember? He hunted us down a thousand years ago, and he thrust a blade into my belly."

Stix didn't mean for her voice to shake as she said this. Kahina had been so steady when she'd relayed her own story a month ago, when she'd *shown* Stix why the Rook King was their enemy and the Raider King was their future, their friend, the only one to finish what Eridysi had begun. But whenever Stix tried to explain how the Rook King had killed her . . .

Stix rubbed at her eyes. There were cuts on her brow, dirt in her tear ducts. But she scrubbed and scrubbed and swallowed a fresh surge of tears.

"He stabbed me too," Owl said. Or Dirdra or Saria or whatever her name was. There was a cautiousness to her tone, like a mother who didn't want to upset an already unhappy toddler. "But it was a regular blade. Not the one you stole from the Sightwitch in the mountain."

Cold swept over Stix.

"Where is the blade?" Owl asked.

Stix didn't answer.

"Do you have it with you?" A pause. Then a head shake. "That's a silly question. The blade sings to me, just as it sings to us all. *Death, death, the final end.* And I do not hear it now, so you must have left it behind." Her little face pinched up, blunting her features into the child she really was. "It's a good thing you don't have it. Now neither of us need fear the final end."

Stix set her jaw warily. She knew what Eridysi's blade could do, and the looking glass too. She'd finally read Ryber's diary, and she'd visited the workshop inside Sirmaya's mountain that had helped her remember more. Above all though, Stix had spoken with Kahina, mining the older woman's memories for answers about her own past. And until right now, Stix had believed she knew the full shape of what had come before and what needed to be.

But right now, right here, she stood with a child who was disrupting everything.

Stix planted her feet more firmly beneath her, groping for water in the soil as she did so. It was as impatient as the trees to move again; it had flooded onto this land so long ago, and it moved so slowly through the soil. It ached to flow, to fly. To rush and charge and drown.

Nearby, the mountain bat did not move, but its eyes blinked and blinked . . . and it flicked its tail like one of Stix's cats.

"I will ask you again, Owl, and I want a direct answer this time: Whose side are you on? Do you support the Rook King?"

Owl sighed, her little shoulders deflating. She was suddenly a lost, shivering child in a terrifying forest that wanted to claim her. "I am *not* on his side, but rather on the side of the Witchlands. And that means I cannot let you go back into Poznin—it means, that although you have gathered all this water . . . I need only splay my fingers to hold it in place."

She did it so easily, so fast, Stix had no time to comprehend Owl's words. The child simply spread her hands wide, and the connection Stix had *just* forged, the water she had *just* assembled in the soil . . .

It squeezed away. Compressed downward as the earth wrung it out like a sponge—and in a tiny pocket of her mind, Stix recalled a Sightwitch learning rhyme Ryber had once sung to her:

Earth encloses Water,
Water drowns the Air,
Air snuffs out the Fire, blazing everywhere.
Aether shines on Void, shadows turned to light.
So Void seeps into Earth and, softly laughing, wins the fight.

A useful rhyme that Stix wished she'd remembered before she'd started this fight she could not win—before Owl had shifted her weight, and in doing so, sent three of the largest rock columns scuttling sideways.

Except the attack Stix expected never came. Instead, a hole in the ground was revealed.

Stix had to squint to find any details without her spectacles, but even as she gaped, she knew what descended before her: a doorway into the mountain. A doorway into Sirmaya's ice.

"A portal," she said, awe briefly supplanting outrage or fear. "It's a new one, isn't it?"

"Yes," Owl replied. "And soon, you will come with me inside. But first: there are innocents who need us, just as they did a thousand years ago."

"What innocents?"

Owl lifted a hand, and Stix thought it was a quelling palm meant to silence her. But then she realized Owl pointed upward. "The innocents of this forest who are about to be burned alive in their homes."

FORTY-TWO

✳

There were two small blessings in the loss, as far as Vivia could see—and she clung to them like rafts in a storm. First, the Hell-Bard Lev had grabbed Vivia's pack on their escape through the workshop. In that pack was Vivia's healer kit, which meant they could tend both Zander's bleeding and the Empress's.

Which led to the second blessing: Vaness was not dead. Of course, she also wasn't waking up, and Vivia could see no reason. Like Vivia and Zander, she'd used too much magic. The blood on her face gave her away. But Vivia and Zander had awoken—so *why* wasn't Vaness awakening too?

"I'm bound to Air," Lev kept saying. "And there's nothing wrong with her lungs. Otherwise, I'd help."

"It's all right," Vivia kept responding. Except it wasn't. Not really, because nothing was all right. They were still within sight of the megalith on which the mountain door had formed—but it was closed now. Because of course it was closed now.

The Empress had been right. *What if this magic is simply fickle, as you yourself suggested, and the door seals up behind you? Then you will be stuck inside the mountain for all of time.*

Yes, Cam was stuck. Vivia had no idea where the boy was.

And now here *she* was stuck—with Vaness and these Hell-Bards—hundreds of leagues from home.

Keep your mask on, Little Bear. You have *to keep your mask on.* She was the leader now; she was the ruler in charge.

It certainly didn't help that the river through the trees beckoned and crooned. That a breeze pushed through the jungle, hot and sticky. And tasting like thunderstorms with tantalizing rain.

Vivia gritted her teeth against it and stayed seated, cross-legged, beside the Empress on her bed of asphodels. The night sky, thick with constellations, turned Vaness's copper skin to silver. It made her look less like a woman who'd almost died tapping into her magic, but like a story maiden about to be woken by her Heart-Thread.

Vivia cleaned blood crusted under Vaness's nose, while beside her, Zander murmured, "I have seen her do this before. I can carry her, if we need to travel."

Vivia had seen it before too, and she was angry. Vaness *knew* this would be the consequence. She'd had this kind of response to the iron since childhood—now magic was so much harder to control. So why keep the shackles on herself? Why tempt herself constantly?

That, you know perfectly well, isn't why you're mad.

"We'll camp here," she said, keeping her voice even. Her ire locked inside. "At least until the Empress wakes up."

"Yes, Majesty," Lev replied, and Zander—who was still a bloodied mess himself—lumbered to his feet, head bowed.

The minutes passed. The stars slid west, exactly as the stars at home did. Yet illogically, they felt brighter here. Razored and inescapable. Especially the Sleeping Giant, forever pointing north—which was no longer the way home.

After clearing a spot for a fire, Lev aimed south toward the snaking Amonra to fetch water. Zander meanwhile stayed near, foraging through the shadowy underbrush of the buzzing, clicking night.

The Empress slept on. Crickets silenced once the fire began. Moths, meanwhile, fluttered in. The orange glow drifted outward like a veil, too sharp in this peaceful clearing of white and yellow flowers. Too unnatural in a land few humans dared to cross.

Vivia kept thinking she heard giggles. That she saw childlike shapes within the trees.

You must be the Nine of Hounds, those girls had said to Cam. *Do not be frightened. Nine is sacred inside this mountain, for only with nine can any of us ever think beyond.*

Over and over, Vivia imagined the scene from the workshop. A thousand times, at least, but like her Witchmark when she rubbed too much, the memory was starting to swell. To change color and bulge with pain at the edges.

Zander eventually returned to camp. He settled beside Vivia in the shadow of an oak. "I found these, Your Majesty." He offered his cupped palms to Vivia, where fat gooseberries glinted green and ripe. "They're safe to eat."

"I'm not hungry," Vivia told him, and it was true. The thought of eating anything made her gut cramp.

Zander grunted. Then shoved a handful into his mouth. He'd cleaned his own face, so no more blood stained his lips or beard.

"You're a powerful witch," Vivia found herself saying as he grimaced against the sour berries. In the distance, a raven cried. "I've never seen anyone manipulate wood before."

He chewed. Swallowed. Cleared his throat. "I don't know if I'm powerful, Your Majesty. I was brought to Hell-Bard Keep when I was young, so I never had a chance to study it."

"Does it overwhelm you? The magic. Do all these trees and flowers and vines *clamor* at you to be used?" Vivia made an almost frantic motion around her head, trying to imitate the onslaught she always felt from the water.

Now Zander frowned. "Maybe? I definitely think I've got more connection to the plants now than I did when I was a boy. But who knows?" A shrug. "It was so long ago. And I *do* know it's nice to be here with the plants instead of inside that mountain without them."

"Of course it is. Because you're not trying to get home." Vivia didn't mean to sound dismissive. She didn't mean to sound cruel. The words just popped out, and she wished right away that she could snap them back in again. For all she knew Zander *was* trying to get home. He had been a Hell-Bard so long—surely he *did* have a place he wished for.

But if Vivia's words bothered the man, he gave no sign. "Maybe, Majesty," he agreed without malice. "The way I see it, though . . . Well, I've been a lot of places in my life, and while they were almost never the place I thought I needed to be . . ." Another shrug. "They were *always* the place that needed me."

He shoved the second handful of gooseberries into his mouth, and with nothing more than a soldierly nod, he pushed to his feet and strode away.

He didn't get far—there was nowhere to go, after all. And Vivia could already hear Lev's return, tramping through the underbrush with water sloshing in her bags like the sweetest of wines. She was the opposite of Zander in gentleness and solemnity, but Vivia had to acknowledge, Lev wasn't the opposite in loyalty. These two Hell-Bards had proven themselves.

Empress Vaness had been right about them; Cam and Vivia had not.

Vivia swatted a gnat from her eyes. She didn't want to think about Cam. Or the mountain or the ice or what the *blight* she was going to do now to get home. Just because she was sitting still didn't mean she could let madness overtake her.

So she didn't. Instead, she stood as Zander had. Instead she barked, "Watch the Empress, please. Keep the bugs off her." Then she set off the same way Lev had just come from, to face the Amonra. To face the waters always calling to her.

Over the last month together in Noden's Gift—often on their nightly chats beside the Well—Vivia and Vaness had discussed what might be going wrong with magic. Was it actually a *wrongness?* Or was it simply a gift they'd not yet learned to utilize? Was magic actually expanding in strength, or were Vivia and Vaness simply weakening in their control?

They'd had no answers, and it had become a problem that would have to be dealt with later. For although other witches in the settlement had also felt their magics surge, none had experienced the same barrage. They could still function, and technically so could Vivia and Vaness. As such, this particular problem would have to wait until *after* Vivia had reclaimed her throne. Priorities were what they were.

Vivia wished now that she'd looked harder for answers.

The waters of the Amonra formed a thick, writhing beast before her. Starlight reflected and pulled. To the west, Vivia could just glimpse where oaks relented their hold on the earth and the massive stones rose instead.

Use us, the waters lapped, reaching for Vivia's toes. *Join us.*

She nodded absently at them. She was going to have to listen to them soon. And it wasn't as if she hadn't done so before, a month ago, when she'd carried herself and the Empress on tides far, far across the Jadansi. Away from Noden's Gift almost all the way to the Pirate Republic. It had exhausted Vivia then and overwhelmed her, but it hadn't *killed* her.

Surely that counted for something?

Join us, Little Fox. We belong to you.

"Yes," Vivia agreed, her voice eaten by the night's thrum—and her skin eaten by mosquitoes that thrived this close to the shore. "You do, but I can't join you yet."

Something about those words made her face scrunch up, as if there was some important lever she'd just pulled. Sticky heat pressed against her. She stared again at the stones that marked the western edges of the Contested Lands.

But no insights came to her. No more levers she could try. Just mosquitoes, buzzing their high-pitched keen into her ears. She swatted at them.

Mud shifted underfoot. It knocked a branch into the waters, and the waves grabbed for it like sharks fighting for chum.

Until the waves soon realized it was wood and not their little fox. Then they let it drift away.

The branch hit a weak current. It spun once, then glided out toward the heart of the Amonra, where it would eventually drift east, then south, before slowly, slowly reaching the Jadansi.

Oh, Vivia thought, and suddenly she had an answer. An insight. An idea. One that made her smile with sharp teeth into the night. She spun on her heel and left the river.

To call what Zander made a *boat* would have been an insult to boats everywhere. But it *did* float and it *did* have space for four people—even if one of them was stretched out and unconscious.

Which Vaness still was, although Vivia kept murmuring in her ear, "Please, Empress, wake up. No one else can order me around as you do." Vivia insisted on being the one to carry Vaness to the Amonra, her pace shambling and ungainly. Not once did Vaness stir; she simply slept on.

"Does it have a name?" Lev asked once they were all together at the shadowy shore, eying Zander's creation. "'Cos I'd like to propose the *Commander*."

Zander grunted, a sound caught between humor and grief. "Yeah. That's a good one. He'd love knowing a boat that small and ugly was named after him."

Vivia was too tired to ask who *he* might be. Or to care that gnats were now zapping at her face. The boat *was* small, and it *was* ugly. No mast, no sail, no wave-cutting shape. It was more raft, actually, with green leaves still attached and sap oozing out of wounds left by Zander's sword.

It had oars, though, which Vivia was impressed the Hell-Bard had thought to include.

It would also float, and as far as Vivia was concerned, that was all the *Commander* really needed to do for them.

Lev clambered aboard first, reaching back to help Vivia with the Empress. They were at a slight angle thanks to the shore. Vivia almost tripped over a knobby branch . . . until the branch groaned downward, vanishing into the other gnarls and lines of the boat.

"Let's try not to kill any royalty," Lev said lightly. "Really don't feel like

going back into a Marstoki prison. Or"—she shot Vivia a grim side-eye—
"I've heard Nubrevnan prisons are even worse."

"Sorry," Zander muttered. The flush on his face looked almost gray in
the first hints of dawn. "I'll fix any other rough spots once I'm on board."

"It's fine," Vivia assured him. Because it was. The man was clearly struggling against his magic, and Vivia had no desire to push him harder. They
had what they needed; he'd done what she'd asked of him; a few forgotten
branches wouldn't kill anyone.

With Lev's help, Vivia draped the Empress along the raft's center.
They'd all peeled off layers, and now they used their armor and coats to
create a covering like the forts Vivia and Merik used to make in her old
"fox's den." It would keep the sun and insects off Vaness.

At least until she wakes up. And she *was* going to wake up.

"Ready?" Zander asked, still slouched on the shore.

Vivia nodded and tried not to think about the waters she was about to
coast upon. About how much louder they would be once they were directly
beneath her.

Zander grunted and shoved. His boots plowed into the soft bank. Mud
scraped under the *Commander.* Then the Amonra licked a welcome at the
raft's bow and dug rivery fingers into its woven hull. Moments later, Zander hopped aboard. The boat tipped. Water splashed against Vivia.

Swim with us, Little Fox!

Zander settled, as did the *Commander,* and he reached for an oar. "No,"
Vivia told him, pushing away from Vaness, now hidden under leather and
cotton. "Let me do it, Hell-Bard. You need to rest."

The man didn't argue. Instead, he crawled close to the Empress, lay
down with a hand over his eyes, and promptly fell asleep.

The shoreline shrank as Lev and Vivia rowed them toward the river's
deeper, faster heart. Fishes slithered, cutting through the waters that Vivia
could never disconnect from. Shelled creatures scuttled in the substrate.
She heard owls and saw bats, dark shapes that blotted out a few lingering
stars.

Use us, the waters begged. But always, Vivia exhaled against them. The
potential consequences were too dire; she couldn't risk losing herself to
waters that might never let go. She kept her focus instead on keeping their
course true, right down the center of this mighty river that began far to the
west in the mountains of Vivia's home.

FORTY-THREE

✳

Nothing could have prepared Iseult for the Cleaved. She'd seen them through Esme's eyes in the Dreaming. Hundreds of bodies around the Air Well, standing and trapped in the worst kind of stasis. Still, it wasn't the same as being physically in their midst, breathing the same damp air. Touching the same frozen soil.

And for the first time since Esme had arrived as a weasel in Cartorra two months ago, carrying pages of Eridysi's diary in her sharp predatory teeth, it hit Iseult with full, step-stumbling force that the Puppeteer had been punished too lightly. That by saving her life, by *binding* her soul to an animal, Leopold had given Esme a second chance she did not deserve.

All of these children and aunts and partners, all these soldiers and traders and beggars and students—they were simply in the wrong place when Esme had learned to use her magic.

And when the Raider King urged her to do so.

All of these lost souls, their Threads severed from warmth, movement, love—that was Esme's doing. And the Raider King's too.

As he led Iseult past them, his own Threads focused inward and his eyes unseeing of all these people he'd consigned to this fate, Iseult forced herself to stare at him. To nurse a growing fury, a hardening resolve. He might now be armored, but there were gaps at his joints. Her knife could slip in, sever a key tendon while her other hand claimed his sword.

She'd need that blade at his hip if she wanted to fully end him.

They were almost to Esme's tower now. Iseult recognized it against the sky, even if she'd never actually been inside. There was a resonance to it. Another old place, where the walls between this world and the Old Ones' were thinner.

Now, it was crowded with Threads. Determined, orderly Threads bound together in a common task Iseult couldn't discern from this distance. And Ragnor pointedly did not take Iseult nearer, even though she knew it was the most direct route to the Well. Instead, he steered her down a smaller alley, then across an overgrown courtyard, where vines had crept over the Cleaved and snow had gathered on their feet.

Iseult made herself look at each face in the dawn shadows. *I will fix this. I will heal the Well and free you.* Then she made herself look again at Ragnor. His left armpit had the largest gap when he moved.

"Are you well rested?" Ragnor asked in a voice that was too kind. It hinted at the father he might have been to Aeduan . . . had raiders not attacked his family and set him down this path.

"Yes," Iseult told him. Then, as he led her onto another small back street, she added: "Why are you taking me this way? What are all your raiders doing?" She pointed toward the Threads east of them.

"You mean why did I not include these plans on my desk for you to read?"

Iseult's nose wiggled. "Yes."

"Because as much as I want to trust you, I cannot."

"Trust *me*?" Iseult half sniffed, a sound that was pure Safi.

"Indeed." Ragnor's Threads brightened with earnest intensity. He opened his hands, gloved in thick leather. "For I have something I am hoping you will do."

Ah, so this must be what Kahina had referenced accidentally. "What?" Iseult asked.

Ragnor didn't answer. They were on a street crowded with so many Cleaved, it was like saplings reaching for sunlight.

This was where Esme had died, her Threads snipped away. Her army suddenly left with no one to animate them. Iseult had seen Esme's final moments, directly through Esme's eyes. She recognized these particular Cleaved huddled right here at the foot of the hill where the Air Well lived.

As Ragnor moved easily, comfortably, *horribly* around the abandoned Cleaved, Iseult found each step harder to claim. There was a vibration in the air. It made the snow look sloppy and loose, made Iseult's skin chafe beneath her many layers.

It's the Well, she thought. Although whether she could sense that because of her magic's connection to Threads . . . or because she was the darkgiver, and *this* was where Lady Fate had been leading her all her life, Iseult couldn't say. All she knew was that Ragnor seemed not to sense it.

She also knew that this Origin Well would not heal as easily as the others before it had. Iseult and Safi would need every droplet of magic they had to bring this magical spring back into life. To finally heal Sirmaya and all of the Witchlands.

The weight of that task made Iseult's feet drag through snowbanks. *Stasis*, she thought. *Separate yourself from the Threads of the world. You know what you have to do.*

The hill seemed interminable. More Cleaved. More death that wasn't death. Until at last, Ragnor crested the hill with Iseult just behind. Six oak trees, branches barren and trunks pocked, circled the Well, which had frozen over save for a central gap where water blinked up at the dawn.

Such dark water. Like a pool of Severed Threads. It even wriggled like the Threads of the Cleaved as snow fell onto it. Although the sun might climb higher east of Poznin, it didn't reach here. This place was a timeless gray.

"The Wells," Ragnor said, stopping at a crooked edge where snow gave way to ice, "were never meant to be ours, Iseult. Magic was never meant to belong to the people." His voice took on a coarse quality, as if the gray that lurked around them was changing the very nature of his throat. *Or as if we are stepping back in time.* "Sirmaya created the Paladins as conduits of her power. Then six of the Twelve died and their power bled into the land.

"For one thousand years, we have been stealing Sirmaya's magic. Draining it away. You know this is true. She has no strength left."

Iseult did know that, but when she spoke, her voice was weaker than she wanted it to be. "But how does cleaving the W-Wells help Sirmaya? How will that restore Her strength?"

"Consider it with your logical Threadwitch mind, Dark-Giver. If you and the light-bringer heal this Well, the magic might briefly heal across the Witchlands. But Sirmaya will be drained again after that. Again and again for all eternity."

"But that is why the Cahr Awen exist: t-to heal again and again."

"*Is* it why you are here, though?" Ragnor elevated his chin slightly, a military man addressing his troops. "What if you broke the cycle instead? What if you stopped the draining before Sirmaya could die? We could let Her claw back the magic She needs until life and land are stable again."

Iseult blinked at Ragnor. Her lashes wanted to freeze shut. Her nose had lost all feeling. Not that she noticed; her mind was too wrapped up in Ragnor's words—because, against her better judgment, she could follow his logic. "But cleaving the Wells will kill people."

"And so will healing the Wells."

There was no missing the threat in Ragnor's tone—and Iseult's mind shot back to all the Threads scurrying through Poznin, all the streets he would not let her see.

"There are political ramifications to also consider, Dark-Giver. The Wells go beyond magic, beyond even our Moon Mother. You must remember, the nations and empires of the Witchlands have fought for centuries over who controlled the Wells, convinced that possessing them would increase their power, their worth, their claims to rightful control. If there are no Wells, that stops."

"But . . ." Iseult shook her head. "They w-will just find something else to fight over."

"Will they? Or will a new era of peace be ushered in with the right rulers at the helm?"

Iseult couldn't help it: she rocked back a step. It felt as if she were staring at Eron fon Hasstrel. A different twenty-year plan with a different solution for the same problem. The same insistent, single-minded obsession on Ragnor's face and in his Threads. "Rulers chosen by you?" *Rulers like Safi, who do not want to be one. Like Mathew and Habim, who make matters worse.*

"No. Rulers who are chosen by the people. Not by Wells, not by Paladins. I . . ." Ragnor hesitated. His chest swelled. Then he turned away. Cold clarity and certainty still gripped his Threads, even as his words bordered on fanaticism.

"Did you know," he asked quietly, "that this city was once ruled by elected leaders?"

"Of course I know." Iseult's tongue shrank beneath the comfort of an easy answer. "This city was the capital of the Republic of Arithuania. It collapsed because of the plague."

"Yes, the plague that wasn't really a plague, but rather a curse from three empires who felt threatened. They introduced a slow, seeping thing into the earth." Ragnor paused here to remove his left glove. He dropped it to the snow, a smear of darkness on white. Then he unstrapped the bracer over his left forearm. It too fell to the snow. Lastly, he pulled up the sleeve of his thick wool gambeson.

Black lines ran down his skin, pooling at the top of his wrist. It looked almost like Iseult's Witchmark. Almost like the waters of the Well, ready to reject all light and magic.

Iseult swayed.

The Raider King was slow cleaving.

"This Well," he continued matter-of-factly, "was cleaved long before Esme got to it. Carefully and crudely by three empires who wanted to end what they saw as a threat. The Puppeteer . . . I introduced her to it, and yes, she finished the job by building her Loom. But this misery began long before we arrived."

Iseult felt her neck stiffen. Felt all of her muscles brace as if they were about to get hit—hard, *hard*, by the power of a thousand truths slamming into her.

Then it came. Ragnor had one more missile to launch her way. One more explosion to topple her to the snow.

"If you can provide me with an answer, Dark-Giver, for why this"—he dragged a gloved thumb down the oily lines marking his skin—"has spread and worsened over the decades, then I will change my course immediately. I will give you and the light-bringer access to the Well. I will disband all of my forces and walk away. There will be no fight left in me, and I will let you fix what ails the Witchlands and Moon Mother. So tell me now: Why has cleaving worsened with each Well you have healed?"

Iseult swallowed. Her tongue bulged, bigger than ever. So much pressure, she thought she might choke. Because wasn't the answer obvious? *Don't ruin this, Iseult. Don't falter.* "Because Moon Mother i-i-is dying, so cleaving has spread."

"Except," Ragnor countered, a mere murmur to be swallowed up by the trees, "with each newly healed Well, cleaving has only spread wider, poisoning more and more each time. People like me, with no magic inside them at all.

"So again, I ask: Why has cleaving worsened? Why, as you have healed more Wells, have more people died instead of getting better?"

FORTY-FOUR

✳

The river moved too fast. Safi was used to the sea, to streams, and even to sharp, churning rivers—but this stout, glutted python? She'd thought it would be sluggish. Slowed by winter's breath across its cold skin. Instead, the current sped so hard, so fast that no matter how desperately Safi slammed her heels onto the icy shelf along the shoreline, she couldn't keep pace with the blip of pallor that marked Merik in the water.

And soon, the blip was gone.

It didn't help that the ice was unpredictable. Some places, it held her weight with sturdy ease. Other places, her foot would smash through and feel the river's teeth.

Behind Safi, Merik's advisors ran. Ahead, Aurora darted back and forth, corkscrewing inside her winds. Every few moments, she would dive into the water, disappear for several agonizing seconds. Safi's feet would hammer, a wild gallop next to the three people with her. The ice would groan. Break. Slide. Slip. Then Aurora would emerge again, her fur sodden, her wings limp, and her magic over storms waning.

Every dive, she grew weaker.

"Stop," Safi shrieked after the hound's fourth attempt. Her voice was reedy and pinched in the frozen air. "Stop or you'll drown with him!"

A poor choice of words. The word *drown* sent Aurora yowling back toward the open slit of river. There was no sign of Merik in there now—at least not from where Safi and the others ran. He might have sunk to the bottom. He might be trapped somewhere under the ice, right under Safi's own feet for all she could see.

She needed a plan.

She needed her Threadsister here to help her make one.

At that thought—at the fist into Safi's brain that reminded her *Iseult is missing too*—Safi skidded to a slippery, knee-wrenching stop. Her companions stopped beside her, and even Aurora slowed, her winds spinning her backward toward Safi, toward the shore. *A plan, a plan, we need a plan.*

Merik's advisors stared at her. They'd all lost their hoods now, and a distant part of Safi's brain was shocked to see how young two of them were. Round, red-faced children who had suddenly been thrust into the highest-stakes chaos imaginable.

Safi could relate to that.

A plan, a plan, we need a plan. They were all looking at her. Even the storm hound, who'd hauled herself to a whimpering, whining stop on the ice. She dripped water; frost clung to her fur.

"You," she said to the girl with the rifle. "Keep your eyes on the city in case raiders come. You," she told the boy, "try to get the storm hound out of here. She's a huge target. And you—Loued, was it? How powerful a Herd-witch are you—" Safi broke off as a new noise wailed. It drowned her voice like the river drowned Merik. A howl like Aurora's . . . except blasted by a horn.

No, by horns, plural. *Many* horns, deep, rumbling, and magnified by bloodlust across the rooftops of Poznin.

Safi rounded toward the city, her jaw slackening. What did those alarms mean? Were they for Merik or something—some*one* else? If Safi had to choose between Merik or Iseult, the answer was easy. It would be Iseult. Always. But gods, how about she get through this *without* having to choose? That would be so much better.

The two young advisors and Loued stared at the city. Aurora too, her hound body floppy and lost. Until Safi barked: *"Move!"* Then she grabbed Loued's shoulder and pushed him onto the ice. *"Use your magic! Control a creature in the river and find Merik!"*

The man's exhales were as white as the ice underfoot, and he stared at Safi with bafflement while horns blared on. "Animals, Loued. Herdwitch-ery. Find Merik."

This time, the man understood. He nodded. Faster, faster. "*Ahtset!* Yes!" He stretched out his hands as if he were a weaver at the loom. As if he were Iseult reaching for Threads. His eyes flared green.

Then they flared white as a summer's day. All of his body, in fact, lit up like a star had ignited from within. *Or from above,* Safi thought, as she realized all of the ice, all of the shore, all of the forest and the Windswept Plains beyond were brightening with the same unnatural sunshine.

And she knew, before she felt any heat or heard any flames, what she would find when she turned again toward Poznin. Because hadn't she been here before? Trapped in fire while a ship burned around her. But there was no Empress of Marstok to save her this time. No Vaness made of iron.

Safi twisted, the movement as sluggish as if she were the one held by the river, and there it was: seafire comets lancing across the sky. They aimed toward Last Holdout.

For a brief space between moments, Safi heard the crackle and roar of the conflagration. Louder than the horns, she *heard* the hiss and snarl as seafire rocketed across the river. And although she was a hundred feet or more below the closest comet, she felt its heat on her face, on her eyeballs, in the aether of her soul.

This, she thought, *changes everything.*

She rounded for the young advisors. "Get back to Last Holdout. Now, *now.* Flee the forest, take nothing."

"Rora," the boy protested. His eyes were wide, the pupils reflecting a forest in flames.

"Leave her." Safi wagged her head. "She can survive this." *Maybe.* "But Last Holdout cannot."

"What about Merik?" the girl asked, her voice almost lost to the horns. "We can't leave him. He's our leader. He's our king."

True, true, true. There was so much conviction in her voice, in her spine, that Safi's whole body sparked from within. A purifying flame to chase away the black seafire.

And in that moment, with all the noise and heat and death crashing down, Safi had a sudden vision of this girl leading armies of her own one day. *Armies that will belong to the King of Storm Hounds.*

She squeezed the girl's shoulders. "He will not drown," Safi promised, trying to match the girl's conviction. Trying to impart her own truth with each word. "Loued will make sure Merik gets out of this alive. Now *you* make sure he has people to come home to."

The girl snapped up her chin, obedience aging her face ten years. "Yes, we will." She spun away, snagging the boy as she went.

In seconds, they were flying across the ice—comfortable in a way that Safi and Loued were not. As if the two kids had crossed this river before. As if the winds of dawn were coming to their aid, sweeping behind them and gliding them right into the trees.

Safi rounded back to Loued. His eyes were closed, his hands still outstretched. He rocked. His lips moved. And Safi knew without needing to ask that he had found creatures beneath the water.

He would locate Merik. She was certain of it. She just had to make sure no seafire hit him before that happened.

Or can hit Aurora, she realized with a jolt as she lurched around in search of the great beast. But the storm hound was gone. She'd taken flight from the river's ice and now she was nothing more than a shadow spiraling south across the ever-brightening sky.

FORTY-FIVE

✳

Iseult had no answer for the Raider King's question. *So tell me now: Why has cleaving worsened with each Well you have healed?* Her hands went to her collar, cold and wet. Then fell limp at her sides. Her nostrils flared. Her tongue was stiff and lifeless as her mind scrabbled ineffectually for a reason, an explanation, a worthy reply for the man before her with his patient, serious Threads.

But every cohesive sentence got stuck to her tongue like flies on sap. Nothing she could conjure resounded with the same thunderous certainty.

So tell me now: Why has cleaving worsened with each Well you have healed?

Iseult's ankles began tremoring on the snow. Only years of Threadwitch training—of stasis, in her fingers and in her toes—kept her from collapsing at the intensity of what Ragnor had just asked . . . and at the answers she didn't have.

It truly felt as if the sun had moved to night and the moon had moved to day. As if the land had flipped inside out, and nothing looked quite real anymore. A small voice, almost lost to the confusion, squeaked inside Iseult: *Do not falter. Safi and Aeduan need you.* But the voice was too small to mean anything—and besides, weren't its conclusions based on false information? Wouldn't healing this final Well only make cleaving *worse*?

Cold clamored against her feet. She rested scarred hands upon her thighs. And a strange, peaceful quiet settled over her as stasis rearranged into something new and logic laid claim. Was it really possible for Alma to be wrong? For Safi and the Cahr Awen souls to be wrong? And Leopold too, and Monk Evrane, and so many people—could all of them be wrong? Were Iseult and Safi truly making cleaving worse by healing the other Wells?

Ragnor gazed at Iseult, his face creased with such sympathy, it actually hurt to look upon him. *Threads that build, Threads that bind, Threads that break.* He possessed them all, spinning across his soul. Brightest of all, though, were the Threads already broken. The grieving blue core of him as pure as Sirmaya's own ice inside the mountain.

People had died to save the Witchlands, and more people would die to finish this. But how many people could be saved? How many Republics of Arithuania could form and flourish without empires to ruin them? How many displaced lives—Nomatsis, Baedyeds, and yes, even Purists and Red Sails too, could find safe havens without empires to dominate or Wells to control?

Life is the price of justice, Aeduan had said once to Iseult, quoting this very man standing before her.

Do not falter! a voice squeaked again. It sounded like Safi. It sounded like the Cahr Awen souls. It sounded, even, like Leopold. *But does it sound like me?* Iseult wasn't sure. Her logic mind was trapped between two possibilities that might both be true.

Ragnor shifted his weight upon his knees. The sword sheath at his hip clinked. "'Six turned on six,'" he recited. "'And made themselves kings. Then one turned on five, and stole everything.' That *one* was the Rook King. My former master. He tricked me, Eridysi, and the Paladins who wanted only good for this world. He tricked us into killing the Exalted Ones. Then one by one, he killed each of us too.

"Or he tried to." Ragnor opened his hands. The exposed clots of cleaving still glistened. "Sirmaya protected me, Dysi, and my girls. For a thousand years, we slept in Her ice. Then one day, Dysi and I awoke to find the world had changed. No longer did six all-powerful tyrants enslave and massacre the people. No longer was magic confined to twelve Paladins chosen by Sirmaya. Instead, witches lived everywhere across the land.

"The world Dysi and I had known was gone, and everything we'd fought for had been relegated to legend.

"As for my daughters, they were trapped inside this . . . this sleeping ice, and nothing I did could get them free again. If not for Aeduan—whom Dysi gave birth to right there inside our frozen tomb—I would never have left my girls. But my new son needed me, and Dysi needed me too. *The goddess will release them when the world is safe,* Dysi promised, and I had no choice but to trust her.

"So we stepped into the day, and instantly, we knew that all was not as it seemed. The signs were everywhere—the little songs Lisbet had sung to us, the warnings she'd told Dysi a thousand years ago. We saw those warnings all around us." Ragnor paused, his Threads flickering with something that was almost pink amusement, but mostly pale disgust.

"The people of today didn't even know that Lisbet was the Sightwitch who'd seen the prophecies. All her visions were attributed to Dysi and called 'The Lament.' An apt name, at least, since we could easily see Sirmaya was dying—and is still dying, because magic, Iseult det Midenzi, was never meant to be ours.

"If we do not stop the flow of power out of our goddess, then not only will She die, but everyone else will too."

Iseult listened, unmoving despite the snow sinking into her clothes. Into her hair. She had pieced together tiny fragments of this story from Eridysi's diary, but most of it was new information that her brain couldn't appropriately catalog. Aeduan had two sisters? Eridysi was his mother and he'd been born inside the mountain? The Lament was not written by Eridysi but by someone else?

Do not falter. Do not let these tales confuse you.

"Why," she said as flatly as she could, "are you telling me all of this?"

"Because we must cauterize these wounds. We must save Sirmaya before it is too late."

"You mean you need me to cleave the Wells. That's it, isn't it? W-without Esme or Corlant, there's no one left who can do it, so now you are turning to me—even though for months, you've tried to kill me."

"No." Ragnor shook his head. "I've never tried to kill you. Capture you, yes. But I have never intended for you or the light-bringer to die. Tools should not be penalized for being tools." His right hand—still gloved—moved to the sheath at his hip. Then with the practiced ease of a soldier, he withdrew his sword. Steel flashed.

Iseult sank back, her left arm rising defensively. Her right arm groping for her boot. But she stopped before retrieving the knife.

Because Ragnor was not attacking.

Instead, he held the blade toward Iseult like a merchant showing his wares. And it was no ordinary blade. For one, the steel was shattered all the way to the hilt. For two, hovering over the jagged sword's edge were three wriggling Severed Threads.

Sever, sever. Twist and sever. Threads that break, Threads that die.

"What is that?" Iseult asked on an exhale. A single swipe of that steel, and Threads would shear beneath it.

"This is the source of your power. *This* is what makes you the Cahr Awen. Eridysi made the blade. Then the Rook King used it to create you and the light-bringer."

A wave of recognition rolled over Iseult. As if she was suddenly a Truthwitch; as if she suddenly knew Ragnor spoke true. This blade was a mirror. This blade was a piece of herself.

Do not falter. Do not let these tales confuse you. She pressed her lips together. *He is the reason for the Cleaved. He will see slow cleaving decimate the land.* The proof of this was everywhere Iseult looked.

But then, so was the proof of Ragnor's words. Cleaving *had* worsened with each new Well healed.

One truth, however, did not negate another. If there was one thing Iseult had learned from Safi over the years, it was that two things could simultaneously be true. Right and wrong were not clear sides on a coin; good and bad did not adhere to easy lines.

Do not falter, the voice ordered again, and this time, Iseult knew it was her own. *She* believed in healing the Wells because *she* believed in the Cahr Awen. And above all, Iseult believed in herself.

So she finished sinking low, fingers reaching for the knife. She felt her boot, wet with snow. She felt the hilt, warm from her skin. Then she levered upright, her leg lifting to carry her forward. She would need to disarm Ragnor first, then aim for that gap in his armor.

But Iseult was a few fractions of a heartbeat too slow. Ragnor saw what she intended. His Threads flared. His eyes widened. And although belief and certainty propelled her forward, Ragnor moved faster.

He sprang like an asp, and the broken blade was his fangs. It happened too quickly for Iseult to follow. Too fluidly for her to fight.

The broken blade pierced her abdomen. Through fur, through wool, through flesh, through muscle and stomach wall. No pain, for the steel was too sharp. No comprehension, for Ragnor moved with more skill than any opponent she'd ever seen.

Sever, sever. Twist and sever. Threads that break, Threads that die. The broken sword went all the way into Iseult, right up to its crossguard. She swiped with her tiny knife, her muscles still acting out the instructions her brain had provided them. *Attack at the gap in his armor.*

Her knife grazed skin. It cut muscle and sinew, releasing hot blood into the dawn. But it did not stop Ragnor.

"Take comfort," he told her as he pushed against her shoulder and withdrew the shattered blade. "Your death will not be wasted, Iseult det Midenzi."

Iseult fell backward then, the steel withdrawing from her by the same route it had entered. Her body hit the frozen ground. Her eyes sank shut.

Above, the sky sang with snow.

Kullen,

I sit in your tomb right now, writing this. There are two holes in the ice where the girls once slept. I expected to find that, which is why I came here. This morning, instead of pulling the usual cards, I instead drew four new ones: *the Nine of Hounds, the Twins, the Giant, and the Knife.*

The Nine of Hounds has always been Cam, with his nine fingers. You might not remember him, but he was the ship's boy with me on the *Jana*—and he is my Thread-family.

The Twins, meanwhile, can only be Lisbet and Cora from a thousand years ago. So I came here to find them, and sure enough, their tombs are empty. I would have sent the Rook to explore for me, but . . .

He has gone again, and I'm trying to pretend my heart isn't hurting because of it.

I can't stay long. The ice comes for me, and the whole mountain rattles. I keep thinking of the old skipping song Tanzi loved to sing:

> *When the sky splits and the mountain quakes,*
> *Make time for good-byes,*
> *For the Sleeper soon breaks.*

I can't let Sirmaya break, Kullen, but I also can't stay in the Convent or the mountain or the Crypts. Not if the sisters are awake, not if Cam is near and I might find him.

I'm sorry, though. *Goddess,* I'm *so* sorry that I couldn't find a way to wake you. I see all the letters I wrote you, just lying here untouched on the floor. And now there's a diary beside them as well—Eridysi's. The other half of what I gave you over a year ago to read.

I didn't put that diary there, Kullen, and I don't know who did. But I am going to take it, in hopes that there are clues for what I am meant to do . . .

I am no longer the last Sightwitch Sister. I have no idea what that means for me.

I love you, Kullen. My Captain. My Paladin. Ever since that day in the mountain when I chose to ignore the Rule of the Accidental Guest and to help you instead, our Threads have been bound. And they will remain bound for as long as I live, as long as I breathe. I am not giving up on you. I'll come back when I can.

Good-bye.

—Ryber

FORTY-SIX

✳

They all felt it when Iseult died.

Alma and Gretchya, too far away to help. Evrane on a shoreline, not far at all. Owl inside the forest where seafire burned, where ice and rock collapsed around her. Habim and Mathew hundreds of leagues away. Aeduan, so high in the Sirmayans and struggling to breathe. All of her Thread-family felt it.

And above all, Safi, running on the frozen river mere miles away.

She felt the Threads that bind tear asunder. She felt her heart cleave in two. And she felt the broken blade enter her as if she were the one being killed. As if it were *her* blood coming out so fast that her organs were shutting down and her mind was detaching from its body.

A hundred Cahr Awen souls screamed inside Safi. A mourning, inconsolable sound because the dark-giver was being ripped away. Safi screamed too, with all their voices and her own. Her body fell to the ice. Backward, exactly as Iseult had fallen.

When Iseult died, Safi died too. In fact, if not for the Cahr Awen souls inside her, she would never have moved again—and everyone who'd ever been bound to her would have also felt her death as it severed her Threads from the world.

Instead, a Marstoki Herdwitch who had no reason to care if Safi survived this moment, who had no loyalty whatsoever to her or her cause, dropped to her side while his eyes glowed green. His arms dug beneath her and he lifted Safi, inch by inch. The sword at her hip dragged on snow and ice, an anchor trying to pin her down.

It seemed to take all of the man's strength to fight the ice, to control his magic, and to manage the weight of Safi's near-dead body. Once she was on her knees, though, the Cahr Awen souls stopped their screaming.

One minute, they were as loud as the horns in the city; the next, they were completely silent as they raced like worker bees down to save their queen. The souls reached Safi's muscles. *Initiate*, they commanded. And

Safi stood. They surged up to her brain: *You are not actually dead, and the dark-giver's soul is not lost. Initiate and save her. Initiate and move.*

Safi's magic whimpered at that truth. And from her distant, out-of-body vantage, she couldn't decide if she simply wanted her Threadsister's soul to still be out there—and so her belief, her hunger, her *need* made her magic thrum.

Or was it really true? Did the core of her power recognize a fact she herself could not yet see?

Does it matter? the Cahr Awen souls demanded. *Will it change what you are about to do?*

No, she acknowledged. *It won't.* Safi's neck muscles shifted. Her jaw too, and suddenly she was moving again. Cracking her head side to side. Faster, faster, like a dog shaking off a bath.

Safi lifted her head and peered at the seafire-streaked sky. Snow fell thicker. The forest around Last Holdout was aflame. The horns blasted an endless refrain from the city.

But there was more happening than just the enemy's triumph—there were people Safi had connected to during Iseult's death. As if the act of ripping apart Iseult's Threads had woven together all the Thread-family she'd left behind. Safi sensed Alma and Gretchya, their grief nearly as expansive as hers. She sensed Evrane, illogically close and shouting a war cry for the Cahr Awen. She sensed Aeduan, sprinting and focused in a way that Safi also needed to be.

And she sensed Leopold, furious. Violent. Grappling for his Aether-witchery so he could make the world right again.

For a vivid half moment upon the ice, Safi saw the weave of Iseult's Thread-family as if it were a taro game. As if she herself were one of several cards in an expert player's hand—and each card was about to be laid down to win.

The Nameless Monk to double a hand's strength.

The Fool to be played wherever needed.

And the Witch, the Empress, the Sun, and Birth—a winning combination no other hand could beat. No other cards, no other assemblage could ever dominate.

And they are all me, while I am all of them.

Safi stepped away from the man who'd helped her. "Thank you," she told Loued, although he couldn't hear her. The horns and the seafire were too loud—and armies that appeared from seemingly nowhere now clashed upon the ice.

Ice that Safi was going to have to cross somehow, if she wanted to reach Iseult in time.

Iseult's soul was not yet gone.

Safi's quest was not yet over.

Her pace picked up. The dark slash where the river still flowed looked immense and uncrossable. Too vast for only her two legs. But Safi knew—she *knew* because she had the winning hand in her grasp—that she could leap across it. Lady Fate would find a way. The hundred souls pulsing inside her would find a way.

Arrows whizzed by, silent and crunching into ice around her. Seafire hissed across the sky. Twenty paces to reach the river's flow. Ten paces. Safi would make it. The gap was not so big. She reached it. She jumped; her muscles sang with truth and certainty and all the belief she had inside her.

She flew across the river's black waters, wind lashing around her. She still wore only her loose sleeping gown. She imagined she looked like a ghost to the people on the shore.

A righteous, vengeful ghost for the Cahr Awen, and with a sword that sang of truth.

The Witch, the Empress, the Sun, and Birth.

Arrows sliced into the water around her, harmless. Lost. Then Safi reached the other side of the ice. She didn't land easily, and the muscles around her knees felt torn asunder as they tried to stabilize her. But she didn't fall, and the arrows now aimed in great droves could not seem to hit her.

She thrust back into her sprint, the ice hardening with each leaping step she took. More arrows, their fletchings an array of colors. Red, green, black, brown. Like Threads weaving around Safi, connecting her directly to the world.

She darted, she curved, she spun and lurched until she was no longer on snow-laden ice, but on a snow-laden shore. Raiders aimed for her, and Safi realized with remote awe that it wasn't merely arrows giving her the illusion of Threads. She *could* see Threads, just as Iseult did. She had, for reasons she could not fathom, bits of Iseult's magic rousing inside her.

Safi withdrew her sword. It flashed with the reflected light of dawn and seafire. It hummed with the power of a Truthwitch. Then Safi reached the first raider, and she cut. Not their Threads—she didn't have all of Iseult's magic—but their limbs. Their bellies. Their necks and their armor. Anything her sword touched, it carved effortlessly through.

I am coming, Iseult, she thought with each swipe, each duck, each shove. *Do not leave me until I reach you. Do not complete until I am there.*

Merik was dead. This was nothing new because he had been dead for several months now. The only things tethering him to a semblance of life were the Threads that bound him to Kullen, sleeping in the ice.

Yet although he was dead, his body kept sputtering along. Death would shatter it, then Kullen's bound soul would restore it. Right now, it had restored Merik to his false life directly inside Noden's watery Hell.

It was too dark to see anything, and the cold was so complete, Merik could not have moved his limbs if he'd wanted to. The current was so powerful that he could do nothing except be dragged along by it, ever deeper into Hell.

Water had entered his lungs. He'd been dead when that had happened; now that he was slowly returning to life, he could feel the water inside him.

Merik's body died again. From cold, from drowning, from a broken neck. And still Noden's currents carried him toward the final shelf.

Why do you hold a razor in one hand?

So men remember that I am sharp as any edge.

And why do you hold broken glass in the other?

So men remember that I am always watching.

When Merik came into consciousness a second time, his body once more stitching itself back together, his eyes had become ghost eyes. Or maybe that was the light of Noden's Court. Either way, he could see now. Not well, but his dead, dead brain connected to his dead, dead eyes, and his dead, dead awareness sensed streaks tendriling through the water column. Merik was still too broken to fight the current—and really, what chance did he have against Noden? Plus, his lungs were too filled with water to live for long. He would die again at any moment.

But at least in all this cold, there was no pain. No frustration either. His time had finally come, and not even Kullen's Paladin Threads could keep him bound to life. Noden wanted Merik, so now Merik would go.

He drifted. Onward, onward while the shadows coiled closer.

Then he realized what he saw, and he let his dead eyes close in supplication. These were Noden's Hagfishes. They were going to escort him past the final shelf. He felt their slippery skin against him. He felt their muscles twist and tighten around his arms, his legs, his neck. They were somehow even colder than he was, and were he still a living man, revulsion would have kicked in.

But he wasn't alive, and his belly was filled with water. So he felt nothing but gratitude because this, surely, would speed up the process. This, surely, would mean it would all be over soon.

He was not afraid of death—he'd been trapped on the final shelf for so long now, he knew the abyss was waiting for him. He *was* sad, though. He didn't want all those souls in Last Holdout to suffer at the hands of the Raider King. He didn't want all those Cleaved in the city to stand forever, trapped like Merik had been in a life that wasn't life at all. He hoped that Loulou might take over. With Sky and Revan beside him, he would lead well—

One of the Hagfishes that had slid around Merik's neck now snaked into his mouth. Its small head pushed through his teeth. Then it pushed and pushed to reach his throat.

Now the revulsion switched on. Now, bones that had been shattered were repaired enough for his muscles to engage. For instinct to unreel and Merik's fingers to claw at the creature trying to swim *into* him.

He gripped it. He pulled. The other Hagfishes embraced him, like shackles. Like Threads that bind and will never let go. And the Hagfish at his mouth forced its way all the way down Merik's esophagus.

Merik died a third time.

But not before he felt the strangest thing happen inside his chest: water pumped out of his lungs.

Then came a voice he knew almost as well as his own: *You don't get to die before I do, Threadbrother. We're still needed in this fight.*

A light brightened before Merik. *Ice*, he realized, and it occurred to him—in a cloudy, unformed part of his dead brain—that perhaps he wasn't in Noden's abyss at all and perhaps these weren't Hagfishes. Maybe he was still in the river, and that pallid blue coming closer was nothing more than the surface and a dawn sky.

His feet caught on something that latched into him with such gritty severity the current was forced to release him. The Hagfishes were able to relax their control and, one by one, release Merik until there was nothing between him and the cold.

The last to leave was the one in Merik's throat. It withdrew, wriggling and graceful.

Merik's feet dragged over silt. Vegetation scraped against his legs. Then his head bumped against ice that slushed apart at his touch. Light pierced his dead eyes. Sounds pierced his dead ears. And a touch, gentle and warm, reached his shoulders.

Warmth coursed through him as a head leaned over his body. She was upside down at this angle, but there was no mistaking her face.

Sun-browned and silver-haired. Haunting, wise, and painful in a way Merik had not known his chest could still feel. "I cannot believe it," Evrane told him, her hands clutching his face. "I cannot believe it, yet here you are, Merik. Delivered to me by Noden Himself—and oh my nephew, it is so good to see you."

FORTY-SEVEN

Iseult was in the Dreaming. Her body, still bound by a heretic's collar, was beyond saving without magic. There was too much blood across the snow. Her eyes had no life in them, and the winter would freeze her quickly like this.

Still, the Moon Mother had not yet reclaimed her Threads, and so here Iseult stood—a spectral version of herself—while somewhere in the city, horns blasted. They were dampened by the Dreaming. Muted into a distant musical undertow as Ragnor faced off against his most ancient enemy.

"Come, Rook King," Ragnor shouted, waving the bloodied blade that Iseult had recognized as a piece of herself. "Come, my liege. I see you there. This glass my wife made shows all, no matter what tricks you may try to play with it." With those words, Ragnor lifted a broken looking glass and held it before him like a torch. Its square frame was nearly empty save for a few shards of clear glass clinging to the edge. "I see you, right there. So stop hiding, Rook King, and face me."

Iseult saw him too, in the Dreaming. He was a Paladin's ghost, broadened by dark furs and shining with a silver crown. He stared at Iseult's soul, and she stared back at him. "I cannot save you," Leopold told her, his grief as pure as Ragnor's. "There is not enough power left in the Moon Mother. I cannot save you like I did your friend. Sirmaya does not answer—"

Ragnor charged at the Rook King.

And suddenly the ghost was gone from the Dreaming. In his place was Leopold beside the Well. He whipped sideways before the broken blade could pierce him.

He was fast.

But so was Ragnor. Incomprehensibly so. A master above all masters.

"My life for hers," Leopold shouted. "I will give you my life for hers! You can have me, Ragnor, if you let me save the girl."

The girl, Iseult thought vaguely. *Not the dark-giver.* She wasn't sure what that distinction meant—only that it was there.

"No." Ragnor swung again at Leopold, and this time, as he swirled past in his armor, the moon sigil on his chest looked bloodied and cruel. His Threads too, the forever grief now dominated by focus and violence. It might not have been his first choice to kill Iseult, but he was using her death to his advantage.

And it occurred to Iseult that perhaps this had been his long-term aim all along. That he had *wanted* to lose battle after battle so that he and the Rook King might one day face off.

Ragnor had called Iseult a tool; now he'd found a way to use her.

"You have always believed yourself so clever, Rook King, but it was never your brain that won our wars. It was never *your* strategies or even *your* armies. They marched at your whim, but it was my command they followed. It was me they always trusted."

Leopold blocked and dipped, his feet tangling in snow. He had a weapon, but his rapier—long, sharp, gleaming—looked weak against the broken blade Ragnor swung. In the Dreaming, the Severed Threads coiling off the sword made it seem whole.

They reached for Leopold like tentacles. *Death, death, the final end.*

"You poisoned my thoughts," Ragnor continued, his words reverberating through the dawn. "You poisoned our minds—each of the Six. Dysi. My *daughters*. You tricked us with your tales of rebellion and salvation, and then you killed us one by one."

"I did not betray the Six." Leopold scooted aside as the broken blade and its Threads hissed toward his eyes. "And I did not kill Dysi or your daughters or take your son—"

"But you would have if Sirmaya had not protected us! Do you deny it? *Do* you?"

Leopold did not, yet there was a flood across his Threads that told Iseult he didn't merely regret what had happened a thousand years ago, but it was *the* regret that had haunted him ever since. *So if you did not betray the Paladins, Polly,* Iseult thought, *then who did?*

So many questions.

So many answers she would never get unless she somehow escaped this Dreaming and returned to life.

"We were Threadbrothers once," Leopold said.

"And Threadbrothers do not betray each other." Ragnor rushed him again. Leopold barely evaded. His feet were slipping on this ice. His breaths were coming in fast. He was flagging, and soon he would lose. His skill with the rapier was simply no match for Ragnor's hate and rage—or the broken blade's bloodlust. That steel wanted to end Leopold. It wanted to ensure he was never reborn again.

Oh, Iseult thought, and suddenly a small click of understanding sifted into her dream mind. That blade: it was what had killed the Exalted Ones permanently. It was what had ended them before Leopold . . . or someone else had turned on the Six. But what, then, was the glass that Ragnor had tossed to the snow?

And why are both items broken?

Iseult's spirit legs took her five steps across the Dreaming. Metal clanged and breaths rasped. Boots thumped and armor creaked. Threads hovered at the edge of her awareness, each set unnaturally bright in their own way. Leopold's with his Paladin soul and loneliness. Ragnor's with his all-consuming righteousness and grief.

She had almost trusted the Raider King. She had almost let his arguments trick her.

And she *had* faltered. She *had* failed.

Iseult knelt beside the looking glass, sunk into the wet snow. She reached for the handle with dream fingers, but she couldn't grasp it—for it was real, while she was not.

Threads uncoiled from it. Not Threads that break, like those quavering off the blade, but rather Threads that build. And seeing that tickled a memory inside Iseult's mind. Many memories, in fact, that had gathered dust because she'd hidden them away.

Memories of watching Gretchya weave together Threadstones and of herself failing to do the same. The Threads had always slipped through Iseult's grasp; they'd never braided and wound as she'd wanted them to.

These Threads, however, didn't run or evade Iseult. Instead, when her dream fingers reached again for the handle, the Threads that build reached for her in return. They swirled and stretched. They strengthened and grew, grabbing for Iseult's soul, melting into her wrist like snow. Power hummed inside her.

It made Iseult think of how Safi had always described her magic when it responded to truth. *This*—whatever it was—was true. And in that moment, it *was* Safi's. Iseult was connected to her Threadsister, their souls bound. Their Threads woven together.

Then it was done. There were no more Threads unspooling from the glass. Iseult was locked to it, and it was locked to her. Blade and glass. Moon and Sun. Initiate, complete.

Hurry, Safi, Iseult thought. *I need you.*

True, true, true.

FORTY-EIGHT

✳

Stix was no longer reduced to a weakling. Power surged through her, strong as river rapids. And like the rapids, Stix's magic was whittled to a choppy point. Everywhere she looked, the forest burned, and nothing she did could quench it. *Nothing* she did could put it out. Yet all these people were going to die if she and Owl did not find a way.

Stix forgot about Ragnor or his cause. She forgot about the Cahr Awen or the Rook King's wickedness. She forgot even that she did not trust Owl or know what the woman-child really wanted from her. What mattered right now was that they both fought against the seafire that burned this settlement hidden in the forest.

This was why Stix existed. *This* was why Sirmaya had made the Paladins: to protect the people. To protect the Witchlands.

Last Holdout, Owl had called it as they'd raced through the woods. *We must empty Last Holdout.*

Stix had found a strange place made all the stranger by the smoke and the heat and the black, black flames. But it was familiar too—as if Stix had been here in one of her many past lives. The people were new, though, some dressed like Purists, some like Baedyeds, and some like poor beggars forever trapped in the Skulks of Lovats.

Stix didn't care who they were; she just wanted to keep them alive.

Her magic frothed inside her. She swung and she swooped, claiming water from the river, from the soil, from the snow falling in the sky, and with each droplet, she built a wall. Ice would not stop the seafire, but it would slow it. And latticed within the ice was stone and soil riven from the earth by Owl.

Nothing they did was fast enough, though. Or high enough. For despite the shield of earth and water, wind always sent sparks circling around to ignite on branches and winter trunks.

Stix dripped sweat. Heat scorched against her. Inch by inch, she and Owl guided the people out of the settlement and north, ever north, toward a new doorway into Sirmaya's home.

We must get these people into the mountain, Owl had said, *and into your under-city, so we can finish what we tried a thousand years ago.*

Baile and the others had never finished their mission—not before the Rook King had turned on them and the Exalted Ones had descended. But now . . . now Stix's Paladin soul could finally finish. She could close the circle they had opened so very, *very* long ago.

With that thought, Stix felt the past rise up and claim her. Felt the flames roar from Lovats and his Paladin wrath.

Just get them to the under-city. This is all Baile can think of as she rushes the people toward the doors of Paladin's Keep. There is a secret way under her home, and she will fit as many people through that doorway as she can.

Somehow Lovats knows what the Six have planned. Somehow, he pounced upon Baile in the night with his jade ring made of curses and his magicked hold over her searing in her veins. He is one of two Paladins of Fire, but unlike Rhian—Baile's closest, oldest friend—he uses his flames to dominate and destroy. This whole city, named for Lovats and built with stone carried across the Witchlands by slaves, now burns beneath his rage.

He hunts Baile, and although she uses all her magic, all her waters, she is not strong enough to fight the pain his ring-bond sears into her. She can scarcely see for the agony of it, a thousand sparks scoring her from the inside out. She feels her skin burning like paper over flame. Her organs, her lungs, her brain. But she keeps moving, keeps dashing water against every attack that Lovats flings her way.

These people will get into the under-city that she, Bastien, and Saria have built for them. Then the Rook King Elias will arrive with Eridysi's blade. Death, death, the final end, it sings, and when its steel touches Lovats, his Paladin Threads will fray apart—and cut him forever from this world.

Soon, they are under Paladin's Keep. Baile's cats are charging into fire to protect their master. They are small, they are fast, and their claws are viciously sharp. Some reach Lovats; many do not. Baile cannot save them, and so she lets them go. She already weeps from the pain; she will spill tears for her cats later.

When the last of the city's citizens has entered her secret door below the Keep, Baile thunders in too. She doesn't bother to shut the door—there is no point. Lovats knows where they are going; the door and its lock are laughable for a power as vast as his. Baile instead calls more waters to her. More, more, every ounce she has ever bewitched inside the city's Cisterns. The waters love her as her cats do, and so the waters come.

They flood the under-city. The foxfire meant to light the stone streets turns the water green as it rises. Not so high as to drown, but high enough to soak the floor and reach to Baile's knees. She calls more, more, from each tunnel that she bewitched because Lovats made her; she pulls the currents. There is so much here, more than when she could reach aboveground.

Lovats and his fires cannot burn this place.

Stix reached the clearing filled with stones. She still fought the seafire, but now Owl had many more rocks to add to their defense. The columns slithered and reshaped, until there was a vast dome stretched overhead. What little sun had pierced the clouds now vanished until all that remained was a lone beam pouring down like the light into a Nomatsi tent. The heat from the seafire cut off. So did the smoke. But Stix and Owl were not done yet. These people couldn't stay here, because although the wall would stop the flames, it wouldn't stop the soldiers blasting with them.

"Into the doorway," Stix shouted, pushing at bodies she didn't know with faces she had never seen before. "Follow the stairs down and we will guide you to safety!"

Wide eyes stared at her, stunned or confused or terrified. But there were others shouting. Urging them to listen. A boy and a girl in Purist gray. A Baedyed with eyes glowing green. They yelled at people who would listen, and they shoved at people who would not.

Outside, the forest burned, heating the stone wall. Soon, if they could not get into the mountain, they would all cook like crabs in a pot.

Lovats is stronger than Baile realized. Or perhaps she is weaker. Her cats are gone, her waters are limp, and the pain from the ring-bond is snapping her spirit in two. That strange, awful ring that Portia, the Voidwitch Paladin, made for Lovats.

"She told us what you planned," Lovats said, glee building in his eyes and fattening his pupils. "She told us what you would do. You thought she was one of yours, did you not? Your little six meeting in secret? We knew. We always knew, because she has always been one of ours."

Baile cannot fathom this. She hurts too much. There is no space inside her to follow words or logic.

"I won't go in there!" This came from the hooded girl. She stood at the lip of the hole, with its spiraling ramp into the mountain, and she held up her hands in the Purist sign against magic. "I won't go in there—we can't go yet."

Stix didn't speak much Cartorran, but in some past life she must have. She understood the girl as if this language were her mother tongue, and when she grabbed the girl's shoulder, a voice that wasn't quite her own emerged: "You must or you will die."

"Merik," the girl said. "Our leader."

"Gone." This was from Owl, who now stood on Stix's other side. The heat swelled with each passing second. "He is not here, and you will die if you remain." This was all Owl said before she scurried past on her child's legs to join the others down, down toward a magicked—and now glowing—doorway.

A growl sounded nearby. It was almost lost to the seafire's roar, but Stix felt it rattle in her intestines. She didn't have to turn to know the mountain bat was there, menacing. *Go into this mountain, child, or I will eat you.*

The young woman shook her head. "Blessed are the pure," she rasped. "Blessed are the pure."

"Come on, Ulga!" yelped a new voice, and a boy sprang up beside her. "We can't help Sky or Merik if we're dead. Come *on*." He flung his arms around her and towed. It was a desperate movement, made from love. They were family; he wouldn't let her roast here.

The mountain bat growled again. And the girl, Ulga, deflated into the boy's arms. He pulled. She followed.

Lady Baile floats on her waters toward the under-city's other side. That is where the Cisterns are, and she wants Lovats to follow her there. Anything to get him away from the people.

A static sensation scampers across the waters into her body. It is not Lovats's flames or his laughter, though, and when Baile forces her breaking neck to look at the door, she sees a figure in black furs stepping through. On his head shines a silver crown. In his hand gleams a silver sword.

Elias. The Rook King. He has the Paladin blade that Eridysi forged, and now Baile can finally stop. He will kill Lovats. It will all be over.

Except that this is not what Elias does. Instead, he strides past Baile, splashing water across her body, her face. He does not look at her, does not even seem to see her floating there. "Lovats!" he thunders, his voice echoing off stone even as flames and smoke engulf. "The doorway is open. You can go through!"

This makes no sense to Baile, and although it hurts more than she knew anything could hurt, she makes herself and her skeleton rise. All the way up until she can see into the doorway that Elias just left through.

A battle rages there. Flames, smoke, stone, and ice. Winds and lightning too. Then Bastien is at the doorway instead. His scarred face is a mask of more fury than Baile has ever seen.

He spots Baile and rushes to her. Waves lap and spray over her in his haste. Then he is beside her. Lifting her up. "We must hurry, my love," he says, and Baile realizes he is weeping. "We must get away before Elias can destroy you. He has already killed the others. I will take you to safety, and then . . ." He does not finish his sentence before scooping up Baile with a grunt of exertion. Of exhaustion.

But she doesn't need to hear his words to know what he means: I will take you to safety, and then I will destroy the Rook King.

In that moment, she realizes that Elias did not in fact have the Paladin blade. It is tucked into Bastien's belt now, vibrating with its power to kill immortal Threads.

Death, death, the final end.

Stix wiped sweat off her brow. She remembered now—how everything had collapsed inside the mountain. How the Rook King had betrayed them all.

But there was still one piece from a thousand years ago that was missing. One memory shaped like the girl who now watched Stix through smoke and sparks. She was just a child in this life, but her strength was as vast as an earthquake.

Stix knew she stood no chance against Owl.

If only she could remember *why* she might need to.

With another rub at smoke and heat upon her brow, Stix stepped into the mountain.

FORTY-NINE

※

Safi sprinted as if she was not in Poznin. She sprinted as if she and Iseult were on the streets of Veñaza City, racing to be the first back to Mathew's. As if the day were hot and the sun high. She was the light-bringer, the world-starter.

The Witch.

The Empress.

The Sun.

And Birth, she thought as her arms swung higher, her knees pumping almost to her chest. She ran with the speed of a hundred Cahr Awen. She fought with the power of a Weaverwitch and a Truthwitch combined. She saw the weave of the world, and felt its truth. Nothing could stop her.

They tried. Raider after raider, but she was always one beat ahead. A shift of Threads, a warning of what was to come.

A raider came at her from the left. A Red Sail, and with the now-familiar lines of the slow-Cleaved across his face. He had two cutlasses, his movements were graceful. At another time, Safi would worry that she'd met her match. But what good was steel against her Truth-blade? What did his grace matter when she was as fast as a hundred souls bound in Aether? He swung his blades, two arcs aimed inward for her neck.

All she had to do was swipe, duck, and there went his cutlasses, cleft in two. He was startled, as every other fighter had been before him, and in that moment, she swung across his abdomen.

Blood sprayed hot against her. It landed on ice . . .

Ice, she realized, that was moving. Retreating uphill, as if summoned. She had no time to study it before light erupted and sizzling heat smashed a wall behind her. Then Safi sensed a Stormwitch's Threads, yellow, sharp, focused, and coming this way.

Safi dove sideways, barely escaping three more lances of lightning. One sliced against the back of her head. She felt the heat of her own blood rise.

A smell like metal burning overwhelmed her—as did the scent of her hair on fire.

She'd never faced a Stormwitch before—never even seen one except from a distance at the Weatherwitch Guild in Veñaza City. *Steel*, she thought, *is not going to help me here*. No matter how sharp her blade, it would only be a liability now.

Safi leaped for a narrow side street. Here the ground was so dry, it was almost desert. No frost to slip on, no soggy moss like Merik's forest. Just dry, dead earth . . . Which was wrong. She thought back to the ice moving on the avenue. Could that be where all the moisture was going?

The Stormwitch stalked into the alley behind her, wearing a uniform Safi didn't know—black with a red moon. It was terrifying, as was the woman now lifting her hands. Safi barely careened out of the alley before two more bolts cracked out.

A new cacophony met her on the street beyond. So many people on the move. Threads spun and slashed, disorienting her until she had no idea where she was in the city.

Then came more lightning. Safi barely dropped before it sliced across her head. She smelled metal again and more burning hair. The lightning hit a Baedyed man. He screamed as his whole body shivered and burned. Safi scrabbled sideways before the next attack came—and ran right into a familiar square of troops wearing familiar uniforms.

How they were here, she didn't know—but she would use them.

"HELL-BARDS!" Safi shot up as tall as she could, thrusting her blade toward the sky. "TO ME!"

The Threads around her shifted with surprise, awareness, purpose, as the Hell-Bards who spotted Safi realized who she was—and realized what they must do: protect the Empress.

There were other soldiers with them. Cartorrans from the army, the navy, personal guards. They too heard her cry and swarmed. So now, as lightning smoked and sizzled through the dawn, it did not reach Safi. The lightning found other targets to incinerate from the inside out. The stench of burning hair, cooking flesh—none of it was her own.

Safi ran on. She had to. She *had* to finish this journey. She *had* to reach Iseult before it was too late. Her heart could break for Cartorran lives lost later. For now, there was only chasing in the same direction as the ice that snaked across the cobblestones.

Four Hell-Bards sank into position around her, moving instinctively into a square. She didn't know these guardians, but her mind turned them into familiar faces. Caden, Zander, Lev. She wished it was them; she knew it was not.

She and her Hell-Bards reached a new avenue. Trees stretched wide, branches dipping down to the cobbles, and all around them, wooden spikes had been stabbed into the ground. There would be no getting across this intersection. No aiming directly for the Well from here. "That way." Safi skewed right, and her Hell-Bards skewed with her. In the distance, she heard pistols fire. She heard flames roar. And lightning—still there was that pop and crack of a Stormwitch hunting.

Do not stop, the Cahr Awen screamed inside of her. *Do not slow.*

New sounds erupted. Firepots, she thought, exploding nearby. She felt the heat of them, but they were not so close as to slow her or the Hell-Bards.

Until one of them did get hit. A flash of light, a cry of pain, then the Hell-Bard on Safi's right fell. Smoke plumed.

Still, Safi didn't slow; nor did the other Hell-Bards. They were on a road cleared of stakes. The ice, though—it was here and retreating, as if the earth itself were being sapped dry.

Safi couldn't guess why, but it felt important. It felt like she needed to keep following it.

She pointed, and her three-sided Hell-Bard shield launched up a hill. They crested it in moments. Threads gathered behind. Many, *many* Threads all chasing this way. *Please,* she prayed, *don't lead me wrong, ice.*

She sprinted onto a crumbling road, but rather than find the Well, she found only an empty pond bed filled with bodies and surrounded by the remains of a house. *Only three walls,* she thought, gaping at it. *Just as I have only three.*

Safi searched for a new road, a new escape, but there was nothing. Only people, Threads, raiders with weapons and witches with magic. She saw fire, rock, ice, and wave.

This was a dead end.

She and her Hell-Bards tried to double back, but were met with more of the same. The ice had tricked Safi. The Cahr Awen souls inside her had been wrong. Now these three Hell-Bards, whose faces she'd never seen and never *would* see behind their helms, would die. As would Safi.

Lightning arrived. A giant explosion that hit the Hell-Bard on Safi's left. Their armor and helm roasted them in seconds. The remaining two, their weapons drawn, sank low and prepared for the same. They would fight until they couldn't, to protect the Empress who had once been noosed like them.

"No," Safi tried to say. "We'll surrender. We'll surrender." She lifted her arms to show her guards how.

But it was too late. A spear made of stone shot through the Hell-Bard at her front. A blade of ice sliced into the one behind. Then there was no one standing, except for Safi.

She had only moments. These people were here to kill her. They would never let her reach Iseult. Their Threads throbbed with shared bloodlust.

The lightning soared out. It hit Safi. First, she locked up as tall and as strong as her body could ever be. A magnified, all-powerful version of the Witch, the Empress, the Sun, and Birth.

Then she burned and burned and burned.

Merik wished he could say this was his first chaotic reunion with someone important. He wished he could meet the people he loved in *easy* conditions that afforded time for conversation. Instead, here he was, one of tens of people being tended by healer witches inside a sagging tent. Painstones pulsed, filling the space with pink light as Merik was literally dragged on a litter toward a mat at the back. He heard the sounds of war outside, but he couldn't see any of it.

The person dragging his litter dropped it. "Noden save me." Evrane half leaped, half fell to his side. "You were dead, Merik. You had no pulse. Your bones were shattered, there was water in your lungs. Yet here you are, waking up."

"Well," he ground out from a throat that didn't work, "you must have been expecting I'd wake up, if you brought me here."

She didn't respond. Her dark, dark Nihar eyes were wide with horror, forcing Merik to look away. Every shame he'd ever carried from childhood was suddenly churning to the surface, as if the Hagfish in his mouth had sucked it up for examination in the light. And this was the greatest shame he could imagine: being a mostly Cleaved man who clung to life through a Threadbrother trapped in the ice.

There was no dignity in that. No Nubrevnan strength.

He tried to push upright. His muscles resisted. Or maybe that was his spinal column, finally giving way after too many deaths.

"Not so fast." Evrane gripped Merik with strong, ungloved hands. They were winter-reddened and flaking from cold. And ah, there it was: the familiar chant of her magic to weft through Merik's body.

The sensation of being a boy again ballooned hotter. "You can't help me," he told her, as he tried to push her away.

She gripped him harder.

"You were dead," Evrane repeated, and this time, she closed her eyes. Her grip was strong as the Hagfishes had been: "You had no pulse. Your bones were shattered, there was water in your lungs. But . . ." Again, her magic chanted through him. "My witchery reaches you, and that means—no matter what strangeness I feel on your blood—there is still life left inside you."

Hye, Merik wanted to say, although suddenly he couldn't speak. Evrane's magic coursed through him, sparkling and real. He was still a boy, but not a cowering one any longer. Not a shamed one. This was the crash of the Jadansi on the Nihar shore. This was the river beside the Origin Well, still clean when all the rest of the land was dead. This was all the between moments when he hadn't been looking and his aunt had quietly loved him simply by being there when no one else in his family had been.

Merik wanted to say something. He wanted to *do* something. But this was the problem with rushed reunions in the middle of a collapsing world. Cannons blasted outside. Horns bayed in the distance like wolves on the hunt. Soldiers—many limp and losing blood—were being rushed into the tent.

Merik couldn't stay here; whatever he might want to say or share with Evrane, now could not be the time.

"Who fights outside?" He drew in his legs to stand, and Evrane finally released his arms. "When I fell into the river, there was no battle."

"And the battle was only just beginning when I retrieved you. I am here with Cartorran soldiers and Hell-Bards—although the Raider King had anticipated us."

"How many of you?"

"Not enough. Only twelve thousand."

And Ragnor has at least double that, Merik thought. But there was no need to say it aloud. Evrane must know, just as she must know that Ragnor had the better position defending behind his walls.

"The Cahr Awen forced your hand, didn't they." It was an observation, not a question. "They left too soon, so you had to leave too."

Evrane's dark brows jumped. "How did you know that? Have you seen them?"

Merik nodded, and in quick, crude strokes he explained how he'd found Safi—but not Iseult. How he had a small encampment in the woods called

Last Holdout. And as he spoke, he saw Evrane's face lose color. She spoke, rasping and almost inaudible in the rising tumult of the tent. "Your people, your Last Holdout—it is gone. The entire forest is consumed by seafire. No one could have survived that attack. Merik, wait!"

Merik didn't wait. At the word *seafire*, he'd shot to his feet. And although Evrane shouted after him, he had no capacity to hear her. She had her battle, and he had his. She had her cause, and he had his. All his life, she'd put the Cahr Awen and her vows above all else. Merik had resented it as a boy; he understood it now.

But he couldn't do the same.

He reached the world beyond and found a battle raging. With flames, with ice, with arrows to batter into shields. Siege engines mired in earth too soft for them, loosing iron shot after iron shot at a city that had been quiet for decades.

And to the east, Merik found the forest exactly as Evrane had described it: the same thick, clotting seafire that had been his first death months ago now devoured the haven he'd built for lost souls.

Did I do this? he wondered, as the magnitude of what happened bowled over him. *Did I do this by entering Poznin and catching the Raider King's eye?*

The answer didn't matter. Not right now, for Merik's course of action wouldn't change. He had people who needed him, and if any might still live inside those flames, then he would be the one to find them.

After all, he could not die like normal men.

Merik heard Evrane shrieking, begging for him to wait as he kicked into a run. As his winds slung closer, taking strength from the healing magic that still glittered in his veins.

Once his fight was over, he would rejoin Evrane. Then, he too would fight for the Cahr Awen against the Raider King. But not before Merik saved his own people. Not before he was the king they needed him to be.

FIFTY

✳

Never had Stix focused so much energy into such a confined space, never had she had to stay so perfectly concentrated, perfectly connected to the magic coursing through her. If her attention lapsed, if she lost even a droplet of the water she'd fought to find, then it was a long, *long* way down for her and the people of Last Holdout.

So much ice inside this mountain, yet so little that she could touch—because Sirmaya wasn't willing to let it go.

Beside her, Owl did the same with whatever earth and rock she could claw from Sirmaya's grasp. They both stood, feet planted, stances low, and arms outstretched for balance, upon a sheet of ice thin as paper, beneath which was a sheet of even thinner stone. Inch by cautious inch, they stepped across the gaping abyss that filled this cavern. But like walking on a frozen river, one false move and the ice and stone beneath them would give way.

It didn't help that Sirmaya wanted the magic inside Stix, inside Owl, inside all the people, huddling close and following. *Come, come, the ice will hold you.* It stretched and spanned in feathery tendrils all over the massive cavern of Paladins' Hall. Easy to tell apart from Stix's ice because it glowed, it throbbed, it whispered with black shadows. Yet for some reason, as hungry as it was, *that* ice made no move.

It was as if something had happened that had chained it in place; now it could do nothing but watch and salivate while food sauntered by.

"Thicker," Owl cried in her child's voice. "You *must* make the ice thicker!"

What about you? Stix wanted to snarl, but she dared not speak. Dared not lose focus. If she did not cross this gap, then she would not reach the door into Lovats. And if she did not reach the under-city, then all of these people would die.

And, if Stix was wholly honest with herself, there was another reason she wanted to go to Lovats.

At that thought—at Vivia's face forming in Stix's mind—two droplets broke free from the ice, followed by a great *crack!* across the surface. *Shit, shit.* Stix crouched lower in her stance. Anything to keep balance, anything to keep her weight even and the ice intact. They were only halfway across the cavern.

"Wait," Stix croaked, as she realized the path she was trying to forge veered away from Owl's. "Where are you going?"

"You need that water." Owl pointed to a gush of liquid that poured out from the doorway into Poznin—the doorway Stix and Kahina had used to reach the Raider King's armies. Most of the water pouring out of it had frozen like a river in winter, but there was still a narrow current slithering down, pooling over a lip of stone, then dropping into eternity.

"I can reach the Nubrevnan door without that water."

"No" was all Owl replied, and there was little Stix could do to argue. She needed the reinforcement, weak though it might be, of Owl's stone. Otherwise, she and these hundreds of terrified people would never cross the abyss.

No regrets, keep moving, she thought, invoking Vivia's words. Stix couldn't second-guess. She just had to keep moving. And if, when she reached that waterfall, she didn't like what Owl said or where Owl tried to go . . . well, then that water would be the advantage she needed.

Stix did not breathe. Every fiber inside her body was alight. *One more inch of platform. One more inch of platform. Not too far now. Another inch of platform.* Voices murmured or sobbed or whimpered. Stix ignored them, just as Baile had ignored the people in the under-city. Not because she didn't want to help them, but because the only way she could was by powering forward.

At least Stix didn't have a ring-bond breaking her from the inside out as Lady Baile had.

That thought made Stix think of Kahina . . . and *that* thought made her stomach kink. A thousand years ago, Rhian had been Baile's dearest friend. A mentor in much the way Kahina had become for Stix.

You will find her. Once you know these people are safe, you will find her, and together, you will finally deal with the Rook King.

Soon, the weak waterfall vibrated against Stix's magic, and like a harpoon launched at a shark, Stix aimed all of her magic at it. Her witchery lanced deep, deep into the heart of the liquid, freezing it instantly. Ice exploded outward. Thousands of crystals to fly and assemble until suddenly their flimsy bridge became an avenue. As strong as the bridge crossing the river into Poznin and covered in just as many people.

As Stix worked, reinforcing all she'd built, spirit swifts whorled upward from the chasm. They reminded Stix of the swallows that nested beneath the Water-Bridges of Stefin-Eckart. And when the Aether-bound creatures swept against her, an exultant song trilled into her skull. *Good Paladin, strong Paladin.*

Stix finished her bridge and hurried onto the stone platform where the doorway into Poznin awaited. The water, sourced from that city, was nothing more than a trickle now, as if Stix had drained the city dry. Beside her, Owl crouched on her knees and quivered. But there was no emotion on her face. None of the grinning, gulping triumph that Stix felt.

"We still have far to go," Owl said, pointing across the chasm at the door that would actually take them into the under-city of Lovats. "And we're running out of time."

"Hye," Stix agreed. Now that she had access to so much water—water that was not the goddess's—she could get everyone to safety much more quickly. She lifted her arms, then cast them forward in a punch of strength and power. Her witchery crunched out a second bridge to span the cavern.

"This way," Owl shouted in her small voice. "This way."

At first, Stix assumed the child was addressing all the people of Last Holdout, who hewed close to the icy center of the bridges while galaxies seemed to dance beneath them and blackened ice watched hungrily.

But then Stix saw that Owl waved her arms. That she had gathered rock beneath her and had vaulted herself up, high as Stix. Then higher. "This way! This way!" And it was then that Stix saw to whom Owl shouted: new people thronged into the mountain from a different doorway.

Stix knew them. Of course she knew them, smeared though they were without her spectacles, she *knew* the Carawen monks in their distinctive white cloaks and hoods.

Lady Baile had known them too, but they had been soldiers in an army for the Rook King a thousand years ago, back when the Monastery had been nothing more than a fortress atop a mountain.

"What," Stix snarled at Owl, "have you done?"

Baile stands surrounded on all sides by thick forest and white-capped peaks. Snow falls, and nearby, a river churns, its dark waters spanning a stone bridge. Elias, the Rook King, strides toward her.

He has found her. Here, where she and Bastien tried to flee into the Ohrin Mountains.

Elias points beside Baile, and she tries to turn her head . . . but she can only slide her eyes sideways to where a woman lies on her back, a broken blade thrust through her belly. Silver pools around her, glowing with power. Magic entwined in her very blood, and where the raw magic moves, rifts gouge into the rock.

Two paces away, on his knees and crying, is Bastien. He looks at Baile. "I am sorry."

It is all right, Baile wants to say, for it is not his fault he couldn't save her from the Exalted Ones. Yet no words come; she can't part her lips to speak.

Bastien doesn't turn when the Rook King arrives. He doesn't turn when the king calls out, "Is your fury quenched? Is your wrath complete?" Nor does Bastien turn when Elias yanks the shattered sword from the Exalted One's gut.

Only when the king comes to a stop before him does the man finally twist his head. "I will find you," the scarred man rasps. "In the next life, I will—"

The king slices off his head. Bastien's words break off. Blood sprays, mixing with the silver.

Then the Rook King fixes his gaze on Baile, and she realizes that he holds a different sword. It is not the blade to kill Paladins—although that is clutched in one hand. Instead, it is a simple soldier's sword, now bloodied with Bastien's life. "It will all be over soon," Elias tells Baile before his blade arcs out and crashes against her neck.

Only as the sword cracks against stone does she realize why she has been locked in place. Only when it cuts through the rock—three swings it takes him—does she realize she was encased in granite. Saria's granite.

It was not only the Rook King who betrayed the Six. It was his Heart-Thread too.

Blade bites flesh. Baile dies.

"What have you done?" Stix's magic snapped off, her bridge unfinished toward the under-city. She would destroy it and her first bridge if she had to. "What have you *done*, Owl? You said we were going to help people, and now you betray me? I remember, Saria. I *remember* what you did a thousand years ago."

"I do not think you do." Owl blinked like a real bird from atop her stone perch. Her silvery hair shone almost blue in all this ice.

"You helped Elias and turned on Bastien and me."

"No." Owl's face scrunched into a sneer. It added years and lines to her skin. "You know the words of the Lament: *six turned on six, and one turned on five.* But it wasn't Elias who betrayed you, and it wasn't me. In Elias's strange, frustrating way, I think he was trying to fix what went wrong—and he is still trying to fix it to this day. One reincarnation after another, focused on the same problem year after year."

"But those soldiers are *his*." Stix flung a pointed finger at the monks. "Just as the Cahr Awen is *his*. And now you have brought them here." As Stix watched, more monks poured through the distant doorway. Two by two, they filled the mountain like white termites. "I trusted you." Stix lifted her other hand, ready to dismantle her first bridge. Burst the ice into instant steam and plummet the monks into darkness.

She would *not* let the Rook King's soldiers enter Poznin.

Owl moved, fast as an avalanche. Two stone shackles that latched on to Stix's arms while the girl herself sprang down from her stone column. "Your queen needs you." Owl's eyes glowed a pure, pure brown—and they pulsed too, as if bound to the heart of Sirmaya. "And her people need you. I have not betrayed you because I am *not* him."

"You encased Lady Baile in granite a thousand years ago."

"To protect her! I failed, though. Elias killed me too. He killed Saria, his own Heart-Thread, with a plain, unmagicked blade just as he killed Baile. *You*. So believe me: whatever it was he had planned that day and whatever it is he plans now, I have no part in it."

At those words, Owl aimed a small arm at the first bridge. The monks were approaching fast, vague features taking shape. One, however, was at the lead, sprinting far faster than any other monk behind him.

"Stix, you are needed in Nubrevna," Owl continued, "because everything is about to change, and *that* is where you belong. Both of us will need to be ready for when the past returns to life, so don't let the same fury that blinded Bastien blind you."

Yes, the spirit swifts seemed to chime. They flapped upward, dazzling colors and light into Stix's weak eyes. *Listen to the Earth Paladin. Poznin is not your home; the king here is not the one you must lift up and serve.*

"We are on the same side." Owl lifted her tiny chin. "The Rook King Elias played me too, a thousand years ago. But now the Queen of Foxes needs you. All of Nubrevna needs you, so get these people into the under-city and I will join you there."

FIFTY-ONE

✳

The Truthwitch wasn't dead when Aeduan reached her. She should have been, but she was not. Perhaps the Cahr Awen souls protected her, perhaps there was some other magic at work. But the light-bringer was not dead when Aeduan fell to her side.

Carawen monks flowed around Aeduan, charging from a magicked doorway Owl had led them to. While Aeduan and Lizl had sprinted across a bridge of ice and stone—ice that had not retreated from Aeduan's path—he'd seen the *other* ice throttled at the edges of his vision. Panting and shimmering. *No,* he'd thought at it. *No, don't move. Please, leave me be.*

And it had. Somehow, that awful sentient ice left him alone, so the journey progressed steadily. True.

At least until Aeduan felt Iseult die.

It was like a hundred arrows cutting him all at once. Like the flames of his childhood burning anew. Her Threads snipped, and the sudden absence of her—the abrupt *severing* of their connection—carved out all of Aeduan's insides. It squeezed, it wrung, it ripped while the six old wounds . . .

They punched outward with fire. Literal flames that he would have sworn he could see smoking, just like the arrows that had once razed through his mother into him.

"What is it?" Lizl asked, seizing Aeduan before he could topple off their paper-thin bridge into star-swept nothing. "What's happening?"

Aeduan couldn't answer. He had no voice, he had no words; he had only smoke inside his lungs. And for a brief flicker of a breath, he had power too, gathering inside him like a starving storm. As if the six wounds had decided not to kill him, but to reinforce him. Forge his muscles and bones in flame.

"The Cahr Awen," he rasped, locking eyes with Lizl. Her blood had always smelled of speed and daisy chains, of a mother's kisses and sharpened steel. Right now, Aeduan could sense none of it. "They need us now. We have to move."

"Yes," she said. And when Aeduan resumed his run, Lizl followed. He was the first monk to enter Poznin; she came mere paces behind.

The air reeked of rot and smoke, and a dry pond bed slanted upward. Long-dead bodies littered the ground, bone-dry, while cattails, pond scum, and snail shells rattled in the wind.

Blood scents crashed over Aeduan, witches and raiders and soldiers. Then he smelled the Truthwitch, right there—*right there* at the top of the hill where a body lay smoking into the awful dawn.

Aeduan ran to her, while behind him Lizl burst from the mountain. *"FOR THE CAHR AWEN!"* she screamed, and at those words, the opal in Aeduan's earlobe pulsed. Just as it had when Leopold had used it to summon the monks beside the Aether Well.

More monks toppled from the mountain. More monks shouted for the Cahr Awen and charged into battle.

And Aeduan's heart surged. Illogically, a buoyancy coursed through him. A vibrating certainty that, even if he danced to Leopold's command, this *was* the right course. The Cahr Awen needed him. Iseult needed him.

Without knowing he did it, Aeduan joined his fellow monks in a roaring cry:

I guard the light-bringer and protect the dark-giver.
I live for the world-starter and die for the shadow-ender.

Steel flashed around Aeduan. White cloaks flipped and streaked as hundreds of Carawen monks, trained for this moment, fought in a battle they'd thought was months away. Many, like Aeduan, had never been true believers; they'd simply followed where the money went. But now—now they could not deny. They *would* not deny, and their certainty lent Aeduan even more strength.

He reached Safi. She had been hit by something all-consuming that had scorched parts of her hair and her skin. Her eyes were closed, but she still breathed—and the meadows filled with dandelions still beat inside her. At her side was a sword, sharp and silvery. Untouched, somehow, by the ash and blood that filled every other inch of this city.

It pointed at Safi like an arrow. Like the Sleeping Giant aiming north.

Aeduan sank to the ruined earth beside Safi. Her blood still pumped, still flowed—even if her heart was badly weakened—so Aeduan could command her. *If you have to take control of me and walk me like a puppet to that Well, then I expect you to do so.*

Aeduan didn't want to, but he would. He would claim *her* Aether. He would guide *her* blade.

Iseult had once described to him how it felt when she controlled Threads. It had been a confession, and he'd seen in her a need for absolution. *You have controlled people against their will. Please tell me it is all right.* But it was not all right; it had never been all right. Aeduan had told himself he needed to control others because he placed the cause—his father's cause—above all else.

It had been easier that way than to reckon with what he was. With the demon and the monster inside him. With the dog named Boots whom he'd killed all those years ago.

This was the first time, though, that someone had actually told Aeduan, *Yes, it is all right if you control me,* and there was power in that. A trust he'd never deserved.

Bloodwitches cannot do this, the fon Grieg son had said. *They cannot control people like this, freezing them. Killing them.*

I assure you, Aeduan had replied. *I am a Bloodwitch.* And he was—one with a cause that he'd chosen and that he embraced fully in this moment wrapped in death.

Aeduan latched on to each layer of Safi's blood. On to the dandelions and the meadows and truth hidden beneath snow. "Move," he commanded in a voice too low to cut through the battle. "Rise."

Safi's eyes opened. She was confused, but she obeyed. Her muscles switched on. Her heart pumped stronger. And with Aeduan's hands behind her, gripping her at the armpits, she stood. One endless second stretched past. Two more. Then Aeduan was able to release her. To step back, snatch her clean, true blade off the ground.

"Yes," she rasped as Aeduan offered it to her. And as more Bloodwitchery coursed into her so she could grip it. So she could sheathe it in leather blackened by heat. "Yes."

It was all the acknowledgment Aeduan needed to continue on, toward Iseult. Toward the Air Well.

I guard the light-bringer, the monks bellowed over the hammering clash of metal and flesh, *and protect the dark-giver. I live for the world-starter and die for the shadow-ender.*

Lightning singed. Aeduan ignored it. He was two bodies now, his own blood so closely bound to Safi's that he could feel all the Cahr Awen souls inside her. They had no blood, so his magic could not control them—but they were fireflies in the forest. The ones he'd wished upon months ago, hoping that someone might one day want him to stay.

Now it wasn't only Iseult who'd answered his wish, it was her Threadsister too. She needed Aeduan; she *needed* the magic that had cursed him his entire life.

My blood, I offer freely. My Threads, I offer wholly.

My eternal soul belongs to no one else.

Safi grew stronger as Aeduan's magic wove deeper into her blood. Her heart pumped with the same rhythm as his—a rhythm to match the booming vow of the Carawens.

Claim my Aether. Guide my blade. From now until the end.

In a tucked-away corner of his mind, Aeduan knew this could not last forever. He felt his old wounds throbbing. He felt them bleeding inside his clothes. But for now, he was standing. He and the light-bringer were walking, then *running*, and whatever flames decided to erupt again . . .

They would be a problem for later.

"She . . . is . . . not dead," Safi wheezed. Aeduan had one hand clasped tight over her right forearm, and she in turn clutched his left. Their hearts still beat as one. "Iseult . . . can still be saved."

Aeduan did not respond to this. Raiders had seen they were escaping—aiming uphill toward the Well—and their blades flashed as they redirected their attacks. Aeduan drew his own sword. Safi drew hers, and by the time the raiders reached them, it was not merely their hearts that moved as one, but their entire bodies.

They parried, they blocked, they spun. They carved and cut in unison.

Aeduan's opal warmed in his ear, and vaguely, he realized that he and the Truthwitch were not the only ones moving in synchrony. All the monks—*all* of them—were swinging and dipping, kicking, pummeling, and thrusting with exactly the same rhythm as Aeduan.

Which was exactly the same rhythm as Safi.

She is controlling us all, he thought, and he recalled what Leopold had said about making these stones centuries ago. Clearly they were more than simple opals meant to summon aid; Aeduan was no longer the puppet master, but rather the puppet controlled by the Cahr Awen.

I guard the light-bringer. Safi stabbed. The Carawens stabbed.

And protect the dark-giver. Safi deflected. The Carawens deflected.

I live for the world-starter. They all slashed.

And die for the shadow-ender. They all swept.

My blood, I offer freely. My Threads, I offer wholly. They all scooped low and drove blades into abdomens and elbows.

My eternal soul belongs to no one else. They all hook-kicked jaws and knees.

Claim my Aether. Guide my blade. A final slice through the neck.

From now until the end. Heads rolled from bodies.

It was carnage, and the raiders and Purists and black-uniformed soldiers who'd sworn fealty to Aeduan's father, the witches and Nomatsis and lost, cast-out souls—they could not stand against this onslaught.

Many fled, while those who did not tasted Carawen steel and saw flashing opals before they died.

FIFTY-TWO

✳

Iseult felt it when the lightning struck Safi. But just as Safi's Threads kept Iseult from fading into death, now it was Aeduan's Threads that kept Safi moored.

Iseult felt him through her bond with Safi. She *felt* his magic pushing through her Threadsister's veins. And when Safi's strength grew, regained, swelled, Iseult grew stronger too. More tangible, more *real*. Her steps through the Dreaming felt sure, and she knew as she stared down at her bloodied body and lips that had turned blue, that she could crawl back inside. That she had enough life, for now, to return her body into being.

It wouldn't last long. Not without a way to heal that hole in her abdomen, the muscles and organs past repair.

Iseult crouched beside her body, ready to slide down into it and haul herself inch by ruptured inch toward the Origin Well. Its waters might be dead, unable to heal or help or finish the building process that the Threads in that broken glass had begun, but it needed only the Cahr Awen to restore it. Iseult was one half; maybe her shadows and darkness could offer something for the Well, even if the Well could do nothing for her in return.

But that was when three things happened, spread apart like heartbeats. First: Leopold finally saw his moment and struck. His rapier cut into Ragnor's face, directly into an eyeball, and though it was sloppy and desperate, it was also deadly.

Second: the Raider King fell, his Threads so blue, so bereft, so despairing. And he murmured a single word into the rising dawn.

Ignite.

It gusted across the Well and snow and dawn. It resonated against Iseult's Dreaming ears, then it kept going. Out past the hill and down the avenue into Poznin, where it reached its mark. Firepots sparked to life beside barrels of seafire.

And the third thing happened: Iseult's soul returned to her body.

There was no way forward. Every alley, every avenue was filled with shadowy flame. The heat was incredible, and the speed—the *speed* at which the city burned. Safi had never seen anything like it. When she'd been on the Empress of Marstok's ship, it had also happened quickly. A single eruption, and only Vaness's magic to protect her and Safi both.

But now, it was *hundreds* of such explosions. More seafire than Safi had known could consume the earth. And because of it, she and Aeduan were losing ground. Moving *away* from the Well instead of toward it.

Threads blurred with the seafire. Too many colors to track or comprehend. Too much smoke. Too much death. Safi wanted Iseult's magic to go away now; she wanted the Cahr Awen to stop too, with their screaming and jostling: *So close! Do not stop!*

I'm not, she wanted to scream back. *Knifey won't let me!* And it was true. Although Aeduan no longer applied the harsh, almost chain-like control he'd used when he'd first revived Safi, he kept her moving. Kept her focused, like a hand on unsteady terrain.

Never would Safi have imagined that she and the Bloodwitch who'd first hunted her—first *prompted* her to flee Veñaza City—would be so tightly bound. She still didn't like him very much, but at least she had no doubt where his loyalty lay.

He was a Carawen monk. He was her Threadsister's Heart-Thread. And he was the Knife, a card that added strength to any taro hand—or took it away as needed.

The other Carawens still fought around Safi and Aeduan, warding off raiders who dared come this way. The biggest enemy now was the unstoppable flames.

As Safi and Aeduan wheeled onto another street, a sight lifted before them: the Cleaved. Tens of them stacked in frayed rows with Threads black and wriggling.

"Stop," Safi said, and Aeduan obeyed. His witchery slowed her heart, his hand gripped her tightly, reining her in. And she realized with razored frustration that she was not actually moving as much on her own as she'd believed. That really, only Aeduan's power and momentum had carried her this far.

The lightning had cooked her organs and baked her bones.

"This is useless," she said. "I have no idea where we are or how to get—"

"I can get you through!" A small figure hopped up beside Safi. She wore Baedyed garb with a headscarf pulled low. Her face was streaked with black. "I can get you to the Well. That's what you want, right? That's what the other one told me. Your friend."

Safi had no idea who this girl was or where she'd come from. One moment, Safi was next to a smoke-shrouded Cleaved; the next she was staring at this girl.

"You've seen Iseult?" Safi asked.

"Before all this, yeah." The girl waved at the smoke choking the sky. "She said you'd need to get to the Well, and I know a way to get you there. She gave me a map, and I know where they put the seafire barrels. There's one place they didn't reach. But getting there will be . . . hot."

"You're from Last Holdout." Safi recognized the girl now, even if they'd never spoken. "Sky?"

The girl nodded, and Safi looked at Aeduan. "She's telling the truth."

"S'more raiders coming, though," the girl continued. "They'll follow us to the Well."

"No," Aeduan said flatly. "They won't." Then he turned and shouted, "Lizl!" A monk, strong and swaggering, appeared from the clot of white cloaks and focused Threads. She had blood streaked across her cloak and authority in her bearing.

"It's Abbot Thewan to you," she barked, and to Safi's shock, humor warmed the woman's Threads. As if the world around her weren't collapsing. As if she and Aeduan had just met on the street, and oh, what a coincidence to see you here!

It wasn't at all what Safi had expected when she'd heard Eron and Evrane mention the Carawens' new abbot. In fact, Safi would bet she and Lizl would get along swimmingly if they were anywhere *but* here. Yet now, that woman was going to blockade the road, and in all likelihood, she would die. One more person on Safi's conscience. One more sacrifice to heal the final Well.

Aeduan lowered his fire-flap to murmur something Safi couldn't hear. Then that was it. The woman reached for the opal at her ear, bowed low at Safi, and shouted, "We hold this line!"

No, Safi wanted to say. *Don't do that.* But Aeduan came to her elbow, his magic cranked into her, and his witchery once more claimed control. "Go," he ordered Safi. Then again to Sky: "Go."

The young woman *went.* Fast as a rat in the sewers, she set off, and Safi and Aeduan chased after her. Around the Cleaved and into alleys, all while the seafire burned.

"Through here!" Sky shoved into a building where the door had long since rotted off the hinges and the windows had collapsed into holes. "There's a door in the back!" She vaulted easily over broken floorboards and collapsed walls, familiar with the space even as smoke rolled across it.

Safi's eyes streamed tears. She could hardly see, and she certainly couldn't breathe. But Aeduan had her, and the Bloodwitch didn't let go. So onward, they followed Sky.

Until smoke erupted. A volcano of heat so thick it knocked Safi into a nearby wall. Then the seafire itself clawed into the building. Aeduan towed her back the way they'd come, but the seafire easily followed. Nothing in its path was an obstacle; everything it touched became fuel.

They toppled onto the street. Sky was gone. Safi saw no sign of her scrappy figure or Threads, and now this building and all the buildings near it burned.

Safi clutched at her hair. Half of it seemed to be missing. Half of her sleeping gown too. This couldn't be the end, though. This couldn't be all that was left for her and Aeduan.

He slid in front of her, and gently, he lowered her hands from her hair. Gently, he gripped her biceps. His blue, blue eyes bored into her. "Do you trust me, Truthwitch?"

"Yes," she replied without hesitation. *True, true, true.* "I trust you, Bloodwitch."

"Then brace yourself, for you are about to feel great pain."

FIFTY-THREE

✳

H old on," Leopold said, his arms wrapped around Iseult's bloodied thorax. "Please, hold on."

I hope he means figuratively, Iseult thought, *because literally is impossible.* But of course he meant figuratively, for although Iseult had managed to crawl her spirit back into its body, she hadn't moved far since. The heat of the seafire bore down. She felt it through the trees around the Well, and she felt it over her bond with Safi.

How had everything changed so quickly? Iseult had been quietly planning inside the Raider King's tent, savoring her pause and logic, and now the whole of the Witchlands was aflame. *How very Safi,* she thought, *for a plan to go horribly wrong.* She wanted to laugh at that. She wanted to share it with Leopold and watch him chuckle too—then have Safi show up and crow, *Goat tits, Iz, you're supposed to be the clever one.*

Instead, Iseult would be lucky if she did not die and float once more into the Dreaming.

Leopold lifted her. It should hurt, but Iseult was too detached to feel anything. His words, *Hold on, please, hold on,* echoed as if they were in a cavern. She sensed as the heretic's collar fell from her neck—a weight releasing. A gust of hot, hot air.

Goat tits, Iz, when you told Sky you found a route to reach the Well, I assumed you meant a tunnel or something. Not a city consumed by seafire.

I know, Safi, but it's not really my fault the city ignited. Plus, I doubt you actually talked to Sky, and this conversation we're having isn't real.

Oh, but I did meet Sky. And who needs Threadstones with our magics connected?

Iseult's bones rattled. Blood spurted, although there wasn't much left to keep spurting. Leopold was walking her toward the ice-crusted shore of the Well. "It's dead," Iseult wanted to inform him. But of course the words wouldn't come.

And of course, he knew it, anyway. After all, he'd been trying to get

Safi and Iseult to travel here all along. His schemes, his armies, his maps and drawings and *insistence* that Iseult and Safi listen to him . . . Well, he'd been right, hadn't he? They'd done it their way and they'd failed.

"Drop her." A voice cut across the Well, command honing it razor-sharp. Threads of pure, pure flame. *Admiral Kahina.* Of course she would come here. Of course she would be able to cross through the seafire advancing on all sides. "I don't want to kill that girl, Rook King. She and the other one have done nothing wrong. So if you drop her, I won't hurt her. Otherwise . . . well, she is a weak shield against my Paladin flames."

"I was wondering when you would arrive." A falseness scuttled over Leopold's voice. But he did as Kahina ordered and gingerly lowered Iseult to the earth. She was at the Well's edge, and cold, cold snow soaked against her.

She could see across the Well from here—and see Kahina as the woman wrapped her body in flames. The fire flickered and licked, transforming from a desaturated gray to vivid orange. Because this was real fire. *This* was the fire of the Moon Mother, not an alchemical cruelty built by humans.

Kahina attacked. Leopold vaulted, and a new fight began. One that Iseult could not follow, even if she'd wanted to. Her eyes drifted shut. She let her magic observe instead. The Fire Threads burning like a flame hawk; the Aether Threads sparkling like spirit swifts. Two Paladin souls who, despite their stark differences, were evenly matched.

Almost evenly matched. Kahina had one edge that Leopold did not: a thousand years of simmering rage. Where Leopold's Threads were defined by a lost, lonely core, Kahina's were defined by vengeance and a certainty that the entire Witchlands had been wronged by this Paladin right here.

In the end, Ragnor had only been a man when he'd faced the Rook King. A brilliant, perhaps once-kind man, but still only skin, muscle, blood, and bone. Kahina, however, was raw power, and Iseult didn't think Leopold would survive this fight.

But she could do nothing to help him. She could not cleave, she could not move. She was an amalgamation of her Threads and Safi's Threads and whatever had been held inside those broken tools gathered by Ragnor.

Sever, sever, twist and sever.

At those words, Iseult thought of Esme. She thought of the white weasel who'd died here and all the Cleaved now caught in the seafire to burn. Innocents who'd never deserved what came for them. Hundreds of bodies with Severed Threads and no Puppeteer to free them. Unless . . .

Unless.

The Well was *right* there. Dead, yes, but perhaps Iseult was looking at it wrong. Perhaps she was asking its dead waters for the wrong thing. After all, it had been a Loom once; all those warping, wefting Threads might still be in there, waiting to be used again.

Iseult opened her eyes and dug deep inside herself. First she found a drop of strength in her muscles. Then she found a trickle. Then she had enough current—from Safi's Threads, from the Threads of a broken blade and glass—to finally lift a single arm. It was so, *so* slow mountains could have grown before she moved an inch.

But she did move. And she did dig her fingers into the earth. And she did pull her body forward.

Iseult's soul was not yet gone.

Her quest was not yet over.

It was without a doubt the stupidest thing Aeduan had ever done. It was the sort of decision one made when the choices were between certain death and almost-certain death. That *almost* made all the difference. He needed that *almost*, and he had no choice but to rely on it.

If you have to, then you will take control of my blood. Whatever consequences might come from that, we'll reckon with them once the Well is healed. The consequences, Aeduan feared, would be dire, but they were all he had left now. Any burst of power he'd found inside the mountain was gone. His wounds were not simply weeping, but gushing. So heavily they soaked his clothes through.

He was losing a lot of blood. It was weakening him far faster than his magic could keep up with.

But there was still that *almost*, and he had to cling to it.

As Aeduan walked Safi toward the seafire, he removed his salamander cloak. Every nerve inside him fought against that. All he wanted was to run, *my child, run and never look back.* Yet Iseult had walked through fire to save him, so he would walk through fire to save her.

He and Safi were close to the flames now. Aeduan saw nothing else. Felt nothing else. His eyes wanted to pop from the heat—and that was only the beginning. "This will hurt," he warned again, although he knew Safi couldn't hear him. He draped his salamander cloak over her. He towed up the hood, and he fastened the fire-flap as if she were a child who needed dressing.

A final time, he said it: "This will hurt," but this time, it was not for Safi. It was for himself.

"You're not protected—" Safi tried to shout at him, but Aeduan had already reined her blood to his. He was already sending her muscles onward. She would go first; he would walk behind.

The fire devoured them. Aeduan had felt flames; he'd survived burns that no one else could; and he'd died by seafire too, beside the Aether Well. But he did not stop. And he did not let Safi stop either.

Run, my child, run. Straight ahead. Straight through. There was no sight, no sound, no touch inside the flames. All senses ceased to be, and there was only pain. Smoke to clog lungs, fire to peel off skin. While inside Aeduan's chest, the six wounds would not stop bleeding.

They made it twenty-seven paces this way, before Aeduan realized his plan wasn't working. That because he burned, his body was trying to heal—and because of the six old wounds, he was running out of blood to heal with.

His control over Safi was failing too, and she in turn was burning. Through the salamander fibers, flames kissed her. Aeduan tried to run faster, to push his magic to fresh heights. Somehow, he kept going. Somehow, there were still pieces of him that did not burn. Pinpricks of light from the Truthwitch herself, he realized, that he could latch on to.

Physically, he grabbed hold of her, his fingers spasming and cruel.

Magically, he latched on to her too, injecting the hot viscosity of his blood into her veins. And mentally, Aeduan screamed: *Run, my child, run.* Then he ran. With the Truthwitch leashed tight, he ran through the seafire and chased after an *almost* that might only be ghosts in the trees.

Straight ahead. The light-bringer was almost there. Aeduan had *almost* finished what he needed to do. He had *almost* survived with the Truthwitch beside him, and that *almost* was all that mattered.

The heat morphed against Aeduan as he finally reached the end of his magic. As the last of his blood boiled. His steps flagged. His lungs, choked with flame, gave out. He thought he must be near the Well, but he couldn't see to confirm.

Run, my child, run.

He kept running. He kept pulling Safi in the salamander cloak that could not protect her forever. *No,* he realized as he tripped over an unseen rip in the road. *She is pulling me.* They had traded places. Her muscles still worked, her mind was still free. And although she could have left him behind—could have sprinted ahead to the Well and to Iseult—she hadn't.

Part of Aeduan hated her for that. *He* was not what mattered here. Leave him to the seafire and the pain. He was done. A husk. A Bloodwitch with no blood, only heat solidifying in his veins. But another part of him—a part that sounded so much like his mother—whispered: *You are not done yet. There are still debts owed and a knife that must go claim them.*

Then they were through. The flames melted off Aeduan and the temperature against Aeduan's skin cooled. Smoke billowed, and his body was lost. But he was out of the seafire, and the Truthwitch was too.

He collapsed.

FIFTY-FOUR

✳

There was blood coming out of Aeduan. So much blood that screamed of both wrong and truth simultaneously. Worse, when she tried to drag Aeduan, he simply would not move. It was as if he was anchored there, and thrice, when Safi's head swiveled at the right angle, she thought she saw six arrows pinning him down.

So she left him. She didn't want to, but she *had* to. She was so close to the Well. Only another ten paces up this path and the Well would span before her. Orange light flared, and with it were wild, violent Threads. So intense, Safi could hardly look at them.

She reached the top of the hill. She finally beheld the Air Well of Poznin.

It was nothing like she'd thought it would be. Based on written descriptions, based on flashes of memory from the Cahr Awen, there were supposed to be oak trees here. There was supposed to be calm, quiet isolation. Instead, there was fire and there was chaos. The oak trunks burned with red flame. The waters rippled with shock.

And there was Leopold, fighting with a rapier, his Threads ablaze in silver. He was so fast as he winked in and out of this world, using the Dreaming to jump around the Well. Then there was a second person, wreathed in fire—the same fire that consumed the trees. It spewed from her mouth, from her hands on a scale that made Habim's Firewitchery look laughable. Her Threads were even brighter than Leopold's.

Another Paladin, Safi thought, already dismissing the woman. She wasn't Iseult, and so she didn't matter to Safi's mission.

Next, Safi's eyes found a body in black, a hole stabbed through one eye. Safi lunged toward it . . . but saw in moments it wasn't her Threadsister. This was the Raider King. *This* was Aeduan's father, dead. Gone. No more Threads to bind him into life. *True, true, true.*

Fifty years ago, the Republic of Arithuania had collapsed in a long, drawn-out death. Today, Ragnor's empire had collapsed in mere hours.

A trunk cracked nearby. Sparks cascaded. The tree—one of the Well's oaks—fell, trailing heat behind it before landing on a bare patch of ice. Embers flew.

The five others would soon fall too. *Where, where, where is the dark-giver?* the Cahr Awen souls screamed. *Find her and finish this! Death, death, the final end is waiting!*

Leopold spotted Safi. From across the Well, he saw her, and his eyes went huge. It was not a look of joy or triumph, but one of horror—and a matching white lay claim to his Threads.

The Firewitch saw Safi too and acted faster than the seafire's eruption. Faster than time itself, and with no warning at all in the woman's Threads. She launched a ball of fire at Safi, and Safi had only enough time to see how pure the fire was, how white its heart and how vast its fury, before it reached her.

Except it never made contact. Suddenly Leopold was before Safi taking all the fire, all the rage. It hit him square in the back, in the head, in the legs, and spewed past him on either side.

But it didn't reach Safi.

And Leopold had enough time before he roasted alive to say five words: *She is in the Well.* Then Leopold's Threads faded to shadow. He fell, close enough to the Well that his body hit the ice. It crunched; he fell through into fire-lit waters. Then he vanished. One more body to add to the countless strewn across Poznin.

She is in the Well.

Safi ran like she'd never run before. Her sprint across the river was a slog compared to this, her race through Poznin a stroll. She was faster than she'd ever been, born on the Cahr Awen souls and the nearness of Iseult. This Firewitch would not get in the way.

"NO," she heard the woman scream. Then again in her head, *NO.* And with that command, pain speared out from Safi's thumb. A sharp ignition of heat before her whole body was wrapped in it. It felt like having her magic removed with the Hell-Bard's noose. And like with that Loom-bound magic, Safi found herself compelled to do something that was *not* her own desire.

I do not want to hurt you, a voice said. Familiar, though Safi couldn't place it. *You were never my target. You were always just his tool. He made you, and you do not deserve to die for that. So stop, Empress. Stop and our bargain will be concluded.*

Bargain. Tool. Empress. Meaningless words in Safi's skull. She grappled and brawled against them. She could *see* the Well—she could *see* how the waters were moving because Iseult must be drowning within them.

Then Safi saw it again: the weave of the scene as if she were a card in an expert player's hand. *In Sirmaya's hand.* Leopold the Fool had just been played where he was needed, after Aeduan the Knife had increased Safi's hand. Now the Paladin of Flame Hawks faced the Witch, the Empress, the Sun, and Birth.

Suddenly Safi knew whom she faced. Because they had played cards against each other in Saldonica. It was Kahina, Admiral of the Red Sails, whose ring had left a magicked mark on Safi's thumb. *I will let you win this fight, and my crew and I will depart,* Kahina had said while her forearm had cut off air into Safi's throat—and cut off thoughts into Safi's brain. *In return, though, you will owe me. Anything I want, I will one day collect from you. Do we have a deal?*

Safi'd had no choice then but to agree to Kahina's terms. She had no choice now as the consequences of that agreement racked through her. Wave after wave of spine-snapping pain. Just as Safi had writhed and fishtailed under Kahina's grip on that Hell-Bard ship, she was writhing and fishtailing all over again.

No, she thought. It couldn't be over this close to the Well. Not after everything she'd sacrificed. Not after so many others had sacrificed for her. She pretended she was back in that game. That Kahina had just dealt out eight cards. *Flip.* Safi pushed herself against the pain and the fire and the desperation in her viscera to obey Kahina's command. *Trade.* What was Safi missing? What path still waited before her? *Reveal.*

The Witch. The Empress. The Sun. Birth.

Then Safi remembered. When she'd agreed to Kahina's demands to save Caden, Zander, Lev, and all those Hell-Bards, she'd choked out a few final words before all her air was gone: *Two conditions. I will kill no one for you, and I will not give my own life.*

And there was her answer. There was her strategy. *There* was how Safi would win this latest game against Admiral Kahina of the Red Sails.

True, true, true.

Safi's magic suffused her. Every spark of Truthwitchery inside of her saturated her organs, her muscles, her pores. It cleared out the rot of the day, of the death, of the smoke and flames and cleaving—and the lies of all this pain. Kahina couldn't kill her with the ring. Their bargain would not let her.

Safi pushed back into a run. *Initiate.*

There was the water, there was the Well. She hit the edge of the ice. She leaped up, out, over . . . and finally toppled into the dark. Cold encased her. The power of Kahina's jade ring released her. And Safi swam, down, down to the heart of the Well. To where she knew the Solitaire, the Traveler, the Moon, and Death awaited her.

Her fingers brushed Iseult's skin. *Complete.*

Safi's quest was finally over.

LONG AGO

Long ago, when the gods walked among us, there was a monster who wished to become a man. He knew only Moon Mother could change him, so he went out to find her. Rumor was she could be met sometimes in the Sleeping Lands, so he traveled there. And each night of his journey, he prayed to her in the sky, begging her to grant him the gift of humanity.

When he finally reached that border between the safe lands and the lands made all of ice where night lives forever, the Moon Mother heard him. And she actually answered: "Yes, I will grant you this wish, Little Monster. But you must first find me six pots of honey."

"I can do that," the monster agreed, already thinking of a beehive he'd found in the south.

"No, no, this is special honey," the goddess said. "And the pots are not easily obtained. In fact, only a monster such as yourself will be able to do so. Now listen, and I will tell you where they are.

"Follow the Bat in the mountains, to find the soil and stones.

"Follow the Fox and the Iris, to find the tides of home.

"Follow the Hound and the Giant, to find the winds and the storm.

"And follow the Hawk moving eastern, to find what flames have born.

"Follow the Rook to the snowcaps, and you'll find the soul that begins.

"But it's in the pitch-deep darkness, that you'll find where all things end."

When Moon Mother had finished her rhyme, the monster frowned and shook his head at her. "I don't understand. Those don't sound like places where honey might be found."

"And I told you, this is special honey. Trust me, Little Monster. You will find what you are looking for. And once you have finished, return to me. Here, inside the Sleeping Lands."

The monster was confused but also excited. He would find the six pots of honey. He would finally become a man. And so, for many months, he traveled and he searched. First, to the west where the mountain bats thrived. He met men—many men—and while most cowered away, some were kind. Some helped him find honey.

The monster feared, though, that it was not the special honey the Moon Mother had wanted him to collect for her.

But onward he went. South. North. East. High, and finally low. In each place, he found what the Moon Mother had described: tides of home or winds and storm or snowcaps where the soul began. Yet never could he find anything but regular honey from regular bees. And after many years of travel—sometimes tracing back to places he'd already gone—he finally had to accept these six pots of regular honey were all he was ever going to find.

So he returned to the Sleeping Lands. "Moon Mother," he called. "I have done as you asked and traveled where you led. I found honey, though it is not special. Please, please, will you make me a man anyway?"

The goddess arrived. She did not smile, but instead looked sadly down at the little monster. "You found honey, but you are right: this is not the special kind I asked for. And so I cannot make you a man."

"But there was nothing else in the places you sent me! I found no special honey. I found only people and beasts and tides and storm and flames and mountain. I found pain and love and violence and beauty. But never any special honey. Please, Moon Mother. I have worked hard and traveled far."

"No, Little Monster. That was not our agreement."

At first, the monster was angry. He had endured so much for so long. He had learned to be kind even when people were cruel. He had grown physically stronger after many fights against sea foxes and flame hawks. He had seen the most stunning, heartbreaking peaks of the mountains and their glowing, terrifying depths. Yet after all that, now the goddess was not going to give the monster what he'd asked for?

Yet the longer he stood there, the ice of the Sleeping Lands swirling around him yet never quite reaching him, the more he realized that Moon Mother was no longer frowning. Instead, she watched him, waiting, as if she knew something he would eventually realize too.

"Oh," he finally said, and a laugh popped from his chest. "I do not need to become a man."

"No," she told him, and the smile that spread over her lips was as bright as the heavens above. "Because you were always good enough as you are, Little Monster. No human could have done all you have done or seen all you have seen. And certainly, no human could have done it with the same grace and patience that you have shown. But listen—I will give you a small gift for all your troubles."

The goddess knelt and offered the monster two things. First: a necklace that smelled of a sky singing with snow and meadows drenched in moonlight. Of sun and sand and auburn leaves falling. It smelled, in fact, like all the places the little monster had visited.

"This necklace," Moon Mother explained, "will remind you of who you are and how all your adventures have shaped you. And this . . ." She offered him the second gift: a small knife sharp as starlight. "This will help you build the world anew, Little Monster. Your world, for the choice has always been yours."

The monster bowed his head. "Thank you, Moon Mother. For everything."

"No, thank you, Little Monster. For my lands are better for having had you in them."

PART 2

Complete

FIFTY-FIVE

✳

It was another hour before Vaness awoke. Dawn had traded its gloaming for true sunshine—just faint tendrils to curl through steam rising up from the river. Zander slept. Lev slept, too. Vivia kept watch, steering with an oar whenever the river tried to sling their raft toward shore. She never saw people. Never felt any other vessels slithering through the waves.

It started with a twitch on the Empress's left hand. Then a shove of her right foot. Then an imperial: "Where in the holy hell-fires am I?"

"Thank Noden, you're awake." Vivia knocked a gambeson aside. It made her admiral's coat topple onto the Empress's face.

In seconds, Vivia had all the layers off the Empress of Marstok and was helping her rise to sitting. Vaness looked significantly less imperial than she'd sounded with her hair fully loose and tangled around her face. With blood still crusted in spots across her cheeks and rips in her sailor's uniform, from where treacherous ice had not been kind.

"Water?" Vivia offered Lev's leather bag to Vaness. The Empress swatted it aside.

"Where are we?"

"We're . . . on the Amonra." Vivia's voice shook, and though she wanted to speak Marstoki for the Empress, it wouldn't come. All she could get out was Nubrevnan.

"The Amonra? In the *Contested* Lands? Gods, Vivia, what happened to the mountain? How long was I unconscious?"

"Half a day, at most." Vivia said this as flatly as she could. The oaks on the shore were golden now. The river a warming pink beneath the mist. "We were all frozen for much longer, though. At least a week, we think. The Sleeping Giant has moved in the sky, and the moon has grown."

"And where are the others?"

"Zander and Lev are here." Vivia motioned to the sleeping lumps wrapped in fog behind Vaness. "But Cam . . ." She couldn't finish it. She couldn't say it.

Vaness gave a little whimper. She swayed, and Vivia lurched to catch her. *No, don't pass out again. No, no, I need you.*

But Vaness didn't pass out. Instead, she sank against Vivia like a child who needed a hug. And distantly, in the farthest reaches of her conscious mind, it occurred to Vivia that this empress had never really known her mother or father. That she'd had no one to hug her for so very, very long.

And neither have you, Little Fox.

Below them, the river crooned without relent. Reached for Vivia with waves that wanted to climb aboard and caress. But Vivia shut them out, and in quick, poorly defined strokes, she explained how she, Zander, and Lev had awoken in the mountain. How they'd escaped through the first doorway they'd found—which had taken here. And how eventually, Zander had used his magic to make a boat.

"This," Vaness mumbled into Vivia's chest, "is not a boat." The imperiousness in her voice had melted away—leaving her words as loose and knotted as her hair. As filthy and torn as her clothes.

"I was worried about you." Vivia held the Empress tighter, tighter against her. She would *not* cry, she would not lose herself to the storm clouds in her lungs, here where the water salivated.

Vaness, in turn, dug her face into Vivia's shoulder. It was exactly the sort of intimate moment they'd avoided so judiciously in Noden's Gift, where there'd always been an audience, always been expectations. There was an audience here too, and expectations that Vivia maintain the helm. That she keep her bear mask firmly locked on—and not from the Hell-Bards, but from the entire river begging her to dive in and join it.

Vaness smelled like iron and salt. "I love you," the Empress said quietly. So quietly, Vivia thought she must have misunderstood.

Vivia withdrew and found the other woman's eyes. Dark, even in this rising dawn.

"When I saw the ice take you," Vaness went on, sitting taller now. Bringing her face close to Vivia's. "I thought we were done. I thought I would never see you again and never get to tell you how I felt."

Vivia stopped breathing.

"I do not expect you to say the same, but at least . . . At least now you know."

Vivia wanted to say the same to this Marstoki woman before her, ripped and battered but never broken. The words were right there, in Vivia's throat, trying like the waves below to crawl onto her tongue. To escape and set her free. *I love you, too,* she wanted to say. Then she wanted to kiss Vaness, deeply—even if that thought terrified her because she'd never kissed any-one before. Because royalty could never know if someone wanted them or feared them. Would love them back or use them.

But then, Vaness has always been royalty too. She has never had any reason to lie to me. Nothing to gain, nothing to lose.

Vivia's lips parted. The words *I love you too* built inside her lungs . . . but never went any farther.

Because suddenly, Vivia was dying. Physically, mentally, inside and out, she felt as if the Threads that defined her soul were abruptly shorn away. One moment, she was here on this living raft with Vaness and the two sleeping Hell-Bards.

The next, she was clutching at her throat and completely unable to breathe.

And she wasn't the only one. Vaness too was toppling forward. Lev, Zander—both were spasming upright and gasping at the thick, damp air of dawn.

Water sloshed at Vivia, spraying across her with the same sense of floundering. *What am I? What am I supposed to be?* It warbled into Vivia's heart, into her intestines, into all of the folds of her brain. *I was water, and now I am not.*

That was when Vivia felt it, rumbling up through the woven branches of the *Commander.* Up into her legs. A voice hewing through her muscles like the shadow of an eclipse: *You have taken what is mine, Little Fox. Now I will take it back.*

Far to the east in Azmir, Habim Fashayid gasped for air. It felt as if some-one drained his lungs with a bellows, drained his veins with a syringe. Be-side him, his Heart-Thread Mathew also wheezed.

They had been bowed over a desk in their private quarters, staring at Aetherwitched miniatures that showed a losing, failing battle in Poznin. They could do nothing to help; the troops they'd sent west to protect the Cahr Awen were still crossing the Sirmayans; everything Eron had planned was happening months too soon.

"What is this, Habim?" Mathew's voice was tight, his pale face folded with pain. "What . . . is wrong with us?"

Habim couldn't answer. There was no breath inside him. Instead, he toppled away from the desk, toward a balcony. His boots slapped on white tiles; his muscles operated on instinct, no real guidance from a brain claimed by panic. *I cannot breathe. I cannot breathe.* He was not someone to lose control; he was a Firewitch general, after all, and he had bested Baed-yeds and Dalmottis, Cartorrans and Nubrvenans.

Right now, though, Habim felt as if everything inside him had been left to burn in the sun.

He half ran, half stumbled to the balcony's doors. Iron shutters clanged as he fell through and gaped at the city far across Lake Scarza. This was the former Empress's balcony, and they had a full view of Azmir from here. Mathew fell against the railing beside Habim—and they were not the only ones emerging into the sunnied day in search of understanding. Soldiers, servants, Sultanate members: the gardens suddenly crawled with people panicking exactly like Habim and Mathew.

"The Fire Well," Mathew gasped. "Something . . . is wrong with the Fire Well."

"I feel it too." Habim's own voice was a deep, diaphragmatic tangle that did not want to exit his throat. Sparks sprayed off his skin. He couldn't see the Well from here, but he knew where in the city it was—and he also knew something wild was amassing there. Like the small cyclones that writhed across the Sand Sea, like a water spigot dancing on the Jadansi. There was water and dust and flames spinning upward. Higher, higher, straining for the sky.

And the sparks still gathered on Habim's skin, but now as they were drawn away, Habim saw exactly where they went: into that building tor-nado.

"Your magic," Mathew said. He reached for Habim.

And Habim leaped back. "Stay away," he tried. "I cannot control—" He never finished this thought, for at that moment, the cyclone reached its zenith. Light seared out, brighter than the midday sun. Then heat flew too, carrying with it dust, power, and pain across the city. It was like a thousand flame hawks winging into the day.

The explosion crossed the lake and reached Habim. It flung him against the palace's outer wall. He lost sight of Mathew, he lost sight of Azmir and the sky. Then a voice shivered through him, ancient and strange: *This does not belong to you, Firewitch. I will take it back now.*

Caden had never felt an earthquake in the Ohrin Mountains. As far as he knew, such movements of the ground did not happen in Cartorra. They were for the Sirmayans and the unsteady rocks that lived there.

Yet here he and Alma ran while the forest rattled around them and the earth split beneath their feet. The horses who had served them so well these past days had bolted into the trees at the first trembling of the earth. Now branches fell, trees snapped, and only Caden's grip on Alma seemed to keep her going.

"The Moon Mother," she kept gasping. "The Moon Mother was healed, but it's gone wrong. Healing her has gone wrong."

Caden felt it too. It was like a bone that hadn't been set properly: things had been better for a time, but now the misalignment had revealed itself. Now the bone was shattering.

He wanted to respond to Alma—to say, *Yes, I feel that too*—but he found he couldn't get enough breath into his lungs. Fire beaded on his skin like sweat—*his* fire siphoned from *his* witchery.

Only his training kept him moving. These were the crooks and crags of his childhood, and although he wasn't sure to where he and the Threadwitch ran, he knew that *this way* was good—because *this way* was in the opposite direction of the Earth Well.

And somehow, Caden knew the Earth Well was the source of all this madness.

Even the trees leaned as if they wished to flee. Wildlife flew, sprinted, buzzed everywhere Caden's eyes landed. Pebbles too, inexplicably crawling across the ground like ants racing toward a mound—except they traveled toward the Well instead of away from it.

"Your Threads," Alma shouted over the crunching earth. "What's happening to them, Hell-Bard? They're fading and changing!"

"Magic." Caden's voice was a hoarse exhalation. "It's leaving." He had felt this before—except this was worse than being lashed to the Hell-Bard Loom because it was slow. Drawn out. The noose had been a searing, instant agony; this devastation was a protracted, torturous pain.

If Caden didn't keep moving, he knew he would pass out from the intensity of it.

That was when Alma suddenly clutched at his neck. At his shirt's collar, forcing him to stop while she ripped the Threadstones from his gambeson. They winked in the morning—yet it wasn't sunlight reflecting on the gems so much as light flashing from within.

"They're near?" he rasped. "Is that what this means?"

"No." Alma snapped the three leather thongs from his neck—and it was easily done because flames still pooled on his skin. The fire ate through the leather and clothes too, not that he noticed. Not that he cared. The loss of his magic, the moving pebbles and toppling trees—they were all external, meaningless, *unthreatening* things compared to those flaring gemstones.

"No," Alma repeated, louder as her Threadwitch stasis seemed to take hold of her once more. "They're not just in danger now, but dying. Yours too, Caden. Yours too." Her eyes, round and silvery, locked on to Caden's face, as if she searched for some sign that he wasn't dying. That he wasn't shedding flames like a wildfire in a windstorm. "What have we done? What have we *done* to Moon Mother?"

FIFTY-SIX

✳

When Iseult broke from the surface of the Air Well, it was to find almost nothing had changed. Seafire still burned, snow still plodded down, and sounds like a distant battle still echoed over the dawn.

Nonetheless, everything was different. For the world now had Threads.

There was no other way to describe what Iseult saw: Threads, everywhere. In the ground, over people, melting across the rapidly warming waters of the Well, and brightest of all, searing in vivid streaks across the sky.

It was blinding. Overwhelming. Especially after everything that had just happened to Iseult—after death and the Dreaming and the *nothingness* that had almost followed her forever.

As she paddled in the Well and gulped in dawn air, her attention gravitated to one spot beyond the Well's shore. Strangely, these new Threads of the world did not reach there. Instead, the blazing colors scuttled around like rats avoiding poison.

That was when Iseult realized what she was looking at. That the smoldering corpse in the distance was Aeduan. Her Bloodwitch.

Iseult swam then. Fast and with such panic rising through that her she didn't notice Safi shouting and chasing after. She didn't notice Admiral Kahina, striding around the Well like an animal awaiting a meal. Nor Leopold fon Cartorra, slipping out of the Well's waters and limping slyly away.

All Iseult had the capacity for was Aeduan.

She reached the edge of the Well before Safi. Winter air blasted over her, and the Well's embrace fell away. Cold, wet, Iseult staggered over snow, blackened and cruel. Faster, faster, until she was sprinting toward her Bloodwitch.

She had seen dead bodies before—there was a stillness to them that life could never mimic. It was unsettling on a stranger. It was incomprehensible on someone she loved.

And it was made all the more damning by how these new Threads avoided him. As if their colorful magic was repelled by his death; as if he frightened them with his emptiness.

Iseult reached Aeduan's side, but rather than scrape off snowfall, or check for any pulse, she simply grabbed hold of his arms. He was frozen to the touch. Ice crunched off him. *"Help!"* she screamed at Safi. *"Help me!"*

Safi did not help. Instead she ground to a halt at Aeduan's side and gawped at him. "Where's the blood?"

Iseult ignored the question; it was a pointless, illogical thing to say because what did blood matter now? *Blood. Witch. Blood. Witch.* All that mattered was getting him to the Well, and if Safi wouldn't help, then Iseult would simply do it alone. As she had done before, after all, beside the Aether Well.

"Blood," Safi repeated stupidly. "Where's all the blood? And the arrows?"

With one hand still on Aeduan, Iseult reached for the tapestry of Threads skating past. Fire had fed her at the Aether Well—had given her the necessary strength to carry Aeduan. So all these Threads ripping and reeling past could feed her now.

But it was as if Aeduan's toxicity had crawled into Iseult too. The Threads reared away from her fingers. Back, back, sideways, around. No matter how Iseult swiped or pawed, the Threads would not let her touch them.

"Go!" Safi shouted now, and Iseult saw her Threadsister had finally moved. Was finally helping her. Together, they hefted Aeduan's stiff body upward. Snow kept falling. Ash fell too. Swords clanged and pistols sounded. It took all of Iseult's strength to walk. To breathe. She was not restored by the Well, but instead weakened by it.

Or weakened by something else. She had almost died, after all. And now her Bloodwitch *was* dead—again.

Except there was more missing from Iseult than that. Like a vital organ had been carved from her abdomen. And worse—although Iseult didn't know yet that it was worse—a wind was assembling. It billowed against Iseult and Safi, flapping and flipping with Threads. Reminding Iseult in a vague, dreamlike way of the wind-flags that hung throughout Tirla.

It took a hundred lifetimes for Iseult and Safi to reach the Well. Aeduan's boots tore as they towed him over rock and ice and flagstone. His clothes too, sloughing away across his chest, ripping from the six holes already there.

With each new rip, more skin was revealed to the Thread-filled dawn—and it was not the skin Iseult had seen, had touched, had kissed. This was pale and shimmering, as if he were a rock with veins of ore weaving through him. And where his old scars had been, there were now dark, awful scabs.

Blood, Iseult thought. This must be what Safi had meant, although it didn't matter. Not now, not here. Once Aeduan was in the Well, the holes would heal. *He* would heal.

Iseult's muscles shook, her lungs quaked. For some reason, the Well kept moving farther away. No matter how fast she or Safi moved, its waters kept drawing away. And Iseult didn't want to, didn't mean to, but her pace stopped. Her grip on Aeduan's frozen arms released. He fell like a block of stone at her feet.

Blood. Witch. Blood. Witch. The words screeched through her, booming in time to her heart. In time to her blood. In time to the organs that felt as if they'd been removed. *Mhe varujta. Te varuje.* He was dead and frozen and she could do nothing but stand here and watch as the Well drained—literally *drained* before her eyes.

All while the weave of the world broke around her.

"What do we do?" Safi shouted. "Where do we go?"

Iseult shrugged stupidly. The wind beat her hair against her face, fanged and growing hotter by the second. Her eyes burned. Her lungs could not get enough air.

Then came a smell like petrichor and lightning. The heated winds turned to razors and slammed into Iseult like a hundred swords. So sharp, she could do nothing but scream. So all-consuming, she lost any sense of Safi, of Aeduan, of herself.

And it was, as Iseult felt herself lift and detach from the world, that she heard a voice rippling out from the crushing winds and the fraying Threads. It spoke in a language that was almost familiar, almost Arithuanian, almost tangible and real.

At long last, it seemed to say. *At long last, we are awake and can reclaim what belongs to us.*

The battle is supposed to be over, Safi thought, gaping at a sky turned to black with storm. *The battle is supposed to be over.* The Cahr Awen had finished their mission. There was nothing left for her and Iseult to complete. This was meant to be, if not a happy, exuberant moment, then at least a moment of triumph. Because finally, *finally* Safi and Iseult could rest.

When Safi had surfaced from the Well, she'd seen the Sleeper's Threads searing across the sky, great bands of color that wavered and danced—just like the old Nomatsi tale that Iseult had told her when they were children.

But then the Well had begun boiling and shrinking. And then a storm had spun into life. A shroud of cold and heat to snap Safi into its maw like a crocodile. Winds cycloned around her. Feral, furious, with lightning to clap and snarl. It lifted Safi, so high, so fast, she could do nothing but watch as ground vanished and violence punched in.

"Iseult," she screamed, but her Threadsister was being carried a different way. And no matter how hard Safi reached for her, no matter how wildly she twisted or spun, she could do nothing against the winds that claimed her.

Safi still wore her nightgown, burned and sodden and frozen. Her sword was still belted at her hips, and it hit her with bruising force over and over again. Her hair turned to ice against her skull. Her ears popped like gunshots. She thought she heard Iseult screaming.

Only when she was thirty feet, fifty feet, a hundred feet above the earth did she finally see what had become of the Well. No more water, no more bubbling heat. Now, it had all been made flesh: a person with pallid, grotesquely long limbs and strings of white hair. With laughter that rolled out like thunderclaps and winds that shredded off her, thick with rain.

Exalted One, Safi thought, remembering what Iseult had taught her about the origin of the Wells. *Paladins so wicked, they had to be slain a thousand years ago.*

But they hadn't been slain. They couldn't have been because there was one right here, dragging herself into life below.

The creature swiveled her gaze upward, and when her glowing eyes found Safi's, she grinned with too many teeth, shaped all wrong for a human. Then the storm snapped Safi sideways. She lost sight of anything—of Iseult or the earth or Poznin, burned and ruined.

The battle was supposed to be over, but there was no denying it had only just started.

Safi was so cold. She was so hot. The laughter pummeled and thrashed around her. Until suddenly, when Safi thought it could get no worse—that *surely* this was what waited at the bottom of the hell-gates—a new sensation exploded into her.

Emptiness. Complete and total emptiness.

This must be death, she decided, because she knew only absence. It devoured her, encased her, infused her until she could do nothing but crumple inward. Her mind, her muscles, her senses.

She forgot all about the storm that had claimed her. There was only a hole widening inside her and the storm carrying her ever higher into oblivion.

FIFTY-SEVEN

✳

Merik's home was gone. There was nothing left of Last Holdout. He stood in the center of the charred, scorching remains of the refuge he'd built, and he wondered how there could be so much hate in something as simple as fire.

He didn't know what to do, so he stood there while smoke plumed around him and embers burned into his boots. The only thing left of this place was the stone shrine, twenty paces away, turned to shadow by smoke.

Snow fell. Thick, wet, freezing flakes that had been ensnared by the clouds for weeks. Now they fell, as if the sky itself wept for what had happened. Merik wept too, for the people who'd been here. For the target *he* had painted on this place when he'd gone into Poznin.

The horns no longer blasted from the city, but the battle clamored on. Louder. Crueler.

He wasn't sure when he sank to the smoldering soil—to the earth that had been soft enough to sleep upon. In a numb, meaningless sort of way, he sensed his knees were on fire.

How had everything gone so wrong? How had he failed so badly, *again?* Always the disappointment. Always the one who hurt those who got near.

The Fury never forgets, he thought. *Whatever you have done will come back to you tenfold, and it will haunt you until you make amends.*

That was all he'd ever wanted to do: make amends. *Fix* everything he'd ever broken. But every step Merik had taken forward had meant two . . . three . . . a thousand steps falling back. Everyone he'd ever loved was always left ruined or cursed or dead. Kullen. Cam. Safi. His sister. Even his own mother all those years ago. How many times could Merik's body die, only to come back so he could destroy the world again?

Eventually, the burning in his knees prompted him to haul himself upright. In the distance, he could sense things had changed—although he could pinpoint no reason. The battle sounded the same. The war for the Cahr Awen still raged, and he needed to pull himself and his winds together so he could fly that way. So he could still *try* to wring some use from his ever-failing soul.

He was just stumbling away from the embers, sucking winds to him, when he felt his magic shift. Like a wind snapping into a new direction or a whistle piercing through total silence: whatever had been a reliable constant inside him was suddenly gone.

Just . . . gone.

Merik fell. A lurching, brutal fall that shouldn't have hurt as much as it did—but that sent him once more to his knees. He couldn't breathe. He couldn't see. He was again choking on Hagfishes that weren't Hagfishes, and death was coming for him.

He prised up his head, fighting to see against dark, writhing winds that he could no longer feel with his magic. They crushed into him, fists that wanted to shove him down. He couldn't fight them. He was beyond weak; he was beyond dead; he was simply empty.

Ah, it is he who would be king, said a voice Merik felt more than heard. *So close, and so easy to find. But do not worry, Little Hound: it will all be over quickly, the end of everything.*

Paladin, Merik thought, and old words surfaced in his brain—sentences from a book in Kullen's apartment he'd found months ago: *The Paladins we locked away will one day walk among us. Vengeance will be theirs in a fury unchecked, for their power was never ours to claim.*

Merik knew, with a sickening, violent certainty that such a Paladin had now awoken—and now vengeance would raze the Witchlands until there was nothing left.

At that thought, the ancient voice scuttled up Merik's neck and tickled into his ear. A living voice that said, "Why, look at the little hound, cowering before his master."

The winds softened. The blackened cyclone stopped its spinning. And finally he could see who spoke to him: she was like a bird's skeleton bleached by time and sun. There were echoes of what she might have been—pale, blond, powerful. But now, she was a crooked, stretched-out creature with arms that were too long for her body and fingers with swollen knuckles. Her head was hammered thin and long, her eyes distended and glowing.

"I can see you do not recognize me, but long ago, I was exalted. Long ago, these plains belonged to *me*, and all knew the name of Itosha." She smiled, an unnatural expression that revealed teeth too straight. Too sharp. "I will enjoy teaching the world my name again."

She settled onto the carpet of ash that had once been Last Holdout. For a creature of such distortion, she moved with carnivorous grace.

Merik pushed to his feet, ungainly and weak. He swayed once he was upright—but he didn't fall over.

It made the creature laugh. "Oh, Little Hound. You have no Paladin here to protect you. And no magic either—which must hurt so very deeply. Although . . ." Her smile returned, no longer amused, but instead hungry. "Nothing will hurt as much as what comes next."

She slashed out, a whip of pure wind to reach for Merik.

Time stretched long. As if each heartbeat were a lifetime, each breath a generation. No, Merik had no magic. This monster was right about that. Whatever had once been the source of his witchery, it no longer lived inside him. Where Esme's collar had cut Merik off from the source, now there was no source. *No Well either,* he thought—although that realization was deep, deep in the crevices of his brain.

Where Merik also found a tiny pocket of something else.

It blustered and blew inside him. A corner made of Threads that bound him to a different Paladin far, far away inside the sleeping ice. Merik had used those winds before, when he'd fed himself on rage and hungered for vengeance. They'd been brutal and electric.

Now, the winds were the smile of a Threadbrother who wasn't gone, but only sleeping. *Take them,* Kullen said from his tomb.

So Merik did.

When Itosha's wind finished its whipping arc, Merik spun sideways on a burst of freezing, summoned air. Hoarfrost laced around him.

There are advantages to being a dead man, he thought, smiling just as Kullen would have.

Then he made a wind whip all his own, and he attacked.

Vivia was empty. Where for weeks she'd been resisting the magic always lapping and singing, now there was nothing at all. No connection to the waters of the Amonra or the fog still rising into the sunrise.

She'd wondered in the mountain what it would feel like to lose her Tidewitchery—for the waters to snap off into silence. Surely her pained resistance against that magic was infinitely better than having no connection at all.

It *had* been.

Now she knew with merciless certainty that the possible deluge of her tides *had* been far better than having no tides at all.

"Gone," Vaness croaked, her eyes bulging and terrified.

"Gone," Vivia agreed, and something that might have been despair flashed across the Empress's face.

"Why?" This came from Lev, who crawled toward them from the back of the raft. It made the *Commander* rock and sway. "Why do I feel like I'm being noosed all over again?"

"Magic," Zander now choked. He was the only one who had pushed to standing, although his posture was half collapsed. "It's gone, I think. I think magic . . . is . . . leaving."

Those words made no sense to Vivia. Magic couldn't just disappear. It couldn't just *punch* out of a person like water ejected from a drowning man's lungs. Someone had to *take* it, like the Hell-Bards with their Loom.

Maybe someone is, she thought uselessly. *Maybe Noden Himself has decided He will lay claim to everything.*

Their raft was rocking now, tipping everyone on white chop that Vivia could see, but that she couldn't *feel.* As far back as her memories went, she'd been bound to that water. Now it was simply something she observed. Something she fought against on this raft that was . . .

"Breaking!" Lev barked. "This rutting thing is falling apart!"

The Hell-Bard was right. The oak branches that Zander had wound together were now sliding apart. As if the branches had forgotten how they'd been ordered and arranged.

Vivia, Vaness, Zander, Lev—they would topple right into this roughening water. And they would drown, because no matter how well they might swim, this river had become ravenous. *Yes,* said a slippery voice in Vivia's mind. *You will all drown, and I will delight in watching it. Because I was drowning for so very, very long, and now it's your turn, Little Fox, Little Hawk, Little Bat.*

"Paddle," Vivia barked, clawing to her feet. She might not be able to control the water, but she had other instincts inside her. Other training and power. "Get us to shore! *Now!*"

They made it a few feet. Lev on one paddle—which was already crooking and changing in her hand—and Zander on the other. *Row, row.* Vivia, meanwhile, shoved her legs off the back of the collapsing raft and kicked as hard as she could. More white foam to add to the already churning river.

But they were too slow. Or too weak. Or maybe simply too late to fight back against a magic so vast it could command not only the Amonra, but the steam now roiling to life around them. An unnatural fog that heated toward boiling.

The branches of the *Commander* cracked. Vaness screamed and Vivia reached for her, straining to cross water now burbling upward. Ripping them apart. But she couldn't fight this river. She couldn't fight these branches.

She did, at least, manage to grab on to the Empress. *We've survived this before. We've drowned and lived. We've faced a navy and kept breathing.*

Silly words from a silly mind trapped inside a sinking body. She couldn't hold on to Vaness because the waters wouldn't let her. Like they'd done to the raft, they now shoved up to separate. Vivia lost the Empress's hand. She lost sight and sound and breath.

The last thing she saw before the river crashed up to cover her—and to claim the woman she loved—was something heaving through the fog. A blobbing, almost formless figure, like a fish from the deepest pockets of the Jadansi. It called to a piece of Vivia that wasn't her magic over tides, but was some other cluster of key Threads that defined her.

Then slimy gray skin clamped around Vivia's waist and gurgling laughter filled her. "There you are, Little Fox. Let us find the others, shall we?"

Vivia was yanked down into darkness.

Kullen,

We were wrong.

We were wrong and the Wells should not have been healed. I need to fix this. I *need* to make this right before it really is too late.

The Rook King had it all wrong.

And the Raider King had it wrong too—although I suppose out of everyone in the Witchlands, he was the closest to seeing the truth. I understand that now, from this diary left for me. I have read the whole thing, you see? I had the second half before, now I have the first . . .

And oh, by the Sleeper, it was a text meant to be read whole.

I must now track down the missing girls from the tombs, Lisbet and Cora. They were the Raider King's daughters and the closest Eridysi ever had to apprentices. Lisbet was the most powerful Sightwitch who ever lived, so if anyone will know what to do, it is she.

Yet only in death, could they understand life. And only in life, will they change the world.

—*Ryber*

FIFTY-EIGHT

✳

High in the Sirmayans, the Aether Paladin called Nadje shivered on a flat stretch of earth beside a crater that had once been the Aether Well. He tried to stand, but his muscles were confused and displaced. His time in the Bloodwitch's body had reminded him what weight and muscles and organs felt like, but that body had moved like hot wax from a candle.

Nadje's actual body was more like wax that had cooled.

Slowly, achingly, he rose. And the land that had been his home for so long now sharpened into detail around him. Fir trees and spruce. Snow. Mountains, craggy and harsh against a gray sky. He had never thought it beautiful when he'd been trapped inside the watery prison. Now, he was struck by how beautiful it really was.

"What a gentle awakening compared to the others," came a voice Nadje knew. Then there was the figure attached to it, materializing out of the Dreaming only a few paces away. He held a simple white robe, which he offered to Nadje.

Nadje took it, savoring the texture of the fine wool on his fingertips. "Are all the others awake?" Nadje's voice was deeper than he remembered. Like a drum rattling beneath a symphony.

"They are all awake."

"And Rakel?" Nadje slipped into the robe. His muscles glided more easily now. "What side has the Exalted One of Water chosen?"

"That we will have to see. You are the first I am visiting."

Nadje smiled. It was a strange but not unwelcome sensation across his cold cheeks. "I am honored, Rook King."

"Do not be too honored, Nadje." The other Aether Paladin opened his hands like a performer. "We have work to do, and less time in which to do it than I had planned for. You must go to the Contested Lands."

Nadje nodded, slowly. "Like the prophecy says? The final battle has begun?"

"Yes. Twelve must meet now on the lands long contested—and you are part of that Twelve."

Nadje nodded. He had known this was coming; his time in the Bloodwitch had prepared him.

"I will take you to the Contested Lands," the Rook King continued. "In the Dreaming, if you think your spirit can handle it."

Could his spirit? Nadje closed his eyes. Grit scraped against his eyeballs, and it was a delicious, multifaceted sensation that he never wanted to end. He was free now. Free to fix what he'd done wrong a thousand years ago. Free to repair all that he had broken.

Assuming he could survive whatever came next.

"I will not be able to stay with you." The Rook King set his hand on Nadje's much higher shoulder. "For the dark-giver needs me. But I will take you to where I have arranged for the Lament to finish."

Nadje opened his eyes. "I will do whatever is necessary for Sirmaya."

"Good." The Rook King offered a smile. Sad. Even heartbroken, as his fingers tightened on Nadje's shoulder. "And perhaps, if Rakel will listen, there might still be some hope for her yet.

"Now come, Nadje. Brace yourself, for what comes next will be uncomfortable for a soul as old as yours."

FIFTY-NINE

✳

Stix reached Lovats to find the city falling apart. It was like watching a toy tower tip over: where once there had been structure, now there was only wobbling collapse. Noise crushed her. Stones, tides, people, beasts. Everything was lost as magic was guzzled away. Stix might not understand the *why* or the *how*, but there was no missing the countless people whom she passed on the streets—they grappled for power that no longer answered to them.

Only Stix still seemed able to command the elements.

But worse than the lost witcheries—so, *so* much worse—was the loss of other magic. Anything that had ever been assembled by witcheries was now breaking apart.

Including the Water-Bridges of Stefin-Eckart.

Which was why Stix ran as fast as her legs would carry her, toward the southern bridge. The ancient Stonewitcheries and Tidewitcheries that had assembled it were gone now; the bridges were collapsing; all the ships and souls atop them were going to die.

Stix shot off down a side street that would take her to Hawk's Way and then to the river now emptying inside its canal. As she ran, she pulled her magic to her. It was more than she'd ever felt, or ever known she could tap into.

She'd gotten glimpses of it when she'd fought in the Slaughter Ring and encountered her past lives. And she'd gotten tastes of it when she and Kahina had—in secret—helped Vivia and Vaness battle the Dalmotti navy.

But this . . . it was so much more.

And it made Stix think of something Ragnor had told her a month ago: *Magic was never meant to be ours.* He'd meant humans *and* Paladins; he'd meant they needed to let Sirmaya have what She needed in order to heal because it was the only way to prevent a much worse fate for everyone.

Stix had believed Ragnor then. And now, she *felt* the truth of his faith.

In ruthless detail, here was the full expanse of her power. And here was the entire land collapsing because all of its magic was surging into her.

The Cahr Awen had won. The Rook King had prevailed.

And so many people would die because of it.

Stix reached Hawk's Way and the sharp canal that carved through Lovats. The River Timetz was draining from it, and it was like watching water poured from a pitcher. Out it gushed, renouncing its magicked route to follow gravity instead—which led directly into the valley surrounding Lovats. Anyone not crushed by toppling stone would drown. Tens of thousands of people would die, first from this devastation. And then tens of thousands more when crops never grew again.

Unless Stix could stop it.

Stix leaped onto what remained of the river, summoning waves to catch her. She was the Paladin of Water, and this was the city she had protected for a thousand years. She would not let the madness of the world, of the Rook King, destroy everything.

Though we cannot always see
the blessing in the loss.
Strength is the gift of our Lady Baile
and she will never abandon us.

A frizz swelled in Stix's chest the nearer she came to the collapsing water-bridge. Stone by stone, it was falling apart. Sand sliding through an hourglass. She was practically flying by the time she reached it—and by the time she *saw* the hundreds of ships flailing backward. Ferries, frigates, galleons. Nothing could survive this. They rocked, they yawed, and the draining waters trawled them toward total emptiness.

"No," Stix commanded in a voice made of waves. "Stop."

The water obeyed, and the sound of ice forming cracked across the city. Briefly louder than the bridges collapsing, louder than the screams and quakes and boats crashing onto farms below.

The ships froze in place. Crooked, dangling, and with six of them halfway off the bridge. Yet beneath the ice, stones still fell. More sand from the hourglass.

Stix jetted onward. There was still so much river ahead, so much death and loss she had to get to. These bridges were vast and crowded.

In a blur of heartbeats, Stix reached the end of her ice, where the gap between this stretch of bridge and the next was massive—far too large for old Stix to have ever crossed with any speed. But she was not *that* Stix anymore. Nor was she Lady Baile. Nor was she any life that had been lived by this soul inside.

She was simply the Paladin of Water. And so these hundreds of feet of empty air were laughably small. A power as rich and untapped as hers? She could topple mountains if she wanted to.

Ice erupted outward, assembling a new bridge from anywhere there was water to be found. From the river draining; from the river already collapsed into the valley; from the clouds that drifted by, no longer carrying swallows or gentle breeze—

Winds suddenly crashed against her, wild and charged. These were unnatural winds birthed by magic and targeting this way. They slammed into Stix's back.

No, Stix thought, wrenching around to face them. *No!* She could not fight right now. She might have more power than she'd ever felt before, but a battle—it would ruin the city. It would take more lives.

Except when she fastened her weak gaze into the winds, she spotted no single enemy. Instead, there were nine creatures—massive, winged, savage—flying toward her from the west. One single hound hurtled at the fore, a vibrant blur of gold-and-white sunrise.

And on the storm hound's back was a small figure in Nubrevnan blue who whooped as he shot by.

Cam, Stix thought. She didn't need spectacles to recognize him. She remembered his voice—and she remembered, like a fledgling just finding its wings in her skull, a moment from inside the mountain. It had happened months ago: Ryber had drawn her gold-backed cards for Stix.

Lady Fate. The Paladin of Foxes. The Nine of Hounds.

She'd said the card meant Stix could trust Cam to reach Vivia, to pass along the necessary warning about the Raider King . . . But what if it had meant something more? Because now Stix could feel other shapes cresting through the waters of the bridge. Massive creatures she'd connected with back in Saldonica.

Yes, she thought as they came to her. *Help me.* Tears she hadn't known were brewing now crawled free, offerings to the wind and the waves.

Then it wasn't merely storm hounds retrieving ships and holding the bridge intact, but sea foxes too. They twined through the water, melting Stix's ice in an instant. And while the storm hounds' winds blasted up from below, the sea foxes' currents drove ships straight toward the plateau.

A new water-bridge built using the most primal of all powers. The most wild of magics in the Witchlands. It wouldn't hold forever, but it didn't need to. All the city needed was enough magic to get people off these bridges and onto safe ground.

So Stix shot forward, carrying herself on waves all her own, and she got to work getting Nubrevnans to shore.

SIXTY

*

Safi wasn't merely swallowed in cold and heat, in blizzard and rain, lightning and thunder, she became them. Literally, *became* them.

Because once the emptiness had passed, then the storm had pummeled in to fill her up instead. Threads vibrated through Safi, connecting her to every throb, every waver, every heartbeat in these winds. In the whole thrice-damned universe, for that matter.

She couldn't escape it because she *was* it, and every slash of airborne magic flayed Threads and emotions against her. So much rage and hate and hunger—yet sadness too. Regrets of such profound depth, there was no name for them. There was only the blue and the blue and the blue.

Until, just as the prior emptiness had faded, the fullness eventually fell away too. A gradual peeling of Threads, of storm, of emotion and thunder until there was only Safi.

And she was so very, very far from the ground.

Safi began to weep. Not because of the death that would break her whole body when she hit the earth below, but because of what she saw.

The battle *was* over, and they had lost. The entire Well was gone. Decimated. A hole in the earth where there had once been, if not life, then at least the possibility for it.

Even that spark of potential was gone now. There was nothing left behind. No Iseult. No Aeduan, no trees nor stones nor snow. Even the seafire had vanished in a wide, jagged circle near the Well.

We lost, Safi thought as tears cut over her frozen face and slung upward, gifts to the unfeeling sky while she fell. *I'm so, so sorry, Iseult. We lost, and I could not say good-bye.*

Iseult was spinning. Flying faster than she'd ever experienced in her life. Threads. Magic. Rage. *Ragnor was right. We should not have healed the Wells.*

That certainty hit Iseult almost as hard as the impact that came next. It felt as if the earth leaped up to meet her. Her spine snapped and her brain slammed against her skull.

Then she realized she was no longer in the storm of unbridled Threads, no longer in the real world at all, but instead in the gray nothingness that was the Dreaming. One heartbeat stuttered by. A second and a third. Until Iseult melted back out of the Dreaming and found herself at one of Middle Sister Swallow's shrines.

No, she was at *the* shrine where she, Safi, and Aeduan had camped only two days ago.

It was unchanged. Wholly still, wholly silent because the cataclysm that had struck Poznin hadn't reached this far. But it would eventually— Iseult could see that in the Threads scuttling across everything. Lacy and vibrant and sucking through the land.

Iseult's heart boomed in her skull for several long minutes as she crouched there, bent upon the snow. The brightness of the Threads, the cruelty of the storm, the impossibility of Aeduan's too-still, too-dead, crystal-veined and bloodied body . . .

And Safi. *Where* was Safi? *Where* was Iseult's Threadsister?

Iseult's organs pounded with a stasis she didn't want—one that held her in place like a prisoner chained to the ground. She panted. She shook.

Until her legs gave out, and she knew in a detached way that she was convulsing on the snow. She also knew there was nothing she could do about it. She saw nothing but shadow, she felt nothing but pain. It was as if her body couldn't adapt to a sudden emptiness—or her brain couldn't comprehend why there was so much space now, when before she had been so full.

Full of what?

Searing silver Threads stretched across her. Then came a voice she knew well. "It will pass," Leopold said. "The power of the blade is gone from you now, but your body will adapt. I promise, Iseult. I would never hurt you."

But you already have! she wanted to scream at him. *You have taken everything from me!* Because that was the truth of it, wasn't it? Ragnor *had* been right. Safi and Iseult should never have healed the Wells.

"Where is Safi?" she rasped out. "And . . . Aeduan?"

"Safi is safe. Or she will be shortly. And as for the Bloodwitch." A tip of Leopold's head. A bounce of his shoulder. "He fulfilled his purpose as Lady Fate's knife, now there is nothing left."

"I don't b-believe you." Iseult shook her head. Each movement sent Threads—of sky, of wind, of dawn—rippling above her like pebbles dropped into a pond. "*Save the bones, save the bones. You can do that again, like you d-did with Alma.*"

"I cannot."

"Cannot or *will* not?"

"Cannot," Leopold said softly. "Everything near the Air Well has been destroyed, Iseult. Gone. Eliminated—"

"No."

"—so even if I wanted to, I could not bring that Bloodwitch back into life. There is no corpse within which to bind his soul."

Iseult's head shook faster. Snow and soil scraped against the back of her head. "Why? How is that possible, Leopold? What d-did . . . what did we *do*?"

"Ah." He draped a cool hand on her brow, and like a maestro leading a symphony, he reached out to brush the weave of the world. Iseult could scarcely see him, but the Threads—the Threads were inescapable.

They shivered. They sang.

And before Iseult's tearing, aching eyes, an image formed.

"Long ago," Leopold said, his voice rhythmic and beautiful, "when twelve gods walked among you . . ."

Long ago, when twelve gods walked among you, six chose to use their powers for devastation. They called themselves the Exalted Ones.

The others, who simply called themselves the Six, worked in secret to stop the wickedness razing their land. A Sightwitch aided their fight, fashioning a glass that could find and reveal Paladin souls. Then that Sightwitch forged a blade that could sever Paladin Threads.

The Six's plan was to track down each Exalted One and kill them. If the Exalted Ones' Threads were severed, they could not reincarnate.

The cruel gods would be dead.

But one of the Six betrayed their fellows, and the rebellion was stopped before it could truly begin.

One Paladin—the Rook King—tried to salvage the situation as it all came crashing down inside a mountain. He and the Paladin of Air used the blade to kill the Exalted Ones. But that was when the true horror of what the Six had done was revealed: the blade did not kill the wicked six at all. It only transformed them into Wells, leaking their Threads into the land rather than returning their Threads to Sirmaya.

Because the Rook King did not know who within their ranks had betrayed the Six, he used a simple steel blade to kill the remaining gods. They would re-incarnate into new bodies, after all, and he could use that time to find out who had double-crossed their rebellion.

First, though, he set out to destroy Eridysi's blade and glass, so that no one could ever misuse them again. But it was not within his power to destroy the tools; all he could do with his mastery over Aether was bind the powers of the blade and glass into humans.

The Cahr Awen, he called them, and to protect them, he transformed his army into their guardians.

Over the next decade, the Six returned with new bodies. They did not trust the Rook King, and they believed he had betrayed them on that fateful day in-side the mountain. So the Rook King fled and hid. As the centuries passed, he tried to uncover who had truly betrayed them all.

Meanwhile, unknown to any of the Six, one of the Exalted Ones still lived: the Paladin of Void, Portia. In the chaos, she had been able to trade places with one of the Six, and so she had died by a real blade instead of being slain by Eridysi's. And for centuries, she worked in secret, killing each new iteration of the Rook King's Cahr Awen.

With each killing, she claimed more of the brutal powers of the blade and glass. Given enough time, she would have taken all the power she needed. She would have been able to make a new blade and glass—and in turn use those tools to kill all remaining Paladins. Then only she would have been left to con-trol the Witchlands.

But the Rook King discovered this—and at the same time, he finally found his answer of who had betrayed the Six: Midne. Bound by the first Loom, she had had no choice. And her warning had allowed Portia to switch places with her.

The Rook King worked quickly to counteract Portia's plans. He claimed control for the newest dark-giver and light-bringer before Portia could reach them. Then he killed Portia.

Yet even when her latest reincarnation was removed once more from the Witchlands, that did not change the other great problem that a thousand years had revealed: Sirmaya was dying.

For you see, humans had used magic without caution. They could not help themselves. They wasted power, draining Sirmaya, Thread by Thread, thinking there would be no consequence. Even as cleaving razed across the land, growing worse each day, humans thought themselves untouchable. The problem was al-ways someone else's.

So this left only one solution for the Rook King: he had to heal the Wells. He had to bring back the Exalted Ones and let magic and Sirmaya return to what *they were a thousand years ago. Let the goddess's Threads blaze in forgotten colors across the sky, beacons for Her children to follow home.*

Then and only then could the Rook King start fresh, restoring balance to the Witchlands.

Iseult watched as Leopold's tale unfolded before her. It was not simply a performance she watched, assembled by an Aetherwitch who controlled Threads to build a glamour. No, she was *there*, caught in each scene like a ghost.

Here were the Six, close enough to touch inside Eridysi's lab inside the mountain. She felt the cold that breathed forever off the stone. She saw how each of the Paladins looked in their ancient bodies—Bastien with his scars and festering rage at the Exalted Ones, Baile with her calm steadiness, Rhian with her clever smile. Even the Rook King, handsome and hard with dark hair and a silver crown.

Iseult watched as Eridysi focused all her time, all her life on crafting the blade and the glass. It was a brutal, desperate determination that filled her. And Iseult watched as two girls bounced and played nearby. They were Ragnor's daughters: Lisbet and Cora. Aeduan's sisters from before the sleeping ice could claim them—sisters whom Iseult had only just learned about from Ragnor.

Iseult also saw Saria, the Earth Paladin, as she quietly built magic doorways into the mountain. And she saw Midne, the Void Paladin, crushed by Portia on the Hell-Bard Loom.

Now there was Ragnor, younger, brighter, and stoically competent as he ordered armies wherever the Rook King directed from his fortress in the sky.

Until at last came that fateful day in the mountain, when the Exalted Ones descended on the Six. When Midne betrayed them—unwillingly— and a battle of unmatched, raw power ensued. Iseult felt the Rook King's horror, followed by his cold detachment as he did what he thought he must do. As he and Bastien eliminated all of the Exalted Ones.

They never realized that Portia had replaced Midne. They found a mutilated body with a golden chain, and they believed it to be their friend, slain by normal means. And when they found the one they thought to be Portia, they didn't believe her cries to the contrary.

The Rook King and Bastien slew Midne with Eridysi's blade.

Then, as if this was not awful enough to bear witness to, Iseult watched as the Rook King killed all of his remaining friends. Bastien, Baile, Rhian, and even his Heart-Thread Saria. The only people he let go free were the pregnant Eridysi, his general Ragnor, and the two daughters, Lisbet and Cora.

It was all real, vivid, *tangible* to Iseult as if she were right there with Elias, living through it all. Wells formed. Magic changed. Witches became commonplace. And the Cahr Awen were born and reborn century after century. Until the day that a young imperial prince named Leopold saw an ancient tower and the memories of his past lives were triggered inside him. It was then that Leopold had realized what he was—and what he must do to save the goddess at the heart of everything.

It was a magnificent show, unlike anything Iseult could have imagined. She felt each of the Rook King's emotions, each of Leopold's. And not simply because she could see and interpret the Threads, but because the glamour wove directly into her. Directly through her. It played at her own Threads as if she were one more instrument inside Leopold's orchestra.

Because she was.

She always had been.

Iseult came back into her body gradually. No more shadows. No more pain. She simply lay on the snow while Leopold gazed down at her with a look that said, *I would never hurt you.* Somehow, he still believed that.

For several seconds, the ghost of the Rook King lingered upon him. There was the hard jaw. There was the silver crown. Then that too fell away, and there was only a prince, green-eyed and golden-haired.

Iseult blinked as the final glimmers of the glamour melted like dewdrops off a flower. Here was the biting cold. Here was the shrine. And here was the snow slanting against her, carried by a burgeoning wind that flew toward Poznin. It bit against Iseult's cheeks and scraped at the old scars across her hands.

Above all, it struck flint on steel inside her heart.

Anger, she pinpointed instantly, and she couldn't help but smile. Because *this* was an emotion that was useful to her. *This* was a feeling she wanted to be embraced by. Its fires warmed her muscles, sharpened her senses, and ground her body and mind into many years of training.

She had been a tool for so long, filled with Threads that had never been her own—and that had been placed there by this Paladin kneeling beside her. But he was hardly the only person who'd ever treated her as a tool or tried to hammer her into what they wanted her to be.

Make Threadstones, lead the tribe.

Protect Safi because no one can protect her like Thread-family.

Be the Cahr Awen and heal the Wells.
Do not heal the Well and instead cleave them.
Save Moon Mother before it is too late.

So many expectations. So many years spent trying to be what everyone *else* wanted Iseult to be—and all that had led to was disaster.

"I trusted you," she said softly, searching Leopold's face for some sign of humanity. Of regret. He was so beautiful—even more so now, for it was not merely the distant Well that reeled Threads of magic into it. Raw power bled into Leopold as well.

Before Iseult, he was becoming a god.

"I even cared for you," she continued, and with tender caution, she tried to rise. Leopold reached to help her.

She shook him aside.

"After all that time we spent together in the Sirmayans, Leopold, h-how could I not care for you?" Iseult reached sitting. Now her eyes were only a few inches below Leopold's. Wind pulled at his curls. Snow fluttered on his lashes. "But everything you've ever said to me was a lie.

"You never worked with Eron fon Hasstrel, but m-merely tricked me with a book from my childhood. And you didn't kill Corlant so I wouldn't have to, but so I wouldn't form a new Well with the power of the blade inside me.

"And you certainly never loved me. Not really."

Leopold's Threads tweaked with scarlet frustration—and a glimmer of that aching, lonely blue. "Of course I loved you. And I still do."

"But only because you *made* me. Only b-because I was a looking glass to find what you needed. A blade to be stabbed into hearts you couldn't reach yourself."

Now Leopold's cheeks twitched. "Yes, I did make you, but not because I *wanted* to. I had no other choice, Iseult. It was the only way to save Sirmaya."

"Maybe." Iseult shrugged one shoulder, imitating the mask of boredom Leopold always wore. Cold seeped into her legs. Her hair swatted against her face. "But I really don't care if it was the only way. Just as I don't care what h-happened a thousand years ago or a hundred years ago or even three decades ago. What I care about is what happened today. What you did *today*, at the Air Well."

Iseult inhaled here, letting the cold fortify her and stasis slide into her toes. She did not shout, she did not emote. "How long do we have?" she asked.

"Before . . . ?" He let the word trail out. His Threads flashed toward muddy confusion.

"Before the Exalted Ones are awake, Leopold. Before your ridiculous plan"—she pointed to the Threads, traipsing, twirling by—"is finished and magic is gone from the Witchlands?"

An upward tilt of Leopold's chin. "This cannot be undone, if that is what you are asking. And it does not have to be, for I already have another plan set in motion. One of the Exalted Ones will join my side against the others. He is called Nadje. You knew him when he—"

"No." Iseult released a sigh. "I don't c-care about your plans and schemes. Don't you see that? The Exalted Ones are *your* fight to wage and *your* history to reckon with. Not mine, and certainly not the innocent people of the Witchlands."

"But they *are* your fight to wage." His green eyes flashed. His Threads too. "For the Lament is not yet complete. You and Safiya must topple nightmares still and build us anew, while the Six and I—"

"No." Now Iseult snarled. Now she pushed to her feet, stronger than she expected her body to be—and certainly stronger than Leopold expected, for alarm scattered across his Threads like meteors. "I am done with that stupid Lament. It has locked you onto a path, and now you're i-i-*incapable* of thinking beyond.

"So while you might *say* what happened at the Well can't be undone, I don't believe you. I reject that answer. I reject the Lament. I am not the shadow-ender, and Safi is not the world-starter.

"We are *done* being your tools. We are *done* being a blade and glass you wield with a flip of your hand, and we are *done* being Threadstones meant to shatter in a Void Paladin's grip.

"The Cahr Awen was a lie you created a thousand years ago because, like a-always, you refused to act directly. But I will live that lie no longer, Leopold, and now that the magic is gone from me? Now that there's a . . . a h-hole inside me where the blade used to be? I say *good riddance* and *good-bye*."

Iseult squared herself before Leopold, her chin tipping high. He did not recoil, although his Threads paled with ashen uncertainty—a shade at odds with the sunrise glowing behind him.

"I was right," she said, holding his gaze, "when I called you *am-lejtu* back in Cartorra. But I was wrong about why. You're n-not a life sleeper because you don't want Thread-family. You're a life sleeper because even after centuries, you don't understand what it takes to give love and receive it."

Leopold sighed. A sound like the earth collapsing. Like a cave-in from which nothing would ever emerge and no Threads would ever grow. For half a breath, as Iseult watched the prince's eyes sink shut, she felt each shiver and shadow of his sadness. It filled her up. Saturated her like a bonfire.

And for that half a breath, there was no denying that he was magnificent, this lonely god of old.

Then the moment passed, the blue grief passed too, and when Leopold opened his eyes, it was with the smug, wicked glint of Trickster.

"You're right, of course." He bowed his head. "As was the Moon Mother in that fable you so love to tell." He dipped close to Iseult's ear and murmured : *"For I love no one but myself, and I will always be alone."*

He vanished then, as Iseult knew he would do, because the truth was that Leopold fon Cartorra—the Rook King, the Trickster god of old—was a coward who only ever snuck or hid or schemed. But there was one small problem. It had been Leopold's problem from the beginning: because he never acted directly, he couldn't understand anyone who did.

So he wasn't ready for what came next. He wasn't ready for Iseult.

Or for her rage.

The moment before his body faded into the Dreaming, like smoke vanishing into the sky, Iseult grabbed at his Threads. At the searing silver core that made him a Paladin. At the forever-grieving heart of blue. At all the shimmers and shades cascading into him, filled with agonizing, bone-scorching heat.

Iseult grabbed on to *all* of them.

And then she simply held on.

SIXTY-ONE

✳

Merik had not flown with such power in months. Perhaps ever. He felt unstoppable. Like Noden incarnate. His winds came to him with only a thought, and he took flight out of the forest.

The monstrous Itosha followed—as he knew she would. As he *hoped* she would. For this was his home. This was *his* Last Holdout. He'd failed the people he'd vowed to protect, but there were still so many others left vulnerable. The Cleaved army in Poznin. Aunt Evrane and all the Cartorrans she had come with.

Even the raiders, the Purists, the Nomatsis who would have happily killed Merik only yesterday. They must all have lost their magic now. Just as Merik should have too. *There are advantages,* he thought once more, *to being a dead man.*

He rocketed high above the burned tree line. The Paladin followed, screaming and cackling as if this were the greatest joke she'd ever heard. Lightning slashed. Merik spun. It should have hit him; it didn't.

Then he was high enough to see what little remained of the forest—and far more shocking, what little remained of Poznin.

There was a crater where the Well had been, as if a comet had fallen from the sky to gouge out building and forest and stone. To erase all that had ever been. And still seafire burned down avenues and through buildings, with its black smoke to clot the sky.

Even the river had changed, churning and chopping with a violent speed like Merik had never seen before.

Another slash of lightning. Brilliant, scorching, thunderous. Merik flipped sideways, instinct moving his winds faster than his mind ever could. He needed to lead this monster called Itosha away from here.

Merik saw her again as he spun. She grinned, clawlike hands shooting up. More lightning spewed from her fingertips. Merik saw it coming; he flipped easily aside.

"So fast!" she crowed. "But with power that is not your own, I see."

How she knew that, Merik couldn't guess. He just knew that *she* was suddenly much faster too. She slung toward him, her hair streaming behind her. Her grin leering in close with those unnatural teeth.

A shark's maw.

Merik flung out his own hands. Winds slammed outward from them like a shield. They thrust him backward before plowing into Itosha. They didn't hurt her; he hadn't thought they would. But they at least distracted her.

Merik dropped now. No winds, only gravity. He fell like the dead man he was toward the *other* part of the forest, which had not burned away as Last Holdout had. Here, trees still stood—as did the stones, in that otherworldly space his people had so avoided.

Yet smoke did gather in some pockets. *Good places,* Merik thought, *for hiding.*

Ten feet above jagged tree branches, Merik yanked wind to him. Just enough to clear a trail below—but not so much that all smoke fled.

He hit the earth.

And now, he ran. No magic, no winds.

Itosha shrieked from above, a sound like a bird of prey. Gone was her amusement. All that remained was the hunger. Her winds billowed downward. She did not land as Merik had, but instead blasted away the smoke.

Light and air closed in, exposing him like a mouse on the field. Then more winds attacked, this time razored by frozen rain.

Merik didn't stop. Rain sliced into his back. His head. Fresh wounds that sent blood into the storm spitting down. And always, Itosha's screams chased behind. *Little Hound! Little Hound! I see you, I see you, you cannot get away.*

Then the Paladin herself descended, carried by a funnel of electrified air. She ripped through the trees, cracking apart ancient trunks as easily as matchsticks.

Merik gave up running. Instead, he exploded forward on Kullen's magic. His limbs flung back with the force of it. His body flipped nearly horizontal. He wove, he spun, he raced around trunks and stones.

So much power—had Kullen always had this? Had he *always* commanded this enormity of wind, as if he were not merely a witch controlling power but a vector through which all air could channel?

No, my king, I did not.

That voice was so unexpected, Merik lost control. Just a stuttering of a moment, but enough for him to almost slam into a tree. He swerved. His shoulder rammed. His arm ripped, and pain filled him.

And he felt as Kullen laughed. A warm chuckle that sang of their boy-hood on the beach, and of hot Nihar sunshine. *Be careful, Threadbrother, for I can't protect you from in here.*

"Where?" Merik tried to ask as Itosha howled behind. "Where are you? Are you awake?"

Yes and no.

"I don't understand."

You don't need to. Kullen smiled then—Merik felt it bloom across their shared Threads. The strange, terrifying smile of a man who'd always been more comfortable alone than with others. *These are the days that make sense to nobody except Ryber and the other Sightwitches.*

"Is Ryber with you?"

Merik never got an answer. Not before a fresh screech hit him. A joyful, piercing sound that matched the winds scorching Merik's back. Itosha was about to catch him; they both knew it.

Not yet, she won't, my king.

It was at this moment that power coursed into Merik with such inten-sity, he could do nothing but be carried along with it. Winds flogged him from behind, but they were *his* winds under *his* command, and they knew how to carry him. How to lift him out of the trees, out of the seafire's smoke and into the dawn.

Itosha followed, but she'd lost ground. She had the power of storm brimming inside her, yet in the end, Kullen's magic across these Threads of binding were faster.

Merik flew high, high, until the forest disappeared below. Until the breath in his lungs felt too thin and his vision spun. Still, he kept climbing. He would reach the clouds. He would lose himself there, then lose Itosha.

But that was when Merik saw someone else. Someone who had no power, no winds, and who simply fell, streaking like a white-clad cannon-ball toward the earth.

Safi spun, out of control. She grabbed and flailed at empty air. The river would break her. Then feast on her if Merik didn't change course now. Yet if he *did* change course now, he would lose his chance to lead the Exalted One away from Poznin.

Many for the sake of one. It was exactly what he'd punished Safi for on the *Jana.* But maybe it didn't matter—maybe there was no evaluating cost in that way. A life was a life, and he couldn't let hers crash into a place he couldn't save her from.

Hye, Kullen murmured at the same moment Merik made his choice.

And so—with his Threadbrother's vast power to drive him—he changed trajectory. Sharp and hard, the move made Merik's brain crush against his skull. Made his organs climb into his throat. His vision went fully black. He lost sight of Safi or the clouds or Poznin or Itosha still chomping at him with lightning and sharpened rain.

But Kullen's winds knew what to do.

Merik hewed through the sky. If Safi was cannon shot, then he was the destruction that came in the aftermath. He drew more power to him, more winds, more speed—and all with a sense of certainty and an awkward smile that had always had faith in Merik's strength, even when Merik had possessed none.

Behind him, Itosha laughed.

Safi had done this before: she'd felt her eyes sizzle, her heart fry, and each breath taste of burning death. This time, though, she wasn't inside the mountain. This time, she was flying in a storm over Poznin, and she was certain she was going to die.

She screamed, a bereft sound lost to the winds. A sound swallowed by the eternal *crack!* of lightning.

Then, just as it had in the mountain, her body slammed against something solid. Something frozen while strong arms flung around her. "*HANG ON!*" Merik bellowed against her.

So Safi hung on, even as her mind fought to catch up. *I've done this before. Haven't I done this before?* Winds charged beneath her and Merik. They rocketed up, up away from the river while the storm pressed down and the Exalted One in the skies tried to squash them, boil them, keep them from getting away.

Lightning slashed. A mere arm's length away, so bright that the world turned bright and fully revealed Merik's face before Safi. Dark, wet hair pressed against his head, while the scars along the side of his face shivered with a silvery glow—as if Threads ran through them.

Never had Merik flown Safi with such strength. It was as if his winds were muscles to be flexed. Extensions of arms and legs. He didn't carry Safi, so much as cocoon her. In his embrace, in his magic.

Above them, fresh tempests shook loose, and a voice penetrated Safi's skull: *Little Hound! You cannot get away from me! You should not have slowed.* Below, dark waters slung past, alive and writhing. Ice no longer covered any part of the river—but Threads did. They laced through, and there was no missing the masses of silver scoring within like sea foxes.

Safi and Merik left the river. They returned to the smoking remains of the forest. Nothing looked familiar. If Safi had been in this part of the trees, she didn't recognize it now. Trunks blurred into rocks bled into charred earth. Smoke seared into her mouth and eyes. And Threads— always there were more Threads, slithering through the soil like snakes returning to a charmer.

Merik held Safi fast against him, hugging her like the lover he'd briefly been. And gods below, what she wouldn't do to go back to that moment by the Jadansi, when the only trouble she'd faced was a Marstoki empress who wanted to claim Safi's magic for her own. When she'd said to Merik, *I have a feeling I'll never see you again.*

Safi laughed. A hysterical sound that lacerated her lungs. She was seeing Merik again, and *gods*, what a thrice-damned miracle that was.

Faster they hurtled, while more unquenched rage thrashed behind them. Boiling, relentless, alive. And just as she had done two months ago, clinging to Merik inside the mountain, Safi lost all sight, all sound. Static expanded inside her, scratched against her skin. She dug fingers like anchors into Merik's hair. Her face pressed against his neck while her thighs squeezed him with all her strength.

He didn't let her go.

Until, as abruptly as he'd caught her, he *did* let her go. It was with winds more *desperate* than *graceful* this time, and he toppled them both to the charred earth where skeletal trees burned like dying candles around them.

"Hide!" Merik ordered, his voice a scratching, stretching thing as he yanked off his coat.

"Little Hound, I am coming for you!"

He shoved the coat into Safi's arms, and now his dark, dark Nihar eyes fastened onto hers. "Safi, listen to me: *hide.* Itosha is on her way, and I will do everything I can to get her away from here, away from Poznin."

Itosha, Safi thought. So that was the Exalted One's name. Before she could answer—argue that Merik could still hide with her; explain she knew what this monster was; or at least insist that Merik keep his coat, foolish man—a burst of air shoved Safi backward. So sudden, it almost knocked her legs out from under her.

Merik had taken flight, and in seconds, he was gone, with only a flare of smoke through the trees to reveal he'd ever been there.

Safi stared after him, too stunned to move or hide as he'd commanded. At least until Itosha's winds crackled into her, sparking with electricity. *That* spurred her back into action, and Safi flung herself behind a burning beech moments before the Exalted One arrived. Cackling, howling, the creature streaked past. Her body was nothing more than a stripe of furious white, but with Threads—*so* many Threads—shoveling into her and propelling her ever faster.

Merik could never defeat something like that. Safi wasn't sure he could escape it.

This time, the winds that knocked into Safi did claim her legs. She hit moldering earth. Her eyes screwed shut from impact, from heat. Embers scorched her skull. And in the endless slog of time it took to reclaim her senses—and reclaim muscles that still hadn't accepted she wasn't falling—a roar of glee filled the forest.

And Safi saw that same glee brim across Itosha's Threads. *No,* Safi thought. *Not Merik.* But there was nothing she could do except sink into the moment. Let the scalded palms of her hands and scorched soles of her feet push her back to standing.

She launched into a run.

SIXTY-TWO

※

After getting everyone off the second water-bridge, Stix carried herself on ice and tide back into Lovats. Scores of people were dead. Numbers beyond counting had fallen from vessels or been submerged and crushed on their farms.

It was more than her mind could fathom, and the only thing that kept her sailing—kept her reaching for this endless spring of magic inside her—were Vivia's words: *No regrets, keep moving.*

Hell-waters, she prayed her queen was safe. For now, finding Vivia would have to wait. There was simply too much work to do. Too many lives that still needed saving inside of Nubrevna.

And Stix could never abandon them.

Especially because Ragnor had been right; the Rook King had not; and the proof of that was all around her. *Thank Noden no other cities in the Witchlands rely on magic as much as this one does.* There would be destruction everywhere across the continent, no doubt, but at least no other city was built almost *entirely* from witcheries like Lovats was.

At that thought, a question came, as sharp and brilliant as a beaming sun: *Why is that?* Why was *this* city, which had been named for an Exalted One from a thousand years ago, so dependent on magic? And was it important—was there something *there* that Stix ought to recall and use?

There was no time to consider this, or even to really let the thoughts fully surface. Because then Cam and his storm hound were before her. Winds battered. People fled, not knowing that this creature and its rider had saved them—or perhaps too driven by unshakable fear to care.

Stix leaped at Cam, and the hug she gave was enough to lift him off his feet. They hadn't spent much time together before she'd sent him to warn Vivia against invading raiders, but she could easily say then—and she could especially say it now—that she'd never encountered anyone more loyal and true.

"How are you here?" Stix asked, finally letting him drop back to his feet. "How do you have these creatures with you?" She twisted to the storm hound—a small one compared to the beasts still slinging across the skies.

And . . . she'd seen this small one before, hadn't she? When she'd chased the man she'd believed was the Fury?

"I don't have an easy answer, sir." Cam grinned his charming grin, dirt smeared across his face, and his hair was damp from floodwaters. "But I was told to come here by two girls inside the mountain. Sightwitches, they are. And they said I would find Aurora, and she would bring me here. That's her name." He grabbed for the hound, and with the ease of a boy and his puppy, he nuzzled against the creature's massive neck. "Aurora, this is Captain Stacia Sotar."

Aurora's only answer was to blink.

"The girls told me," Cam continued, "that only *I* would know this city—inside and out—well enough to help it, and then—" He broke off as a new figure staggered to their side.

Without spectacles, Stix didn't recognize the man. He leaned on crutches while bandages encased his right leg. There were so many people, fleeing or limping or searching for loved ones, that one *more* person trailing this way scarcely registered.

Until a voice filled her brain: "Stacia."

Shock swelled through her. After all these months, she'd thought there was no one she wished to see more than Vivia. That no face could lift her up so high, and no voice could steel her heart.

She was wrong.

"Father," Stix croaked.

"Stacia," he replied.

Even as his city fell apart, he was ever stoic, ever strong. And it was that strength that had always kept Stix's waters smooth. Growing up with powers that often overwhelmed, with her white hair that made others laugh, with weak eyesight that meant advancing in the navy would be a struggle . . . She could never have done any of that without this man right here.

And now, he could not keep standing without her. She grabbed for him, both arms sliding around him to keep him from falling off his crutch, and for several seconds, they held each other. Two Sotars in the city they both had always loved and protected.

"You're hurt," Stix tried to say.

But her father only shook his head. "I will survive. Which could not have happened without your powers. Or your creatures." He looked at Cam now, his eyes almost skimming past Aurora as if afraid to look upon her directly.

And Cam, a well-trained sailor, snapped his posture high. "Sir." He bowed, fist to heart. "I'm here with sea foxes and storm hounds to help the city. Just tell me where we're needed."

"The Cisterns," Sotar said right away, as if his mind couldn't grasp the enormity of what Cam had just told him—of magic creatures coming to save the city—and so he defaulted to training. "They're collapsing, and waters are flooding into the Skulks."

Stix hissed. "And the under-city? Is it flooded too?" She had *just* taken all those people there. Had she *just* led them from one death into another?

"I don't know if it's flooded because no one can get in."

"I can."

Stix and Sotar snapped their attentions back to Cam. Gone was the boy's earlier smile. Now there was only a stern slant to his jaw. He looked older. He looked indomitable. "I grew up in the Cisterns," he explained. "I know every passage, every entrance. And this must be"—his attention flicked to Stix—"what those girls in the mountain meant when they'd said only I knew the city well enough to help."

"Then we'll go there immediately. And I will summon the sea foxes." Stix shifted as if to ease her father back onto his crutch.

But his posture gave way and a bark of pain left his throat.

Another hiss from Stix. "You *are* hurt, Father. Let me heal you. I have some skills—"

"No, no." Her father tugged weakly. "There are healers gathering at the temple on Hawk's Way. I will go there. You are needed in the Cisterns and the Skulks."

Stix couldn't disagree, but she also couldn't leave her father like this. She wasn't sure he could keep standing, much less get himself all the way to that temple on the canal. So she flashed a sharp look at Cam and said: "I'll meet you in the Skulks."

"Hye, Captain." Another salute from the boy. Then he grabbed for Aurora, and charged winds once more spiraled them into the sky.

"Come on, Father," Stix murmured, taking all of his weight onto her. "Let me carry you like you have always carried me."

The creature that had claimed Vivia was unlike anything she'd ever seen, ever imagined. A nightmare that had once, perhaps, been human, but had spent too much time as *something else* to ever truly be human again. There were two legs, two arms, and a head with two eyes and a mouth. But there were no ears and no nose. Only a curved, bloated shape like a fish left to rot on the waves.

"You never came to visit me," the creature said as she hauled Vivia through the waters with kelp-like silver hair that tendriled around Vivia's neck and arms. "Not like some who came before, who swam in my waters and healed themselves with my pain."

Vivia had no idea what this meant. And the river shoving into her throat meant she couldn't answer. There was nothing she could do but kick and claw against her captor.

Until even that seemed futile. Until Vivia was so exhausted, so drained, she knew that continuing to fight would only let the monster win faster.

Growing up, there'd been a cat that Vivia had loved. It had always hung around Pin's Keep, and her mother had fed it whatever scraps the shelter had had left at the end of each day. *A good mousing cat,* Jana had always said. *You can tell by its six fingers.*

It *had* been a good mousing cat, but the mousing had also been one piece of the calico's personality that Vivia had hated. Because whenever he'd caught a mouse—or rat or sparrow or sometimes fat wolf spiders—the cat had never just killed them outright. He'd always played with them for a while, carving off of their lives bit by bit with a savage swipe of claws or a chomp of fangs.

Once though, Vivia had walked into her fox's den in the palace and found the calico there, far from his usual home. It had been after Jana's death, and Vivia hadn't seen the nimble mouser in months. Now here he sat, in the middle of her rug, a rat dangling from his mouth.

The poor rodent was barely alive. Its little chest wobbled, and its whole body hung limp in the calico's jaws.

"No!" Vivia shouted at the cat. "Drop it." Then without thinking, she grabbed on to her magic.

Glass shattered, water attacked, and the cat ran—although not before dropping the rat onto the rug.

Vivia, crying now, inched toward the dying, sodden creature. She was going to have to kill it herself, wasn't she? Please, Noden, don't make her do that. *Please,* there'd been so much death in her life lately. Don't make her end this animal to save it from pain.

But as she knelt beside the rat, reaching tentatively toward its gray fur, the rat suddenly sprang up. No more wilted spine or rolling eyes. Just sheer determination to hang on to the last breaths it still had.

In seconds, it had scampered from the room, vanishing under a door that was now open—because now little Merik stood right there.

Oh no, Vivia thought. *Did he see?* He must have. He *must* have seen Vivia trying to hurt the cat to save a rodent, and oh hang her, what if he told their father? Serafin would bellow and blare about showing strength by killing vermin . . . About acting fast before one's prey could escape.

"Don't tell him what you saw," Vivia blurted.

Merik recoiled. He was a small boy, and gentle like Jana had always been. "What . . . did I see?"

Vivia blinked. Was he toying with her? Had he really seen nothing? *No,* she decided. He was simply being nice, being understanding. So she nodded. "Exactly," she told him. "That's exactly what you have to say."

True to his word—or perhaps genuine ignorance—Merik had never tattled on Vivia's weakness to their father. He'd never brought it up with Vivia again, either. And for years after that, Vivia had thought she'd seen the rat lurking throughout the palace. A bit roughened up and scarred, but still hanging on to whatever last breaths it still possessed.

And now, being carried down this river by a beast as cruel as the calico had sometimes been, Vivia was determined to be the rat. Not a fox, not a bear, but a lowly *rat* that was impossible to kill because it knew how to wait for the right moment.

Vivia would wait. She would survive. She didn't need her magic to win against a target bigger and more deadly than she. She just needed wits and patience.

She let her whole body go limp in the monster's grasp. Let herself float along like another *Commander* to sail uselessly out to sea. She didn't know where she was, where Vaness was, where Zander or Lev were—or if they were even still alive. There was only the sky, brightening overhead, cresting with colors too beautiful for this much pain.

Thank you, Merry, she thought. *Thank you for keeping my secret.*

SIXTY-THREE

✳

Sky wasn't much of a soldier. She wasn't much of a spy. And she definitely wasn't much of a diplomat. But there was one thing she was good at—other than her magic, of course: staying alive. And when she saw that empress lady run into the seafire with the Cleaved . . .

Well, Sky had decided that was *not* going to be her escape route. Especially since she still had the book with the map. The one the other woman, Iseult, had given her.

Problem was, there weren't any routes from that map that she could reach. Seafire burned down so many streets. And even after a great *rattle* had shaken the city in a way that Sky figured must have meant something good had happened at the Well, nothing about her own circumstances had changed. If anything, the quake had made it all worse. Three buildings toppled over right before her, kicking up more seafire and smoke.

And Sky abruptly found she couldn't breathe. It happened like a thunderclap: one moment, she was upright and scouring for a way out of this wretched place . . .

And the next, buildings were falling and she was doubling over. *This belongs to me,* she heard, even though there was nobody there. *I do not want to, but I fear I must take it back now.*

The suffocation ratcheted higher. A fist to close over her throat. Then her mind. She felt like she was being drained of some fundamental part of herself, and she grasped clumsily at the ground. At the air. At her own head as if maybe whatever was leaving her could be kept inside.

It was an animal that finally roused her. A blur of white at the corner of her weeping eyes. Furtive movements that meant something else lived—and something else wanted to stay that way.

Sky wrested her head high enough to see what was passing. It was white, it was wriggling, and oh yes, it was very much alive. Because animals—like Sky—were awfully good at surviving. *So get up, Skyvenjetsa Drakora,* she thought. *Get up right now and move.*

Sky got up. Her muscles rebelled and screamed. Her lungs too, and for several heartbeats, she could do nothing but cough and hack and try not to fall again. But then the intensity of the unexpected pain finally cleared.

And so Sky finally moved. A stumbling run. Then stronger, faster, after that slip of white squirming beyond.

Within two blocks, she was close enough to recognize the animal as a weasel. It wore its winter fur, which was a real blessing. Had it been dressed in black, Sky would never have seen it in all this soot and ash.

Twice, the weasel looked back at Sky. Twice, its nose twitched before it kept running. Which meant Sky kept running too. For now, it was leading Sky *away* from the Well, and that seemed like a good thing. Because now that the quake had stopped its aftershocks, a new chaos was setting in: winds. *Bad* ones that kicked up seafire and sent it flying onto new roads and houses and humans.

A *lot* of humans. Most of them already dead, but quite a few who simply stood there, as lost as Sky had been. Or trying, like her, to stumble out of here. Sky ignored them all; she still had her Baedyed gear, and she didn't know who might see her and think *enemy* or think *friend*. Too many Cartorran soldiers here, and Red Sails and all those monks in white too.

Sky pounded onward, leaping and gasping through her scarf as she tried to never lose sight of that weasel. But then the weasel finally hit an avenue filled with smoke so thick, she couldn't see anything but blackened shadows that sang with seafire.

Sky wiped ashen tears from her eyes. The winds were kicking harder, and now thunder rumbled. She had never hated this city more, and now she hated that weasel too.

Except, no. Something was changing. The shadows were shrinking, and a flicker of white could just be seen darting and swerving through. The weasel was close to the ground, and she'd found a way through the seafire.

Sky was about to chase forward after it, when something fell before her. It came so hard, so fast, she leaped backward, yelping. Her arms flung over her head. She dropped to a protective crouch. Several smoky seconds boomed by.

But nothing else crashed down, so Sky unfurled. She needed to move. She needed to *not* lose that cursed weasel before it escaped through all this black smoke. That was when she saw it, though—what had landed before her.

A sword. It was still sheathed, and she recognized it immediately. The woman Safi had been wearing it at her hip when Sky had tried to help her.

344   ※   Susan Dennard

Now here it was. Just *stabbed* right into the charred cobblestones with the bottom half of its sheath split apart. "Well, shit," Sky said to no one as she snatched up the blade. Leather scraped off it to reveal pure silver to a dawn made of storm. "Well, shit," she said again.

Then Sky ducked low and dove into the gaps of seafire where the weasel had just sped away.

Where the hell-waters am I? Merik thought as he blasted into the mountain. He'd made it through a magicked doorway and was almost certain Itosha would follow him, but it was proving to be a minuscule blessing in the loss.

For this was not the vast hall crawling with ice he'd expected, but a snaking tunnel filled with water and half-thawed bodies who screamed at Merik as he passed. A cacophony of sound that overwhelmed almost as much as Itosha's attacks had. *Follow the grain! Forced to change!*

I am! he wanted to scream back. *I have no other choice!* And he didn't, for the tunnel was too narrow, too unpredictably curving for him to tap into Kullen's magic. All he could do was sprint and occasionally launch himself faster on winds fed by his Threadbrother.

Then all blessings vanished when, after a steep rise in the tunnel, the voices snapped off. Merik knew right away it meant Itosha was with him inside the mountain. And *she* was able to fly.

Move, Kullen roared into Merik's mind. *Go, my king. Go!*

"What do you think I'm doing?" Merik snapped—a waste of breath as his vision blurred with panic.

That way goes to Paladins' Hall, Merik. Keep going, and then take the brightest door when you get there.

"Why? What's through it?" Merik veered past hanging limbs encased in wet ice. Past faces with silvery eyes. "Are you there? Are you in that hall?"

No. This was all Kullen said, but Merik could feel—across their Thread bond, across their many years as Threadbrothers—that there was more to that word than what Kullen was letting on.

He didn't like it, but he also had no chance to press for more answers because Itosha was *right there.* She carved through this tunnel with far more speed than Merik had, since unlike Merik, she wasn't trying to avoid the bodies in the ice. She just crushed them as she flew.

Merik saw the tunnel's end ahead. He saw the melting ice release its claim in a crooked, raw hole. Merik had been in this mountain twice before; there'd never been a passageway like this one before.

Move, Kullen commanded, and power burst again inside Merik. He shot as if from a pistol into the vast cavern called Paladins' Hall.

There was no ice now. No summoning song for sleeping. No whispers of *Come, come, the ice will hold you.* It was just a vast abyss inside the mountain, where several doorways glowed.

The ice is gone, Merik thought at Kullen. *Does that mean you're awake? Does that mean you've been set free?*

Kullen gave no reply beyond a fresh surge of power. It hurled Merik toward a new door glowing brighter than any other in the cavern. It stood upon an island of rock in the center of Paladins' Hall—a central platform that Merik was certain hadn't been there before.

Warmth sparked against Merik. Inside him too, and he remembered that feeling. It was a sense of star-spun power, and it had fed him faster, higher the first time he'd come here, with the Northman.

Now, since it fed to him through his Threadbrother, there was a new dimension. One of strength, of love, but also one of crushing sorrow—

No, Kullen barked, and cold slapped through Merik's lungs. *Focus on flying, my king. Get out of this mountain. Get Itosha away from here.*

Merik obeyed, rocketing across the dark abyss that filled the cavern. There was the galaxy he remembered, forever swirling in the mountain's heart. And there was the door he needed to use.

The magic pulsed against him. Then it grabbed hold and sucked him through. Seconds later—after his whole being had been pulped and then reconstructed—Merik erupted into a new place. A hot, baking place where no storms darkened the sky and where green dominated red soil.

Don't slow, Kullen commanded. *She is right behind.*

How do you know? Are you awake? Where are you, Kullen?

I am where you left me, Kullen replied, and again, Merik could feel there was more to this answer. Something his Threadbrother was intentionally holding back. But—again, *again*—Merik could do nothing except resume flight with a fresh torrent of power.

Not a star-spun power, but a Paladin-shaped one, tender and old.

Merik flew into a new day.

No. Leopold's panic blazed through his Threads into Iseult. He hadn't expected her to do something this excruciating—or this profoundly *stupid*.

But stupid was the one thing no one ever saw coming.

Iseult's hands were on fire as she held on to Leopold's Threads. Her body was getting pounded to dust. But she couldn't let go of him—no matter what he did, she *couldn't* lose him. He tried, his eyes huge and his body moving like a dancer's. Like a fighter's. First, in the Dreaming, he dipped and spun and *tried* to shake Iseult free.

But he couldn't.

So then he ran, his body streaking so fast, it snapped Iseult almost horizontal in the immaterial space between worlds. She was like a banner on a ship. The wind-flags in Tirla.

Still, Leopold could not get rid of her.

So he leaped out of the Dreaming. Gray smashed into seething Threads and hard earth. Golden grass, but without snow—as if these were the Windswept Plains to the south where winter had not yet taken hold.

Leopold tried again to wrench Iseult off him. His face was flushed, his lips too, and his Threads glowed with such intense determination, it darkened the sea green of his eyes into forest shadow.

Never trust what you see in the shadows.

Iseult should never have trusted Leopold—and she would never make that mistake again. Nor would she let go of him. He sank low in his stance and lurched sideways. The move tore Iseult forward like a dog on a lead.

The fraying weave of the plains smashed once more into gray. The intensity of the shift obliterated Iseult's senses. Wiped them all away so that there was nothing but her and Leopold. His silver cloak. His many Paladin faces, wavering across him. Ghosts of the past he could never escape.

She might have pitied him for that curse. She might have felt something other than rage if he'd only *told her the truth*. If he'd only *acted directly*. And Iseult couldn't help but wonder—in that little corner by her left lung—if this was exactly what Moon Mother had felt when Trickster had saved her from the storm in that legend of long ago. Had she stared at the creature before her and marveled that he thought himself so clever he could marry a god?

Iseult wasn't a god.

But she wasn't quite human either.

Lightning flashed. Winds beat. Snow cut against her. They were out of the Dreaming once more, where peaks towered wicked and young against the sky. These were the Sirmayans—the Rook King's old home.

Leopold reached for Iseult, his body lithe and trained. But Iseult was lithe and trained too. In fact, this was exactly what Aeduan had taught her to evade. So when Leopold lunged, she twisted. She swept. He dodged her counterattack, although only barely. His Threads erupted with white panic.

And *still* Iseult held on. The fire of his Threads saturated her veins, burned behind her eyeballs and up into her own Threads. Fuses she knew existed even if she couldn't see them. They'd caught fire when she'd tried to hold on to Corlant.

But she wasn't that Iseult anymore. She wasn't chosen. She wasn't special. She wasn't a blade or a Threadstone or the dark-giver half of the Cahr Awen.

She was just herself. A Threadwitch who'd never made a Threadstone. A Nomatsi hated wherever she went. And it would be enough, not because Iseult was chosen, but because she was *choosing*.

For Safi. For Aeduan. For everything Iseult had ever believed about herself—and for everything Safi and Aeduan had ever believed about her in kind. Her mother too. And Alma. For Mathew and Habim and Monk Evrane.

The blizzard vanished. The Dreaming engulfed Iseult anew—and this time, Leopold spoke to her. His voice was as desperate as his Threads. No masks to hide behind, no Trickster self to mock and jeer.

"You *must* release me, Iseult! You *must* finish what we started!"

"No." She smiled at him, her fingers squeezing tighter. He no longer ran. He simply stared at her.

"We will all die, if you do not."

"Good." She laughed. "Death is what we b-both deserve."

He didn't respond to this. Iseult didn't know if he even heard her, since now they were snapping into a forest where the earth itself writhed. Root and rock and branch scuttled by as if answering the call of a master—and all of them moving with the Threads of the world, still sucking away.

Soon, there would be nothing left. Soon, the end would be complete. Death really *was* what they both deserved.

So Iseult kept hanging on.

SIXTY-FOUR

✳

As Safi careened through the burnt forest, she had the distinct sense she was following a path someone else had made for her.

She'd been shoved onto tracks like a mine cart before, by her uncle in Veñaza City during the Truce Summit that had changed everything. By Vaness when she'd served as the woman's Truthwitch in Marstok. By Henrick once she'd become his wife—and had later been bound to the Hell-Bard Loom. Then by Leopold as he'd manipulated and lied and spewed out pretty words to convince her to traipse across the continent after Iseult.

Now, Safi was almost certain she was locked on someone else's tracks again. The question was, whose? Leopold was the most likely answer—always acting in the shadows. Always angry when no one obeyed his whim. And, if it turned out to be him, could Safi break free? For that matter, should she?

Very safe and very alone. It was what she'd thought about Leopold in Praga, when she'd first started wondering if maybe he couldn't be trusted. Now here she was again, very alone . . . but most certainly not very safe.

She could still see Itosha's Threads, far ahead—although they were hazing in a way that worried her. As if the Exalted One were somehow leaving, somehow sinking down into some place Safi couldn't follow.

Because they are, Safi realized when she finally broke from the trees. Before her was a clearing filled with column-like stones that she would wager a *lot* of coin weren't natural. There was a pattern to them, a circling inward like the markers on a highway.

Oh, something tickled in her brain. *That's important and you should remember it.*

She hugged Merik's coat to her. It smelled like woodsmoke and rain, and she was glad to have it. Snow fell now in clumping, wet flakes that soaked Safi's body. Gone was Itosha's electric storm; now it was the forever clouds unloading.

She dug forward. *This way, this way, on these tracks someone else had* placed for her until she reached a hole in the ground of spiraling black stone where snow did not gather, nor melt, but simply vanished.

The Threads of the world shivered into the hole, following the ramp like a whirlpool. Itosha had gone that way. Which meant Merik must have as well. So Safi would go that way too, picking up speed as she spun downward. As Threads wormed past her in brilliant lines. More colors than Safi had ever heard Iseult describe; more than Safi's eyes could fully separate; and more than this magic (that wasn't really *her* magic) had ever before encountered.

What the *hell-gates* was going on?

Safi felt the sputter of a mountain door. Felt the familiar and agonizing gravity of it as it towed her inward like the worst kind of riptide. This time, as she was torn apart, she had the engulfing sensation that *someone else was there*. A giant, inescapable being that observed her without malice or love. Just curiosity as Safi passed through.

Then Safi was rebuilt. Restored. And dropped inside the mountain—or at least her addled brain *assumed* it was the mountain. Logically, it had to be. It looked different though: a tunnel filled with melting ice instead of a cavern.

Everywhere she turned, glowing blue seemed to ooze and bleed. In some spots, she thought she saw bodies. In others, it was just limbs exposed and thawing.

A hand grabbed at her hair.

"Weasels piss on me!" Safi jerked away. "Don't touch me—no, no. Get off, get *off!*" She ran, her gait stumbling and desperate. To the right, ice had been gouged in huge pieces, lightning had scored stone, and Threads trailed where Itosha had been.

More bodies. More melting ice. More hands and occasionally mouths too, shouting about lands long contested and fissures in the ice and five turning on one. There was one particular refrain, though, that kept leaping out above the others.

"*Think beyond. Think beyond.*"

Beyond what? Safi wanted to scream back. But there were no fully formed faces for her to latch on to—and there were still too many hands grappling. Nightmares she couldn't escape no matter how fast she pushed her legs or how many swivels and turns the tunnel made.

Until at last, Safi did finally escape the wretchedness. She *did* finally reach a fork in the mountain with only stone. It was jagged and rattling, as if the mountain had only *just* opened it up, but the chaotic, exuberant Threads traveled this way, so Safi would too.

She ran. She chased. She didn't stop. Not until the rift through the mountain reached its end. Not until she stumbled out into the part of the mountain she'd visited before. Paladins' Hall spread before her, both exactly as she remembered and also completely changed.

No longer did the mountain itself attack, but instead the Exalted One. First came the cackling squall that signaled Itosha. She'd been slowed by the narrowness of the tunnel, but now she gusted and chanted from the cavern's heart: "You cannot escape me, Little Hound. I will follow wherever you try to go."

And Itosha did follow, cycloning into a new doorway. A massive, shimmering thing of lucent blue hovering on a platform in the middle of the abyss. It was a full moon all eyes would latch on to, no matter how bright the constellations that shone nearby.

The sense of being placed onto tracks hit Safi again. So hard in the chest that she staggered into stone. Her vision spun, shrouding her view of the cavern.

Think beyond, quavered voices against her neck. *Think beyond.*

The mountain started moving again, a brutal lashing side to side as stones ripped down and dust choked. Shards of rock fell, so sharp they cut at Safi's scalp, her arms, her legs. Then came a voice, so like Itosha's and yet so different.

"You should not follow him, Itosha. You should change your course before it is too late."

"Coward, Ferisien. This is our chance."

"*This is your doom,*" the voice replied. And then it was no more.

Safi shook her head, wobbling like a dog as she tried to latch on to her senses. Her vision was clearing; the mountain was calming; and sure enough, she could see a new upthrusting of rock that had formed across Paladins' Hall. A bridge made of stone that hadn't been there before.

But a bridge Safi could take all the same.

Once more, she staggered into a run. And once more, she did not stop.

The temple on Hawk's Way was as old as the city itself. Time had smoothed away the Hagfish columns at the shadowy entrance. *Six of them,* Stix noted as she helped her father inside. *Always six.*

How much of the past had always been embedded here? How much *more* had they all forgotten of the living history that was reborn today?

As she had hobbled her father through the city, Stix had directed healing magic into him. It wasn't a skill she'd used often—or ever, really. She had always been more comfortable as a fighter, defender, sailor on the seas.

But magic was different now, and the power inside Stix was dimensioned in ways her Paladin memories knew how to use. She sent warmth into his blood. Clumsy, but soothing against the pain that shuddered through him. And she kept his blood *inside* so no more would fall on to the cobblestones.

He'd lost too much though, and what he needed more than anything was rest.

The air turned cool as Stix guided him deeper into the temple. Sunlight faded, replaced by two lamps above a statue of Noden on his throne. It was almost funny now, knowing what Stix did. The god all Nubrevnans had worshipped for centuries did not exist. There were no Hagfishes at his side in an abyss. There was, instead, a goddess sleeping with spirit swifts and shadow wyrms inside a mountain.

On the statue's left was a fresco of Lady Baile. Noden's Right Hand, and Stix's own self from a thousand years ago. Her skin was painted like a starry sky, while her fox-shaped mask shone blue. She held golden wheat and a silver trout, and the copper urn resting before the image was filled to the brim with wooden and silver coins.

Before her figure, tens of people had gathered. There were no cots or mats, but she recognized healers from Pin's Keep. Trained medics—some with magic, some without—moving through the rows and clumps of injured.

It was too many hurt and broken and dying, and suddenly Stix was afraid to leave. Not merely because she feared for her father's life—although she did—but because she could do good here. She was a fumbling healer, but she could learn.

You will return, she reminded herself as she eased her father down against the cold wall. *You will return after you help Cam with the Cisterns, for you are Lady Baile and you will never abandon them.*

"I'll be back," she told her father, releasing her hold on his blood. Instantly, she felt it start leaking anew. But it was a slower trickle now, for the journey here had given his body enough time to start repairing itself. "Just hold on, Father. I'll be back very soon."

"I know." He smiled. A brief burst of sunlight in these shadows. Then he slumped down and his eyes drifted shut.

Stix turned to go, making herself *not* look at all the bloodied and half-drowned people around her. The broken limbs and bodies drained of life. The Cisterns had to be the priority. She *would* return.

Her gaze briefly flickered over the other fresco. Noden's Left Hand, the Fury. Normally, there were no offerings in this urn, for no one wanted the Fury's eye to find them, lest they be judged. Now, though, there were nine people bowed low before him, murmuring and begging, some with injuries. Others with injured ones in their arms.

They thought Lady Baile had forgotten them, so they begged out of desperation for the Fury to turn his cruel eye their way. *I will be back.* Stix bit her lip. *I swear, I haven't forgotten you.* She picked up her pace, aiming for the Hagfish columns.

But she never reached them. Not before a sound knifed into her ears. Into her mind. Then electricity rammed into her spine.

It was like a thousand firepots beating at her from the inside out. She felt her skin burn, paper over flame. She felt her muscles give out and her body crumple downward.

The ring-bond. It is my ancient ring-bond just like long ago.

No one approached Stix. No one even seemed to notice she was suffering. After all, she was just one more person in the temple who needed help after calamity had struck.

Stix grabbed at her throat, at her eyes, and she searched frantically for any sign of where that old, old enemy might be. Then she saw him, coming from behind Noden's throne as if he'd always been there.

"Hello," he said in a voice that had always been too soft, too kind for the cruelty that lived within. "You have changed greatly in these last thousand years, Baile. I, however, am the same as I always have been." He smiled now, his face as beautiful as she abruptly remembered it had been—and a perfect match to the stone Noden nearby. Because of course, the city hadn't created their god out of nothing . . .

They'd simply renamed a person who really *had* come before.

Time might have changed the tales, the memories, the title, but his likeness—there could be no denying who Noden had been inspired by all along. The Exalted One Lovats had the same broad shoulders over a supple waist. He wore the same curls, silver and gleaming.

He came to a stop before Stix. She curled onto her side, wheezing. *Those are the rings,* she thought. *Those are the rings we are bound to.* There were three on his right hand, and Stix remembered now: this was why her city had so much magic.

The Exalted One, Lovats, had bound the Six with jade rings crafted by Portia. Midne had already been claimed by Portia, so she was untouched. The Rook King had been too powerful for domination, so he had also been left alone. But the four elemental Paladins? They'd had no choice but to kneel, to serve, to *build* this city that Stix had just worked so hard to save.

One ring was missing now, and that was the ring Kahina wore.

Lovats dropped to a crouch beside Stix. Somehow, he was even more beautiful than he had been a thousand years ago. The silver of his hair glowed like moonbeams.

He ran a hand over Stix's face. There was nothing she could do to stop him. She was aflame. She was dying. The pain shattered every bone, lacerated every vein. "I missed you more than any of the others, you know. And now, here you are. The first face I find upon waking. But do not fear, my love. I have no plans to claim vengeance. No desire to hurt you—or anyone else. I am changed, you see.

"Now stand up, Baile."

Stix's muscles convulsed. Then obeyed, shoving under her. Cranking her upright.

Lovats smiled at her, only a few inches taller than she was. "This version of you is so lovely. You always have been, though, for your soul is ever constant." Again he stroked at Stix's face. He leaned in too, as if he might kiss her . . .

But he paused, mere inches from her lips. "Come with me now, Baile. I command you."

The pain exploded, and again, Stix lost control of her muscles. But rather than collapse to the stones, Lovats simply caught her. Lifted her like a Nubrevnan groom with his bride.

The pain will stop, my love—she heard crackling inside her skull—*if you would just stop fighting against me. Can you not see that you have already lost?*

SIXTY-FIVE

※

Iseult saw Poznin from above, brutalized.

She saw forests burned to ash.

She saw more mountains and hot white shorelines baking under a morning sun. She saw waters—and briefly, she was even dunked within them, as if Leopold hoped he might drown her into submission.

Still, Iseult held on. And with each leap into the Dreaming, each leap into a new dying corner of the Witchlands, the heat of Leopold's Threads faded into something almost bearable. Or maybe Iseult's body simply lost the ability to feel pain. After all, stare too long at the sun, and eventually you'll go blind.

But let her go blind. Let her hands and body lose all feeling. She would not allow Leopold to escape, and she would not let him walk free and un-damaged. He was *not* worthy of a god; it was past time that his mischief had consequences.

Green forests. Limestone and lakes. Leopold's Threads shifted from panic and fear to fury and hate. In the Dreaming. Outside of it. No matter how he pivoted or pulled, attacked or assaulted, he could not get Iseult to release him.

"Let a man have his secrets?" Iseult asked as they once more glided through the Dreaming, so thrice-damned calm with its snow and its gray and its nothingness. "How many t-times did you say that to deflect me from finding the truth?"

"I have never hurt you—"

"You have *ruined* the Witchlands. You have *killed* Aeduan."

"Then fix it, Iseult." Now Leopold's Threads blazed into something new—a shade of such godlike power, Iseult's eyes screwed shut against her will. Her grip didn't weaken, though, even when he sank low again and tried to snap her loose.

They tore out of the Dreaming. Humidity clawed in. And green and sunlight and warmth.

And Threads. So many Threads, burning and untamed, racing toward a master—or maybe several—west of here. A storm rallied there, accumulating thunderclouds like the hurricanes that sometimes struck the Dalmotti coast.

"That storm," Leopold said with wide, glimmering eyes, "is only the beginning of what awaits if you do not take the next step. The seas and rivers of the Witchlands will boil. Mountains will collapse, and all the people will burn. Unless you find Sirmaya and build us anew. I told you I had a plan, Iseult, and this is it." He opened his arms to the hot, sticky lands around them still thrumming and singing with life. "*In light,*" he recited, "*twelve will meet on lands long contested, while in darkness, the shadow-ender will topple nightmares and the world-starter will build us anew.*"

"That means n-nothing to me."

"It is the Lament, Iseult, and it cannot be ignored."

"It can be. I told you already, I'm done with that *goat shit.*" Winds brushed against Iseult now. Charged and smelling of rain, but not a storm yet. Not deadly. Just hot and burgeoning.

Leopold's Threads were hot too. They rolled against Iseult, through her, gradually claiming mastery over her primary senses. As if by stopping, her body now had no choice but to focus on the pain scorching into her through this god right here.

Her hands were ruined. She couldn't see them through the Threads, but she didn't need to. If Corlant's Threads had left scars . . .

I don't care.

"Three of the Twelve are here," Leopold continued. "I lured them here, by bringing the rulers they are bound to. That is what all those Threads in the distance mean. Rakel and Itosha have followed the king and queen they were created to protect. Ferisien will follow soon, and Lovats too.

"The final battle will begin, but only *you* can finish what Lisbet saw a thousand years ago. It is what your Moon Mother wants you to do. *The sleeper falls into the sky, awakening, so spring can finally weave.* It's all written, Iseult."

"Listen to yourself." Iseult could do nothing but laugh, a barbed, high-pitched sound. The pain was thickening within her body. "You lured the Exalted Ones here, using people as bait. All because you were too cowardly to ask directly."

"I am asking directly now." His cheeks twitched. "I am asking *you* to finish what must be finished."

"And I am responding," Iseult said, "with the answer *no.* Because that is my right, just as it's the right of everyone you *lured* into this disaster." Her lungs were struggling to cooperate. There was so much green here, thick and humid. And so much sunlight too. A vibrancy of life that didn't belong in a place where the world would soon be ending.

And the Threads, of course. Always the Threads. Except, as Iseult watched them, they changed. No longer squirming with the same intensity. No longer racing with the same speed—because they didn't need to. Their new homes were here; they'd reached their new masters.

In light, twelve will meet on lands long contested.

Iseult had been here before, in the Contested Lands. With Aeduan. She'd saved him by cleaving a Firewitch, repaying one life-debt of many— and forging the first strand of Heart-Threads that she would wear for the rest of her life. A short life, perhaps, but a life she wouldn't let end without some meaning behind it.

After all, she might not be chosen, but that didn't make her powerless.

Mhe varujta, she thought, and she finally let go of the Rook King. Leopold's Threads reeled away from her. Vibrant blue relief erupted across them . . . before turquoise alarm took hold. Iseult glanced down. Her hands were, indeed, smoking and raw. But good. Perhaps it would make what she was planning to do hurt less.

She turned away from Leopold fon Cartorra. "No," he called at her back. "No, Iseult, you are no match for those Exalted Ones, nor for the ones who still have not arrived. You cannot stop them."

She ignored him, and Iseult det Midenzi—who was nobody special at all—walked into the light of the Contested Lands.

For days, Caden and Alma had traveled alone on a road ever westward, and an hour ago, before this quaking and collapse had begun, Caden would have said he felt no closer to the Threadwitch than he had when they'd first met in the Nomatsi tribe. She was inscrutable, and conversation had always been perfunctory. *Where do the Threadstones lead? West. We must keep going west.*

But now, in this moment, Caden knew all he needed to know about her—and he'd never felt more certain that she was as loyal, as brave as any Hell-Bard he'd ever served with. The steely determination that had settled into her muscles was the only thing that kept Caden going.

Good enough, he thought, and although he still could hardly breathe through the magic that wanted to leave him, he shoved whatever remained of his strength into letting Alma tow him along.

The ringing in his ears magnified with each step. The wind that beat against them both blew harder—dry and thick with dust. This way was danger—*this* way was where the chaos of the moment aimed.

It was where they'd aimed ever since they'd left the tribe and the Solfatarra. A doorway he'd traveled through before, and *the* doorway where the Bloodwitch had found Lev's and Zander's nooses.

Then there it was, glowing through the trees: a magic access into the cursed mountain. Blue light seared outward, and although Caden's whole body felt aflame, he also felt the scratch of powerful, uncanny magic against him.

Alma slowed to a stop. Her panting breaths were lost to the forest still thrashing around them. "They're through here."

Caden heaved a nod and dragged himself around to face her. To grip her biceps and make her look at him with her silvery eyes. "You don't need to go in with me. It will likely be worse in there than out here—"

"No." Alma clutched Caden's arms. "You promised to get me to Saldonica, Hell-Bard. If I leave you now you cannot do that." Then she smiled at him, and it was like the first sunrise Caden had seen after he'd been set free from the noose. Color, life, dimension—they all washed over him in a way he had forgotten was possible.

"I will do all I can to protect you," he told her.

"I know," she replied, still smiling. "And remember that Moon Mother lights our path, so Trickster cannot find us." She tore away from him now, although her hand held fast to him, and she guided him to the doorway, pulsing and brilliant.

Magic scraped against them, and for half a moment, Caden no longer felt as if he were dying. As if the fire of his witchery were being sucked away.

He also felt an itching, inexplicable urge to look backward. Because something wrong, something hateful was back there—something he needed to witness before it was too late.

He turned.

And he saw. It was a figure, stocky and stonelike, more mountain than human with a skull that melded directly into their shoulders. And on their strange, earthen face was the grin of someone safe in the knowledge of their triumph.

The figure waved.

Then Caden and Alma were subsumed by the mountain's magic.

Do not snag the weave.
Do not snag the weave.

How many times had Gretchya or Alma or even Esme too said that to Iseult? Well, Iseult wasn't just going to snag the weave. She was going to completely obliterate it.

For half a mile, she ran through oaks and hot winds. Clouds gathered, but they couldn't fully block the sun. They couldn't shut up the birds and insects and whispering leaves that lived here.

Sometimes, she imagined she smelled coffee, fresh-brewed from Mathew's shop. Sometimes, she imagined she heard Safi laughing like she'd just won at taro. Twice, she *did* sense Leopold nearby. A flicker in the shadows of dappled trees. A murmur of desperate, yet cunning Threads.

He never stepped into her path, though, and he never tried to stop her.

Iseult lost track of time. She lost track of her exhausted body or her mangled hands. She thought of Aeduan, over and over again. Her final image of him was so broken. She wanted to summon a different version of him. *Any* version. The one who'd met her gaze across a canal in Veñaza City. The one who'd dived into a river to save her. The one who'd held her hand and walked her through hundreds of raiders and monks locked in place by his magic.

Her feet kicked at ancient, rusted armor from battles long forgotten. Ferns and flowers brushed against her.

Why so much fighting? Iseult had asked Aeduan as they'd crossed these same forests where humans might never live, but where other life always thrived. *Is the land so valuable?*

At the Monastery, he'd answered, *they taught us that when the Paladins betrayed each other, they fought their final battle here. Their deaths cursed the soil, so no man can ever claim the Contested Lands. I think it is all a lie, though.*

Why?

Because it is always easier to blame gods or legends than it is to face our own mistakes.

Yes. Iseult could see how true that was. No one had cursed this soil; the final battle had not even come yet—it was happening here *now* because a Trickster god had made it so.

Eventually, a shape hefted itself up from the forest, as if the earth itself were coming alive. Then a scent like soil and time curled into Iseult's nose, and to her shock, she felt her lips twitch with a grin.

"Hello, Blueberry. Is Owl w-with you?" She would not be able to hold back her tears if Owl were to appear, in this place where Aeduan had first found the child and saved her.

But the mountain bat only swatted his tail. It made a nearby boulder hop.

"I need to get close to that Exalted One in the distance. The thing making all the skies build with storm."

He opened membranous wings and squatted over to offer Iseult his back. The ground rippled around him—literally rippled like waves, because while magic might drain from the Witchlands, it was not abandoning the creatures to which it had always belonged.

His fur was hot and sunbaked. Iseult couldn't fit her legs across him like a horse, so she stretched herself flat against his back instead. Iron and stone scuttled up, moving with Blueberry's guidance from the forest floor. It crawled over Iseult's legs, her ankles, her waist and bound her to the bat like shackles.

Smart, she thought, since she couldn't use her ruined hands to hang on to him—and she would need these useless things soon, once they were near to the Exalted One.

Blueberry hefted himself up. Dust and ferns blew wide around them. White and yellow asphodels too, so beautiful. So alive. Then Iseult held her breath, closed her eyes, and the mountain bat took flight.

SIXTY-SIX

✳

Well, the weasel had turned out to be useless, and Sky kept thinking of something her mam used to say: *Over the falls and into the rapids.* Sky might have gotten out of the seafire, sure. But now she was in the middle of the rutting city where, instead of flames, there was a giant hole filled with *ice*.

And not normal ice either, like she was used to finding all over this city and Last Holdout. This was weird, veinous ice that carved across the ground in evenly spaced lines like the spokes of a wheel. And all those spokes moved toward a single mound where wet snow gathered.

The mound looked an awful lot like a corpse, and sorry, but Sky had had enough of those to last a lifetime. She shivered. She was literally the only thing alive here other than the weasel. Nothing moved except the snow, slopping down. There wasn't even a wind, which was about as unnatural as things could get here on the *Windswept* Plains. Also, hadn't this whole area been the Well? That's definitely what the map in the book was saying, but if a whole Origin Well could just disappear . . .

Blessed are the pure, Sky thought—and this time, the voice in her head sounded like Priest Corlant's.

She pulled out the book, fingers numb. Teeth chattering. If this *was* where the Well had been, then there was supposed to be a tunnel on the other side. An old hypocaust that had heated baths centuries ago . . .

Yep, Sky found it. Straight ahead. She just had to circle left around the gaping hole she didn't want to study too closely. She returned the book to her pocket and shifted, ready to leave.

But the weasel had other plans—and now it wasn't even pretending to be a normal animal doing normal animal things. It raced right for Sky, white as the snow, and it chittered and purred, curling its tiny form around Sky's boots.

Then an image formed in Sky's brain. Although *image* was overstating the clarity of what appeared there. It was more like a *feeling* laced by vague shapes, and that *feeling* indicated the snowy mound ahead.

"You . . . want me to walk over to that mound? Where all the ice lines are going? No way." Sky snorted. "I ain't doing that. I'm going over to that old hypocaust, and I'm getting the hell-pits out of here."

The weasel didn't like this answer, and after zipping up Sky's body, it bit her on the face. Just *bit* her, right on the nose with wicked fangs and claws to stab into Sky's neck.

Sky punted the weasel off her, squawking with surprise and pain. The weasel hit the snow ten paces away, but she was down no more than a heartbeat before she got to her little feet and hurled forward again.

Sky ran; part of her was ashamed to be fleeing a *rodent*, but most of her was wondering what this cursed creature was and why she, Sky, had gotten trapped in this completely unhinged reality of ice craters and weasels.

Her feet pounded into ice veins on the ruined earth, and each time they hit, a ringing walloped through her. It didn't hurt so much as stagger Sky with the intensity of its response—and it reminded Sky of this one spot on her elbow that always knocked her silly whenever she bonked it. This ice wasn't just weird, it was alive. It was *part* of some greater being.

Nope, Sky didn't like this and she didn't like that weasel and she didn't like that she was close enough now to the mound beneath the snow that she could see blood trailing outward from it. Six trails moving on the wheel spokes . . . until they froze, forming the very veins Sky couldn't seem to avoid.

The weasel chittered anew, and fresh feelings and images filled Sky. *The sword*, it seemed to say. *Drop the sword.*

Sky obeyed. She flung the sword at the mound. To her horror, though, the sword didn't just rotate a few times through the air, then land on its side like it *should* have done. Instead, it found a path all its own and stabbed right into the mound. Fully vertical, exactly as it had when it had landed on the cobblestones before.

The ice veins all rang at once. The mound groaned.

And Sky gave one more *Nope* before running with all her heart away from that mound, that ice, that sword, and that weasel.

Heat roars. Wood cracks and embers fly.

"Run." Blood drips from his mother's mouth as she speaks. It splatters his face.

With arms stained to red, she pushes herself up. She wants him to crawl out from beneath her. She wants him to escape. "Run, my child, run."

But he does not move, just as he did not move when the raiders first ambushed the tribe. Just as he did not move when his father drew his sword and ran from their tent. Or when the raiders reached their doorway, loosed their arrows, and then his mother fell atop him. She had hidden him with her body until the raiders had moved on.

"Run," she whispers one last time, pleading desperation in her silver eyes. Then the last of her strength flees. She collapses onto him.

The six arrows that pierced her body slam into Aeduan. Pain and punctured breath and blood, blood, blood. Always the blood.

He is pinned by cedar and corpse. His mother is dead.

And now there will be no running. Now there is only flame.

He begins to cry.

Aeduan watched himself. He stood where the raider had stood when he'd loosed the six bolts into Dysi's back. He stood at the mouth of their tent—except there was no tent now. No walls or battle raging in the tribe. All that surrounded Aeduan was fire and shadow.

Death follows wherever you go, yet by the grace of the Wells, you always outrun your own.

All he had wanted that day as a child was to join his mother and escape the flames. But death had refused to claim him. His mother's body had kept away the full brunt of the fire's force; his magic had healed his wounds.

Demon. Monster. You're bound to the Void, a cursed beast with 'Matsi poison running in your veins.

Eventually, Dysi's body had burned away. Eventually the arrows in Aeduan's chest had too, leaving only white-hot heads trapped inside his chest. And eventually, Evrane's gentle face and gentle hands had found Aeduan among the debris.

For so many years, Aeduan had relived that nightmare. Only once before though had he hovered outside like this, watching as his mother died and his wounds oozed blood upon the floor.

Now here he was again.

Yet rather than watch as the vision ended with Evrane carrying Aeduan away, the memory continued. Rain kept falling. Smoke kept rising from flames buried deep in the wreckage. As he had done beside the Aether Well, Aeduan turned to see if he blocked someone from entering . . .

That was when he saw a new figure. Staggering, frantic, the man dove into what remained of the tent. He flung, he searched, he wept and shouted: "Son! Where are you, my son!"

It was Aeduan's father, too late to save those he'd loved. Too late to do anything, for even Dysi's corpse was gone now. There was nothing at all for Ragnor to find. Nothing at all for him to save.

He scoured and crawled anyway, and for a time he vanished from Aeduan's view, as if he searched wider, farther than the nightmare would let Aeduan see. Then Ragnor returned and collapsed to his knees in the middle of their ruined home.

As Aeduan watched Ragnor's heart break, he felt his own break too. For how many nights had his own father relived this carnage? This failure? How many times had Ragnor, like his son, died that day? And how many times, like his son, had Ragnor been alone in this nightmare with no child, no wife, no escape? He'd had only the darkness and himself, the nightmare and himself.

As the vision continued onward, Aeduan sensed his father's blood transform. From frosted baby's breath and sleeping ice, from loving hounds and nighttime songs, a new shape emerged: *bone-deep loss and flame.*

All these years, Ragnor had blamed himself for what had happened that day, and Aeduan knew precisely how such blame could warp you. How it gave death meaning and life a twisted light.

Aeduan had been a child trapped in the wreckage of war, and Ragnor had been a father trapped in the same. Ragnor had not done this—he had not *caused* this—yet he had lost his life to it all the same.

One need not be evil to become it.

Ragnor lifted his head. His hazel eyes found Aeduan's. The tears streaking down slowed. "Ah, my son. I failed you. I failed her."

"You didn't, Father. You tried to protect us from the flames."

Ragnor frowned, glancing around at the nightmare—and seeming to realize, much as Aeduan had, that none of this was real. "Here. Yes, I did." A slow nod. An inward puzzling that made his brow furrow. Then again, his hazel eyes found Aeduan's. "But *there*, at the Well—I failed your mother. She warned me the Wells should not be healed. She *warned me* that only more death and violence would ensue. And I tried. By the Sleeping Goddess, I tried."

"What did she tell you, Father? You've always said it was her cause that you aimed to finish, but what was it?"

"She said the Cahr Awen were not real. That they were a lie to make us all believe someone would save us, when the truth was that no one would. *We* hurt Moon Mother. *We*, the people of the Witchlands, hurt her. For you see, when the Six and your mother and I made the Wells, we cut six deep wounds into the goddess. But those wounds could never heal because we never understood that no one can save us but ourselves."

Ah. Aeduan felt his breath unwind. A release of air held too long. Six Wells. Six wounds. And a desire to give death meaning by forever blaming oneself. Aeduan had learned that lesson the hard way, hadn't he? Months ago, in this same nightmare with the same flames and the same falling rain.

No one could save him but himself.

Four long steps carried Aeduan to his father. He stared at the face so much like his own, half hidden by shadows and pain. Ragnor had been a loving father long ago. Now he was nothing more than a ghost filled with aching memories.

Just as Dysi had been.

With careful hands, Aeduan gripped Ragnor's shoulders. "Father," he said. "It is done. There is nothing here, and you can let go now."

His father nodded. A tired movement as he gazed back at Aeduan. "She told me you were special, you know. *Born in the Moon Mother's own ice,* she always said. *And that which is closest, she cannot see. A strand fallen from the weave, cast adrift on winds of flame . . .*"

His father did not finish. Not before he crumbled into black nothing and whispered away. But Aeduan already knew what came next, for he'd heard the lines of the Lament before. Inside the mountain, inside the Moon Mother.

A knife with two sides. Blood on the snow, he thought.

He looked down at his shredded clothes. At the six old wounds exposed into this nightmare. They'd bled away his life and strength for so long. But no one could heal them. No one but himself.

SIXTY-SEVEN

※

On the one hand, Kullen had not led Merik astray. The brightest doorway had led Merik to a place where no settlements clustered in the forest and no boats slid down the nearby river. There were no plumes of smoke from cooking fires or mines; no signs of humanity at all.

This was the Contested Lands, and it was a hot, green place broken only by a canyon filled with stone.

As Merik flew ever higher into the sky, it occurred to him—vaguely, distantly—how very similar those megaliths in the nearby gorge looked to the stones he'd just escaped near Poznin. Different colors, different shapes, but still a mark on the landscape that someone in the sky might see.

Just as someone from the ground would see Merik.

And Itosha did spot him as soon as she burst into the light. Thunder and storm clouds spewed up from the earth with her. Laughter split into Merik's skull, except now, rather than declare her joy at finding Merik, she bayed out something else entirely: *Sister, you are here!*

Merik knew right away that this was bad. One Paladin was already too much for him. Two would be unstoppable. *Who is it?* he asked. *What does she mean by sister?*

Another Exalted One, Kullen answered, and for the first time, fear bled across their bond. *It must be Rakel, the Paladin of*—

Merik didn't hear what came next. He didn't need to, for a new voice crawled deep into his viscera. It was made of shipwrecks and decay. Of dead fish and endless tides—and of a hot, craggy shoreline where Merik had spent his childhood.

Water, he knew right away. *This monster has mastery over water.*

Merik turned, flipping his winds until he found this new Paladin. She hefted her body like a crocodile onto the river's shore, unmissable. Unmistakable. Where Itosha had been stretched by time and cruelty, this creature had been compressed into a pulp of gray limbs and bloat.

And she dragged a person behind her. Unmoving and unknown. Yet as

Merik watched, as he once more changed his trajectory to try to save them, the figure *did* move. And suddenly she was *not* unknown. Suddenly, she was terrifyingly familiar: his sister. Half-drowned, but rising.

And now grabbing at something long and sharp on the shore. She stabbed it into the Paladin, who screamed with a voice that spewed into the sky.

The Paladin retaliated. With waters so vast, so violent, there would be no escaping them.

No, Merik thought—and at that same instant, Itosha, still squalling behind him, shrieked the same thing in her ancient tongue: "NO." The word rattled through her winds, her rains, creating a thunder all its own. "NO."

Merik snapped toward her, expecting a fresh attack. Except it was not at *him* that Itosha directed this ire. A new creature scorched the skies toward the river—massive, winged, and the color of moss and soil.

A mountain bat, Merik knew because Kullen knew.

But the bat was not alone. There was a person on its back, her eyes glowing. Her hands smoking—and her mouth too, as if she were cooking alive.

In that moment, Merik recalled what Safi had told him about the Cahr Awen, about how only she and the Threadwitch Iseult could heal the Air Well.

Now that Threadwitch was right here.

Itosha shrieked. She writhed, her pale hair flinging out like barbed whips. Her winds flailed in uncontrolled directions. She no longer cared about the little hound. She no longer seemed to sense that Merik was there at all.

Thank you, Merik thought at Iseult, and in that moment, he knew there really could be no accounting in the way he'd always done. *One for the sake of many. Many for the sake of one.* Life was life, and it was always worth preserving.

Hye, Kullen agreed, and with his magic to fuel Merik ever onward, Merik aimed for his sister.

The pain that consumed Iseult was different from the pain she'd felt with Leopold. This was the pain of hurricanes colliding. Of monsoons building and blizzards crashing down. She felt as timeless as the sky and as ephemeral as a cloud.

Itosha. That was the name she thought this Exalted One wore, and she was the creature who'd crawled from the Air Well. She was the power Ragnor had tried to keep Iseult and Safi from awakening.

Like Leopold, Itosha wanted to lose Iseult. Unlike Leopold, the Exalted One's thrashing was far more deadly. Leopold hadn't intended to hurt Iseult; he'd only needed her to release him.

Itosha, meanwhile, aimed to destroy. She attacked with winds, with lightning, with hot rains and frozen gales. Water shredded Iseult's clothes until there was no fabric left. Until it was skin that cooked. Then her muscles and sinew.

The lightning, meanwhile, was content to simply *eradicate* with each new crackling charge. Iseult became the heat, the light, the explosion of sound all around her. *Crack. Consume. Crack. Eradicate.*

Distantly, she knew that Blueberry did his best to evade each attack. But he flew on wings, while Itosha flew on raw, undiluted power taken from every Airwitch in the land.

And as much as Iseult *tried* to sink into herself—to finish this fight she had started with whatever Weaverwitchery she still had left—Itosha wouldn't let her. Because with every slash of Itosha's magic, Iseult also felt the slashing of her Threads. Of her emotions, more raw and undiluted than even her magic was.

The Exalted One was furious and hungry, and above all, she was *afraid*. She had spent so many years drowning—now it would all end? Like this? With a wretched body she didn't recognize and pain, pain, pain?

Iseult *knew* she had to drag these Threads to her teeth and sever, sever, twist and sever, but how could she do so when she was so locked into an Exalted One who wasn't ready to die?

Shock waves beat into Iseult's elbows. Her ribs. Her organs. She saw nothing but the Threads. She heard nothing but the crackling core of a Paladin made of storms. *I thought you would be stronger,* Corlant had said to Iseult when she'd tried to do this to him. When the dark current at the heart of his Void magic had defeated her. *But there is still time for you to become the dark-giver you were meant to be. The shadow-ender the Witchlands needs.*

Everyone had a different idea of what those titles meant. Of what Iseult—and Safi too—were supposed to do.

And now you have your own idea, she thought. *Now it is time to finish this. You are not your mind. You are not your body. They are merely tools so you may fight onward.*

Iseult opened her mouth. She chomped down.

Nothing happened. Only more heat to ignite her skull. Only more pain—hers and Itosha's—to rattle, rattle, *shatter* into her teeth and eye sockets.

Oh no, Iseult realized as smoke filled her nasal cavity. *I am no longer a Weaverwitch at all. I am no longer bound to the Void, because there is no Void.* She was only the magic that the first Nomatsis had brought out of the east, only the Threads unbound to Moon Mother.

Not only had Iseult's power as Eridysi's blade been removed from her when she'd healed the Well, but *everything* else had too. And now Itosha's storm would finish its destruction. Iseult's body would be pummeled and cooked, while her mind would finish collapsing into the strength of Itosha's Threads.

There would be no completing what Iseult had initiated. There would be only oblivion.

When Safi left the mountain, she found herself in a land subsumed by storm. It was like Poznin all over again, except now it wasn't winter, it wasn't cold. There were no evergreens or soft earth. There was only heat and oaks and dry soil. *This is the Contested Lands.*

Safi had been here before, with Vaness, with Caden and Zander and Lev. There was a sharpness to this landscape she recognized, built by sunshine and the absence of humans. As if this place was what *all* the Witchlands could be—content and brimming with life—if people and their worst instincts would simply get out of the way.

Hot, fat droplets hit Safi's already blistered scalp, shoulders, hands, while the winds that accumulated froze like winter's coldest breath.

For several uncountable moments, Safi felt detached from herself. As if she were watching a performance unfold upon a stage. She knew she was in this forest where oaks groaned and ferns ripped from their homes. Where water cut down in fat lines and soaked the dry soil. Where insects and animals fled for their lives at the edges of her vision.

She also felt the winds gasping against her and the rain digging in. What she didn't feel, though, was herself.

She followed these other feelings, these external Threads, her body a weathervane until she found Itosha in the sky with storms churning around her—storms that were focused on one small speck flipping and diving through the rain. Winds lashed at that speck. Lightning tried to cook it.

Love and dread, Safi thought, for that small speck was a mountain bat.

And on it was a person who somehow held on to the storm's Threads, clinging to them like a child holding a thousand kites.

There was only one person it could be. Only one person who could make Safi's heart instantly swell—make her muscles regain all strength and certainty.

"Iseult," Safi gasped, and without another thought, she hurled herself forward. Through trenches dug up by rain. Past torn-up trees and over massive roots that groaned against the winds.

She had to blink rain from her eyes—and mist too, which had begun to rise in the forest with Threads of Waterwitch blue lacing through it. What was Iseult doing? What was Iseult *going* to do? She couldn't hold on to those Threads forever. They would kill her if the Exalted One did not.

Unless, Safi thought, *there is something else that we can bind the Threads to.* She thought of her Truth-lens, she thought of her sword, and she thought of how she'd been able to make those things with the skills of a Threadwitch.

Then she thought about how Iseult had never been able to . . . and something about that scratched at the nape of Safi's neck. There had been those rocks near Poznin, arranged in a way she'd thought meant something. Those rocks weren't here, but . . .

She knew where there were others like them in the Contested Lands.

"I'm coming," she panted as mist pushed into her mouth. "Hang on, Iseult. Like you did before."

SIXTY-EIGHT

※

When Aeduan awoke from his nightmare, it was to find a sword had pierced his belly. There was an uncanny stillness draped over Poznin. A brutal cold, too. It didn't bother him, so much as fold into him. One more dimension to add to the many dimensions that filled him after the dream.

He inhaled, savoring the scent of a sky singing with snow. Of meadows drenched in moonlight, and of sun and sand and auburn leaves falling.

That was the scent of the Sleeping Giant. Aeduan recognized that now.

With a wince, he crunched upward onto his elbows. It hurt—the sword was all the way through him. But he gripped the hilt with one hand, and in a single, easy move, he wrenched it out.

A groan unwound from his throat. Blood spurted. Then the wound crusted over with ice he was beginning to . . . not understand, but at least *recognize*. He set the sword beside him. It was the Truthwitch's blade—he'd already found it once, and now here it was, delivered right to him.

Its sheath was gone. Burned away like so much of this city around him.

Aeduan patted at a pocket on his thigh, where the necklace waited. Despite many rips and tears that had shredded his clothing, this little gift from the Truthwitch still remained. And like the sword beside him, the bits of quartz and glass hummed with a purity of purpose.

"This necklace," Moon Mother explained, "will remind you of who you are and how all your adventures have shaped you. And this . . ." She offered him the second gift: a small knife sharp as starlight. "This will help you build the world anew, Little Monster. Your world, for the choice has always been yours."

"Thank you, Moon Mother," Aeduan said to the snow falling around him. "For everything."

A breeze stroked across him, tender like his mother's kisses had once been—and filled with more love than any little monster really deserved. *Run, my child,* she whispered again, just as she had in the nightmare. Just as she'd always told him, whenever he'd needed it most. *Run.*

The Bloodwitch named Aeduan stood up, and he ran.

SIXTY-NINE

✳

N o!" Iseult tried to scream. "No, *Blueberry, no!*" He was flying her away from the Exalted One Itosha.

Maybe Blueberry's hurt? Maybe he's dying? Iseult couldn't easily see. Her vision was devoured by these Threads that wouldn't break, wouldn't die. The only way she knew they plummeted down was because of the occasional spurts of awareness: sunrise in the east. Clouds, black and boiling. Forest filled with chopping waves. Sandy, striated megaliths surrounded by fog.

"No!" she tried again, letting her throat rip and the last of her air burst forth. "No, *don't go this way!*"

Blueberry kept going that way. Straight down as more boulders launched, propelled by Threads that warned of their approach. Treetops zoomed in, smears of green that split into Iseult's consciousness.

She thought hail might be hitting them.

Behind Iseult, the Exalted One Itosha howled. She was still leashed to Iseult, but Threads wouldn't stretch forever. Eventually Iseult's grip would give out or Itosha would yank Iseult off this bat and kill her.

One final scream for Blueberry. "No, *please!*" But he still didn't listen. Instead, he whipped them into a canyon filled with rocks that Iseult knew well. There was the Amonra. There were the red and yellow striations that had eroded into a column-filled canyon.

And there was the *exact* stone where Iseult had cleaved the Firewitch to save Aeduan.

Beside the stone was Safi. It made no sense, how she could be there, but then, hadn't Iseult learned at least one truth by now? *Threads make decisions the mind cannot.* Safi and Iseult didn't keep finding each other—again and again across the Witchlands—because they were some chosen Cahr Awen pair; they always found each other because they were Threadsisters. That bond, that love, that *choice* would always bring them together.

Blueberry skidded to a rough landing. Earth and ferns and flowers ripped up, moved by his magic and his enormity. Iseult felt the shackles connecting her to him give out. But she couldn't move even if she'd wanted to. Everything she had was being funneled into her fingers, her knuckles, her palms.

Do not let go. Do not let go.

"Please, let me go." These were the words of the Exalted One. "*Please, let me go. Do not bind me again. Do not leave me to drown for all eternity.*"

Hands came to Iseult. Urgent and rough. They dragged her, by wind and by foot, to the pillar where Iseult had given in to the severing, severing, twisting, and severing.

There was no Aeduan here now. *Blood. Witch. Blood. Witch.* There was only the stone soaking up a hot rain.

"All right, Iz," she thought she heard Safi say. "I'm taking the first of these Threads. You've got to trust me—do you trust me?"

Always.

"Then let go."

Iseult loosened her fingers. Her knuckles, which were past broken and fully shattered, shook like the world around her. It was a wonder she could move the muscles and bones at all. A wonder there was any agency left inside her. But her grip did loosen. Her fingers did splay.

Safi grabbed hold. One by one, her inexperience evident, but not stopping her, until the last of Itosha's Threads wove out of Iseult's fingers into Safi's.

The Exalted One screamed.

The ease with which Safi had made her Truth-sword was *nothing* like what she did now. She'd made that tool in the stutter between heartbeats, looping and knotting exactly as she'd practiced with her Truth-lens. Intuition had been all she'd needed because it was *her* magic on a single blade of steel.

Now . . . it was like the worst test from Habim. Words like *Korelli Double-Fastening* or *Vergedi Inverted Knot* kept emitting from her brain. And Safi wanted to shout, *I am not a Threadwitch! I don't remember what any of those words mean!* She'd read exactly *one* book on Threadstones, and all of those names were useless if she couldn't recall how to apply them.

She wanted to ask Iseult for help. Her Threadsister must remember all her lessons from childhood, even if she'd never been able to do what her mother wanted so desperately—and what *she*, Iseult, had wanted so desperately too.

But Iseult had curled too deeply into herself. She was nothing more than a black-clad mound on the muddied earth by Safi's feet. Which meant that if this task needed completing, it would have to be Safi and Safi alone.

If you wanted to, Safiya, you could bend and shape the world. Her uncle had been right about that, and here she was, literally holding on to the weave of the world. To the Threads that defined air.

And *oh*, here was the Arlenni Loop. Here was the Vergedi knot—which yes she could see how to invert if she flipped her left wrist sideways. And all right, sure, Safi would braid these Threads over there together, anchoring them deep into this rock before her. One rock was not enough to hold all of this, so when it could contain no more power, Safi shuffled sideways to another one.

Rains still sliced down, although gentler now. No more hail. No more scalding winds. Instead, there were simply more Threads. More power. More spirals and twists and knots . . .

And pain. It scored through Safi's fingertips and up her arms. It flamed into her skull like a lantern. But Safi had felt pain—she had *become* pain beside the Well when Kahina had tried to keep her out of the waters. This was no different, except now Safi had a purpose: she was undoing the mistakes of the Well.

She was bending and shaping everything, with Iseult right beside her. Exhausted, but alive. Threadsisters to the end.

With each Thread bound to stone, the world quieted. The storms softened. The screams and agony of the Exalted One faded—as did the screams and agony inside Safi. Until at last, there were no more Threads left to bind to stone. No more air storms or winds or thunderclaps. Just a defeated creature, fallen and bound.

Itosha crashed to the earth near Blueberry. Her Threads throbbed in time to her heaving breaths. Her birdlike body was crumpled and compressed. She didn't look as Safi approached.

She did speak though: "This will not hold me. You can tie me, but it will not hold forever."

"No," Safi agreed. She too was heaving and hurting as a hundred new bruises and cuts made themselves known across her body. "It won't hold. But . . . well . . ." *We'll figure that out then. Initiate, complete.*

She stumbled past Itosha—ancient, sad—and aimed back the way she'd come. Back to Iseult and the first pillar, where yes . . . already, Threads were loosing. Already, air magic was wavering free and building once more into Itosha.

But there was something else happening too. A vacillation in the Threads of the land, as if the very fabric that defined this canyon around them was ripping. It was as if someone came this way with scissors to snip-snap through the weave of the world.

Iseult, Safi thought. *Oh gods, what's happening to Iseult?*

The world shivered and smeared before Iseult. Safi had taken the Threads from her, then she'd bound them in ways Iseult could sense at the edges of her magic . . . Already, however, the magic was tugging free. Even with these massive stones and all of Safi's cleverness, it wouldn't be enough to hold the Exalted One down.

So training took over. Iseult was nobody special, but that didn't mean she couldn't find more inside to give.

She staggered to her feet. She readied her stance, arms lifting. Fingers opening. Itosha would break free, so Iseult would be ready. Probably. Maybe.

But that was when she saw it all change. The Exalted One's Threads shivered . . . then tightened. Then *froze* in a way Iseult knew because Iseult had seen it so many times before. First at a lighthouse by Veñaza City, when he had tried—and failed—to control her. Then hundreds, thousands, *countless* times since.

Moments later, he was there. A figure in white coalescing before her. Her Bloodwitch, back from the dead again.

Threads whispered off Aeduan, exactly as they had at the Well. It left a line through the weave of the world like a ship cutting through water, and although Iseult had no comprehension of how he could be here, she knew she couldn't look away.

Blood. Witch. Blood. Witch.

Twice before she'd thought that Aeduan carried himself as if he came from another time. As if he had walked a thousand years and planned to walk a thousand more. Now, she had no doubt it was true—and that a thousand years was, in fact, a very short time for a man with a heart like his.

She watched him walk ever closer. His pace never slowed. Until at last, Aeduan came to a stop before her. Iseult was upright, if barely. He didn't touch her or reach out to assist. And she made no attempt to reach him. His clothing was as ruined as it had been in Poznin. She could see his six old wounds, bloodied and raw.

She wanted to touch them. She wanted to touch *him*. And she wanted to cry and say, *How are you here, Aeduan? Please, please, don't go again.*

But she didn't. And instead she kept watching as he dropped to a kneel before her, just as he had in the snowy forest near the hunting lodge. As he bowed his head—where ice and snow still rested on his brown hair. Rather than offer vows, he instead offered her two tools.

A necklace and a sword. The necklace and sword Safi had made before they'd lost the power of Eridysi's blade and glass. They radiated cold, and just as Threads avoided Aeduan, the weave of the world fled those tools.

Not because Aeduan was dead, but because he was alive. As were these tools.

Iseult reached for them, her hands so broken she wasn't sure she could actually hold them. Her palms and fingers were blackened and shaking, but they obeyed her command. Enough, at least, that she could grip the hilt. A jolt of familiarity surged through her—yet there was something else too, for this was not merely the blade Eridysi had made. This was not merely the magic that Leopold had bound to people centuries ago . . .

This was a new blade, and it sang with truth. It sang with certainty. And above all, it sang with snow and meadows drenched in moonlight. With sun and sand and auburn leaves falling. With every magic that had ever been, from every place that had ever felt the goddess thrumming beneath it.

A song, Iseult realized distantly, that Aeduan echoed as well.

Iseult dragged herself around to face Safi. Her Threadsister was stumbling closer, her clothes and hair torn, her body sodden and spine exhausted. Her eyes—always the color of the Jadansi's wildest waves—gaped at Aeduan like the ghost he was.

"Knifey," she said, "you have great timing." She grabbed the necklace and draped it over her head in a surprisingly strong move.

Then together, Iseult and Safi turned to face the Exalted One, still collapsed twenty paces away. Itosha seemed to know what items Iseult held and Safi wore. She seemed to know what awaited her.

And she could do nothing about it. She was held in place by the power Aeduan had always possessed to freeze, but a power that was now fueled by something so much vaster.

"Have I not suffered enough?" Itosha asked as Iseult and Safi took one staggering step after another. "We were always awake, while the world feasted on our bones. Do not curse me again."

"No," Iseult said as she came to a stop before the Exalted One. "No one deserves that much pain." At these words, Iseult glanced at Aeduan. He no longer knelt beside the stone, but simply stood, watching her with his eyes the shade of sleeping ice.

"Please," the Exalted One begged now while Safi studied her Threads through a Truth-lens. "Please do not change me again."

"There," Safi said quietly, pointing to a cluster of silver shot through with blue. "Start there."

Iseult obeyed. *While the right hand distracts,* she thought as she slung out the sword, *the left hand cuts the purse.* She sliced through Itosha's soul.

The Exalted One screamed. It was not a scream of pain, for she didn't cleave—she didn't even die. She simply lost all of the Threads, one by one, that had made her more than human. Made her bigger than a mere witch.

Safi found more clusters of Threads, more key connections that bound Itosha to Sirmaya and to the Witchlands. Eridysi and the Six hadn't known what they'd initiated in the mountain a thousand years ago. Nor, Iseult thought, had Leopold known despite all these centuries he'd spent trying to undo it.

There was no going back. As Ragnor had said: there was only breaking the cycle. Stepping outside.

And thinking beyond.

As the last of Itosha's Paladin soul slipped away, released into a continent that needed the magic back, ice crackled slowly—achingly—over her crooked body. And by the time the girls were done, there was nothing left but a coffin of impenetrable cold where Itosha had once been.

Come, come, the ice sang, with the same tune that echoed off Aeduan and that the mountain had sung before him. *Sleep, my daughter. Come, come, my ice will hold you.*

When at last it was complete, Iseult turned to her Bloodwitch who still stood beside the striated rock, stoic and ancient. He had not moved this entire time. The only thing that had changed about him since he'd handed over the new blade and glass were the wounds on his abdomen.

The highest on his chest had healed over. No scar, no blood.

Five wounds remained.

Iseult exhaled. She wanted to laugh. She wanted to find Leopold fon Cartorra and gloat into his face: *Do you see how wrong you had it? Your stupid Lament meant nothing.* But instead, Iseult dropped the sword to dry, hoarfrosted earth and staggered toward her Bloodwitch.

He opened his arms.

Iseult slid her blackened, aching hands around him. One breath they were like this. Then a second. Before arms slung around them both.

"Goat tits, Iz. Can we agree to never do something like this again?"

SEVENTY

※

This water knows us. This water chose us, Vivia thought uselessly as the river flung her and snapped her, like the calico had with his rats. Vivia had been towed ashore, where she'd seen a rusted sword from battles long ago. She'd snatched it. She'd attacked.

But it hadn't been enough.

Because it always seemed that Vivia was never quite enough.

She had always felt so powerful in the underground lake that had belonged to her and her mother. Through that lake, she'd been able to connect to every droplet of water inside the Lovats plateau. All the way up into the Sirmayan Mountains. Some days all the way out toward the sea. She'd felt so tiny, so inconsequential, and it had filled her with a tender, nurturing awe—for there was a comfort in knowing that the world and Nubrevna would spin on, even when Vivia did not.

Now, the awe she felt was shaped like despair. She was tiny and inconsequential in a different way. The water no longer knew her; the water no longer chose her. She was a dead rat who hadn't quite died yet, but there would be no soft-hearted princess to save her.

Until there was. Or rather, there was a soft-hearted prince.

Vivia felt him, in the waters beside her. A bond that was not built from magic or tides or winds. These were Threads no master could take from Vivia—because they had been made so very long ago in a fox's den where two children had felt safe.

Merry, she tried to say.

Vee, she heard him reply. Then she was no longer in the waters but instead on the shore where waves crashed and hot wind flayed against her. Entire trees cracked down.

As one, Vivia and Merik turned to face the whitecapped waters hurtling toward them. The flood would hit them in heartbeats. Two rulers. A sister and a brother who'd never really known each other, and only recently tried.

The onslaught arrived.

Out flung Merik's arms. Wind, tides, power. A wall of magic to meet white foam. He slid, his planted feet dragging him backward across the gouged-apart riverbank. And he roared, a sound that tore from his throat. Sent his jaw slinging low as more winds, more power coursed out of him.

How, Vivia wondered. *How does he have such power?* Had she been wrong to believe magic was gone? She'd seen Zander lose it. Lev and Vaness too. And Vivia had felt it all leach out of her.

Her hair slapped against her face. Cuts she hadn't known were there stretched wider as Merik's winds slashed and fought. More, more. An untouched well that must come from deep inside him . . .

The Well, Vivia thought, and she remembered what the monster had said in the waves: *Ah, the little hound I used to watch over. It is time to take back everything we gave you.*

Merik had grown up swimming in the Origin Well of Nihar.

Vivia had grown up in her underground lake—a place where she'd only ever felt safe. Watched over. And long after Jana had left this world, the lake and its foxfire spokes had been there.

Yes, a gentle voice whispered. *I am so very far from you, Little Fox. But I can still give you what you need. I never forgot why I was made. You need only ask, and it will be there.*

"Who . . . ?" Vivia choked out. "How can a . . . a lake be inside in my head?"

Because I am a lake no longer, the voice answered. *I used to be known as Midne before I became the Void Well. I used to serve and protect, and I vow that right now, I will do so again.*

At those words—incomprehensible as they were—Vivia felt her waters return. Not *these* lethal rapids of the Amonra, but *her* waters. Unbound by droplets and limestone, by tributaries or mountains.

She felt as she was returned home.

And Vivia took that power. No rage, no hate, no love, no past. Just power, letting her reconnect to the waters that frenzied around her—but that now she could control again.

Vivia lifted one leg, stepping forward, pushing herself, pushing the waters. A second step became a third. One foot after the other into the waters that this beast had tried to take from her.

And beside her, Merik walked too. Their steps matched. One. Two. *Fight. Push.* Three. Four. *No regrets.* Five. Six. *Keep moving.* His winds never faltered.

Until suddenly, their magics grew bigger. As if leashes had been shorn.

As if dams had been broken. More power *slammed* into Vivia, and she could do nothing but redirect it outward. Launch more river, more wave at the beast who fought with tide, with ice, with steam, with pain.

Vivia and Merik were in the middle of the river now, the waters cleared around them. Wet silt sucking them down as they pushed, stepped, fought. No regrets, *still* moving.

The monster roared, her massive form briefly faltering in the face of these two Nihars.

That was when the iron launched in. A hundred blades from battles long ago stabbed deep. Punctured hard. And when Vivia turned, she found Vaness was only paces away. *Her* empress. *Her* Ironwitch, and with fury scored across her beautiful face and violence in her dark eyes.

"I," Vaness screamed as she staggered to Vivia's side, "am Empress of the Flame Children! I am the Chosen Daughter of the Fire Well. I am the Most Worshipped in Marstok and the Destroyer of Kendura Pass. You will *not* claim me today."

Hye, Vivia thought. *And you are the woman I love.* She'd never been more certain. Never felt more pride and power and hope. All this time, Vaness had been trying to teach Vivia how to not simply trade her little fox mask for the mask of a bear, but how to *know* that being the fox was enough. Because Vivia was enough and she always had been. It was in her blood, in her heritage, and above all, in the truth that she was *here*, still fighting, when almost all others would have given up.

So Vivia Nihar joined the chorus. "I am the Chosen Daughter of the Void Well. I am the rightful Queen of Nubrevna and the destroyer of the Dalmotti navy. And *I* am the Little Fox you cannot drown."

Over and over, Vivia bellowed these words at the face of the bloated monster that could *not* have her. She might be made of pure magic, pure water, but she still was no match for three rulers with entire kingdoms that they would die to defend.

As if he thought the same, Merik joined in the war cries too: "I am the Leader of Last Holdout. The son of Jana and the Prince of Nubrevna. I fight for one and I fight for many. *You cannot claim us.*"

And with one final push—*no regrets, keep moving*—the monster in the waters shrieked terror, pain, defeat.

Then she fled. A calico who had learned some rats were not worth fighting.

Merik felt everything change when the one called Rakel finally fled. It wasn't just that the magic around him shifted—or that the monster's attacks were gone and this wrecked shore was left in quaking silence.

It wasn't just that Merik's own winds had returned, either, or that a new spring had filled him halfway into the battle.

And it wasn't *just* that everything in the world had fallen silent. No more storms, no more Itosha, no more battle . . .

It was that the power inside Merik had shifted. Where his own winds were trickling into existence once more, the ones that belonged to Kullen were now fading.

No, Merik thought as he dragged himself away from his sister and the Empress of Marstok. Away from the countless questions he wasn't ready to contend with. *It's not the magic of Kullen that's fading. It is Kullen himself.*

"Where are you?" The words climbed from Merik's throat, coarse as rusted knives. "Kullen, where are you?"

Kullen didn't answer.

Merik found himself once more running. Then flying, up through the forest. Up over the wrecked trees. "Answer me!" he screamed—both from his lungs and from his mind. "Kullen, where *are* you?"

Only silence. Too much silence, and the faster Merik flew back toward the mountain, back toward that cursed doorway that had brought him here, the more ice clotted inside his belly. Not a sleeping ice, not a timeless ice, but the kind that came with death.

Merik slammed to the earth before the door. Itosha's storms had toppled oaks and flattened undergrowth. Lightning had scarred and burned. But it was meaningless destruction compared to what now suffused Merik.

He toppled into the mountain.

Instantly, the frizz of starlight hit his body. He stood on the central platform. All was calm. All was peaceful. The doorway now glowed behind him, as if nothing at all had happened or changed outside this mountain.

Merik flew once, a haphazard, panicked wind. Nothing like the targeted power he'd had only *moments* ago against Rakel, against Itosha.

"Where are you?" he roared, and his voice sent echoes across the cavern. It sent bursts of winged galaxies flying upward.

There was the door into the ice tomb ahead. No longer did ice clog its entrance, no longer did ice hunt a prince and his hound. Now it was as calm, as peaceful as the rest of the mountain. The ice that glowed was the ice that had always been there—ice for Sightwitches.

It had no interest in Merik as he shot through and bellowed out, "Kullen! Are you here? Answer me!"

"He can't." The voice that spoke was one Merik knew right away, even if he hadn't heard her in months. Hadn't seen her, hadn't known where in the Witchlands she might be. She stood high above, on the same ledge Merik had leaped off of with Aurora only weeks ago.

Merik flew up, a streak of terror. His muscles, his magic, his mind were all shouting, *No! This can't be happening—not again.* But it was. Merik needed only look into Ryber's silver eyes to know . . .

Kullen was dying.

"Am I too late?" he rasped as he landed clumsily onto the ice beside her. "Is he gone?"

"No. But also . . ." She swallowed. Then nodded. Her eyes—always that Sightwitch silver—were brighter than Merik had ever seen. As if she were no longer *just* Ryber, but something much more.

It was like the very knowledge of Noden or the goddess or whoever it was inside this mountain were rippling out around her. It made Merik think of what Kullen had said over their Threadbond: *These are the days that make sense to no one except Ryber and the other Sightwitches.*

Merik pushed past her, no longer using magic. Relying only on his desperate legs and this ache that was filling him just as the waters and storms of the Exalted Ones had done only moments ago.

Then Merik saw Kullen. He saw his Threadbrother, stretched upon the icy floor. Kullen had always been a lean man, but with massive bones on a long, stretched-out skeleton. Now he was nothing but that skeleton, his eyes sunken. His chest barely moving. His pale hair turned almost as silver as Ryber's eyes.

And although it was not as thick as the tomb had been, there was new ice latticing across his body. A sheet to encase his desiccated hands, knees, feet.

His eyes fluttered open as Merik lurched to his side. They were the blue Merik had always known.

"Is it your lungs?" Merik asked. "Is it a breathing attack? I can get you air. I can fill your lungs—"

"No, my king." The voice that rattled out was stronger than it had any right to be. It made Merik's heart catch. Made tears punch through his eyes. "The problem is not my lungs."

Ryber stepped into the tomb. It was so cold in here—not that Merik felt it—and she wore a thick gray gown and a knife at her hip. Behind her, other bodies assembled, each dressed the same. And each with eyes that glowed as Ryber's did.

They were somber, unknown beings whom Merik supposed he ought to be alarmed by . . . but that he scarcely noticed. All that mattered was Kullen sprawled before him.

Merik tore ice off Kullen's right hand and pulled his Threadbrother's fingers into his. "What's happening to you? How do I stop this?"

Kullen smiled. "You already know the answer to that."

"No, no." Merik's grip turned brutal on Kullen. "Please, Kullen. The grave is still too deep, and I haven't dug us out yet."

"You're wrong." Kullen's voice was weaker now. And the ice lacing over him had reached Merik—although it didn't try to contain him as it had before. "The grave is long since filled, Merik, except for the one you refuse to climb out of."

"*I* refuse?" Merik half choked that word—part laugh, part sob. "Kullen, everything I have touched is ruined. Everyone I have ever loved has ended up cursed or dead."

"The greatness I saw in you is still there."

"There is nothing there."

"Trust me." A tired, terrifying smile. "The Fury never forgets." Kullen's pupils were dilating now. His gaze looking somewhere far, far beyond Merik's head or even this tomb.

Merik barked another awful laugh. How could this be happening? How could he be losing Kullen *again*? Were the first two times not enough? "But how can the Fury haunt me if he is gone? How can I make amends without you here?"

"You already have." For the first time since Merik had dropped beside him, Kullen's own grip strengthened. His longer fingers curled into Merik's as they had done so many times during all those breathing attacks they had fought through together. "And now . . ." A weak breath. "Everything you have done is returned to you tenfold."

One last squeeze.

Then came a burst of life, of light, of love and tempests and thunderclaps that had first rung out millennia ago—all of it surged out of Kullen and into Merik. "Safe harbors, my king."

Kullen's eyes fell shut. His body went limp. Then it went still, not with sleep but with death, death, the final end and a last embrace from the goddess at the heart of everything.

Ryber sank to Merik's side. She did not cry as Merik did, but only chanted—along with every other Sightwitch inside the mountain, now awake and watching.

In the name of Sirmaya, I vow to preserve
All that has come before,
For the past is the only truth.
Once seen, never forgotten. Once heard, never lost.

In the name of Sirmaya, I vow to see
With clear eyes and open mind.
For the world is ever changing,
And the present is the only constant.

In the name of Sirmaya, I vow to protect
The future that is shown
For the Sleeper knows all
The Sleeper dreams all
And there is no changing what is meant to be.

SEVENTY-ONE

✳

Stix wanted to weep, but she couldn't control anything inside her body. Whatever this ring was that Lovats had—*the* ring she'd never been able to forget—it moved her about like a doll.

He carried her through the city, limp in his arms because he wanted her limp in his arms, and everyone she passed saw nothing more than a powerful man helping a broken woman. Without her spectacles, the people of the city blended into a hundred colors and countless sobs of pleading, of loss, of desperation.

Their Lady Baile had abandoned them. Not by choice, but by force.

Stix remembered Lovats now. Everything. How she had agreed to this—how they all had. Bargains that four of the Six had made, one by one, to protect the different peoples they'd loved. And one by one, Lovats had used their magics to build his city.

This city.

But Kahina, Stix thought. *She has her own ring. How?*

The question was useless. Even if Stix had an answer, there wasn't anything she could do about it. She was pain, she was emptiness, and each step that Lovats carried her—thump, thump, thump—splintered her farther apart.

But you have fought this before. She knew she had—she'd *remembered* it so clearly in the mountain only a few hours ago. *What was different now? Why could you push back then?*

Because she hadn't been alone. Owl had been with her—a girl who knew so much more about their past lives than Stix did. Now, Owl wasn't here. Nor was Kahina.

Stix had only herself . . . and only this pain.

She tried, as they left Hawk's Way and wove deeper into the city, to do as Lovats had described. To stop fighting him, if only so she could be free of this torture. But it didn't work. Perhaps because her mind could not switch off her body's most base instincts. Her muscles, her organs, her bones—they wanted to be away from this Paladin of Fire, and no matter how much Stix told them to relax, to relent . . .

Her body would not give way. And so the pain would not give way either.

Every few minutes, she spotted hazy streaks across the morning sky. And she felt—like small pinpricks of freedom—as sea foxes slithered through the city's ancient Cisterns.

Those beasts could no more help Stix than Cam could. She had to figure this out. Alone. With only the limited memories and knowledge she had of Baile and Lovats and the Paladins from a thousand years ago.

Except, as Lovats hauled Stix ever onward, he wasn't the tyrant she remembered. He smiled at passersby or nodded with grave sympathy. He even paused twice to ask if he could help someone that Stix, in her limp pain, couldn't see.

He isn't really changed. Of this Stix was certain, for no changed man would control her as he did now—nor let this pain punch through her like wildfire on dead fields. But he believed himself changed, and perhaps Stix could use that.

"If you . . . love me," she croaked while a sound like wind-drums echoed through the city. While broken awnings and dusty rubble smeared by in her periphery. "Release me. We can . . . speak."

"Soon enough," Lovats murmured, tugging her more tightly to him. He was shockingly strong; Stix didn't think anyone had carried her like this since she was a child—and certainly not for such a distance. "We will speak and you will understand once you see what I need you to see. We are almost there."

"Almost . . . where?"

He didn't answer. Only smiled at her with a smile that, against her will, made her heart ache from the glory of it. From how *much* he did look like the Noden that Stacia Sotar had been raised to believe guided all.

So much history forgotten. So much history *changed* to suit the needs of a lost people. All these hundreds of years, Nubrevnans had believed that the statues in their city were of a god. But that was because they'd *made* the statues in their city into a god. Just as they had made representations of Baile and Bastien into saints.

"Ah, here we are," Lovats said, and the sky opened wide. *Judgment Square*, Stix thought, recognizing the shape of this space and the building's facades. Above all, she recognized the shackles where guilty were subjected to public shame.

Yet where she expected to see the dead white branches of a goshorn oak stretch into view, she instead saw leaves.

Vivid and green, a vast canopy cast her face in drifting shadows. *Impossible*, she thought. This lighthouse-sized tree had been on the verge of death for decades. It hadn't sprouted any green in generations. Now, somehow, it had thousands of leaves. Tens of thousands, and small acorns too that clattered down like rain.

It was here that Lovats finally finished walking. He had reached the trunk, and he lay Stix at its massive base. The pale bark was warm, as were the shadows around her—suggesting the tree itself radiated heat.

It certainly radiated life. Stix could *feel* sap pulsing inside the oak.

"How?" she croaked out, searching Lovats's face. He wore pride in his puffed chest, and self-congratulation on the slant of his full lips.

That was more like the Exalted One Stix remembered.

"The tree remembers me. It remembers the leader that built this place. Do you not hear how much these people cry out for me?" He motioned to the square—filled not with criminals facing judgment, but with the broken, the frightened, the lost. Ten times as many people here than had clustered into the temple. A hundred times as many.

"They have a leader," Stix rasped. She tried to sit taller, and to her surprise, her muscles obeyed. Weak, agonizing . . . but responsive.

"You mean the queen you serve? And where is she now, then? Where *is* this little fox you so believe in?"

South, Stix thought, *in Noden's Gift*. But she didn't actually answer. Lovats didn't need to know where Vivia and the Empress of Marstok had last been sighted. It would only put targets on them—only rope Vivia into this mess that Stix's soul had fallen into a thousand years ago.

She sat a bit taller, and if Lovats noticed, he gave no indication. He was looking at the oak, one hand resting fondly against its bark. "So much has changed here," he said with something almost like regret. "But then I have changed too. I was once a fire fueled by kindling. Quick to spark, and quicker to flame out. But now . . ." He dragged his hand down, bark scraping until his fingers left the tree to touch Stix again. To rest upon her shoulder.

The rings winked, so close, and the one on his middle finger—*that* was the one she remembered. *That*, she was certain, was the one that controlled her.

She thought again of Kahina, who had somehow reclaimed the ring that bound her. Could Stix do the same? *Could* she get that ring off of Lovats and end this?

If only there was something she could use as a distraction. Stix had never been a convincing performer. Acting, donning masks had been Vivia's skill. Not one Vivia enjoyed—that much had always been plain to Stix—but a skill she'd been forced to hone nonetheless. The vizers of the High Council never took Vivia seriously without bluster and bombast.

Stix, meanwhile, had always used the sheer strength of her Water-witchery to cow any who might get in her way. But just as she had no one to help her—no Kahina or Owl or Cam or even a random passerby—Stix also had no magic. Not while Lovats overwhelmed her with his ring.

And whatever curse Stix's soul had agreed to a thousand years ago.

It was, as Stix sat there and felt Lovats caress her cheek, as the Nubrevnans wailed and shambled and wept their way through Judgment Square, that she saw the shadows above her change. Subtle shifts in the leaves that weren't caused by wind or aftershocks through the plateau.

Then she spotted golden eyes within the branches. *Many* golden eyes.

Stix wanted to laugh. She wanted to weep. *Six-fingered cats to ward off mice*, she thought, and with what little control she still had over her muscles, she nodded at all the cats now gathered in the leaves.

A black cat sprang first, followed a fraction of a breath later by tens more. A *hundred* more. Some with six fingers, but many with only five. They were the feral cats of the city, and they had always loved Lady Baile as much as she had always loved them.

The first cat landed on Lovats with her claws and fangs bared. The Exalted One was startled enough to spin about—and to meet, face on, the hundreds more bodies that hissed and yowled from the tree.

Stix sprang too. She had barely enough clarity, barely enough strength to control her muscles *and* grab hold of her witchery, but it was enough. It *had* to be enough.

Ice, she thought at the water all around her, gathered in cobbles, vaporized in the air, pulsing as sap in the tree. *Feast upon him.*

The water obeyed, crushing over Lovats—and over cats too—in an iron maiden of ice. Stix felt Lovats's scream through her magic, through her water. And she *heard* it rip through the cats.

Then came his flames, cooking anything in his way. They roared into Stix. Cooked her eyeballs, her skin, her hair. But she thrust right through. She *needed* that ring; she *had* to get it off of him.

She tackled Lovats to the cobbles. Years of training moved her muscles without thought. *Always, always stay the night for Baile's slaughtering.* Lovats was so much more powerful than she. A god in many ways, and as soon as Stix's arms slung around him, he flipped her to the ground. She landed on irons. Chains and shackles barked pain into her kidneys—but that was minuscule concern compared to the bone-cracking pain the jade ring shot into her.

No, Stix tried to scream as Lovats bore down. As his beautiful face swam closer and his fingers closed around her neck. *NO.* She grabbed at his hands. A chokehold like this was so easy to get out of. She'd practiced it so many times. She'd *taught* it so many times. All she had to do was grab the pinkie and yank. Snap the finger so hard that the knuckle broke.

On a normal human, that would be enough to change the fight's direction. But on a Paladin? On an *Exalted One* as powerful as Lovats? Flames coursed off his body, and Stix smelled burnt hair. Her hair, the cats'. Hell, maybe all of the city burned for all she could see.

No, she thought again, and after fumbling her fingers over his pinkie, she counted inward *one, two.* Here was the middle finger. Here was the ring that controlled her. She felt it, right there, throbbing in time to her own fading, scorching heartbeat.

Stix grabbed hold. For this city, for Nubrevna, for the Fox Queen she would always serve, she *ripped* at Lovats's finger. Because she was Lady Baile, she was Stacia Sotar, and she was *not* abandoning anyone today. Least of all herself.

Flesh tore. Muscles stretched and frayed. Bones snapped, and flames burned, burned, burned. But it was all too fast, too violent for Lovats to resist.

The finger came off entirely—and with it came the ring. With it came Stix's power.

Water pummeled into Lovats then. Sap that finally broke from the tree. Floods that filled nearby Cisterns. Rain that had not planned to break today. It all blasted down in a single, targeted torrent for this man who was *not* a god.

Yet none of Stix's waters ever made contact. Instead, they hit fire and became steam. A great, heaving fog that erupted across Judgment Square and shrouded everything. And as the fog and fires laid claim—scalding and cruel—the weight of Lovats atop Stix vanished.

She scrabbled to her feet, gasping for air and reaching, groping, searching the steam for some sign of which way he'd fled. But even with her magic back and the pain of the jade ring receding . . .

There was nothing to be found. No trace to follow.

Lovats was gone.

SEVENTY-TWO

✳

Caden found his Thread-family in a clearing of flowers that was much too calm after climbing through a mountain where ice had melted, and after running through a forest while a storm had faded away.

The Amonra had flooded past its banks. Now waves lapped against oak trunks and striped boulders. A heavy line in the earth showed where Lev must have dragged Zander ashore.

She was pumping at the man's chest when Caden and Alma reached her. "Wake up, Zan. Wake up." Lev was crying, even as her movements stayed curt and trained. "Zan, buddy, come on." She stopped her pumping to press her mouth to his. Hard puffs of air that sent his chest rising.

Caden knelt on Zander's other side. As soon as Lev finished her breaths, he replaced her. The giant of a man wasn't dead—he could see that in the Threadstone Alma still clutched. In the way she stood there, grave and focused on the air around Zander instead of on the man himself.

But Zander was in danger, and death hovered near.

"I can't heal him," Lev said as Caden pumped. She didn't seem surprised by his arrival. She was too focused on Zander for anything else. Muddy tears streaked her face. "Commander, I can't heal him. I keep trying, but I can't get the water out of him. I'm not strong with this magic yet—I don't remember how to use it—"

"It's all right," Caden said.

"It's not, though. I'm in command. This is *my* mission. I did this—I *did* this."

Caden couldn't answer. There was no time as he tipped back Zander's nose and pressed his lips against the man's. Two hard exhales before Lev was once more pumping at his chest.

Part of Caden couldn't believe what was happening right now. He and Alma had just been in the collapsing Ohrins searching for these two people right here, and now they had found them in the thrice-damned Contested

Lands, where Lev was talking about a mission and being in command. She was soaked but unharmed . . .

While Zander was dying.

Had Caden and Alma come all this way for nothing?

Caden pumped. Lev pumped. Caden shared his breaths, Lev shared hers. Over and over. *Toward death with wide eyes. All clear, all clear. Toward death with wide eyes. All clear, all clear.* Caden wasn't sure when they both started saying it, but it gave them a rhythm to work by. It kept them locked into the moment, into Zan, even as the river lapped through trees.

Toward death with wide eyes. All clear, all clear. Toward death with wide eyes. All clear, all clear.

"He's gone," Alma said. One hand came to Caden's shoulder; her other offered him the emerald that stood for Zander's soul.

It no longer glowed.

"He's gone," she repeated, but Caden couldn't stop. He kept pushing. He kept breathing. He kept murmuring the vow he'd lived by for so many years. This wasn't supposed to be the end. This wasn't supposed to be what he found here.

Eventually, Lev stopped pumping at Zander's chest. She turned away, her shoulders shaking. Caden couldn't stop, though. *Toward death with wide eyes. All clear, all clear.* It wasn't supposed to be toward Zander's death he went with wide eyes. It wasn't supposed to be *here* that it was all clear.

It was only when a fourth person joined them in the clearing that Caden finally stopped. He was crying, although he didn't know when that had begun. He gawped at the girl before him, so small and unexpected with her big eyes and dark hair with silvery streaks. He knew she wasn't *really* just a child, but right now, she looked it. She felt it.

Owl crouched on Zander's other side. No glance for Caden or Alma or Lev as she curled down and rested her head on the big man's unmoving chest.

She and Zander had grown close during their time together in Cartorra, and Iseult had described the Threads winding between them as one of Thread-family. A bond that had been as unbreakable as Caden's and Lev's were to Zander. Caden had known it was true then—he'd seen how Zander had cried after Iseult and Owl had disappeared from Praga . . .

Now, Caden knew it was true all over again. How else could Owl be here? How else could she possibly know she needed to say good-bye?

As Caden watched, his tears fell faster, hotter down his face. The earth around him began to change. The plants first, roots and vines climbing closer so they could lattice across the man they'd briefly answered to.

Then came soil, although it didn't clamber upward so much as crumble down, sucking both Zander and Owl into it.

Within seconds, both figures were gone. Buried and claimed by the earth with only a fresh burst of asphodels to punch upward and mark where they had ever been.

Caden reached for Lev across the expanse of fresh flowers, and together, they wept.

It had not been called the Contested Lands when Nadje had last come here a thousand years ago. It had simply been one more stretch of earth controlled by Lovats in his granite city to the west.

Nadje wondered where Lovats was now.

He was ashamed to admit he still feared that Paladin of Fire—as much as he'd feared Portia. Perhaps even more so, for where Portia had always kept her cruelty close, Lovats had spread it like the wildfires he controlled.

There were no fires here when Nadje had left the Dreaming with the Rook King. There had been nothing at all beyond a sunrise that held no promises of the battle yet to come.

But the battle had come eventually. Nadje had watched it from the edges, too weak to help but growing stronger by the second as the magic of the Witchlands had fed into him. Had bolstered him. He didn't have the rage of Itosha or Rakel; he'd never had it. All he had was patience, and so he'd used that patience until the right moment came.

And that moment was now, as he watched Rakel flee from an onslaught of witches as powerful as Paladins. Three people whose very beings radiated in a way that told Nadje they were special. That they were the sorts of souls who could lead, who could lift up.

He'd forgotten how it felt to be near them—not a real sound, but a sense of ringing from the purest of bells or a feeling like the sun when she rises after a cloudless night. A sun much like what had been rising before Itosha and her storms had arrived.

Nadje found Rakel; she was wounded. A hundred blades from an Ironwitch pocked her heaving form like fishhooks caught on a whale. She would die like this, bleeding slowly on the riverbank, and Nadje could be the one to ensure it. Certainly, that was why he was here, wasn't it? That was what he'd told the Rook King when he'd awoken at the Well. This was the final battle; he was meant to fight in it.

And yet, finding Rakel so broken, rusted blades lying around her . . .

All Nadje could do was stride to her and kneel at her wretched side. Unlike he, who had awoken with—as far as he could tell—his original body, this was not the shape Rakel had once worn. There were remnants here, in the strength of her brow and the underbite on her jaw. But otherwise, she was a creature transformed by too many years drowning.

Nadje had drowned too. He didn't know why it hadn't changed him, but he did at least understand why Rakel had been so focused on possessing Monk Evrane's body—and why, in turn, she'd been so angry when the Rook King had snatched it away.

"You," she said in a voice defined by agony. It burbled with the watery depths of her soul. Blood spilled out.

"Me," Nadje replied, and he took her wet, slimy hand in his. The sun was high enough now and the storm long enough gone that beams cut down, warm and welcoming.

They made Nadje think of when he'd been inside the Bloodwitch's body. Of that smell he'd sensed like sun and sand and auburn leaves falling. That had been Sirmaya's scent; and here it was again—not a smell, but a feeling. A heat. An embrace.

Again, it did not feel like a battle to end times. It felt, instead, like a battle to begin them.

"You chose the Rook King." Rakel fixed her bulbous eyes on Nadje. Only one still appeared to be working. "Instead of us."

"I chose Sirmaya."

"And why do you assume I have not chosen Her too?"

Nadje's brow furrowed. Something about that question prodded his ancient brain and ancient soul.

"Sirmaya gave us all this power," Rakel went on. "It was only natural we would wish to use it."

"But that was not *why* She gave us this power."

"You used it greedily enough a thousand years ago." Rakel tried to smile. It revealed torn gums and shrunken teeth. Her breaths heaved.

A hot wind crossed Nadje, rustling at the oaks. Playing with the asphodels. "Yes," he agreed. "I used it greedily, and now I do not wish to."

"So what will you do, then?" *Rasp. Cough.* "I will die and be reborn. But you? What will *you* do now?"

Nadje's frown cut deeper across his face. She would indeed be reborn.

That was how their Paladin souls worked. But he had no easy answer. The Lament simply said: *In light, twelve will meet on lands long contested, while in darkness, the shadow-ender will topple nightmares and the world-starter will build us anew.*

The Twelve were not here yet. *Or at least,* he thought vaguely, *not the Twelve Paladins.*

The wind whispered louder. Tree limbs shook, spraying fresh shadows across Rakel. Lifting fallen leaves and dust. *And,* he noted, *ringing like the purest of bells.*

"Ah," Nadje said on a heavy sigh. Because of course Rakel was right: they both believed that they served Sirmaya. Just as both the Rook King and Ragnor the General had believed they served her too. Two sides to one knife. Two truths that were not really true.

Nadje tightened his grip on Rakel, and something like sadness twined through him. Sorrow for all the centuries it had taken, all the lives and mistakes and effort, cycling again and again because no one ever had thought to step outside.

But here he was, outside. Feeling his goddess in the clammy, cold touch of Rakel against him. In the earth under his knees. In the breeze and the leaves and this small meadow drenched in sunlight. And with those sensations, he thought again of what a Sightwitch from long ago had seen.

In light, twelve will meet on lands long contested, while in darkness, the shadow-ender will topple nightmares and the world-starter will build us anew.

"I am not going to kill you," Nadje said quietly. "Yes, it would give you that new body you have hungered for . . . but it would not bring you back to Sirmaya. It would not bring either of us back to Her. And that, I think, is what both of us really desire.

"We have earned our rest, Paladin of Water. Do you not think we should claim it?"

Rakel's lips shook. Something almost like tears glossed her fishy eyes. "How?"

"With my help. I can take us both there."

"And what will happen?"

"I do not know," he said truthfully. "But I think it is and always has been a question of balance. When it was just the Twelve, we did not steward magic as we should have. When it was just humans, they did not either. The Rook King wished to give it back to the Twelve. The General wished to leave it with the people. Maybe we should simply give it to the goddess instead and let Her decide."

The sigh that slid from Rakel's throat was one that weighed too heavy. That carried centuries atop it and sought only freedom, only solace. She had let anger stew inside her because it had been the only way to exist inside that Well beside the sea, where her tides had been so close but never within reach.

And Nadje, he had drowned too—but it hadn't stoked a rage inside him. At least not a rage so vast as Rakel's. Not a rage he hadn't been able to claw back from thanks to his time inside the Bloodwitch's body, with its unique history that had given Nadje far more than he'd deserved.

"I want to see Her again," Rakel said.

"Yes," Nadje agreed. "I do too." As he said this, it occurred to him that he already had—or at least that he had seen part of Her, when he'd found the dark-giver and watched her end Portia. He knew now that the dark-giver was nothing more than a tool of the Rook King.

But then, what was the Rook King other than a tool of Sirmaya?

Another sigh from Rakel. Another collapse of centuries and civilizations and pain. "Yes, Nadje. I choose Sirmaya. I choose to let Her start anew."

Nadje nodded. He could not lift Rakel—he was too weak still, and she was too misshapen and changed. But he didn't need to lift her to carry her into the goddess's embrace.

The last thing he saw, before he took hold of Rakel's other hand and winked them both into the Dreaming, was a shape in the trees. A figure in white that he knew instantly because he had worn that shape and body only a few months ago.

And on either side of him were the dark-giver and the light-bringer, the purest of bells to shimmer across the land.

The Bloodwitch nodded at Nadje, and as the walls between the realm that was *theirs* and the realm that was *Hers* fell away, Nadje saw the Cahr Awen too. No longer did they wear corporeal forms, but instead they were simply two sides of a knife. The left and right hand to a goddess.

Then ice carved across Nadje and Rakel.

Come, come, the ice will hold you. Come, come, my children, and sleep. You are forgiven here in the ice, and you will be as you once were again.

The Paladins closed their eyes. Together, they slept.

THE WEASEL

The Weasel hates the Sleeping Lands. It is bitterly cold here. Barren and unwelcoming with no wind to displace snow. No breeze to carry sound. It is always midnight, yet no moon fills the sky. Only the Sleeping Giant constellation shining so bright it casts the world in a perpetual twilight glow.

Occasional shapes disrupt the landscape—if you are foolish enough to brave far. Mounds of snow that might cover forgotten megaliths or might cover nothing at all. Glaciers that thrust up sharp fingers made of pure blue ice. No animals are foolish enough to tread here.

Except, of course, for the weasel.

The only movement comes from beacons of color wavering across the sky, just like the old No'Amatsi tales described. Several hours ago, those Threads were not there.

The weasel shivers before a stone doorway wedged into a pyramid-like glacier at the heart of the Sleeping Lands. She wishes she could leap back through the frizzing blue light. Take refuge in the no less strange, but at least less cold mountain made of starlight. For although her fur might be made for snow, it is never thick enough to ward off the cold of this place that rejects all warmth and daylight.

The doorway gives a quake. It makes the weasel's ears pop and fur ripple. She wriggles toward it, unsurprised when the man who believes himself her master topples through. When she was a human, the general who called himself the Raider King also believed he was her master. But silly men never could learn that she has only ever belonged to herself. And even in this much smaller, much stranger body with no magic and no voice, the last two months haven't changed her.

She chitters at the tall, beautiful man. His pale curls shimmer green beneath the Threads of the Moon Mother. His greenish eyes ripple with other shades like iridescent fish scales the weasel used to see on the hot shores where she grew up.

On Leopold fon Cartorra's shoulder is the bird that the weasel has grown to know in recent weeks. He has spent a thousand years in this world, sometimes playing messenger, sometimes playing spy.

Today he will play a traitor.

The Rook swoops down to flap his wings at the weasel in greeting. He kicks up a fine, almost dust-like snow. It makes the weasel sneeze.

When she was a human, she had tried to come here once—into the Sleeping Lands—thinking perhaps there was some truth in the old tale about the monster gathering honey. But it wasn't true. At least not for her. The Moon Mother never appeared; no task was ever given to her.

Leopold crouches beside his bird and before the weasel. His cheeks tick, meaning someone has made him angry. Very angry.

But the weasel already knew that would happen. The strange sisters from the mountain already told her that.

She purrs as Leopold pats her head and strokes her fur. He was never a bad master, so much as a misguided one. And really, the weasel can relate. She spent her whole life focused on a task that bore no fruit—what difference does it make that he spent many lifetimes doing the same? A failed attempt is still a failed attempt, no matter how long it takes to get there.

"We have more work to do," Leopold says, his voice a tired thing. He is angry, yes, but he is also lost. "No one has gone where I sent them, and they have not fulfilled the Lament as it was seen. So I must start anew. I can sense that magic has stabilized, but this isn't the way She wanted it to be."

"And how do you know that, Rook King?" The person who asks this is a child, her face young but her eyes ancient as she emerges from where she was hiding behind the ice.

Leopold spins toward her. He recognizes her immediately—that is evident in how his eyes flare. How he rears back for half a beat, before snapping his gaze toward the second girl now stepping out after her sister.

He gives a harsh laugh, his eyes sliding back and forth between them. They are both Sightwitches; they have both been gone a very long time. They do not approach Leopold fon Cartorra, but instead take up sentry ten paces away.

"Now you awaken?" he demands of them. "Now She releases you from Her ice? I needed your help a thousand years ago. What good are your visions to me now?"

"Oh, Rook King." This is the younger sister, Cora. "It isn't always about you."

"It never is, actually," Lisbet agrees.

The prince's nostrils flare. He stands taller, which prompts the Rook to clack his beak twice at the weasel. It is a signal that means nothing to Leopold, just as the weasel's answering double chomp of teeth means nothing. But this was their *agreed-upon signal, and after they have both finished, they scuttle and hop out of the way . . .*

Right as the third child finally arrives.

In a blast of stone and power, she thunders through the magic doorway. Fast, hard, and with the mountain to seal up behind her. A zipping of granite. A silencing of magic.

And now Leopold fon Cartorra understands what is happening.

The weasel, if she were still a human, would have laughed. After all, this is exactly how it was in the old fable, when Moon Mother's Little Sister Owl trapped Trickster and the world once more felt peace. He, of all people, should have known how much truth there is in those stories.

"Owl," Leopold says. "You must let me back into the mountain."

"No." *She shakes her head, and her dark hair—loose and tangled like a nest, with silver lines gleaming—flips against her pale cheeks.* "You are finished now, Rook King."

The Rook King's cheeks tick faster. He knows he is in trouble, for the Dreaming does not work here. The walls in the Sleeping Lands are not merely thin so much as torn down entirely. One cannot use magic of any kind, and that is why Owl lured him here in the first place.

Or rather, the weasel and the bird did, bit by bit as they helped the last Sightwitches—Cora, Lisbet, and Ryber—do what needed doing.

"You have failed no one," *Lisbet says, offering a sweet smile that belies her near-infinite knowledge.* "Except perhaps yourself, Rook King. So many years with your Paladin soul fixated on one thing—a thing that never really was."

"You mean the Lament was not real? Is that what you are telling me? But you *saw* it. You *were* the one who told Eridysi what to transcribe."

"Yes, but it was never meant to be interpreted. It was never meant to be collated and used as a guide."

"And yet," *the prince bites out,* "so much of it *has* come true, has it not? The one turning on five, and now . . ." *He opens his arms to them.* "Five appear to be turning on one."

Cora laughs. She is the youngest of the three girls and the silliest at times. "It only *appears* to be true because you're looking backwards. You're fitting what was written to what came before—but you could have just as easily fit other words here instead."

"Yes." *Lisbet nods.* "That is the thing about our Goddess. She dreams what she dreams, and we Sightwitches do our best to make sense of it. But the truth is never so easy and the words—as you know yourself—are never so clear. Sometimes what Sirmaya dreams happens more than once. Sometimes, what She dreams is so strange, we cannot express it in words."

Leopold sniffs, a hateful sound that puffs steam from his nostrils. "So you have cornered me here, in the Sleeper's own land, to tell me that She"—he flings a hand toward the sky—"made a mistake, and I should not have spent the last thousand years doing what I did? Yet I have healed Her, have I not? The sky no longer splits, the mountain no longer quakes."

"Yes," Owl replies quietly, and she extends an arm so that the Rook will fly to her. "And in this, you did well, Rook King."

The prince's cheeks twitch again as he watches his bird obey. He glances at the weasel, expecting her to follow. But she stays where she is, several paces away. Not because she has chosen Leopold's side, but because she recognizes her own sly ways within him.

He has one more trick left to play.

The weasel respects that about him. He coordinated so many and managed so much over the last thousand years. Countless puppets doing as he wished without ever building a Loom. It might not have worked as he'd hoped, but there can be no denying the scale of his accomplishments.

The same was true of Ragnor. Silly men she learned from but never truly served.

Leopold's cheeks are red with cold. His nose too, yet he gives no outward indication that the chill bothers him. He is the poised performer. The prince trained for this moment since birth. Then it comes: the trickery.

He swipes his cloak aside in a flicker of silvery gray, and he withdraws what remains of the broken Blade of Eridysi. It whispers with a sound that is too loud for the Sleeping Lands. That makes the ribbons of the sky flare momentarily with Severed Threads and makes a wind kick up with icy claws.

But where the weasel expects the prince to turn this blade on Owl, he instead turns it on himself. Jagged, cruel edges that are barely longer than fangs—but vicious enough to pierce his clothes, his skin, his abdomen.

He makes no sound. Only a sharp exhale followed by a widening of his eyes as the pain punctures in. His knees give out. He hits the snow. Blood splatters across white.

"That which is closest," Lisbet murmurs, "she cannot see."

"A knife with two sides," Cora adds.

Then together, they murmur: "Blood on the snow."

Leopold sinks down, his life draining fast. And not just his life, but his Threads too. The weasel does not need her old magic to see how the sky soaks him up. How the goddess is taking back what she had once given out to a man she loved.

Owl is the only one to approach Leopold, her steps careful with the Rook now on her shoulder. She sinks to Leopold's side and places her hands atop his. He stares up at her, the sea green of his irises growing duller by the heartbeat.

"I only did what I thought was right," he says.

"I know," she replies, and the Rook hops off her shoulder to land upon Leopold's other side. The bird nuzzles his old master, which makes the prince smile. "But you mistook purpose for love," Owl continues, "as did your old general, and that path never ends well for anyone."

"No," Leopold agrees.

Owl strokes his brow. And slowly, slowly, the prince's eyes close. Until eventually, Owl leans down to whisper something in his ear. Some final good-bye that no one else can hear, save perhaps Sirmaya. He smiles again, more brightly. More true.

Then Leopold fon Cartorra slips away.

The Rook squawks, a sound of both grief and surprise—even though he knew that something like this must be coming. He nudges, he nips. But the prince doesn't respond. And soon, ice scuttles over the body. It seals him in like a tomb.

It also scuttles over the blade, as if reclaiming whatever droplets of magic might still remain inside.

Cora is the first to move, coming to Owl. She offers her a hand. "What did you tell him?" she asks. "Because it gave him great comfort at the end."

Owl swallows, looking first at Cora's hand. Then at the ice stretched before her where a prince will sleep forever.

"I told him that I loved him," she said without inflection. "And that he would no longer be alone."

Cora sighs. "I see." And the weasel feels a similar response unfurl inside her. It is like an ancient hunger loosing. Like pieces of herself being made new again.

She startles when hands suddenly grasp her. She hadn't noticed Lisbet approaching, she'd been so focused on what it might mean to no longer be alone. And now she is clutched. Now she is lifted. Now she is placed upon Lisbet's small shoulder, where she can leap back down . . .

But she does not.

"Come, little cousin," Lisbet murmurs into her white fur, "the Sightwitches are awakening. Enough magic has returned for the world to settle, and there is a new spring we must all prepare for."

PART 3

Witch Light

My dearest Captain,

I know you're gone, but it doesn't feel real to me yet. So many letters I have written to you over this past year—and when I wasn't writing them, I was always thinking of *how* to write them. What words I would use to describe a place, a discovery, a feeling thumping in my chest.

Goddess, I miss you.

And while I know it's not fair, right now, in this exact moment, I hate Merik. You gave up your life for him. Which means he took you from me.

Hye, I know you did what you did because you were *created* by Sirmaya. You lifted up the man you saw as king. But I'd rather have you here than Merik.

Do you remember that time we talked about marriage? We were on the *Jana*, and you said you wanted a proper Nubrevnan wedding with all the fanfare and dancing. I said I would never agree because Sightwitches aren't allowed to marry . . .

A stupid thing to say. I wish I could take it back. I don't adhere to the Sightwitch Rules anymore, and I expect few of the newly awoken Sightwitches will either. (Tanzi *certainly* won't. I've already caught her twice sneaking Cam into her bedroom. Hilga will have a fit when she finds out.)

I suppose I should take some comfort in the fact that Poznin already flourishes beneath Merik's guidance. He's a changed man from the one you last saw in Lejna, and as much as I wish it *weren't* the case . . . I do think your instincts were right. Your Threadbrother will lead the New Republic of Arithuania well, and a peaceful age will prosper there.

Also, if you had not let Sirmaya take your Paladin soul back, then magic would not have stabilized. It would not have returned to witches across the land.

We still need one more Paladin, of course. One more source of magic to fully return to how things were. But that is what Stix and Kahina are focused on. They won't rest until they find the last Exalted Ones: Ferisien, Lovats, and perhaps a reincarnated Portia too. Although Sirmaya has stabilized, no one in the Witchlands can be truly safe while those three still remain.

Stix and Kahina also fear that Midne has joined the other side. Why else did she disappear upon waking? I'll admit I'm not convinced. Although Midne might have been the first betrayer of the Six long ago—the one who turned on five—it wasn't her choice. She was bound to Portia as the first Hell-Bard.

What if she is still bound? What if she hasn't slipped away because she wants to but because she fears causing more harm?

The cards offer me nothing except a verification that Stix's and Kahina's *current* path is true: the Paladin of Foxes, the Paladin of Hawks, and the Giant. Any future information beyond remains a mystery.

As for the Paladin of Bats, Owl, she has remained here at the Convent. The reason is twofold. One: she isn't safe so long as the Exalted One Lovats still possesses the jade ring she is bound to. But perhaps, here where the mountain's magic is strong, she can at least *hide* from the ring for a time.

And, on top of that, here Owl perhaps can grow with something resembling a childhood. (Although truth be told, Kullen, *I* feel like the child whenever I am around her, Lisbet, or Cora. I have no idea how Sister Hilga will manage all three of them as apprentices.)

In Cartorra, Eron fon Hasstrel maintains the helm with the assistance of his longtime advisors: a Dalmotti Glamourwitch, a Cartorran Wordwitch, and a Marstoki Firewitch general. Since the Hell-Bards are now fully disbanded, this is the empire that looks the least steady to me—and my cards confirm this. They are a muddle of different options that might steer true or might steer into chaos.

Nubrevna and Marstok are also filled with chaos, but Stix and

Kahina believe in their rulers—as much as you believed in Merik—and so I must believe in them too.

As for the Cahr Awen . . .

Well, Safiya fon Hasstrel and Iseult det Midenzi could be anywhere in the Witchlands right now. Truly. The girls and their Bloodwitch protector vanished shortly after the Great Collapse (that's what they're calling the day the Wells woke up), and the cards tell me nothing except that they're still together: the Sun, the Moon, the Knife.

The Rook and the weasel bring me interesting animal whispers, though. A tale of the trio being spotted near the Sleeping Lands; another of them in the Contested Lands; and even a murmuring that put them near the Sand Sea.

No matter where they really are, it makes me happy to know that they and *only* they control their hearts, their minds, their bodies, and their destinies. *For only in death could they understand life. And only in life, will they change the world.*

So many things that one vision from Lisbet could mean . . .

I will keep writing to you, my Captain, my Heart-Thread, my Kullen. As I descend ever deeper into the Crypts. As I go where the Goddess and my own heart lead. I am no longer the last Sightwitch Sister, but I still have plenty of work to do. Plenty of new paths to find as I seek out my own future in the Witchlands.

Magic is changed. What stars will we need to think beyond now?

All the love from your maiden north of Lovats,

—Ryber

SEVENTY-THREE

✳

It had been years since the Bloodwitch Aeduan had come here, to the Shrine of the Fallen at the Carawen Monastery. Roughly hewn in an underground cavern, its vaulted ceilings were lit by Firewitched sconces, while thousands upon thousands of opals glittered atop a hexagon of black marble.

Monks bent or knelt throughout these catacombs, some murmuring prayers, most simply silent and remembering. So many of their ranks had been lost in Poznin. *The Battle for the Cahr Awen*, they were calling it, and Aeduan wished that such a title—accurate as it might have been—offered some relief.

But in the end, death was death. Loss was loss. Monk Evrane Nihar had been one more soul of many who'd died in battle, and in the end, Aeduan had never gotten to say good-bye.

He'd never even seen her body.

Now here he stood, in this place that had once been the Rook King's fortress, with an opal in his hand that had once been the Rook King's creation.

At Aeduan's side was Lizl, as broad-chested and high-chinned as she ever was. She'd saved Evrane's opal for Aeduan, and it was a strange debt he didn't know how to repay. Life-debts, he'd always understood. But kindness? Gifts simply because?

He was still sorting those out.

Along with everything else, it would seem. He still didn't fully understand what had happened since he'd toppled his nightmares and awoken to a new incarnation of the blade and glass in his possession.

For that matter, he still didn't fully understand how magic had stabilized. Five Paladins had died; their magic had returned to the goddess and Her Witchlands; now all of the wounds on Aeduan's abdomen—save for one—were gone. No scars left behind. Nothing to ever show where his mother had died protecting him.

Strange, how he missed the scars. Not the pain, not the blood . . . but the memories. And yes, even the nightmares. For without them, what did he have left of his family? No mother, no father, and now, no Monk Evrane.

He supposed it was a small price to pay if it meant Sirmaya was no longer dying.

Aeduan set Evrane's opal on the marble slab. It made a soft clink—one more earring, nearly identical to every other within sight. Every Carawen monk who'd ever died. Every soul ever lost in the service of a lie.

Aeduan knelt before the marble. In a rustle of fabric, Lizl joined him. Together, they bowed their heads.

"We did as you taught us, Monk Evrane." Lizl's voice was so low only Aeduan—and perhaps any ghost left from Evrane—could hear her. "We guarded the light-bringer and the dark-giver, exactly as you wanted. You were a hard teacher, but you were the best this Monastery ever had. The best . . . I ever had."

Aeduan frowned. His fingers itched to tap at his thigh. To check that each of his blades was in place across his chest.

"Nothing to add, Monk Aeduan?" Lizl glanced sideways.

But Aeduan ignored her. His witchery was reaching outward, groping like a man suddenly dropped into darkness. Evrane had always been here. The crisp spring water from her many years near the Aether Well. The salt-lined cliffs from her childhood in Nihar. They were as familiar to Aeduan as the rocks of this monastery and the sting of Sirmayan blizzards outside. How could he be within these walls and not smell her?

Yet there was nothing for his magic to find, so he grappled clumsily at empty air.

Evrane Nihar was gone.

Lizl sighed—a sound loud enough to kick through the cavern like a wind. "Really? You traveled all this way, Monk, so you could offer *no* words of respect?"

Yes, Aeduan wanted to reply. Instead, he mumbled, "I remembered my duty. I remembered who I am." The words were directed at Evrane—a closing statement to a conversation they'd begun many miles southwest of here, on the shores of Nubrevna.

And also, a conversation begun the day she'd found him burning alive inside a Nomatsi tent where swamp and crocodiles stewed. She could have left that boy with the holes on his body, but instead she saved him. Instead, she *made* him become more than the witchery he'd been cursed with.

And see? he could almost imagine her saying, with that infuriating faith of hers. *I was right, was I not? You were more than your magic. And your magic, it would seem, was also more than you.*

"You remembered your duty," Lizl muttered, pushing to standing. "Great. I could have saved you the trouble and done that duty for you. Alone. But I held on to this opal, thinking you'd want to do right by the woman who raised us. But how typical of you, Monk Aeduan. Only ever thinking of yourself."

Aeduan sniffed as he also rose—with more grace and less spite. "Thank you for that, Abbot Thewan. I am grateful."

"No, you're not." An eye roll as Lizl strode on her long legs toward the nearest stairwell out of this underground shrine. It was clear she had more to say, but she kept the words chewed back until they were out of the Monastery's depths and stepping into the cold, wintery night.

The Sleeping Giant's stars flared down.

And Aeduan caught a whiff of sun-drenched meadows on the wind. It blew over the stone ramparts and made his lips twitch with an almost smile.

"I've done as the Cahr Awen commanded," Lizl told him, leading Aeduan north toward her tower. This was not the most direct route, but he appreciated the open air after the cold solemnity of the shrine. "I have . . . I think it was thirteen suitable candidates? They're young, but promising. Like we were at that age." She bared a sideways grin. Then amended, "Or more like *I* was at that age. I'm still not sure about you."

Aeduan let his lips twitch again, and this time in a way that Lizl could see. His cloak snapped around him, carried by the mountain wind. Hers billowed too, but with the old bloodstains that she refused to remove.

They smelled like Natan fon Leid. Like cackling laughter and bloodied knuckles, like endless hunger and mountain cold. Not that Aeduan had told Lizl this. For her, those stains marked change. For him . . .

Well, he'd had enough blood to last a lifetime. Enough bleeding, enough death, enough battle and brutality and red staining snow.

"I know you said," Lizl continued, "that the Cahr Awen wished to travel for a time—to fully sink into this new role they've formed for themselves. And I know you also told me that magic isn't fully stable yet, since there are fewer than six sources to replenish us. But I do think it's important that apprentices be brought in as soon as possible. If we're going to train these acolytes to sense when magic is being abused and overused, it's got to start now.

"And, I think . . . Well, an apprentice for you is even more urgent. The tools you carry will be a responsibility one must learn as young as possible."

"Yes," Aeduan agreed, and while his right hand moved to the Truth-sword sheathed at his hip, his left hand went to a small pouch added to his baldric. There, next to his stiletto, was the Truth-lens tucked safely away.

"Tool-Bearer." Lizl's eyes lingered on the pouch at Aeduan's chest. "Fancy title."

"Stupid title, more like." Aeduan shook his head. "But I understand why the Truth . . . I mean, why the *light-bringer* feels it's important to give the role a name. Whomever replaces me, now and long into the future, will need to know the full weight of what they carry." *And how dangerous it will be if these tools ever fall into the wrong hands.*

"I still think you should take more monks with you on your travels." Lizl slowed to a stop, pausing at a gap in the ramparts that revealed the entire valley and frozen river beyond.

No Aether Well shone. There was only a blank island—and a small cooking fire sparkling in the trees. He had no idea who would make a camp there. It was such an inhospitable place to spend the night, steeped in that same *strangeness* Aeduan had felt in the forests near Poznin. Some residue of the Old One that had been there.

Or perhaps just some remnant of what Iseult had done to save Aeduan's life months before that, when she'd swallowed flames to save him.

Think of Iseult. Reach for the silver taler.

The taler had somehow survived everything that had happened in Poznin. When the smoke, ash, storm, and tide had cleared, Aeduan had found it around his neck. The leather thong had been almost shredded, but a narrow strand had still remained.

He'd immediately returned it to Iseult. Who was, of course, nowhere near here. She and the light-bringer were in Dalmotti, preparing for a new Truce Summit. Still, Aeduan's instincts could not be quelled simply because the brain knew better.

Except then it came: a punch against Aeduan's magic, against his senses, of the silver taler *right* there.

His chest constricted so hard, his breath burst out. A small cloud into the night. His first thought was that this was a game—another trick by the prince of Cartorra to lure Aeduan exactly where he'd lured him before . . .

But the prince was gone. Aeduan knew he was gone because he had—for some intangible, almost aching reason—tracked the lingering scraps of Leopold's scent all the way to a door in the mountain. Then through that door into the Sleeping Lands.

Where only the goddess's ice had awaited him.

Which meant that it really *was* Iseult down there. Inexplicably, she was here; that was her fire; and she must know that Aeduan would come to her.

It took far too much effort for Aeduan to return his attention to Lizl.

"But," the abbot was saying, half leaning against the stones and fully oblivious to his lapse in concentration, "I'll respect your decision to keep it a small party. For now. If you end up targets, though, I'll *force* you to bring more monks—understood? We might have a slightly different mission, now that we know the true origins of the Cahr Awen . . . But we monks are prepared for anything, so we will continue to serve. And to serve the new tool-bearer too."

"Yes," Aeduan replied. If Lizl noticed that he sounded rougher, cooler than before, she gave no sign. "But until we know exactly how the rulers and leaders of the Witchlands will accept—or will not accept—the mandate of the Cahr Awen, then it's easier and safer this way."

"Right, right." Lizl swatted the air, her eyes flitting again to the satchel at Aeduan's chest. "The light-bringer explained all of that to me when she came. *I* am simply asking that you not make this as difficult as you always make things for me."

Aeduan knew this was a joke; he knew he was meant to laugh; but with the silver taler so near, he could barely grind out a smile. He bowed his head. "I understand, and I promise we will not keep you waiting, Abbot."

"Good." Lizl nodded. "In that case, I will make sure the thirteen I have so far are in top shape for whenever you return. I've already got one of Evrane's lessons in mind."

Aeduan's eyebrows lifted. For the first time in several moments, *this* fully captured his attention. "You'll teach them yourself?"

"Why not? You just said how much responsibility and weight these new roles carry. What better way to instill that than having the abbot be their teacher?"

Aeduan saw the logic to this—and also felt a surge of gratitude. His fingers flexed at his side. Once. Twice. "Thank you, Abbot. For this and everything else."

Lizl gave an absent grunt as she squinted into the valley, toward the campfire flickering like a candle in the wind. Then past that and up, up into the steep mountains beyond.

"You know, Bloodwitch," she said eventually, "you still owe me a number of life-debts. Six, I think, was the count before the battle at Poznin. Now, though . . . Well, I'd wager that battle alone added at least another ten." A sidling glance. A crooked smile. "In other words, don't die before I can claim them, yeah?"

This time, Aeduan didn't have to force the smile or the laugh. "Yes," he told her, bowing again, now in supplication. Now with the respect she deserved for the title she'd earned. "I have not forgotten, and if you ever need me, Abbot Thewan, I will come right away to repay you."

She sighed, a sound that was satisfied, but also. . . . *wistful.* Like perhaps she envied that Aeduan would get to leave while she had to stay behind. Yet Lizl gave no final good-bye nor bow—nor even glance as she twirled sharply away. Her cloak streaked white. Her steps clipped out.

And the scent of speed and daisy chains, of a mother's kiss and sharpened steel faded along with the sight of her.

Iseult knew her hatred of the Old One Nadje wasn't wholly justified. In the end, that Exalted One had chosen correctly—and in the end, it hadn't been his fault he had taken Aeduan's body. That he'd hurt Aeduan, and in turn, hurt Iseult and Owl.

Yet as Iseult stared at the jagged crater where the Aether Well had been—while dry, Sirmayan cold crisped around her, while her breath tendriled from her mouth like Threads, while her hands ached inside the gloves she always wore . . .

Iseult hated Nadje.

And she was glad—*glad*—that he was gone.

She was glad that Leopold was gone too. Owl had told Iseult what had happened; Aeduan had told Iseult what he'd seen in the Sleeping Lands. And while she couldn't deny there were shards of grief dug into her heart—as if the looking glass that had once been a part of her soul had left fragments behind—most of her was glad he was gone. That she no longer had to navigate him and his thousand-year Trickster plans.

Or him and his thousand-year-old Threads. Too bright, too dominating for a mind such as hers.

She was a Threadwitch again. And a Weaverwitch of sorts, able to touch Threads. Control them as the Puppeteer once had. But for reasons she didn't understand—but that the Sightwitches were already racing to research and explore—she could no longer cleave. She could no longer sever, sever, twist and sever.

She didn't grieve the loss of that magic.

She almost hoped Ryber and the other Sightwitches never found an answer.

The night's sky, stippled with stars, was unmarred by moon or clouds. Only the Moon Mother's own Threads hovered here—although these days, no one but Nomatsi Threadwitches could see them.

Iseult crouched at the edge of the Well, where snow had banked. Soon, this hole would be filled with that snow; soon it would look solid when it was not.

"You're here."

Iseult almost leaped out of her skin. She spun so fast, jolted so high, that she lost her balance. Her arms windmilled.

Then Aeduan was there, catching her before she could topple backward into the new abyss.

His breaths feathered as hers did. His eyes were near, and she couldn't help but notice—as she did every time she'd looked into them since the Great Collapse—that they were not *quite* the same blue they'd once been. Now there was a ring of silver around the edges. A faint glow like the annulus of an eclipse.

"You're here," he repeated, harsher this time as he pulled her away from the edge and toward her nearby campfire. She'd set up a small tent.

"Yes," she said. "I—I took Blueberry."

"Why?" Aeduan's jaw fluttered with worry. "Has something happened?"

"No. I . . ." Iseult was suddenly very conscious of the fact that she'd come a long, *long* way.

And she was suddenly feeling thoroughly stupid for that decision. *Fanciful fool.* "The T-Truce Summit," she squeezed out, "is all organized. And Safi is in Veñaza City, making final preparations for our new role and title. H-her uncle will be the first to announce it."

Aeduan nodded. They had reached the fire's warmth now, and he released Iseult—although he didn't step away. "I just finished speaking to Lizl. She asked that we not take too long before choosing apprentices."

"Yes." Iseult had expected this.

And now they were out of conversation topics. Which was silly. After everything they had been through together—everything they'd done for each other . . .

"I wanted to see you," she blurted at the same moment he said, "I love you."

Oh. She squared herself toward him. Firelight cast shapes across his white cloak and pale face. His eyes glittered—and the annulus glowed.

"I love you," he repeated, a rigidity claiming his muscles. His face. "I should have said it when we parted on the Windswept Plains. I don't know why I didn't."

"Because you didn't n-need to." It was true: Iseult had known he loved her, even if he hadn't said those exact words. Did the phrase *mhe varujta* not tell her as much every time he uttered it?

Yet, she was discovering that it was one thing to know something abstractly and quite another to find it real and within your grasp. Like knowing that your body and its organs could function without you commanding them . . .

Versus hearing your heartbeat stutter or having your lungs fill so full they ached. All these weeks, Iseult had sensed how Aeduan felt for her.

But now she knew.

He loved her, and she loved him too.

Her throat closed up. Her tear ducts sharpened. And it was—as it so often tended to be with Aeduan—too much. She *hurt* from it even as she wanted this hurting to never stop. So she reached for him, one gloved hand extending.

He stepped in close. Then her arms came around his waist, and she laid her head against his shoulder. Her eyes closed. She breathed in cold air that smelled like Aeduan's armor, like the lanolin he used on his blades, like blood and starlight and the man who *had* walked a thousand years and would—if she asked him to—walk a thousand more.

"I made a vow to you," she said into his neck. "That when this was all over, you would serve no one but yourself, and we would find wh-what it is you want."

He squeezed her more tightly. It pressed his knives into her chest—and also the pouch that held the Truth-lens.

Iseult rested her hand over that pouch for three heartbeats. Then she drew back. Just enough to find his eyes. To hold that gaze of understanding. "I made a vow, yet here we are again, with this lens and this sword." Her hand slid down to the pommel at his hip. "You are y-yet again, serving someone else. It wasn't supposed to be this way."

For several seconds, the only sound was the fire crackling. The wind briefly twisted, and smoke whispered between them. It hazed Aeduan's face. Softened how tense he had become.

Then the wind resumed its southern aim and Aeduan finally spoke: "There is a difference this time, Iseult. I am choosing to become the bearer of the sword and the necklace. I am *choosing* to follow you and the light-bringer wherever your path takes you. It's my chosen cause, and that . . ." A frown. A slight shake of his head. "It's not the same as serving a master."

Now Iseult was the one to frown. She felt her brow pinch, felt her nostrils flare. She supposed he wasn't wrong. When she had been Cahr Awen—when she'd been nothing more than the Rook King's tool—it hadn't been her choice. As much as she'd wanted to be special, she would never have chosen it that way.

Now though, being the Cahr Awen *was* her choice. Iseult and Safi were taking on that title because they wanted it to stand for something; because they *believed* that someone needed to steward magic and ensure it was never abused as it had been.

"I understand," Iseult said softly, and with cautious—and still painful—hands, she cupped Aeduan's jaw. Then lowered his head until she could rest her brow against his. "There are words," she began, feeling her tongue instantly thicken. *Stasis, stasis.* "Th-that the Nomatsis say. In their braiding ceremonies. In o-*our* braiding ceremonies. A Threadwitch who leads the tribe will ask questions, and the couple answers them."

Aeduan nodded against her. "Are you married? Do you have a lover? Are the Threads between you true?"

Iseult swallowed. "You know them."

"I do." His left hand came to her hip. His right hand slid behind to rest on her low back. "And here are your answers: I am not married. You are the only lover I have. And the Threads between us are true. At least." His lips parted. Shut. Parted again. "For me they are."

Iseult's tongue tripled in size. "Y-you aren't the only one who needs to swear this vow. I must too."

"Then do it." He said this in a way that was both playful and also brutally serious. A subtle juxtaposition Iseult had first glimpsed on him in the Contested Lands, when it had been only the two of them wondering who would betray whom first.

The fire snapped; orange light flared.

"I am not married," she told him. "I have no lover . . . b-but you. And the Threads between us are true. *Mhe varujta,* Aeduan Amalej. *Te varuje.*"

"*Te varuje,*" he repeated back, and although neither of them said it, they both knew it was true: now they were not just Heart-Threads to each other, now they were braided in the Nomatsi way. Now they were bound with the Moon Mother's blessing.

Iseult kissed Aeduan then. A tender, almost tentative thing because her insides felt scraped clean. Like everything had been yanked out, leaving only heat and fullness behind.

"It's more comfortable in the Monastery," Aeduan offered after several minutes of delicate lips and gentle hands.

"I—I don't want to be near people." Iseult kissed his jaw. "And the tent is comfortable too. You'd be surprised how many supplies I could fit on Blueberry's back."

Aeduan laughed—it was a sound that, again, was simultaneously light and solemn. "He would be angry if we wasted his efforts."

"Yes," Iseult agreed, and after slipping her hand—sore though it was—into Aeduan's, she led her Bloodwitch toward the tent. The campfire hissed and shuddered as they passed.

And the stars shone like fireflies waiting for wishes to come true.

SEVENTY-FOUR

You are taking too long to write to me, my Queen.

> And you are too impatient, my Empress. There is so still much to
> clean and heal and fix inside my city.

*Mine too, but it is much easier when I know I will see you. Please visit
again.*

> The Truce Summit is next week. I will see you there.

Do not make me wait an entire week, Vivia.

> I thought you were busy negotiating between the Baedyeds and the
> Sand Sea dwellers. You told me just yesterday that you had no time
> to eat or sleep. I certainly don't.

Yes, but you are much more important to me than eating or sleeping.

> And I imagine you are blushing now, in that very sweet way that you do.

*Don't pretend I am the only one who blushes, my Queen. You're much
more forthcoming in these letters than in person.*

> I am trying, you know.

*I do know, and I do appreciate. And I would like to show that appreci-
ation in person. Please. Is it not better for both our peoples if we are at
our strongest? And I am always strongest when I see you. I can send
Windwitches for you, if you have none to spare.*

> Cam will take me on Aurora. Although he keeps sneaking off, think-
> ing I don't realize he's got himself a lover somewhere.

Is that a yes, then? You will come?

Did you really think I would refuse? You, who are the Chosen of the Fire Well?

Tease all you want, Vivia, but I can never tell with you. I was trained my whole life to win arguments, yet I think my tutors would despair if they knew how much trouble I have convincing you to do anything.

Well, your tutors need not despair quite yet. Because you'll see me tomorrow. It'll be late, though. After sunset.

And I will, as always, wait up for you.

Stacia Sotar had been watching Vivia for only several moments from the doorway, but it had been more than enough time to know Vivia was not writing a simple missive to her vizers or commands to her admirals.

She was writing to the Empress of Marstok, and seeing that much pleasure on Vivia's face . . .

Well, Stix might as well pour some salt on the wound that had brought her here in the first place.

She cleared her throat, prompting Vivia to whirl about. Her desk chair creaked. Then her eyes popped wide as she spotted Stix at her bedroom door.

Her face drained of color, and she stood so fast, her chair fell with a scraping thump.

"Noden hang me, is this real?" Vivia's voice was pitchy and strained. It was night outside, so her bedroom's lanterns guttered shadows across her sun-browned skin. "Is that really you, Stix?"

"Hye, Your Majesty. It's me." Stix shut the door behind her. She wasn't at all surprised to find Vivia's bedroom unchanged since she'd last been here, despite so much transformation—for better and worse—throughout Nubrevna. And in four steps, Stix had crossed to the center of the same threadbare rug beside the same iris-blue bed she remembered.

There was a new trinket here, though, added to Vivia's desk: a single iron shackle with a dangling chain. And as much as Stix might tell herself that the reason she'd avoided Vivia in the three weeks since the Great Collapse was because she'd needed to reconnect with the other Six—or at least those that remained . . .

That hadn't been the full truth.

And now, Stix couldn't pretend otherwise.

She dropped to one knee, her fist coming to her heart and head bowing. It forced Vivia to draw up short three paces away. And more importantly, it set the tone—or so Stix hoped—for the conversation to come.

Stix didn't need to look up to know her queen's shoulders would be rising. That Vivia's face would be hardening as she tried to paste on a royal visage.

"I'm sorry I didn't come sooner, my Queen." Stix didn't lift her head. "Duties called me away."

An incredulous exhale. Stix could imagine Vivia's shoulders climbing even higher.

"You're a hero," Vivia said. "This city wouldn't be standing if not for you, Stix. And *everyone* has been searching for you for weeks. Your father, the navy, Cam, and I . . . *I* have been searching for you for weeks. No, for months." Vivia claimed a step closer.

But Stix couldn't make herself look up. Not yet. She couldn't meet Vivia's dark eyes, for it would kill her resolve.

So instead, Stix ground her molars and stared at the rug's crisscross pattern. "I'm sorry I left you without any warning or explanation. I wasn't . . ." Stix swallowed. "I wasn't myself, and there were things—surprises, really—that I had to take care of."

"You mean joining forces with the Raider King."

Now Stix was the one to exhale sharply. "It's not easy to explain, but yes, Your Majesty. It was the right thing to do, joining with him."

"He tried to destroy our city." The venom in Vivia's voice startled Stix. So much so that she finally looked up.

Only to discover Vivia bearing down. One step. Two. Before Vivia dropped to her knees in front of Stix.

Stix felt herself squint, although she didn't need to. She wore new spectacles from the Sightwitch Sister Convent, and she didn't need to strain to see mere inches away. But it was as if the unblurred truth of Vivia was too much for her.

There was a new scar over Vivia's left eyebrow. A cut, too, that hadn't finished healing across her chin. But it was the expression itself that was most different. Old Vivia would never have done this—come so near. Worn such feeling upon her face.

Which is even more proof of why you cannot stay here. Because you weren't the one to peel away her mask.

Stix felt her entire abdomen solidify, like magma suddenly doused by the sea. Because she knew it was true—which also meant she was absolutely doing the right thing. She had made the right call; she simply needed to follow through.

"The Raider King tried to destroy Nubrevna," Vivia said. "Yet somehow going to his banner was the right thing?"

"It is not easy to explain—"

"And you're not even trying." Vivia rocked back until her feet were beneath her. Until she was shooting once more upright and stalking away. It was such real, visceral anger that radiated off her, and Stix couldn't help but notice that—unlike when Vivia had performed her rage countless times for admirals and vizers and even her father—she was not performing now.

This was real. Vivia was seething.

And Noden hang Stix, but this conversation had too quickly spiraled from her control.

"Why did you leave?" Vivia demanded. "*Why* did you go to the Raider King? *Why* did you save this city when magic just . . . just *disappeared* from the Witchlands? And then why did you leave again before I could see you?"

Stix dug a knuckle into her temple. "These are all fair questions, and I will do my best to answer them, but—"

"No." Water splashed from a pitcher on her desk. "No, Stix. Explain now."

With no preamble, Stix tried—as best she could—to execute her queen's command. She described all that she had learned, all she had done, all she had become in the past months. But just as Stix's own mind had rebelled and rebelled against the truth inside her, against the Paladin soul and all its memories . . .

She could see Vivia doing the same.

And Stix could hardly blame her.

Eventually, it became too much. Vivia sat on the edge of her bed, while Stix remained kneeled upon the floor. The water in the pitcher stopped its wild heaving, although it didn't calm entirely. And for many dragging minutes, there was only Stix's voice—as detached and clear as she could make it—filling the bedroom.

Until Stix finally reached the end of her tale. And she finally reached the part she had come here to say: "So you see why I can't remain in Lovats."

Vivia swayed. Her eyes, huge and pale in the fire-lit room, looked at

Stix with something that might have been horror. Might have been shock. "You will leave? Again?"

"Hye." With careful movements, Stix pushed to her own feet. The room spun. "I told you: there are Exalted Ones still out there. And one of them . . . he will come back here. This city is not safe. *None* of the Witchlands are until I find him."

"Why you, though?" Vivia pushed off her bed. "Just because you're . . . you're Lady Baile? A . . . a Paladin? Surely the Cahr Awen can do this. Or the other Paladins you spoke of. That Red Sails Admiral and the child. Leave this task to them. And stay *here*, Stix. Protect us *here*."

Stix ground her teeth. Again, she was squinting. Again, there was no reason. But it was the only way to blunt the agony of this choice she didn't want to make. *Except you do, now that Vivia has found love with another. You don't want to be here to watch that.*

"Do you see this?" From her shirt, Stix dug out a silver chain with a vial attached. She unlooped it from her neck and held it outstretched.

And as she expected—as she'd *hoped*—Vivia recoiled. "Is that a finger?"

"It's *his* finger. The monster who built this city. It belongs to him, as does the ring upon it. I will use these to find him."

"How?"

"I . . . don't know," Stix answered truthfully. "I only know that this piece of Lovats is important." *A sixth finger,* she thought, as she watched it dangle next to her fist. *To ward off mice.* "And until I find him, I cannot stay here, my Queen. But once I do—once Kahina and I have ended him, I'll return."

"Or you will never find him and never return?" Vivia shook her head, and the water in its pitcher juddered with the same furious rhythm. But where there had been outrage on the queen's face before, now there was only cruel indifference.

It wasn't real. That expression. It was just a little fox putting on her mask, even as the water betrayed her true pain.

"I'm sorry." Stix returned the chain to her neck. Then tucked the encapsulated finger back inside her shirt. "I'm more sorry than you can ever know, Vivia Nihar. But I swear to you that I will return."

Vivia's lips seamed shut. She turned away. The water sloshed anew. "Go," she said toward the desk. "Go, Stix, before I say something I know I can never take back."

Stix obeyed. It was the best path for them both, even if all she really wanted to do was fling herself at her Threadsister and *beg* for her to listen, to understand.

She spun on her heel. *Calm,* she told the water in the pitcher. *Be calm and give her the peace she needs.*

Stix was almost to Pin's Keep when Kahina slunk out of an alley's shadow. The spark of her pipe gave her away. Then the woman herself was there, her white hair tucked under a hooded cloak.

"It's done?" she asked.

Stix nodded, finding the word *hye* too hard to utter. Everything hurt. Not on the outside, of course, but on the inside where pain had a way of festering long after an injury should have healed.

"I'm sorry," Kahina said as she pulled Stix against her for a gruff—but ferocious—embrace. This was the softer side of her that she rarely showed anyone. The hearth fire instead of the inferno.

A cat purred against them as they stood there in this half-collapsed street of the Skulks, and Stix found that suddenly she was crying. All the tears she had kept locked away during her many steps from Queen's Hill to here now pulsed outward. Neither physical resistance nor magical resistance would keep them dammed in.

"I'm sorry," Kahina said again. "I did warn you."

Stix nodded against Kahina's shoulder. "You did." The woman smelled of tobacco and woodsmoke. "And I know you're right that this is for the best. For Vivia and Nubrevna—and for the Empress and Marstok too. But . . ."

"But," Kahina agreed, and she finally withdrew. Her hands moved to Stix's biceps and she squeezed so hard it almost hurt. "You will be tougher for this, Stacia Sotar of Nubrevna. Just as I was tougher for my own broken heart. Some wounds might be slow to heal, but all do heal eventually. And as Paladins, we have more time than most. She will age and she will die, yet you will linger on."

Stix screwed her eyes shut. Paladin bodies didn't live forever—although their souls did—but they still outlived most humans. There was so much magic inside them; time simply did not have the same hold.

"Now come, Stix." Kahina released her, smoke puffing from her pipe. "Our little sister is waiting for us at the Convent, and we have so much work to do."

SEVENTY-FIVE

✳

It was amazing to Vivia Nihar, Queen of Nubrevna, how little had changed in Dalmotti since she'd last come here. Hye, there were no naval vessels blocking the bay, and now it was the Doge scraping and bowing to *her* instead of the other way around . . .

Still, the city itself—with its waterways and sticky sea breeze, with its gardens and color and quavering, voice-filled life—none of that had changed. *Great Collapse?* this city seemed to ask. *What collapse?* Only the guilds and their members had felt the pain of what had come, and only the witches in the military. But it had been brief. Mere hours of agony and emptiness before a return to normal.

None of the buildings, none of the alleys or thoroughfares or canals had suffered. No Wells had collapsed and unleashed agony. And now, weeks later, it was almost as if the Great Collapse had never happened.

Certainly inside this ballroom, it had not.

And certainly to the Doge blinking his watery eyes before Vivia, it had not. "Your Majesty," he said with an obsequiousness that was as fake as the new white wig upon his head. "It is good to have you finally reach our fair city. Your brother arrived this morning."

Vivia already knew this, although she'd yet to see Merik. And if she was being honest, she didn't much want to see him. There was only one person she'd come to this blighted ball for, and at the moment, neither she nor her Adders were anywhere in sight.

So Vivia let her face settle into a smile. Just a *slight* tip of her upper lip. Just a dash of vacant boredom in her eyes. "If only you had welcomed me so graciously last time, Doge." She let her smile spread until teeth showed. "Perhaps I wouldn't have felt the need to obliterate half your navy."

With nothing more than a curt nod, Vivia stalked away. The palace ballroom awaited, with its wall of glass, reflected chandelier light, and people from all across the Witchlands, twirling and shimmering like fish in the reefs off Nihar.

Three doors were cast open, each with paths leading into shadow. Vivia sensed the sea that way. Tides and ripples and salted water that no longer threatened to engulf her or drag her down.

It was strange, though, because while her magic had returned, it hadn't felt the same. In some ways, it was steadier. Like a loyal hound always at the ready . . . but also weaker, as if the hound had gone lame in one paw.

Vivia knew she wasn't the only one who felt this. Her favorite captain—*don't think of Stix, don't think of Stix*—who now walked mere paces behind in her own dress uniform had said as much only yesterday. *These tides,* Shanna Quintay had mumbled as she and Vivia had thrust the first currents against their ship, *are as familiar as they are strange.*

Vivia slowed her gait as hundreds of eyes swiveled onto her. She felt Shanna and the three vizers who'd accompanied her stiffen. It took all of Vivia's self-control not to do the same. Nor to check her collar, fix her cuffs. She was here, and she had every plan to keep moving until she found . . .

There. Her eyes lit on a row of black-uniformed Adders, their faces hidden and their eyes glittering. At their heart was Vaness. She spoke with an expression of utter calm to a woman who, from this distance, looked Cartorran. Or possibly Lusquan. Or maybe even Svodish. Vivia wasn't familiar with the intricacies of high fashion in the west.

The closest of the Adders leaned toward his empress. Rokesh was the man's name, and Vivia liked him. Not merely because he would die to protect Vaness, nor merely because he had remained loyal to Vaness during her brief deposal . . .

Vivia liked the Adder High because he was one of the few people in all the world that the Empress fully listened to and fully trusted. That, Vivia knew, was a quality that would matter in whatever future lay ahead.

For both Vaness *and* Vivia, if Vivia's plans came to fruition tonight.

At the words of Rokesh, Vaness snapped her eyes away from her conversation partner. She found Vivia, and instantly, her face transformed. Not perhaps in any way that someone else would notice, but Vivia saw it: a relaxing of her brow. A softening of her shoulders.

And then a twinkling dance of iron beads across the bodice of her blood-red gown. Gone were the shackles at her wrist, but then they had been gone for quite some time now.

With no ceremony at all, Vivia marched right up to the Empress. Then she cut a sharp bow, deep and respectful—and in the style of the Marstoks.

To the evident surprise of all who watched, Vaness also sank into a bow of her own. Fist over heart, head dipped low.

When they both rose, the conversation partner from some unimportant place in the west was gone. And all of Vivia's guests had conveniently dissolved into the ocean of dancers and minglers nearby. The Adders too, had scooted respectfully away.

"Walk with me," Vaness said. She motioned toward the nearest door. "I want to speak without eyes upon us."

Ah, Vivia thought, her throat tightening. *Me too.* She offered the Empress her arm, and Vaness took it with a tiny, almost private smile. Then together, the two monarchs strolled with regal ease toward the door.

It was all a show, of course, but Vivia was pleased at how well they both performed it. Vaness had lost her empire, only to get it back and find some of the changes made had been good ones. That in fact, General Fashayid had uncovered all sorts of cracks in her imperial foundations that needed fixing.

Vivia, meanwhile, was the newly crowned Queen of Nubrevna—but all here knew it was only because her father had died in the Great Collapse. None were certain she had earned the sliver of a golden crown she wore atop her head.

Together, the queen and Empress left the tiles of the ballroom. Twilit air washed over them. The rhythm of the tides pulsed louder in Vivia's veins. Louder, louder as they ambled—with Adders never far behind—down a winding path surrounded by roses and oleander.

"It looks just as I recall it," the Empress murmured. "As does the Doge. Slimy, disgusting man."

Vivia smirked. "I thought the same."

"Of course you did. Here, let's stop at that bench and catch our breaths."

Hye, Vivia thought, even though they'd scarcely exerted themselves. Still Vivia was finding the deeper into these gardens they wefted—and the more distant the music and voices became—the harder it was for her lungs to function. She checked repeatedly that all of her buttons were done up. She smoothed her hair every second turn, and she removed . . . then *returned* her crown thrice.

"I would like to," she began, once they were seated, "that is to say, would you do me the honor—"

"Of a dance?"

"*Ahtset*. But also, would you do me the honor of—"

"A kiss?"

"By Noden, Empress, let me finish."

"No."

Vivia recoiled. "*No?*"

"Because if you finish, then I cannot be the one to ask, and I . . ." Vaness withdrew a small band from her pocket. It was not iron, but a silvery material.

And Vivia's heart crumpled in her chest. "Steel?"

"Hye," the Empress answered in Nubrevnan. "I told you, I only work with it for the most important items. And this . . . well, please do *me* the honor of becoming my bride. I understand there are political ramifications for our nations, but I believe we can—"

Vivia kissed her. A gentle thing of her lips against Vaness's much softer ones. Then a harder thing when the Empress sank inward. When her bones seemed to melt against Vivia, and for once, the iron on her dress stopped moving.

"*Ahtset,*" Vivia murmured between kisses. "I will marry you."

She now felt Vaness smile against her. Then she saw, when she opened her eyes, how the Empress's dark eyes crinkled. It was an expression she so rarely revealed. *Except for me.* Between them both, all masks had long ago fallen.

"You will move to Marstok?"

"Of course not."

The Empress laughed, scooting closer so she could slide her arms around Vivia's waist. Then up Vivia's back. "I did not expect you to, but it was worth asking. My Windwitches are tired of flying us back and forth."

"You could move to Nubrevna then. That would solve it."

Now Vaness's laugh turned sharp. Her fingers too, as she let them dig into the muscles of Vivia's shoulders. "Oh yes, a brilliant plan. My people and Sultanate and soldiers—whom I have only just returned to—will certainly understand."

"Fine." Vivia let one eyebrow cock high. "Neither of us moves. We'll just wear out our Windwitches. And poor Cam and Aurora too."

"There *are* magic doorways." Vaness's perfect eyebrows now notched high to match Vivia's. "We could ask that the Sightwitches open one for us."

Now Vivia really laughed, even as her mind wondered . . . wondered . . . *Would they, maybe?* "Logistics are for later," she said, and with no other words—because really, they weren't needed—she cupped the Empress's face and kissed her again.

And nearby, where the Jadansi forever lapped against the city and salted

winds forever blew, Vivia felt the waves kick higher. Crash hotter, responding to a Tidewitch celebrating whatever was to come.

Merik Nihar, Minister of the Republic of Arithuania, felt a fool as he
tucked himself into a shadow of the Doge's ballroom. He didn't think he
could have been any clearer with Revan's mother—whom they'd found in
Poznin, severely burned, but alive after the Great Collapse: he had not
wanted buttons on his elegant attire for the Truce Summit ball.

Actually, Merik would wager it had been Revan's own doing that the
request regarding buttons had gone unheeded. He did so love his little
unnecessary extras, so here Merik stood with an infernal number of pure
silver beads climbing up his torso, a cascade of molten starlight against
a blue so dark, it was almost black. Meanwhile Merik's collar was high
enough to stab into the edges of his jaw. It rubbed at the scars on his right
side.

Merik's only consolation was that his sister looked as blighted uncomfortable as he was, in her pale gray Nubrevnan Admiralty uniform. Chandelier light glowed across her and her entourage of vizers, and although
she'd met Merik's gaze across the tiled room several moments ago, she had
yet to actually come speak to him.

To be fair, he hadn't gone to her either. He and his lone guest, Sky, had
been cornered almost immediately upon their arrival by a friend Merik
hadn't expected to see again. A man who'd been a Cleaved alongside Merik
in Poznin, and without whom, Merik never would have escaped the Puppeteer's control.

It was this man who'd thrust the killing blow into Esme, and *he*, it
turned out, was nothing short of royalty in the northernmost tribes of the
Witchlands.

The Northman's haggard beard was now a finely groomed one with
beads and gold ribbon; his furs were dyed blue; a velvet purple cloak draped
over one beefy shoulder; and a hammered band of silver rested atop his
head.

The hug that the Northman and Merik shared made tears score in
Merik's eyes. (And also squeezed most of the air from Merik's lungs.) But
alas, the same language barriers that had prevented conversation in Poznin
now prevented it on the dance floor. Sky did her best, but Merik could see
her struggling.

Which was why he lifted both hands and said in Svodish, "We'll be back—and with someone to translate."

That journey led them across the ballroom, onto a patio, into the ballroom again, and eventually behind the columns to a Wordwitch named Mathew fitz Leaux, who stood with another advisor for the Cartorran Imperial Regent.

Sky instantly began salivating. "He's a Wordwitch. That's what that mark on his hand means."

Merik snorted. He knew blighted well what that Witchmark meant, and he was more than a little relieved to see it there. Merik had already drained his entire socializing quota for the evening; he didn't think he could manage another search for a translator.

"Of course I can help you and this Northman," Mathew told Merik in fluid Cartorran. Then, with no effort at all, he slipped into Arithuanian and said to Sky: "Or better yet, I can teach your advisor here how to do it for herself. Would you like that, Skyvenjetsa? To see the words hovering right before you, even though you've never encountered them before?"

"Gods, yes," Sky breathed with delight. "I would love that, sir."

"Excellent. Then let us take a turn about the room, so I may show you some basics." His gaze slid back to Merik; his words shifted to Nubrevnan. "If that is all right with your minister, of course."

Sky flung Merik a pleading glance.

"Go on." Merik laughed. "Just please remember those manners we practiced last week, hye?"

Sky bowed, fist to heart, and with an almost mocking grin, she answered: "Hye, sir. Of course, sir. Right away, sir. I would never forget, sir."

Which prompted Mathew to grin Merik's way. "Oh, do not worry, Minister." He winked. "I have dealt with far less polite pupils than she."

Pupils? Merik thought as Mathew whisked Sky away. *When did we say she was your pupil?* But Merik couldn't chase after to ask—not without abandoning the second Cartorran advisor and revealing poor manners of his own.

Guildmaster Alix smiled at Merik, as if knowing what Merik was thinking. "This is quality needlework, Minister." He gestured to the complex lines sewn onto Merik's cuffs. "And such shimmer on that silver thread—it must have cost a fortune."

"Hye, Guildmaster, it did." Merik bowed his head. "Except . . . that is not your title anymore, is it?"

The man's smile spread wider. "No, you're right. I am Guildmaster no longer. My time masquerading as a tailor came to an end shortly after I met you at the last Truce Summit. Not that I mind being an Imperial Regent's advisor now. It is . . ." A thoughtful pause. Then a twirl of his finely boned hand where a Witchmark used to grace it—but where now there was only pale flesh. "It is much easier to be oneself than to hide, would you not agree?"

Merik's gaze sharpened. The question was clearly pronged on purpose, given that it certainly *appeared* as if Merik was hiding behind this column while all the monarchs, Guildmasters, nobility, merchants, and powerful players of the Witchlands spun and danced, chatted and colluded beyond.

But before Merik could respond as pointedly in kind—*I am here because you and Mathew fitz Leaux were hiding before me*—the former Silk Guildmaster bowed. It was a respectful bow, not mocking as his words might have been. And in seconds, he and his own beautifully tailored clothes had swished away.

Leaving Merik to tug at his collar and frown at the crowded space beyond the column. The air at the heart of the ballroom was quickly turning stuffy. The breeze slipping in through the open glass doors was too sticky to help. Merik should go back out there. He should talk to Vivia, then track down the Northman again—whose name Merik still hadn't sorted out (there were a lot of syllables involved)—and do his best to endure the rest of this night without letting the heat and the crowds get to him.

"Oh, who are you fooling?" he muttered, turning his attention to his cuffs. The truth was that he *had* fled behind this column, and only random chance had placed a Wordwitch back here too.

"Quite the show, isn't it?" a voice asked.

Merik spun about, only to discover the shadows he'd claimed were changing shape before his eyes. One dark corner in particular was now coalescing into a woman dressed in white—a woman who absolutely had not been there several moments ago.

Safi grinned. "Sorry to sneak up on you. Don't be mad at Alix for hiding me. I didn't want to talk to anyone before I could find you. And gods, it took you so *long* to finally make it back here. I was on the verge of sending Alix to track you down."

Merik's mouth hung open like a fish. He knew it did, but he couldn't seem to reel it shut. All he could do was take in the workmanlike cut of Safi's gown. The silken gray breeches that slid out from a knee-length skirt. The fine black boots that reached to her mid-calf. She looked dressed for a fight, not a party.

"I . . . I have been trying to find you for weeks," Merik sputtered at last. "I sent letters and spies and even Aurora, but I heard nothing. Where have you been?"

Safi had the decency to wince. "I'm sorry. I *did* send a letter."

"Hye, and all it said was, *Thank you for saving me. Twice. Yours, Safi.*"

Her wince melted away, a familiar defiance flashing in her storm-blue eyes. "Was that not enough?"

Merik scoffed. "No, *Domna*, it was not enough. It sounded so final, I thought I'd never see you again."

"Why? Did my uncle not explain our plans at the Summit lunch today? How the mantle of the Cahr Awen will now be an apprenticed position that ensures magic is never again abused by humanity?" She tapped impatiently at the symbols on her bodice. "I'm wearing this ridiculous outfit to make the point."

"Your uncle explained everything." A fresh surge of temper sparked inside Merik's chest. "But that still left me with weeks of wondering."

A capitulating grunt. Then Safi sashayed a step closer. Another step and another until she was right up to Merik and could flick lazily at one of his many absurd buttons. Her hands, Merik noted, were scarred in the same way that his face and chest were. But Safi's were newer scars, still red and angry where his had begun to haze.

She wasn't ashamed of her marks.

Merik envied her that.

"If I didn't know better," she said with a tip of her head, "I would think you were worried about me, *Prince*."

He snorted. His attention shot back to her face—which had plenty of its own scars, from blades and sparks and icy winds in a storm he'd tried to protect her from. "Of *course* I was worried, Safi. The last time I saw you was the Great Collapse. For all I knew, you'd written that letter and then flung yourself into the mouth of a sea fox."

"Yes." Safi walked her fingers up his buttons. "That does sound like something I would do."

Merik's temper kicked up another level, and this time, a slight wind kicked with it. Just a twirl of hot air to flip around them. To tug at Safi's skirts and spray her short hair from her face.

"Well, if it's any consolation," she continued, "you're going to be seeing quite a lot of me. In fact I was hoping you might be the first, Merik."

He swallowed. "First . . . what?" She was very near—and those blue eyes of hers were as choppy and unpredictable as the sea.

"The first place we visit, of course. The Cahr Awen must travel across the Witchlands to ensure magic is never drained or misused. Are you *sure* my uncle explained all of this at the luncheon?"

Merik swallowed again. His winds were well and truly coiling now, while his chest ached with the need to . . . to *do* something other than simply stand here while she toyed with his buttons and skimmed her hands down, down, toward the silken belt at his waist. "Your uncle did indeed say all of this, but . . ." *Focus, Merik.* "But he made no mention of your first stop."

"Well, that's because I only just decided it would be Poznin." Safi's grin turned almost triumphant.

And Merik caught both her wrists. She had reached his belt, and that was quite far enough. "Then I suppose that makes you as impulsive as ever."

"You like it."

"Noden hang me, but I do."

"Then I think you will be especially pleased by the music that's about to begin."

He frowned, confusion whittling into the shadows. It whittled into his magic too, cooling his temper like a wind.

That's not your temper, you dolt. It's your magic responding to a woman. Kullen had told Merik that on the *Jana*, and blighted if Safi wasn't currently realizing the same thing. Or at least, that was what the challenge on her face suggested.

Then Merik heard the throbbing strains of an opening movement, followed by the first stamping of heels on marble. And he *felt* as Safi's fingers moved from his buttons to his shoulders, where they could tap and trickle against him like rain against a ship's sail.

"The four-step," he tried to say, although his voice came out rough as the Nihar coastline.

"Hye," she agreed. "I thought we could dance it for old times' sake, and . . . perhaps for new ones, too."

Merik didn't reply. His body told him there was too much danger in the ballroom—for his temper, for his sanity, for his safety. Because if he danced with the light-bringer, then all of the Witchlands would see his scars beneath the glowing chandeliers.

And all would know how much he had changed since he'd last been here.

But then, Merik supposed Safiya fon Hasstrel was as transformed as he was, if not more so. If she could face them all with that gleam in her blue eyes, then surely he could do the same.

Which was why Merik let Safi pull him toward the ballroom's heart. Why, as he felt the bay's humid breeze reach for his magic—and as dignitaries of all colors and sizes and creeds cleared away to watch them—he let himself take the starting position before Safi.

It's why he also let himself laugh. Because he recalled how he'd begun this dance with her the last time. With arrogance and competition and yes, genuine temper. *I don't move, Domna. People move for me.*

How childish; how absurd—and how childish, how absurd for Merik to keep hiding behind that column. Trust Safi, though, to bring out this other side of him.

Moonlight and chandeliers caressed her golden skin and gleaming hair, just as they had months ago. But this time, instead of people murmuring, *Do you see with whom Prince Merik dances?* it was: *Do you see with whom the light-bringer dances?*

Safi smiled at Merik.

Merik smiled at her.

The music shifted; the storm began; and together, they danced for all of the Witchlands to see.

SEVENTY-SIX

✳

Tonight was a dazzling night in Veñaza City. The stars shone with nary a cloud to interrupt their performance, and the city positively pulsed with heat baked into its cobbles from the day. Salt carried in off the sea, scented with jasmine and roses—and with lies and truths too, forever murmuring in that rhythmic way of the Dalmotti language.

Gods, how Safiya fon Hasstrel had missed this place.

She'd especially missed this particular rooftop tucked in the Northern Wharf District, where she found a sprawled-out Iseult gazing up at the Sleeping Giant.

A pot of fresh coffee steamed on the shingles near Iseult's feet.

Safi plopped down beside her Threadsister. "Coffee at this hour?" There were two porcelain mugs, familiar and used. Safi always took the one with the chipped arm. "You'll never sleep, Iz."

"I don't want to sleep." Iseult stared straight overhead. She wore a fine gray suit with a matching cloak that would blend well into shadows. The fabric was light and strong and worth far more than anything Iseult had ever owned in Veñaza City—and Safi would know because Safi was the one who'd had it custom made for her.

She'd also had one made for herself, although right now, she still wore her white half gown over it all.

And right now, Habim, Mathew, and Uncle Eron were likely cursing Alix for helping Safi first sneak *into* the ball . . . then sneak right back out again. But Alix had always had a soft spot for Safi. He *had* housed her for all those years. And clothed her. And fed her too, on occasion.

"Is this done steeping?" Safi grabbed the coffee pitcher and squinted into its murky depths.

"Another few minutes." Iseult finally tore her gaze from the sky. "You don't see them anymore, do you?"

Safi didn't have to ask to know what Iseult meant. "Only if I look through the Truth-lens. Then I see them like I did right after the Collapse."

A nod. Then a grunt as Iseult pushed herself to sitting. "Well, it's different now. They're simultaneously brighter and thinner. Especially the ones up there."

"Yes, well, we *are* still missing one Paladin. There were six Wells, but only five Paladins have given up their magic."

Another nod, but this time, it was accompanied with a pensive frown from Iseult. And also a silence as she set to pouring their coffee. It was such a familiar combination of sounds. A music Safi hadn't known she missed until this precise moment, when the first clink came from the strainer laid over Safi's mug.

True, true, true, her magic sang, swelling in her chest. Prickling at her eyeballs.

Next came the burble of coffee pouring. The slight crunch as thick grounds gathered in the strainer. Another clink and finally a scrape as Iseult moved the strainer to her own cup and finished pouring.

Then both girls lifted their mugs and grinned at each other. A breeze tugged at Iseult's hair. She wore gloves now because her hands were still too raw to leave exposed—and perhaps because, unlike Safi, she wasn't comfortable yet with how they looked.

Safi was frankly just glad they could both still *use* them. What they'd done in the Contested Lands certainly could have ended much worse for them both.

"To Evrane," Iseult said, extending her mug toward Safi. "Th-the Nameless Monk who s-saved me many times over."

Safi's heart twisted. "Saved us both, actually. Even if she was stingy with her knives."

Iseult laughed, a taut sound. Then she and Safi tapped mugs. Steam twirled up between their faces.

After they each took a sip, Iseult lifted her mug again. "To Zander. Who was the best of the Hell-Bards and who w-was . . . a protector for any who needed him."

Safi sucked in. Her nose hurt now with the intensity of the truth radiating off Iseult's words—and off the ache that hadn't left her lungs yet and perhaps never would. "To Zander," she squeezed out.

Their mugs tapped again. They each sipped again. But where Safi thought they might be done, Iseult once more thrust out her mug. "To

Kullen Ikray, as well as e-e-*every* other life we knew and . . . and all the—the ones we didn't. Even the Raider King. And even . . ."

"Polly," Safi whispered. She couldn't pretend she grieved him—she didn't. Not after everything he'd done. But she *did* grieve the boy he'd been before the Rook King's memories had taken hold.

She'd loved that boy, and *he* was worth mourning.

One more clink of their mugs, and after a sniffle, after a dab at her eyes, Safi gulped down her coffee. Both girls did, in total silence save for the ceaseless noises of this city where they had first met. Where they had become Threadsisters. Where they had been trained and taught and honed into the Cahr Awen.

Safi might resent having had all her choices taken from her, but she didn't resent where they'd led her in the end. Or what she and Iseult had—together—been able to do.

After swallowing back the final, dreggy sip in her mug, Safi clanked it onto the shingles, and to her surprise, she found something almost like mischief wiggling on her Threadsister's nose.

"I thought you'd want to spend your evening with a certain prince, Safi."

Safi barked a laugh. "He's a minister now, actually. What a boring title, isn't it?"

"So does that mean you're *not* spending your evening with him?"

Safi waved at the night's balmy air. "There's plenty of time for that later, Iz. Our first destination will be Poznin—which, before you make a snide comment—"

"I would never."

"—does make sense. I mean, if there's anywhere that might have imbalanced magic that needs tending, it's that city."

"Hmmm." Iseult sipped her coffee. "And how long will we be staying there?"

"As long as we need."

"And what if he doesn't want you to leave again?"

"Well, *that's* inevitable." Safi flashed her most cavalier grin. "They never do, you know."

"They?" Iseult pretended to inspect Safi. "What *they* do you mean? Have you got lovers hiding in those secret pockets on your gown?"

"Oh-ho, you're one to tease, Iz, given that you've got a little *godling* who won't let you out of his sight for more than five minutes."

Iseult's lips pursed. "It's been five days, thank you."

"Right. Because you think I didn't notice you sneaking off two nights ago?"

Red fanned onto Iseult's cheeks—a shadow in this grayscale evening. *True*, Safi's magic purred, both to the reaction *and* to her comment about Iseult's not-so-subtle escapade.

Iseult finished her coffee with a loud gulp, then cleared her throat pointedly. And just as pointedly changed the subject. "Since you're here and we've a-agreed we won't sleep tonight, then how about a game of taro? There's a match over by the Southern Wharf. B-big money thrown around there."

Safi's eyebrows launched high. Then promptly swooped down again as she became the one to inspect her Threadsister from head to toe. "Heard from *whom*? You've been hiding since you got into the city, tucked up in this attic with letters and books and charts."

Iseult bobbed a shoulder, her *fake* nonchalance as obvious to Safi's magic as it was to Safi's eyes. "Oh, just a certain Hell-Bard told me. Two of them, actually, who came by three hours ago."

Safi gasped. "They're *here*?"

Iseult stopped feigning boredom. Her face split with an arrestingly truthful grin—something she was doing more and more often in recent weeks. And that Safi would never tire of seeing. "And a Threadwitch is with them. So what do you say?"

"Yes!" Safi scrabbled to her feet. "Let me change, and we can go. Actually, no. I'm too impatient for that."

Iseult snorted. "Was that self-awareness I just heard, Safi?"

"Shut up." Safi grabbed her Threadsister's gloved hands. "Get up and help me take this dress off."

"Are you fully clothed underneath?"

"Of course I am." Safi rolled her eyes.

Iseult whistled. "Self-awareness *and* planning ahead. All in one night. By the Moon Mother, what has b-become of the Safi I used to know?"

Safi grinned, and once her dress was off, she flung it through the open window into Iseult's old attic bedroom. The night's air coursed against her gray suit. The scent of salt and sewage and coffee mingled into her nose. She stretched once, feeling her spine crack and her shoulders roll.

"Rooftops?"

"For as long as we can. You lead the way, Light-Bringer."

"As you wish, Dark-Giver." Safi pushed into a jog, aiming south toward the beating heart of Veñaza City. And when she reached the edge of the coffee shop roof, she leaped for the next slope of shingles.

Initiate.

She *slammed* down. Pigeons burst upward, wings flapping to get out of the way before Iseult bounded down beside her. *Complete.* Safi started running again.

"You have bird shit on your cloak," Iseult called after. "Left shoulder."

"Are you serious?" Safi skidded to a halt, and sure enough, there was a fresh splat of white on her cloak. "Why? *Why* is it always me and never you who gets crapped on?"

Iseult's only reply was bubbling laughter. It floated straight up into the midnight sky. Straight up into the heavens. And Safi couldn't help but laugh too as she chased after Iseult, toward the next rooftop.

Then the next roof after that, and the next and the next, on and on. Threadsisters to the end.

For their quest was not yet over.

It had only just begun.

THE WITCHES OF
SHADOW AND LIGHT

N ot long ago, when the gods began walking among us again, there was a sister of shadow and a sister of light.

These sisters were not bound by blood, but by Threads—and as everyone knows, there is no greater force in all the Witchlands than Thread-family.

One sister wanted freedom from her magic and her title.

The other sister wanted freedom from her magic and her heritage.

And both sisters believed that if they ran far enough and fast enough, they would eventually find a person or a place that could give it to them.

So the sisters did run, following mountain bats into soil and stones. Following foxes on the tides of home. They followed hounds through winds and storms, and they followed hawks into what flames had born. They followed a rook to white caps, where sunlight seared on snow, and they followed a weasel into caverns, where darkness was never foe.

They met rulers and ruffians, pirates and pickpockets, witches and waifs, and together—although, sometimes also apart—the sisters saw more of the Moon Mother's world than any had ever seen before them, save for the goddess herself.

Which was how, together, the sister of shadow and the sister of light discovered that they could only be special if they chose to be. They could only be powerful if they demanded they be. And they could only be free if they looked inward and understood what chains really held them down.

But the greatest lesson the sisters learned was that which all heroes must eventually learn: that what we want is so very rarely what we need. And what the sisters needed, it turned out, was something they'd always had since the beginning.

Each other.

So hand in hand—and with a little monster who'd joined them along the *way—the sister of shadow and the sister of light set off to be as special as they could be in their own way.*

And they went on many grand adventures for all the rest of their days.

THE END

THE TRUE TALE OF THE TWELVE PALADINS

A Guide Assembled by Sister Ryber Fortiza

As the effects of the Great Collapse continue to ripple through the Witchlands and people hasten to ascribe their own stories to what has happened and why—it is the charge of the Sightwitch Sisters to record all that occurred. Our memories, our truths, and our interpretations.

However, to fully understand, we must first assess all that happened long ago to bring us here. As such, what follows is a brief introduction for incoming and aged Sightwitches alike to learn from.

But of course, hold tightly at all times to the Rule of Disputed Truth: *Oftentimes, Memory Records offer different accounts for the same events. As such, all Memory Records are true and all Memory Records are false, for what is life except perception?*

LONG AGO

As the Nomatsi tales all begin: long ago, when the gods walked among us . . .

There were in fact no gods. There was only Sirmaya. The Sleeper, the Sleeping Giant, the Moon Mother, the Goddess at the heart of everything. She created the Witchlands and all that was within, but over time, She saw that people squabbled. They hurt, they stole, they sometimes even killed. *What I need are arbiters,* She decided. *People who will represent me in the world, since I myself cannot go among them.*

As such, She created the Twelve. These Paladins were meant to use their powers—magics only *they* possessed—to maintain peace in the Witchlands. They would find humans best suited to lead with compassion and care, and they would lift up those leaders.

To ensure a smooth transition from one generation to the next—and to ensure varied experience and avoid stagnation of ideas, of culture, of power—the Paladins were not made immortal. Instead, when a Paladin's body decayed with age or was slain, its soul was reincarnated into a new body. (Note: the current Paladins of Water and Fire have told me their bodies live longer than normal humans, presumably because of the natural healing magic within them. Some reincarnations have apparently lived up to several centuries.)

The Paladin soul grows in its new body until a time when a trigger from the past awakens memories of reincarnated lives. This moment also unlocks not only their full Goddess-given mission of venerating the leaders of the land, but also the full breadth and width of their magics.

Thus the cycle went for many centuries, and the Witchlands prospered. People still squabbled and stole and killed, but at least there were the Twelve to keep widespread war from ever taking hold.

But as always happens when power is consolidated into only a few, some Paladins eventually chose to hoard their magic—and then to destroy the leaders they were meant to uplift.

Six turned on six, as the verse goes from "Eridysi's Lament." *And made themselves kings.*

Soon, those wicked six became the rulers instead of mere Paladins, and in their hubris, they declared themselves the Exalted Ones. They were monarchs who used their magics not for peace, but for control. Who did not venerate and assist the best leaders of the land, but instead destroyed them.

War finally razed across the Witchlands. The deaths were immeasurable.

The remaining Paladins became rebels against them. The Six, they called themselves, and they met in secret, deep in the heart of the Sirmayan Mountains where the Sightwitches had (and of course, still have) their Convent. With our own Eridysi's help and the help of her two apprentices, Lisbet and Cora, the Six crafted a plan to stop the Exalted Ones.

Because a slain Paladin will simply reincarnate, they knew

they had to end their souls for good. So Eridysi crafted a blade that could sever through Paladin spirits, preventing the soul from moving to a new body after death.

And she made a looking glass that could be used to find Paladins—to recognize their ancient souls, since they otherwise looked like any other person.

However, the Six's plans were ruined when one of their ranks had the truth wrung out of her. And so the Exalted Ones attacked.

In the end, the Exalted Ones did fall. The blade and glass were too powerful for them to withstand.

But the Six all died that day, too. Not by the severing permanence of the blade, but by a standard sword wielded by their very own Rook King, just as the rest of Eridysi's verse described:

One turned on five and stole everything.

In the Rook King's mind, one of the Six had betrayed them to the Exalted Ones. He could trust no one until he tracked down who—a feat he hoped to accomplish before the Six's souls reincarnated.

Unfortunately, other problems quickly revealed themselves: the Exalted Ones were gone, but their magic was not. Where each of the wicked Paladins had been slain by the blade, a spring had formed. And from that spring, magic flowed freely into the land.

Within mere years, *everyone* in the Witchlands possessed magic in varying amounts.

Over time, the idea of Twelve Paladins was relegated to myths and legends. Their last-remembered figures and faces and names were elevated into pantheons or revered as saints.

Or, more often, they were simply forgotten. Even the Goddess's true name, Sirmaya, was lost to time, remembered only by us Sightwitch Sisters in our Convent.

At least until a day one thousand years after that first collapse when all of the Witchlands were once more taught the true tale of the Twelve. And when once more, all of the Witchlands were shown the full power of a goddess sleeping at the heart of everything.

GLOSSARY

SIRMAYA

Also called the SLEEPING GIANT, the MOON MOTHER, and the SLEEPING GODDESS, Sirmaya is the deity at the center of the Witchlands. It is Her life-force from which all magic is drawn.

Deep in the Sirmayan Mountains, there is a "sleeping ice" that consumes any creature that possesses magic. Sightwitches "sleep" in this ice, rather than die, so that their prophetic magic can be returned to Sirmaya and balance can remain.

However, balance is easily broken, and only with careful tending and conscious purpose can we prevent a second Great Collapse.

THE EXALTED ONES:

• RAKEL:

o Her mastery was over Water.

o She ruled all the coastal lands of the southwestern Witchlands.

o Her soul was briefly forced into Monk Evrane Nihar's body through a process called *possession* (see resources by Sister Komla Inhar for details on this process), before being removed again by the Rook King.

o Rakel was eradicated a second time during the Great Collapse, and her Paladin soul and the magic therein were returned to Sirmaya.

• NADJE:

o His mastery was over Aether.

o He ruled over a small stretch of lands in the far north.

o He was eradicated when the Six turned on the Exalted Ones, although he briefly possessed Tool-Bearer Aeduan Amalej's body before he too was removed by the Rook King. (Again, see resources by Sister Komla Inhar for details on this type of Aether magic.)

o Nadje was eradicated a second time during the Great Collapse, and his Paladin soul and the magic therein were returned to Sirmaya.

- ITOSHA:
  - o Her mastery was over Air.
  - o She ruled over the region now known as Arithuania.
  - o She was eradicated when the Six turned on the Exalted Ones.
  - o She was eradicated again in the Great Collapse, and her Paladin soul and the magic therein were returned to Sirmaya.

- FERISIEN:
  - o Her mastery was over Earth.
  - o She ruled the lands of the Ohrin Mountains.
  - o She was eradicated when the Six turned on the Exalted Ones.
  - o Her body and soul have yet to be tracked down after the Great Collapse, and she is considered a threat to the Witchlands.

- LOVATS:
  - o His mastery was over Fire.
  - o He ruled over the lands south and southeast of the Sirmayan Mountains.
  - o He was obsessed with Lady Baile, and because he knew the Paladin Bastien was her Heart-Thread, he tormented Bastien relentlessly with fire.
  - o Lovats was eradicated when the Six turned on the Exalted Ones.
  - o His body and soul have yet to be tracked down after the Great Collapse.
  - o He possesses rings that can control the Six, making him a continued threat to the Witchlands.

- PORTIA:
  - o Her mastery was over Void.
  - o She ruled over the northwestern stretches of the Witchlands.
  - o She forced the Earth Paladin Saria to serve her with threats to the people of Saria's lands.
  - o And she claimed her fellow Void Paladin Midne's powers as her own, binding Midne to the first Weaverwitch Loom—and creating the first Hell-Bard.
  - o The Rook King initially believed Portia was eradicated when the Exalted Ones were slain a thousand years ago. In truth, Portia was able to kill Midne instead and take her place for the next thousand years, pretending to be Midne.

o Her modern incarnation was CORLANT, a Purist Priest. His body was slain recently, meaning Portia's soul will reincarnate somewhere, someday in the Witchlands. This makes her a continued threat.

THE SIX:

+ SARIA:

o Her mastery was over Earth.

o She is called LITTLE SISTER OWL in the Nomatsi pantheon and known for her quiet, animal-like ways.

o As Saria, she was Heart-Threads with Elias, the Rook King—although they kept this secret because they feared Portia's wrath.

o Her modern incarnation is the young Nomatsi girl, Dirdra, who goes by the name Owl. She is now receiving an education at the Sightwitch Sister Convent, although she spends much of her time in the Crypts and asks for privacy.

+ BASTIEN:

o His mastery was over Air.

o He is called SISTER SWALLOW in the Nomatsi pantheon and known for a fickle temper.

o He is also called THE FURY in Nubrevnan lore and regarded as a vengeful saint.

o He was the Heart-Thread of Baile.

o Bastien's modern incarnation was KULLEN IKRAY, Threadbrother to Merik Nihar, who recently passed in the Great Collapse. His Paladin soul and the magic therein were returned to Sirmaya.

+ BAILE:

o Her mastery was over Water.

o She is called OLD UNCLE in the Nomatsi pantheon and known for patience.

o She is also called LADY BAILE in Nubrevnan lore and regarded as a nurturing saint.

o She was Heart-Threads with Bastien.

o Baile's modern incarnation is STACIA SOTAR, Threadsister to Queen Vivia Nihar of Nubrevna.

+ RHIAN:
- o Her mastery was over Fire.
- o She is called COMET BRIGHT in the Nomatsi pantheon, known for quick rages and quicker quellings.
- o She is now reincarnated as ADMIRAL KAHINA, leader of the Red Sails.

+ MIDNE:
- o Her mastery was over Void.
- o She is called WICKED SISTER WEASEL in the Nomatsi pantheon, known for selfishness.
- o She is also known as the FIRST HELL-BARD because she was bound magically by the Exalted One Portia to the first Loom ever created.
- o She was killed during the attack on the Exalted Ones, and Portia pretended to be Midne for a thousand years.
- o Since the Great Collapse, Midne's body and soul have yet to be tracked down. There is concern she is once more under control of the surviving Exalted Ones.

+ ELIAS, THE ROOK KING:
- o His mastery was over Aether.
- o He is called TRICKSTER in Nomatsi lore, known for sowing chaos.
- o His palace from a thousand years ago is now the Carawen Monastery.
- o As Elias, he was Heart-Threads with Saria—although they kept this secret because they feared Portia's wrath.
- o His modern incarnation was LEOPOLD FON CARTORRA, heir to the Cartorran empire, who recently passed in the Great Collapse. His Paladin soul and the magic therein were returned to Sirmaya.

OTHERS WHO HELPED THE SIX:

+ ERIDYSI:
- o She was a Sightwitch from a thousand years ago who could not see the future like other Sightwitches, but who had an inventor's mind—and a deep connection to Sirmaya.

o She created the BLADE and the GLASS, which were used to kill the Exalted Ones.

> • The BLADE could sever a Paladin's Threads so they would not be reincarnated.
> • The GLASS allowed a person to see a Paladin's soul and recognize them for what they really were.

o However, when the Six's plan failed due to betrayal, Eridysi and her family fled into Sirmaya's mountain. The Goddess froze them in Her sleeping ice.

o The BLADE and the GLASS have now been rebuilt as tools for the Cahr Awen.

• THE GENERAL:

o Also known as RAGNOR AMALEJ, he was the Rook King's closest friend and confidant.

o He also led the Rook King's armies and beloved hounds.

o After losing his first wife to war, he sent his daughters to the Sightwitch Sister Convent, where he met Eridysi. They fell in love and had a son, the Tool-Bearer Aeduan Amalej. Aeduan was born a thousand years later however, when Eridysi and the General were finally freed from the sleeping ice.

o When Eridysi was killed and his son was lost, Ragnor vowed to end all magic. He then became THE RAIDER KING, uniting raider factions across the Witchlands.

• LISBET:

o The older of Ragnor's original children, she was gifted the Sight younger than any Sightwitch before her—and she saw hundreds of prophecies of the future.

o Because Eridysi was the one to write these prophecies down, when they were eventually compiled by outsiders, the prophecies became mistakenly known as "Eridysi's Lament."

o Lisbet was frozen in the ice, but she did not awaken when Ragnor and Eridysi did.

o She is now returned to the Convent, although she spends much of her time in the Crypts and asks for privacy.

• CORA:
    o The younger of Ragnor's first children, she was also frozen with the rest of her family.
    o Like Lisbet, she was not set free when Ragnor and Eridysi were.
    o She is now returned to the Convent, although she spends much of her time in the Crypts with her sister and also asks for privacy.

ACKNOWLEDGMENTS

I started writing this series in 2013, so it feels an impossible task to remember everyone who has helped me in that time. There are so many of you! But I shall do my best—and if I forget you, you have permission to snarl at me.

First and foremost, I need to thank the Witchlanders—both the very first members of my street team back in 2015, and then the many fans who have since joined our epic and supportive community. *Truthwitch* would never have become a bestseller (and in turn saved my author career) without all of YOU. And it is your patience and love that have kept me going over the last twelve years. These books were not easy to write (so many threads—and Threads, haha!) and my life was slammed with more challenges in a handful of years than I ever could have imagined facing in a lifetime.

So thank you. You are my Thread-family, and I owe you everything. I hope, hope, *hope* that this book is everything you wanted. And hey—I've clearly left a few doors open for the future.

Next, I need to thank two people without whom this particular book, *Witchlight*, simply would not exist: Rachel Hansen and Joanna Volpe. You two are the MVPs for this book—there's absolutely no doubt about it. You were both basically on call for two years straight as I tried to figure out this book. You spent countless hours brainstorming with me, read enough drafts to make your eyes bleed, and you helped me fix, edit, and polish everything until it finally matched the vision in my head.

I just have to say it again: thank you, Joanna Volpe. Thank you, Rachel Hansen. I owe you far more than I can fit into these acknowledgments.

I was also lucky enough to have many other early readers along the way, to help me troubleshoot and polish: Callum Carr, (Captain) Shanna Alderliesten, Sanya Macadam, Samantha Tan, and Gracie Oser. Thank you for being the best cheerleaders—while also helping me spot errors that inevitably creep into a plot this complicated!

For all my friends who have supported me through the *many* years that I've worked on this sprawling series, I am eternally grateful. Thank you to Victoria Aveyard, Leigh Bardugo, Tanaz Bhathena, Erin Bowman, Alex Bracken, Kat Brauer, Alexa Donne, Brenna Gibson, Amie Kaufman, Kaite Krell, Rachel Hansen (MVP!), Brigid Kemmerer, Biljana Likic, Cait Listro, Lizzy Mason, Jodi Meadows, Nicki Pau Preto, Beth Revis, Emily Ritter, Melody Simpson, Emily Suarino, Meghan Vanderlee, Sam Walma, Abigail Welborn, and Elena Yip. (If your name is missing from this list but *should* be here, then give me a good smack when you see me next!)

Thank you to my incomparable team at New Leaf Literary: Joanna Volpe (MVP!), Lindsay Howard, Tracy Williams, Hilary Pecheone, Katherine Curtis, Keifer Ludwig, Sarah Gerton, Jenniea Carter, Jordan Hill, Kate Sullivan, Kwali Liggons, and Joe Volpe.

Thank you to the incredible Witchlands audio team: Christina Rooney, Julie Wilson, and narrator Cassandra Campbell (who absolutely makes my series sparkle with all her voices and emotion!).

Thank you, THANK YOU to the *amazing* people at Tor Teen and Tor UK who've helped me over the last twelve years, since I sold this series: Whitney Ross (without whom *Truthwitch* would never have been published!), Diana Gill, Lindsey Hall, Bella Pagan, Aislyn Fredsall, Sophie Robinson, Georgia Summers, Hannah Smoot, Eileen Lawrence, Lucille Rettino, Anthony Parisi, Alexis Saarela, Isa Caban, Jamie-Lee Nardone, Giselle Gonzalez, Sarah Reidy, Cliff Nielsen, Greg Collins, Russell Trakhtenberg, Megan Barnard, Rafal Gibek, Ryan T. Jenkins, Jim Kapp, Michelle Foytek, Erin Robinson, Audrey Iorio, Alex Cameron, Lizzy Hosty, Will Hinton, Claire Eddy, Devi Pillai, Kathleen Doherty, and Tom Doherty.

Then of course, I have to thank my family: Mom, Dad, David, Jen, assorted nieces and nephew, in-laws, and all the extended family upon our many-branched tree.

Above all, thank you to the Frenchman—who fed me, supported me, listened to my endless whining, and who literally kept me alive during the worst parts that 2020–2023 had to sling at us. *Te varuje.*

And last but not least: dearest Cricket, now that the weight of all these characters and stories and complicated plot entanglements is *finally* out of my head and on the page, I promise to play more dress-up, Barbies, superheroes—you name it! I love you forever and then some.